D

Drake dropped ... ...ing his broad back and lo... ... cover-let. "I do believe ... ...rtainly nothing like the da... ...agined as the hideaway of t... ...asked Marauder." He bunched a feather pillow under his head. "Your pillow smells of asters. Beguiling and provocative." He gave her his smile, the slow, easy gesture Cianda thought no doubt had broken a thousand foolish hearts. "Of you, " he added, his voice low.

Mortified at the sight of a man—this pirate—sprawled across her bed, Cianda nevertheless stared helplessly at him, momentarily enthralled. His broad shoulders tapered to a flat stomach rippling with muscle beneath his thin shirt. She wanted to touch him.

The illicit and unwelcome thought shocked her. Cianda assumed her haughtiest demeanor. "You take far too many liberties, Captain Weston. Your rudeness repels me, and your antics grow tiresome."

Drake laughed. Then he moved to stand before her, as fleet and stealthy as a predator. He lifted the swathe of tangled silver hair from her neck, and let the captured tresses rain through his splayed fingers. "Do you believe in fate, milady thief?" he murmured. "In the destiny of lovers?"

His nearness tossed Cianda's senses and thoughts into a confused tumult. "No, I don't believe." she managed, her own voice sounding strange and small to her ears. "Men set out to seduce and call it chance."

"If that's so, then I suppose I'll take my own chances." Before she knew what struck, Drake wrapped his arm about her tiny waist and crushed her against him. His mouth covered hers, consuming her sweet, soft lips in a furious possessive kiss. Cianda responded without thought. It seemed madness to give in to the temptation of illicit desire, but impossible to deny it . . .

CAPTURE THE GLOW OF
ZEBRA'S *HEARTFIRES!*

DANETTE CHARTIER

STOLEN FIRE

ZEBRA BOOKS
KENSINGTON PUBLISHING CORP.

To partners and friends.
And to our mothers,
Barbara Fertig and Dorothy Chartier-Boyer.
Thanks for your constant encouragement —
and for showing everybody on earth our book covers.
And special thanks to our editor,
Debbie Roth Kane,
for your invaluable insights and guidance,
and for letting us have our abstruse words.

AUTHOR'S NOTE

Although most of the characters and events in this story are fictional, the glamorous and mysterious history of the famed Koh-i-noor diamond inspired the dramatic adventure portrayed in *Stolen Fire*. Bits and pieces of fact and lore surrounding the treasure are woven throughout Cianda and Drake's pursuit of the coveted jewel.

We hope you enjoy reading about this fascinating Indian prize as much as we enjoyed writing about it.

Chapter One

London, England, January, 1850

"You are a thief, my lovely Cianda. And you will remain a thief for as long as it amuses me."

Cianda D'Rouchert glared with troubled eyes at the man seated across from her. Pain and hatred struck her with equal force. It had been a long time since she knew which was the stronger emotion.

In a single quick motion, she left her chair, pacing to the night-dark windows. The flickering lamplight behind her favored half her face with a golden glow, masking the other half in shadow. She threaded nervous hands through a spill of fine, silvery hair before voicing the bold question trembling on her tongue. "And if I refuse?"

Godfrey Thorne appraised her over steepled fingers. His cool gray gaze, sardonic, slightly contemptuous, always had the power to unsettle her. "Then some unfortunate mudlark will find the remains of your precious Jamie on the banks of the Thames. Please, my dear—" Godfrey waved a languid hand at the horrified look of protest that sprang to her face. "Spare me any bewailings or rash threats. They are tedious and quite useless. If you had not been so foolish as to attempt to sever our mutually beneficial arrangement, none of this would have been necessary. Your impetuous actions forced me to employ rather uncivilized means to remind you that you owe me your soul. A large debt, and one I intend to make certain you repay in the only way you are able."

"You're asking the impossible."

"From you? I think not."

"If you harm Jamie . . ." Cianda struggled against the blinding fear threatening to crush her resolve. She checked her feelings, calling on all her wits to bargain her way out of Godfrey's newest version of hell. "If you harm Jamie, you will never get the jewels. Never."

"I assure you, he is quite safe and content. For the moment. And I will have all three jewels. You will make certain of it." Godfrey smoothed his elegant hands over the desktop. With a slight frown, he flicked away a speck of dust at its edge. "You're a very clever thief, but it would serve you well to remember that is all you are. Your entire existence is a charade, created and financed by myself. I gave you your name, your pedigree, your security — everything, including young Jamie's life. And I can take it away." He made a quick, cutting gesture. "As simply as that."

The truth, his threats, her heart-fear for Jamie robbed Cianda of the will to defy him. Part of her despised Godfrey. But he had transformed her from a wretched gutter snipe into an image of aristocratic beauty, and her fierce sense of loyalty would not let her ignore that. Still, deep inside, the desire to be free, to quit her make-believe life and discover her own destiny, smoldered; it was a longing she usually kept well hidden.

For now.

She would risk losing everything her thief's skills had earned — except Jamie's life.

"So." Godfrey stood and gazed down at her, as if to emphasize her delicate smallness compared to his lean height.

The lamp flame washed him in amber; warm light reflecting on gray ice. "When do you begin?"

"Now." She flung him a bitter smile. "You've left me little choice."

"Ah, my dear, of course you have a choice. Bring me the trio of gems by July. Or your brother dies."

Cayeux-sur-mer, France, March, 1850

Drake Weston flattened himself in the rude doorway of the alley, cursing the drizzling rain, the man who brought him to this serpent's den, and the two gendarmes who had decided smuggling wasn't an honorable profession for an Englishman on the wrong side of the Channel.

"You'd better make this worth my time, Antoine," he muttered.

Cayeux-sur-mer was hardly his notion of an alluring French port. The seaside village's denizens as often as not greeted strangers with a dagger or a club. And Drake didn't need to be welcomed by misfortune. These days, he seemed to woo it like a rogue in pursuit of a fair maid's favors.

Darting a glance around the corner of the doorway, he gambled the gendarmes had either lost his trail in the rain, or given up the chase in favor of a cup of wine and a warm bed. With luck for a companion, he stepped out of the doorway and strode quickly toward his original destination.

The Dragon Inn, nudged in a murky corner of one of Cayeux-sur-mer's narrow, cobbled streets, hardly appeared a haven from the evening's adventures. The door of the tavern creaked open with the shove of his hand and a breath of sultry sea air drafted in behind him, quickly swallowed by a smoky stench. The scarred, low-ceilinged room reeked with an evil combination of sweat, stale liquor, and the cheap perfume of the doxies who courted sailors with sly glances and low-cut lace.

Drake paused for a moment, ocean-blue eyes prowling the room. Behind the long bar, the innkeeper wiped away a spill of wine with the edge of his greasy apron, casting a surly glance at the newcomer. A few heads turned Drake's way, eyeing him with lackluster curiosity before swiveling back to a hand of cards or a mug of forgettable ale.

Without effort, Drake picked out Antoine hunched over a table in a far corner. He pushed his way through the close-set chairs and bodies and sauntered up with an air of careless bravado. Kicking back a chair, he sat down, tempting the mettle of the wood by leaning it back on two legs and propping black-booted feet on the table.

Antoine Gueret shook his head, vigorously scrubbing his thin weasel's face with a large silk handkerchief. "So — you survive the excitement in Paris. I must admit surprise. I was almost convinced you would not come, that you had tempted *la bonne chance* once too often. And myself, here alone — " He shuddered, rolling his beetle-dark eyes upward. *"Mon Dieu, quelle horreur!* I do not like to think of it! And I am certain you would not waste a thought if I met with my demise in this — this devil's pit."

"Pardonnez-moi, mon cher Antoine." Drake's French slid out with practiced ease. "I was unexpectedly — delayed." He savored the last word, a wicked gleam lighting his eyes.

"I need not ask, no?" Antoine grumbled. *"Mon ami,* you were born with trouble at your side and you will die in its arms."

Drake laughed, gesturing lazily to the serving girl. "At least I won't expire from boredom. Now Lilli here," he added with a raffish smile as the fair-haired girl sidled up to the table bearing a bottle of claret, "She appreciates my adventurous nature. She could make me forget my good intentions to attend only to business."

The girl swatted playfully at his arm, her lips pursed in a

pout. "So you say, *monsieur,* but for all your pretty words you desert me last night."

"Ah, Lilli, a man must earn a living." Drake flicked the ribbon lacing her bodice, bringing a flush to the girl's face. "But later . . ." He slowly pulled the end of the ribbon, loosening the bow.

Lilli shrugged coyly. "I have other admirers."

"But none better, *chérie.*"

"None more daring for certain, *mon capitaine,*" Lilli said with a giggle. The bark of a customer caught her attention and she hastily retied her ribbon before moving away, tossing Drake a coquettish smile over her shoulder.

Slapping a hand to his forehead, Antoine heaved a sigh. "I had treasured the notion you induced me to risk my life in this viper's hole to give your attention to serious matters. But once more, you have dragged me to the foulest point on earth merely to amuse yourself. *Mon Dieu!* You are madder than I!"

"Don't be such an old woman, Antoine." Drake leaned back farther in his chair, linking his hands behind his head. "You brought me here, remember? All the way from Italy with the promise you'd found Thorne's emerald." As the name fell between them, Drake's hands clenched and then relaxed as he forced a cavalier ease back into his manner. Antoine, the little rat, was high-strung enough.

"And I did, *mon cher Drake,* I did. I would not disappoint you. But—" Antoine's bony shoulders lifted in a jerk. "It is gone."

"Gone!" Drake sat up so suddenly he sent the table wobbling and the tankards clanging across it. "Gone? Are you telling me I spent five damnable days at sea, risked my neck and my ship, and wasted time diverting the gendarmes away from you, just for you to tell me it's gone?"

"Quietly, I implore you!" Antoine's eyes scurried about the room. His fingers pleated and unpleated the rumpled handkerchief. "It was in the possession of *le comte,* as I promised, and then—stolen! *Oui, oui,*" he bobbed his head furiously at Drake's disbelieving snort. "It is true, *capitaine* all true. And only hours ago. *Le comte,* the fool, was murdered trying to stop the thief. They say—" He bent over the table, lowering his voice. "They say it was the Masked Marauder. Ah, he is a devil, that one!"

"So the Masked Marauder is roaming Cayeux-sur-mer?" Drake settled back in his chair again. Smiling faintly, he idly circled a finger over the faded label on the wine bottle, feeling an odd sense of satisfaction. "Just as I expected."

"Your expectations often prove to be most unhealthy. You would do best to heed my advice and leave before you find yourself in a difficulty that a sword and a smile cannot rescue you from. Remember in Italy! You thought you had outwitted Monsieur Thorne and his Masked Marauder, but it was the thief who stole away with the ruby and you who ended up in a prison cell!"

"I hardly need you to remind me." Drake's brashness dimmed as the too-recent memory returned to mock him. A thief with no face and the man he most wanted dead had outwitted him. But not twice. Not again. He'd waited, months, and now, the Marauder was at his fingertips.

"Cayeux-sur-mer is an admirable den in which to hide, " Antoine persisted. "And from which to spring. One man already has the Marauder's dagger in his heart."

The corner of Drake's mouth quirked upward, and his eyes held a dangerous gleam. "The devil looks after his own. I intend to get both jewels and the thief, and use them to hang Godfrey Thorne." He lifted a tankard in a mocking toast. "Don't tell me you'd mourn the loss of that particular customer of yours. There's always work for a master lapidary who doesn't ask uncomfortable questions."

Antoine waved a dismissing hand. "As you say. Yet none of this will make a difference if it ends with a blade between your ribs. You cannot always trust those whose coins line your pockets."

"I trust no one and nothing. Ever. Nothing but luck and a kiss in the dark."

"Luck is a fickle mistress, and you yourself have told me many times *les femmes* are the quickest to cut your heart out for want of a bigger prize. I thought, *mon ami,* after Isabelle—" He stopped, letting the name fall between them and shatter into a thousand memories.

Drake said nothing. He didn't want to think about Isabelle. She was six years dead, and he had buried his desire for more than one night in a warm embrace with her.

Antoine waved his handkerchief in an agitated flutter, flustered by Drake's silence. "You have no one at your side. Your own brother betrayed you in Italy, your employer forgot you as dead. If you are careless . . ."

"I won't be. I'm in this for my own satisfaction. That's the only way I do business these days." These days, and from now on. Loyalty, to anyone or any cause, was a foolish conceit he could no longer afford to indulge in. It had cost him too much already. Now the risks he took were for himself only. Drake's hard smile was intended to quell Antoine's admonitions, but the little Frenchman persisted.

"Take care, *mon ami,* you do not confuse business with your personal obsession with—what shall I call it? Is it justice or revenge you wish to achieve?"

Drake leveled a cold glare at Antoine, but said nothing.

Antoine averted his eyes and shook a hand to the side in a careless gesture. "Ah, but no matter, eh? The dangers are the same either way you choose to view this mad pursuit of yours. Monsieur Thorne is powerful. And he would find the greatest pleasure in destroying you. You would do best to forget—"

The crash of the door against the wall chopped short Antoine's warning. Two uniformed gendarmes shoved their way into the tavern, their faces set with aggressive determination.

"Merde!" Antoine slunk low in his chair, his hand sheltering his face. "I told you, did I not, that to come here was madness? How do you sit there, *mon Dieu!* when we are both dead men?"

Drake slowly pushed back his chair and stood up. He picked up the nearly-full wine bottle and flashed a wicked smile at his friend. "I always find the back door convenient. *Au revoir* , Antoine."

Ignoring Antoine's dawning expression of horror and his half-raised hand, Drake took a long swallow of claret, and then swaggered up to the two officers.

He saw the tallest of the men glance in Antoine's direction and stepped in front of him, obscuring his view. "You're blocking the door," Drake said gruffly, his words deliberately slurred. He staggered a little against the man, butting him into his companion.

"Out of the way, you fool," the tall man spat, vainly trying to catch a glimpse of Antoine shrinking toward a speedy retreat.

He tried to push past. Drake lurched forward in a seemingly graceless jerk. His leg caught the tall man's ankle, sending him crashing into a table.

Cards and coins and ale flew into the air, showering the four sailors seated there in an unlikely rain. They scrambled backward, cursing, as the table splintered with a thunderous crack under the weight of the tall man. He ended with his face squarely in a muddle of frothing ale and sodden wood.

His companion's head swiveled from Drake to the growing confusion and back again. Drake held up his hands, shrugging, presenting his best look of innocence.

The gendarme's eyes narrowed in dawning comprehension. But he hesitated a moment too long. With a daredevil grin, Drake tipped the man a mocking salute, ducked around him, and darted out the open door.

Ignoring the shouted spate of angry curses and commands, he sprinted down the rain-slick street. The sound of running feet close on his heels, Drake made a quick turn into a narrow alleyway. The alley twisted and turned and finally branched off in two directions behind a row of smutty stone buildings, perched in a drunken row near the edge of the sea.

Drake gradually slowed to a trot. He paused, listening for the slap of boots on the cobbles. He heard only the rhythmic slosh of the sea chewing the wooden piers, punctuated with the whispers and howls of a capricious wind and the dwindling patter of rainfall.

For luck, he chose another alley, one leading toward the farthest end of the pier. He moved slowly, almost carelessly. But his eyes and ears hunted the darkness for the unexpected.

On the verge of congratulating himself on another fortuitous escape, he nearly dismissed the faint sound trickling from an unseen point in front of him. The sound of a footstep.

He stopped, poised. Ready. For—what? Ahead, the passage stopped dead against a stone wall, then crooked sharply to the right. The perfect place for an ambush. And behind?

As he neared the corner, a slight shuffling noise flattened him against the wall. Slowly, he bent and eased a dagger from the sheath of his boot. Cradling it against his palm, his fingers caressing the hilt, he drew a breath and sprang around the corner.

Whatever he expected—angry gendarmes, a thief on the prowl for easy prey—the anticipation evaporated in an instant. Instead, he found himself challenging a phantom of a woman.

She stood, swaying, illuminated by a sudden shaft of

white moonlight. A baggy overcoat hung to her ankles, draping her body in a cloak of ebony.

Drake stared, helplessly ensnared by an utterly alien sensation: enchantment.

Her face might have spawned legends of sea nymphs and mermaids. An aura of the ethereal made her seem a creature born of ocean mist and dreams, a translucent illusion of beauty. A waterfall of hair tumbled over her shoulders, pure silver plaited with gold in the moonlight. She was deadly pale, her eyes blank with exhaustion—the only sign of her mortality.

For a fantastic moment, Drake dared not move for fear she would vanish.

She swayed a little, stretching a trembling hand to him.

"What the devil—?" He stopped, switching to French. "What are you—?"

"Please." Her lips formed the word without a sound. Then her voice—soft, low, English—floated to him, a bare whisper. "I've got to get away . . . ." She took one stumbling step forward, shuddered, and began to crumple, slowly, as if all her bones were melting away.

Action leaped ahead of thought, compelling Drake to jam his knife back in its sheath. He reached her in two strides and caught her in his arms before she fell.

She might have been a child for all her weight. Her head drooped against his shoulder, spilling silvery hair over his arm. "Damnation!" Drake glanced around him, at an unexpected loss. What was he supposed to do with her?

Leaving her alone, defenseless, in an unfriendly alley chafed what honorable intentions he would admit to. And with the gendarmes dogging his heels he couldn't very well carry her into town babbling an unlikely tale of her falling into his arms.

That left the *Ferret*.

He didn't like it. In fact, he detested it. He would rather

16

face the point of a sword armed with a feather than have a wisp of a woman—anyone, for that matter—literally wrapped around his neck, particularly with the Marauder so close. He'd waited too long to snare the thief, and she would only prolong the agony. Especially if he took her to his ship.

But right now fate offered him a frustrating lack of options. Roundly cursing destiny's poor sense of humor, Drake turned in the direction of the docks.

A familiar chorus of voices froze him in his paces. Angry voices, grumbling in foul-tongued French, detailing what fate they intended for the drunkard who had created chaos at the Dragon Inn.

"I don't mind trouble, but I don't like carrying it over my shoulder," Drake muttered to the woman in his arms. "In your case, I'm going to make an exception." Suiting action to the words, he edged in the opposite way of the voices. Frustration gnawed at him. He fought the inbred urge to confront the obstacle fists first, rather than skulking away from it. Necessity urged caution.

The midnight-darkened alleys provided scant shelter, and Drake was frequently forced to take quick turns and laborious detours to outwit the gendarmes. Nearing the docks at last, he relied on his infamous luck and the long twilight echoes of the piers to shield them.

When the hazy outline of the last pier melted into view, Drake resisted a shout of hard-won victory.

Against the timbered pillars, a sleek schooner pulled impatiently at the anchor lines tethering it to shore. The golden flickers from a scattering of lanterns barely traced the outline of the ship in the thick covering of fog and rain. High on the topmast, the English colors snapped in a gust of wind.

Drake caught sight of the tall, gaunt shadow of a man leaning against a mast on the bow.

Gathering the woman closer, he took the gangplank in

three strides. "Zak! Zak, get the bloody hell over here!"

The shadow at the bow slowly turned and ambled toward them. Zak stopped when he saw Drake, thrust his hands deep in the pockets of a disreputable looking overcoat, rocked back on his heels, and cocked a brow at his friend. "Problems?"

"What does it look like?"

Bending a little forward, Zak used one finger to part the curtain of hair, then peered into the woman's face. "What did you do to her?"

"Nothing, damn it! I'm taking her below."

"Really." Zak looked faintly annoyed. "I can't imagine why, old man."

"I wonder myself. Rouse enough of the crew for a watch. A pair of gendarmes aren't happy with the way I do business."

Zak shrugged. "Not many people are."

"True. But I don't want to invite more trouble."

"Bit too late for that. But then it usually is." With another shrug for Drake's irritated scowl, Zak headed toward the bridge.

Drake took the quarterdeck in long strides. Maneuvering his burden carefully, he slid open the hatch and descended to his cabin. He kicked open a battered door, shouldered his way inside, and laid his burden down on the narrow bunk.

After a moment's faltering, Drake coaxed the two oil lamps in the room to life. The dim flickers danced at the tips of the wicks, flirting with the shadows on the wooden walls of the cabin, the small flames doing little to lighten the somber browns and grays. In the close confines, the sharp tang of the brine simmered and became a sultry heat.

Drake stepped to the bunk, raking a hand through his dark hair as he looked down at the slight figure.

Her lashes brushed fragile cheekbones, dark smudges against the ivory skin. He idly wondered what color her eyes were. Green, he guessed. Deep and mysterious as a tropical lagoon.

Drawing a breath to dispel his uncharacteristic bout of fancy, he bent and jerked open her overcoat. When it fell away, he winced. She wore boy's breeches and a white shirt, torn and dirty. Blood spattered the front.

His face dark, Drake, with a quick yank, snapped the buttons of her shirt. Dark red had soaked through to her thin chemise. He eased the material open, expecting to find a near-mortal wound. Instead, he found a spidery slash just below her breasts. Painful, but hardly cruel enough to have caused the stains.

"What kind of trouble have you been into, lady?" *Blast it all, this is just what I need,* he thought as he pulled away her clothing and tossed it haphazardly into a corner. Giving in to a half-witted whim, he had stuck himself with a woman who was probably being pursued by a jealous lover or a disgruntled customer. "I should have left you in that damned alley."

He ran his hands over her bared arms, exploring for missed injuries. Her skin was cold, yet petal soft. It felt like touching an alabaster figure of some mythical sprite, perfectly sculpted with loving detail, surreal and captivating, inviting his fingertips to savor every hollow and swell.

She was beautiful.

Beautiful trouble, he grimly reminded himself, willing away the sudden quickening of his senses. His unbidden response to her annoyed him, and at the same time roused an uneasiness he couldn't shake off. "Sorry for taking the liberty," he told her as his hands appreciated the curve of her waist. "I wouldn't if you hadn't made it necessary, but you did issue somewhat of an invitation when you landed in my arms. Although I will admit — "

A glitter of green and gold arrested Drake's one-sided conversation. Bending closer, he nudged away the flimsy

19

linen covering her cleavage. Nested between her breasts was an emerald tied with gold.

Dipping his fingers into the dusky hollow, Drake slowly drew out the jewel.

Stunned, he let the gold slide through his fingertips until he held the braided metal rope by its clasp. The egg-sized emerald swung in a hypnotic rhythm, aflame in the lanterns' glow.

A footstep behind him shattered his momentary trance. "So," Zak drawled from the doorway. "Who is she?"

Drake turned and held out the emerald. Even Zak was, for once, without a retort. "It's the Rajput," Drake said, unable to keep the astonishment from his voice. "And she—"

"You can't believe—"

"No, she can't be . . ." Drake mumbled to himself while he hastily rummaged through the pockets of her discarded overcoat. "She can't be—not a scrap of a girl like this. She—" He stopped, drawing out a crushed wad of cloth. Shaking it out, he held up the black silk mask. Even without trying it, he knew it perfectly fit her face.

"She can't be," Zak echoed his disbelief.

Drake stared at the woman, then back at his partner. "She must be. She's the Masked Marauder."

Chapter Two

" 'Ere now. And where d'ye think yer goin'?"

Leaving here. Leaving forever.

"Yer brat's as good as dead. Leave 'im, and I'll give ye a better job than priggin' a few potatoes off a barrow."

Leering eyes, groping fingers, pinching and pulling.

"Ye'll never be nothin' but a miserable sneak-thief lessin' ye learn to spread yer legs with a smile. A warm bed's better than a dead brat, ye'll soon see."

Jamie will not die. Not if I have to steal a pitchfork from Satan. Jamie won't die like Mama, cold and stiff in the corner of the lodging house, with nowhere else to live. Nowhere else to die.

Cianda tossed and twisted in her sleep, tormented by the familiar nightmare, struggling against memories her sleeping mind would not forget. Or were they real this time?

No. Something mercifully awakened her, an insidious whisper of sound, as steady as gentle rainfall. Had she left the window open? She curled closer under the blanket, trying to ward off the intrusion.

The lodging house was frigid and the roof leaked right over her pallet, a constant, taunting drip, drip, drip. But that was long ago. Long ago? She didn't want to remember. Here, soothing warmth cradled her. She didn't need to remember. Jamie was safe now. She was safe.

21

But a niggle of warning prodded her, urging her to remember — what?

A nightmare. As usual, the same one. Yet if it was, it felt frightfully uncomfortable. Her chest and sides ached and her stomach churned. The bed felt hard, her blanket scratchy; the air caught in her nostrils when she inhaled, hot and damp, suffocating.

And her room moved.

Wakefulness doused her like icy water. Her room at the inn, no matter how lacking, never moved!

Her eyes leaped open. The black eye of a porthole stared blindly back. It explained the rhythmic sway. But how had she gotten on a ship? The chateau, she'd been at the chateau. . . .

Memories tumbled over her in a torrent. The emerald. The blade of a dagger and a frenzied run into the darkness. And then —

"I was right. Your eyes are green."

Jerking the blanket to her chin, she swiftly pulled herself up and into a huddle in a corner of the bunk, regretting the movement as pain knifed her ribs. But she forgot the discomfort when she saw him.

Sprawled in a round-backed chair near the bunk, his black boots stretched out in front of him, he studied her with undisguised interest. She scoured her memory for some recollection of him.

The only thought she could muster was the idiotic notion that his looks matched his voice. Dark, provocative, slightly dangerous, with an edge betraying any civilized polish. He had the mark of a ruffian, a days-old beard shadowing his jaw, coffee brown hair carelessly pulled back, his dingy linen shirt split to the waist.

A pirate. Her imagination quickly sketched him at the bow of a sea rover's ship, saber in hand, braced against a stiff sailing wind, challenging man and elements alike. And

22

the captain, of course. Even her overworked fancy couldn't picture him meekly following orders.

Intimidating, yet his bold features were gentled by lines of humor and the sensual curve of his mouth.

He was a man she wouldn't easily forget. Yet she couldn't remember.

Her slight frown dissolved into embarrassment as she realized how intently she was staring. At once, she shook off the feeling and lifted her chin. "I demand an explanation at once, sir. Who are you? When did I board this vessel?"

"A simple thank you would be more in order than ungracious demands, milady." He stretched his arms over his head in a deliberate, languid motion, lacing his hands behind his head. "Allow me to refresh your memory. You begged me to rescue you, and though under normal circumstances I would have had the sense to refuse, you managed to collapse at a rather inopportune moment right into my arms. You left me little choice." He paused, searching her face with eyes as cold and fathomless as the depths of the oceans he sailed. "And you are . . . ?"

"You haven't introduced yourself," she shot back, knowing the delay was feeble at best. "Your manners are atrocious."

"I detest contrived politeness. Just as you must find it annoying to hold your tongue." He tipped her a mocking salute. "Captain Drake Weston, your not-so-humble servant. And you?"

She hesitated. Today? Finally, matching his sarcasm, she said, "Cianda D'Rouchert, your unwilling guest."

He raised a brow. "Very theatrical."

"I'm sorry you don't approve." Cianda's fingers scattered errant wisps of luminous, silver-blond hair from her face as she grasped for some threads of composure among the unraveled tangle of her self-control.

23

"I didn't say that. I prefer it to the Masked Marauder. That is your *professional* name, isn't it?"

A cold snake of fear wriggled up Cianda's spine. Was he guessing or did he know? "Do I look like a Masked Marauder?"

Drake cocked his head, considering. "Not exactly. Of course, I have your mask, your tools — and your clothes. You were wet and . . ." He let the words trail off, grinning raffishly. "Let's just say I'm always willing to accommodate a lady."

"How kind." Cianda absently fingered the soft linen of the voluminous shirt. It smelled of sun-warmed wind — of him. She tried not to think of his hands, stripping away her clothing, touching her bare skin. And what else? She dared not imagine. Stifling the mortifying thoughts, she asked quickly, "What am I doing here?"

"Actually, I'm wondering that myself. Cayeux-sur-mer isn't exactly a pleasant spot for a holiday. And you didn't appear to be enjoying yourself when I found you half dead in that alley."

Cianda scowled at him. "An alley? I don't remember . . . I was at the chateau — " Her sentence snapped off and broke. She slapped a hand to her breast, searching. "It's gone. I had it — you!"

"Me?"

"Where is it?" she demanded, not liking the sudden cunning in his eyes. "It belongs to me."

"Does it? That's very interesting." Drake drew an idle pattern on the arm of his chair. "You're a collector of valuable Indian treasures, are you? I could verify such a claim through the man who originally owned it, but he had the misfortune to be murdered last night. Strangely enough, they found him in his chateau, not far from that alley. Did you say something about a chateau?"

His apparent indifference covered the menace in his

24

voice, like silk draping the blade of a dagger. Unprepared for the rapid hail of events, Cianda stared blankly at him, dumbfounded.

"Nothing to say?" He waited, then got to his feet in one swift move. "Well, I'm a sporting man. I'll give you a chance to concoct an entertaining story while I find you some tea. Although—" Pausing in the doorway, Drake glanced back. "I'd prefer the truth."

When the door clicked shut, Cianda slumped against the wall, her heart thudding in her ears. Of all the trouble she'd been in, all the narrow escapes, the scrapes she'd managed to twist out of, this most resembled a rat trap where the one door leading out emptied into a ring full of blood-hungry terriers.

The truth. He wanted the truth. Cianda wanted to laugh and cry. She had abandoned the truth with her past in the Devil's Acre. Now she relied on costly charades. Reality, truth were frightening, shaming. Pretense fed and clothed her, gave her respectability, a purpose.

She had stolen the Rajput emerald, and made a good job of it, too. The best heist of her unconventional career. But not good enough. To secure Jamie's freedom, she needed all three jewels, or her brother would pay the price with his life.

What she did not need was interference! Time . . . this pirate was wasting her precious time. And time was one commodity she could not afford to lose. Godfrey, in his lust for tension and drama, had issued her a deadline: the jewels by July. He hadn't given a reason for his curious timetable, merely given her the date and the consequences for failure.

Her brother's life now dangled from the fingers of a mad Mephistopheles, a man who delighted as much in creating illusions as he did in dispelling them.

Cianda had convinced herself the make-believe he fashioned for her could become reality. She planned to use her thieving abilities for her own gain, until she saved enough to buy a safe future for Jamie, a sheltered country home where she could quietly retire.

Godfrey preferred the ruse. Now the clock ticked away day by day, hour by hour, minute by minute, the sound of her brother's life ebbing away — No! She must conquer that insidious terror and think. Be logical, calculating. Cianda sucked in a deep breath. Yes. And be calm. Always.

Captain Weston said the count was dead. But not by her hand. Never. Not even if she had to face the gallows at Newgate prison. No, someone else, someone who wanted the Rajput, killed the count, then tried to deal her the same fate.

Think. She must remember! The chateau. She had the emerald, then — an unexpected noise, a scuffle, someone behind her and — damn! It blurred, running away in a confused rivulet of scrambled memories.

Standing in the alley, alone. When had she and Beatrice parted? Plenty of times before she'd gone one direction and her assistant the other for safety's sake. Their plan was standard: reunite at the rented rooms, gather the belongings and leave as they had entered, Lady Cianda D'Rouchert and her lady's maid. Only this time something had gone awry. Terribly, terribly awry.

Someone was carrying her. . . . And then, hands on her body, strong, caressing. *His* hands?

A pleasant shiver chased over her skin. His arms cradling her, and the comforting pounding of his heart under her ear. The smell of salt and sweat, wind and sea.

A rescue? Or did he murder the count? But if he had, why trouble himself with bringing her here, wherever here was? Too many questions, Cianda thought, pressing her fingers to her temples. And no answers.

Only one thing was certain. She had to get the emerald back. It brought her a leap nearer to saving Jamie from Thorne's cruel sport. It was all a grand gaming event to

Godfrey: the quest for rare gems and their lucrative rewards. And no one, not the Queen, not the peers of his realm, not the whole of Parliament, was the wiser for his calculated gamble.

Smuggling jewels out of England under the Empire's pompous, rectilinear nose was Godfrey Thorne's version of a safari for a coveted prize. Only he, finding the actual work distasteful, sent Cianda out for the hunt. But it remained, from the outset to the conquest, always, his game, his rules. His win at her expense. And God help her, this time it would be at her precious little brother's expense if she failed.

Cianda squared her shoulders, as much as her sore limbs would allow. "I won't fail. I never fail." The words were her oath, her insurance. Failure, now more than ever, was not a possibility. No, she must focus on retrieving her emerald and escaping this wretched floating prison.

The Rajput was one of three fabulous Indian treasures. She had one, the Malwi Ruby. And the Rajput was somewhere aboard this ship.

A thud against the heavy oak door scattered her thoughts like startled birds. Drake pushed his way into the room, precariously balancing a cup and saucer. "You'll have to forgive the quality," he said, setting it down on the table beside the bunk. "My chef is still sampling the delights of the port — such as they are — and boiling water stretches the limits of my culinary talents."

Cianda stretched out a hand toward the cup, disconcerted to find herself trembling. The cup rattled against the saucer, slopping scalding liquid over her chilled flesh.

Drake gently moved her fingers. "It's hard to get used to a moving room." He picked up the cup for her.

Uneasy, Cianda started when he sat down next to her and matched her small hand with his large one. "I can —"

"So can I." Drake pressed her fingers around the warm

27

cup, wrapping them with his. Her eyes searched his as he guided the cup to her lips.

The hot, strong liquid slid down her throat, steadying Cianda's nerves. At the same time, she felt strangely light headed. Dark and positive, his powerful presence empha sized her frailty, an advantage she couldn't afford to give him.

Gulping the contents of the cup, she pushed it back in his hand. "Thank you. I feel better now."

"Really? Hmmm . . . well, you'd better let me check you again. That was a nasty slash you took."

Cianda held his gaze, determined not to flinch from his penetrating stare. "It's quite all right. I don't need your help."

"Don't count on it." Drake pressed her back against the pillow. "I don't relish the idea of your dying on my ship. I have enough problems as it is. I did bother to rescue you," he insisted, when Cianda attempted to wriggle out from under his hands. "I don't want the effort wasted."

The deep, persuasive caress of his voice entranced her into obeying. She lay back, letting him draw away the blan ket. His hands lingered over her waist, then slid under her borrowed shirt. Cianda shivered, turning her head away, feeling suddenly hot and uncomfortable.

Drake deftly redressed the gash, his touch gentle. When he smoothed a rough hand over the edges of the bandage, his knuckles brushed the tender curves of her breasts. Cianda jerked, a fiery dart of sensation inciting her nerves.

"How does it feel?" he said, not meeting her eyes.

"It — it's not what I expected. How does it look?"

"Perfect." The low throb in his voice turned her gaze to him.

Slowly, he raised his head, and for a moment, she saw her self reflected in the clear blue of his eyes. Not Cianda D'Rouchert, the elegant French widow, or the Masked Marauder, the midnight thief, but some strange, disheveled creature only he recognized. She caught a breath and, elusive as a fairy's kiss, the mood flitted away.

"Or you will be," he said, the cool cavalier again. "In a few days."

"How comforting," Cianda muttered. Her quick fingers yanked the shirt down and the blanket up.

"Since you're feeling better . . ." Drake dropped down in the chair, stretching his long legs out in front of him. "Perhaps you'd care to tell me about the emerald. And the man you killed to get it."

Bolting upright, pain shooting through her wound, Cianda glared at him, fury firing her eyes. "I didn't kill anyone!"

"You have the emerald. He's dead. Exactly what conclusion am I supposed to draw from those two facts?"

"Draw any damned conclusion you like! I didn't murder him." She skittered the tips of her fingers over her temple, hot shivers chasing over her skin.

"But you did steal the Rajput." His eyes snared hers in a steel blue trap. "Didn't you?"

"And if I did?" she challenged. "What does it matter? You have it now and I'm certain you don't intend to return it."

He answered her with a shrug. "I'm interested in what you intended to do with it. It's not exactly the sort of bauble you dangle around your neck for the world to see. And I don't think you would have gone to all that trouble just to add a trinket to your jewel box."

Cianda's fingers played over each other as she tried to rally her thoughts. Her head throbbed with a numbing pain. She needed to sleep. She needed that emerald. But he had the advantage. And a weighty one at that. "I'm willing to buy it from you," she offered, putting cold business into her voice. "You won't be able to sell it. I can."

"*You* can?"

"Yes, *I* can. I have a buyer who'll pay a fortune for it once I have—" Her words crumbled away as Drake tensed, and she realized desperation had led her to indiscretion.

"Once you have—what? The Koh-i-noor?"

With the sensation of wading into dangerously deep waters, Cianda asked, "The Koh-i-noor?" She feigned innocence. How could he know about the trio? Did he know more than Godfrey had told her?

"In English, the 'Mountain of Light'. Sounding familiar yet? It ought to. After all, you have the ruby. You stole it in Italy, six months ago."

"You're implying a great deal. Why should I find any connection between those baubles?"

"You know as well as I their value as a trio."

But I don't know why! She longed to ask him pointedly, but dared not reveal either knowledge or ignorance. For now, she must remain neutral, as mysterious to him as he was to her.

"Don't bother denying it. I spent five months in a prison cell because someone decided I was a more likely candidate for a thief than you."

"A pity, Captain. But you know what is said about playing with fire."

Drake scowled at her, otherwise ignoring the jibe. "First the ruby, then last night the emerald."

"Which you now have," she spat. "You might have a difficult time explaining that to the gendarmes. As you say, a man is dead and *you* have the emerald. *And,* you've kidnapped an innocent woman. Whose story do you think they're likely to believe?"

To her surprise, he threw back his head and laughed. "I admire your courage, Cianda D'Rouchert. Most women in your dilemma would be succumbing to tears or a fit of the vapors. Or trying to kiss their way out of trouble."

Cianda's lips twitched upward a little in response to his infectious amusement. "You've already scraped me off the street once. Twice would be tiresome. I never cry, and I have no intention of trying to seduce you."

"Then you are unusual."

"What a fine opinion you have of yourself! I've no doubt you think you can smile your way out of anything."

"Almost anything." He leaned back in his chair, appraising her over the tips of steepled fingers. The gesture recalled Godfrey, honing Cianda's desperation to a fine edge. "I'll challenge the devil, or you, Cianda D'Rouchert to get what I want."

Cianda drew in a breath. She was frightened, terrified of losing the jewels she so needed. But he need not know that. Not unless she could use the truth to bargain for her freedom. "What could you possibly want from me? You have my emerald."

Drake smiled, but it was the smile of a predator. "A dangerous question." He paused for a heartbeat, then said with cold deliberation, "I want your employer."

Unable to hide her astonishment, Cianda gaped at him. "My—employer?"

"Lord Godfrey Thorne." He spat the name out as if it were foul poison. "You and he are dear friends, I'm certain."

This time, Cianda didn't bother with pretense. "Godfrey would gain as much pleasure from slitting my throat as he does from his jewels. But no one else can provide him with the kind of gems he wants. If you think you can make a better bargain with him for the emerald—"

"I'm not interested in Thorne's money."

"Then what?" Perplexed, she tried to fathom what he could want. Not the gems, nor the fortune they promised—what?

"I told you—I want Thorne. Dangling from a rope, ide-

31

ally," he snapped, jerking out of his chair. "You help me hang him, and I'll make certain your name and a murder in Cayeux-sur-mer are never mentioned in the same breath. And I'll see you get out of here safely in the bargain."

"I don't have all three jewels," Cianda retorted, wondering why she bothered to converse with a madman. He had to be insane. It was the only explanation for his bizarre plot. "Do you plan to go gallivanting about with me until I can chance stealing the diamond?"

"I'm not interested in the bloody diamond!" Drake slammed a hand against the wall. "I want you to help me use the emerald to spring a trap, after which I intend to return it to its rightful owner, and let you walk away with a fat purse."

"That's ridiculous!" If he thought she would trust him, he really was a madman. She trusted no man. Ever. To men, women existed only as tools to be used for their pleasure or gain. And Drake Weston was obviously no different. "You do not understand my circumstances in the slightest. I won't do it."

"Won't you? Would you rather hang for a murder you say you didn't commit?" His voice struck with hard blows. Raking a hand through his hair, he paced the confines of the cabin with long strides. When he faced her again, the fierceness softened. "Look — we need each other. And it's only for a little while. You'll have your payment; I'll have my rat. It's really quite simple."

Cianda flung up her hands in a quick, agitated motion. "Oh, very simple. Except for one small item. Godfrey won't take the emerald alone. My orders are to bring him the trio." It was a lie. She had no intention of telling him about Jamie, nor of her determination to hide the emerald and ruby from Godfrey as bargaining tools for her brother's life.

"You can find a way to convince Thorne to take only the emerald, I'm certain."

"No. I can't. I need the diamond."

"Lie to him. Tell him it's lost, or it's locked in the Queen's bedchamber. What the hell does it matter?"

"It matters a great deal! There is more, much more at stake here than you realize." Cianda, chiding herself for revealing even a hint of her private torment to him, rushed to attack from a different front. "Besides, how do you intend to convince the gendarmes to let you sail away from France with a fugitive as cargo? Am I supposed to trust your charming manner will get us out of port?"

The uncomfortable expression on his face gave her pause. "Well—"

"What?"

"You're not going to like it," he muttered.

"I already don't like it." Cianda tried to keep from shouting at him. "Nothing you can say is going to make it any worse."

"Don't gamble on that. You see . . ." Drake hesitated, and a premonition of impending disaster revisited her. "You steal for a living and I—"

"Oh no." Cianda closed her eyes. "No."

"Yes. I'm rather quietly employed by a member of the Foreign Office. Sometimes. When he chooses to remember. But I'm self-employed as well, of course." A hint of a smile lingered at the corner of his mouth.

"A British agent disguised as a smuggler. At least I'm in somewhat familiar company," she muttered.

"A smuggler disguised as a British agent, actually. I only work for Lord Palmerston intermittently; when the challenge suits me."

"I see," Cianda said, although she didn't really. He seemed to swing between treating their situation as deadly serious and as an enormous game. "So, Godfrey Thorne is a large enough challenge to tempt you?"

Drake's jaw went rigid. "Thorne is a traitor. I've already

33

stuck my neck out so far to catch him that I can't pull it back intact unless I put the noose around his first. So you see, Milady Marauder . . ." He moved to stand in front of her, his eyes mocking. "We're both in a lot of trouble. And either you help me, or—"

The cabin door lurched open. A tall, thin man wearing a rumpled overcoat, slouched in the doorway. He gave Cianda a brief, disinterested glance before turning to Drake. "Trouble on board." The laconic voice robbed the announcement of any drama.

Alert tension replaced the lazy scorn in Drake's posture. "Gendarmes?"

The man nodded. "I hope your histrionic gifts are in order."

"Me too," Drake muttered. He threw a scowl at Cianda. "You'd better cross your fingers, little thief. And start accepting the fact that you need me as much as I need you."

Arrogant bastard! Cianda glared at the closed door. Accept him, indeed. If Drake Weston believed for one moment she intended to partner with him in his crazy scheme, he was doomed to disappointment. Nothing would interfere with her one aim: to free Jamie.

And yet . . . a thought flashed through her mind, the image of Godfrey, caught and condemned, evidence of his treachery in hand. The vision both gratified and appalled her. Godfrey now threatened Jamie's life, but long ago he had saved it, and hers as well, something she could never forget. Yet Godfrey's downfall would mean her freedom from his malevolent control. It could mean a new beginning for her, for Jamie. Dreams! Foolish dreams! She tossed off the fantasy.

"The only plans I intend to make don't include you, Captain Weston," she said aloud. Moving quickly, Cianda slid out of the bunk. She flinched as her bare feet hit the cool, wooden floor. Her wounded chest throbbing, she took two steps, then stopped, swaying. A wash of dizziness and pain forced her momentarily to clutch at the wall for support. Rallying her wits, she forced her legs to move.

"I've got to get off this ship. Now," she mumbled, searching for her clothes. He'd carelessly tossed her boys' pants and her coat in a corner, and as Cianda hurried into them, she listened intently for any warning sound. As a final touch, she grabbed a hat discarded on a chair. Stuffing her heavy tresses under it, she pulled it low over her face.

As she eased the door open, its hinges creaked in protest. Her heart racing, Cianda slipped into the darkened room. Which way? She cursed the closed doors on every side. For a small vessel, where drapes normally served to partition sleeping and working quarters, this ship was certainly well appointed! Drake Weston must have had the schooner especially outfitted, customized to accommodate an obvious taste for comfort. The frustrating realization only complicated her task.

There was no time to speculate on direction. Choosing the left, Cianda kept her tread light and quick. She prayed she wouldn't get hopelessly lost in some sleeping mate's cabin.

A few minutes later, her fears eased a little. Ahead, a bright square of morning light poured down a steep ladder way. A quick glance told her it led up and out toward freedom.

Her breath came hard and fast by the time she reached the top step, and her limbs threatened to give way to an insidious weakness. *Not yet,* she pleaded with herself. *Just a little longer.*

Cianda put her hand to the top of the railing at the same moment Drake's voice, in terse, angry French, rang out above her head.

"Search the whole damned ship, if you like. I deal in wine, not emeralds."

Crouching on a step, Cianda felt the jutting wood of the

step above bite the small of her back. A grumbled reply—the gendarmes, she guessed—was lost to her as it moved away with the rhythm of forceful footsteps. She froze for an agonizing moment before daring to reach up and peek over the edge of the top stair out onto the deck.

At the railing opposite her, four men stood engrossed in an animated debate. Drake Weston paced back and forth, punctuating his argument with gestures toward the ship's cabins. At last, he strode out of her view, followed by his companion and the two gendarmes.

It was her chance.

Climbing up and onto the deck in one swift motion, Cianda darted to the railing. The murky, choppy water of the English Channel stretched in an endless vista. "Oh, wretched luck. Starboard, not port," she muttered under her breath. Either she chanced capture by trying to make her way to the other side, where the ship faced the pier, or she plunged into a short, icy swim.

An approaching chorus of voices made her decision.

Stripping off her overcoat, Cianda dived overboard.

A shout jumped after her. Drake Weston's voice, commanding her to stop. Cianda never hesitated.

She ducked under the murky liquid veil, her wounds slapping salt water, then surfaced, sputtering and gasping for breath. Swiping stinging streams from her eyes, Cianda ignored the confusion above her head and began swimming for the docks, willing her last reserve of strength to carry her safely to shore.

Lungs burning, muscles aching, her vision narrowed to the wooden piers just ahead. Almost there. She tasted the sweet relief of freedom. A few moments, no more. She stretched out her hands, blindly seeking solid support. Just a yard, maybe two . . .

Her fingers groped against a post. Almost simultaneously, a set of strong hands roughly grabbed her under the arms and hauled her onto the pier as if she were weightless.

"What in the bloody hell do you think you're doing?" Drake Weston's furious face eclipsed a wildly spinning view of sky and pier and shore. "Are you that determined to kill yourself?"

Defeat welled painfully inside her, but Cianda managed a faint, bitter smile. "I don't believe I'll get the chance, Captain Weston," she whispered before closing her eyes to a black oblivion. "It seems you're determined to do it for me."

Drake jerked another blanket over Cianda's still form, bundling it up under her chin. She'd scarcely moved since they'd weighed anchor two days ago. Now she moaned softly and turned her face into the cradle of his palm. Pale and shivering, she looked fragile enough to crumple, like spent rose petals would, in his hand. Drake half expected her flesh to slip like moon-ivory mist through his fingers.

Yet her resource and courage belied the appearance of delicate femininity. Wounded, trapped, she had nearly outwitted him, Zak, and two gendarmes the moment he turned his back. And when faced with failure, she had smiled and come back with some quip about his threat to her safety.

She might be a thief, and possibly a murderess, but Drake couldn't deny a reluctant admiration for her determination and wit.

"Don't let it go to your head," he told her, sliding his hand out from under her small face. He retrieved a cloth and basin from the table behind him, using the damp linen to soothe her heated skin. "You're still more trouble than any woman has a right to be, but I must admit I can't accuse you of committing the usual fatal, female sin; you haven't bored me yet."

Setting the basin aside, Drake stretched back in his chair, fingering the emerald around his neck. Although she'd been unconscious since her plunge into the icy waters of the Atlantic, he was taking no chances with the jewel. Drake sternly reminded himself his unwanted guest had cost him valuable time, forced him to concoct hasty and extensive lies for unfriendly gendarmes, and threatened his plan to snare Thorne.

Drake gripped the jewel crushingly and suddenly in his hand. His vow to see justice done flared with overpowering intensity. He'd waited six years. Six years of watching Thorne amass a fortune in stolen treasure. Knowing Thorne killed to protect it.

He looked down at Cianda, seeing another face. A dead face Isabelle.

Beaten and battered by Thorne's hand.

He couldn't afford to think of Cianda D'Rouchert as a beautiful, intriguing woman. She was the Masked Marauder. A pawn in his deadly game. He would use her, and when he had finished, he could relish the pleasure of seeing Thorne hang.

Slowly, Drake uncurled his fist and held the emerald up to the flickering lantern light, smiling grimly as he watched it swing on its golden rope.

Chapter Three

"You're taking better care of that scrap of a street urchin than I do of Fred."

Drake turned in the narrow 'tween deck corridor to where Zak lounged insolently against an open doorway. A bedraggled, grayish, yellowish, blackish mongrel cat hung over his partner's arm like a worn out dishrag.

"That's not saying much since you don't take care of Fred. Fred takes care of Fred. I'd just as soon toss that filthy fur ball of yours to the sharks, but I must admit I respect his independence."

"*Her* independence, and may I remind you she's the best mouser we've ever had aboard."

"Forgive my lapse. It simply doesn't occur to me that anything so ugly could be female." Glancing to Zak's scraggly red beard and the flame-red strands blazing out of control from the top of his head down past his neck and shoulders, he wanted to add that neither had it occurred to him that anything so wild looking could be human. But he buried the temptation, too tired to do mental combat with so apt an opponent.

Zak shot Drake an offended grimace, and stroked the cat, who, as though insulted, turned her flat, battle-worn face to the side out of Drake's view.

"So," Zak began dispassionately, "are you through playing this little mystery guest game of yours, or must I feign disinterest in your strange preoccupation with that waif yet another day? Really, old chap, you're beginning to worry me. You're the last person on earth I'd ever expect to pick up a stray to begin with, much less to be nursemaid to it."

Drake ground his teeth. *"She's* sick. And wounded. She needs to be watched constantly."

"Naturally."

"Damn it, Zak. I — we need her. Alive."

"Indeed." Zak rubbed the cat's neck. "And you are personally bound to see to it she recovers, no matter how many hours of your very valuable time that task consumes. Or was this meant to be a pleasure cruise? My understanding was that Lord Palmerston had a bit of work in mind for us to accomplish during this voyage." Fred jumped out of Zak's arms, and Zak shrugged and shoved his hands into the fathomless pockets of his baggy overcoat.

"What I am trying to tell you is that I have a strong feeling that woman in my cabin is the solution to our problem."

"I don't like the sound of this already. I sincerely hope you haven't deluded yourself into believing that skinny girl is the infamous Masked Marauder."

"What can I say? I have a vivid imagination."

"You have a penchant for accepting the impossible."

Drake shrugged. "Come on, I'll explain over dinner. And as usual, whether you like it or not, you'll go along with me."

Grumbling into his beard, Zak trailed Drake to the forward end of the 'tween decks. Drake peeked in and inhaled a succulent aroma.

"What's on the menu tonight, Domenique?"

Hovering over a worktable, a grizzly bear of a man attacked a fat piece of salt pork with a razor-edged cleaver. *"Poulet en crème, mon capitaine,"* he answered, his baritone more a low growl than a voice. He tossed the raw meat into a steaming kettle.

"Ahhh," Drake's mouth watered at the thought of the rich sauce and delicate seasonings. Domenique was worth his considerable weight in fresh cream and mushrooms. Besides he'd paid his way more than one time scaring off thieves and pirates by simply raising his cleaver and baring his canines. But it was pure deception. In truth the only victims of the gentle Goliath's aggression were raw hunks of meat and whole vegetables.

"Ze soup you requested for ze mademoiselle iz fini."

"Next thing you know, Dom, he'll have you picking berries for her tarts," Zak said before they moved on to the saloon.

"You won't think you're so bloody clever when I tell you how valuable she is to us," Drake said, retreating from his cook's domain to take his place at the head of the table in the saloon. "If she dies," he said as he sat down, "we lose our only hope of catching Thorne with the goods in hand."

Zak slumped over the table opposite Drake, elbows splayed out to either side, pointed chin resting atop entwined fingers. "I can scarcely stand the suspense."

Drake looked across the table into his partner's familiar, lackluster, hazel eyes, and found an equally familiar dose of doubt glaring back.

He swigged down the tankard of ale a steward set before him and wiped his mouth with the sleeve of his shirt. "By all means, allow me to end your torment," he said, leaning back and kicking his sleek black boots up to rest on a nearby chair. "She is the Masked Marauder."

Zak stared across his ale, waiting. "And?" he asked after a long pause.

"Don't you understand? She *is* the Masked Marauder. It all makes perfect sense."

Zak sighed. "Six and one-half years ago, when I was the

only agent you could coerce into being dragged through hell and high-water on your suicide missions, I was a 'bloody genius.' Now, I'm a fool because I can't take two words, run a thread of coherence through them, and tie them up into a neat little danger-infested plan? No, damn you, it does not make perfect sense!"

"As I remember it, you were as eager to leave American shores behind as I was English."

"Perhaps. But, unlike you, my reputation didn't follow me all across Europe. Obscurity does have its advantages, I suppose."

"You and your clan may be eccentric, Zak, but you can hardly call any member of your family obscure. Your father's theories are taught around the world. And your mother's political essays are equally renowned — and controversial. Even your sister — "

"Enough! Don't you start or I'll have to flee this floating hotel of yours too to find a little peace."

"And leave me alone with Domenique's creations to eat myself into an early grave?"

Zak lifted his pewter tankard. "To freedom then?"

Drake clanked his in response. "And to fate."

Zak cocked his head to one side as though he hadn't heard correctly.

"You mean you can't figure it out?" Drake asked, knowing full well he was being a complete ass. Zak liked him that way. That's why the partnership worked. Drake walked all over Zak, and Zak ignored him. In fact, as often as possible, they ignored each other. A partnership made in heaven, Drake thought.

The steward returned bearing a tray with plates heaped with servings of chicken doused in cream, mushrooms and tiny white onions, a bottle of dry white wine and two glasses. Drake savored his first bite of meat and his first sip of wine. "I realize it may be difficult to imagine, but that

42

slip of a girl is Thorne's jewel thief. And we're going to use her to hang the bastard."

Zak looked up from his plate to a pair of absolutely sober, sea-blue eyes. "That's it. We leave for London today. You've been at sea far too long."

"We are going home. With her. It's so simple. Like a game of chess. We use her as a pawn to set Thorne up to buy the jewel she's stolen, then spring the trap!" Drake slapped both hands on the table sloshing ale and wine and clattering the dishes.

Zak reached out to save his chicken and mushrooms from ending up on the floor. "It's a brilliant plan, no doubt. But, I must ask you to indulge me, just a trifle, by explaining how it is the illusive Masked Marauder has managed to avoid all the constables in London, the Italian police, and every gendarme in France, yet *Voilà!* he — er — she drops right into your arms, or lap, as the case seems to be?"

"We were both after the same thing." Drake pulled the emerald necklace from inside his shirt and let it dangle in front of Zak's face.

"Are you certain it's genuine?"

"My aristocratic breeding may not manifest itself in any other facet of my person, but I do know a genuine emerald when I see one."

Zak reached out and fingered the jewel gingerly. "It's as large as a quail egg. What about the Bean? Didn't he try to get a hand in this? You thought he would. I can't imagine Thorne's ex-head thief is too pleased at being replaced by that — girl."

Drake's mouth was full so he nodded a reply.

"Then what happened? I thought Antoine had information that would lead you to the emerald before it was stolen."

Drake wiped his mouth. "Oh, Antoine had information all right. Faulty information. He's such a jittery little weasel. Maybe his nerves got the better of him and he simply blundered under the pressure. I don't know what went wrong, but it doesn't matter now that we have her."

Zak shot a glance to either side of him and lowered his voice. "How can you be sure she didn't kill the count? It's more the Bean's method of business, but if she is the Marauder . . ." Zak shrugged off Drake's scathing glance. "I don't take the notion of sailing to London with a murderer lightly, even if she is only a scrawny wench."

"I'm not sure who killed the count. But we'll never find out if she doesn't live. Moreover, if she dies, we lose our chance to catch Thorne firsthand when she delivers the goods and he pays her."

"So that's what you have in mind, is it? We're to travel with a thief who's very probably a murderess as well, and expect her to cooperate with us so she can wind up in Newgate with her neck at the end of a rope?"

"I told her she'd have her freedom if she helped us. I didn't exactly explain that the Queen would see to it I suffered a traitor's death if she knew Palmerston had commissioned me to expose her dear Thorne for the mercenary he is."

"That was prudent, and uncharacteristically generous of you. And for your promise, did our guest vow in return not to slit your throat the moment your back is turned?"

"Not yet, but she will. One way or another."

"Forgive me for bringing up the painful past, but this is beginning to sound similar to your last near brush with the Masked Marauder. He—or she—if you will—slipped through your fingers and you wound up in that rat hole of an Italian jail. If I hadn't promised Palmerston your soul, you'd still be there."

At the memory of the wasted months, and the betrayal that caused them, Drake ground his fork into his meat. "Every time you bring that story up, you play a bigger role,

44

you know that? I practically had to beg you to send word to Palmerston. If you recall, you were perfectly content to tour the ruins of ancient Rome and send me the souvenirs. It was I who finally persuaded Palmerston not to abandon me or my plan, despite the minor complication of getting tossed in jail."

"Untrue, untrue. I petitioned for your release, in my own way."

Drake scoffed. "It is true, but that doesn't matter now. What is important is that this time I've got her. And Charles is on the other side of the world in India. He can't interfere this time. And if my older brother values his life, after what he did to me, he'd better stay there."

"Yes, as I remember, you did make that much abundantly clear to him. Still, he is in the Queen's good graces, which is more, my friend, than I can say for you — us."

"Honestly, Zak, sometimes you're utterly gutless. You should be more like Fred." Drake motioned to the cat who was at that moment making a flying leap from a chair up to the table to snatch a leftover chicken bone caught beneath the edge of Zak's knife.

Fred landed less than an inch from the blade, wrestled the bone out from under the cutting edge then dodged the knife by a hair's breadth as it came tumbling down after her. Bone in teeth, she flew out of the saloon in a flash of mangy fur.

"I've lost my appetite," Zak said flatly. "Good night." He shoved his plate aside and followed his cat.

"Don't forget to bolt your door," Drake called after him. "The Marauder might have a few more daggers up her sleeve." He pushed away from the table to go ask Domenique to ladle a bowl of soup for Cianda. If the smell of his onion soup didn't rouse her, nothing would.

"You'd better live," he muttered as he grabbed a hunk of bread and a spoon to add to the tray. "Or, I may not."

45

* * *

A rich aroma wafted through Cianda's dream, the scent of food, real food. Her eyes fluttered open to the image of a dark, imposing form hovering over her.

The velvet stroke of Drake Weston's voice chased away the gray fog of her sleep, startling her into wakefulness.

"Good. You're awake. You can eat this before it gets cold," he said, placing the tray on a stand near his bunk.

Cianda rubbed her eyes, struggling to gather her wits enough to form a coherent sentence; as she pulled herself into a sitting position. "I am famished."

"Thieving and narrow escapes must give you an appetite."

"Whatever it is smells delicious," she said lightly, deliberately ignoring his barb.

"It is one of my chef's specialties. Onion soup with fresh bread for dipping."

"Your chef?" Cianda raised a brow. "Rather a luxury on a schooner this size, isn't it?"

"There are few things I relish in this life. And a well-prepared meal is one of them. Domenique is an indispensable member of my crew."

"It appears he is your crew. I haven't heard or seen another living soul. Except a cat's meow, that is."

Drake sat down on the bunk beside Cianda. She tried to ignore the brush of his back against her sheet-draped leg. The lingering rub of the soft linen and his warm body against her bared skin elicited a heated tingle that swept over her in a rush. Unexpected, uncontrolled, it disturbed her in its intensity.

"You're flushed." The devil in Drake's eyes betrayed his innocent query. He touched two fingers to her face, slowly drawing them down her cheek to her jawline. "Are you feverish again?"

"No," she said, bravely meeting his eyes with a cool gaze. "I feel rather chill. You were telling me about the cat."

46

A faint smile tugging at his mouth, Drake let his hand slip away. "That was Fred. He—she belongs to my partner, Zak. Besides Zak and Domenique, there are fewer than a dozen men aboard." He idly dipped the spoon into the soup as he spoke, blowing on it before offering it to Cianda.

Cianda watched the slow, sensuous motion of his lips as they parted over the liquid. She found herself unwillingly wondering, if he kissed her, would his mouth feel the way it looked? Warm. Soft. Tender. At the same moment, a warning clashed with her distracting fancies. She must be feverish to let any man, especially this man, appeal to her senses in that way. It was foolish and a risk she dare not take.

And it was also dangerously, temptingly exciting. She could never feel safe with a man like Drake Weston. But then, she had never known what safe felt like.

"Here," he said softly, "drink this." Momentarily captivated by the depthless, ocean-blue eyes beckoning her, and the gentle coaxing in his tone, she obeyed.

As she opened her mouth, he touched the spoon to her lips. With an intensity she'd almost forgotten, she relished the taste of food on her tongue. Leaning her head back and closing her eyes, she savored the first bite she'd eaten in days. When she brought her head back up, her hair tumbled over her shoulders in waves of spun fairies' silver and gold. Opening her eyes, she caught Drake staring.

He blinked, an odd expression on his face, as though he wanted to confirm she existed or to make her disappear. Which, she couldn't have said.

"Is that all I'm allowed?"

"What? No. Here. You appear to have recovered. Feed yourself." Drake practically shoved the spoon into her hand, then stood abruptly and set the tray on her lap.

"Thank you. I'd much rather feed myself."

"The sooner you recover the better. I have some things to attend to. Do you need anything else?"

"My freedom," she boldly shot back.

"That's up to you. If you agree to my plan, you'll go free. If not —" He folded his arms, looking down at her from his considerable height. "I'll see you hang. I'd rather it be Thorne, but at this stage, beggars can't be choosers."

"You're ruining my appetite."

"Then I'll gladly take my leave." With a mocking bow, Drake strode from the cabin. Cianda listened for the scratch of the key turning the lock before she returned to her meal. Ravenous, she set the spoon aside and drank from the bowl using the bread to sop up every delicious drop.

"I'll have my freedom, all right. And it won't be at your bidding, Drake Weston," she muttered. Twiddling the spoon in her fingertips, she surveyed the small cabin, hunting for something to assist her in the idea forming in her mind. As she considered and discarded several plans, the spoon slipped from her fingers and clanged against the bowl.

And a solution to her dilemma crystallized in a flash of inspiration.

"Hold on, Jamie," she said with a triumphant smile. "It will take more than one arrogant pirate to stop the Masked Marauder."

Cianda waited until the only noises outside Drake's cabin were the sounds of waves whipping against the side of the schooner. The room was black and she felt at home with the darkness. She sat up and listened in the ebon void. Like a cat in the dark, her eyes adjusted.

Her ears perked. No footsteps topside. None in the adjoining cabin. She'd have to work quickly. If only she could have at least walked the ship one time. But Drake Weston saw fit to leave no clothes in his cabin, save the thin shirt she wore. He'd taken her overcoat — with her jemmy hidden in an inside pocket. He'd even thought to remove his letter opener from the desk. Until now, he had effectively trapped her in his room while he went about his duties elsewhere.

Tucked deeply under the blankets, Cianda had feigned sleep when a steward returned earlier in the evening to clear her tray. She held her breath, lest he notice the missing spoon.

And again when Drake crept in afterward to check on her, she laid perfectly still, as though deep in sleep. He didn't hear her nervous heart pounding beneath the covers, didn't feel her breath quicken when he bent to brush the hair from her cheek. Then, when she felt his fingertips trail down the side of her face, it was all she could manage to conceal the trembling of her nerves.

Now Cianda crept out of the bunk and reached underneath for the spoon she had diligently spent the afternoon and evening fashioning into a makeshift jemmy with an ivory statue. She thought it odd the expensive Indian statue was the only ornament in an otherwise sparsely outfitted cabin. But the goddess had served Cianda well, helping to flatten and stretch the pliable copper spoon where she had broken the handle away from the bowl.

Her makeshift jemmy in hand, she stepped toward the door joining Drake's cabin without so much as the creak of a board underfoot. Earlier, she'd heard heavy boots shuffling about in the next room. The captain's cabin boy should sleep there. If Drake kept a cabin boy aboard, there had certainly been no evidence of him.

Nevertheless, it was a gamble. She'd learned long ago, though, to trust her instincts. And right now, her intuition told her that her emerald was in that room.

She eased her way across the small room to the door. Though she was accustomed to working in near-dark, she felt unusually blinded. "Damn him," she whispered. He hadn't even left her lantern burning, undoubtedly fearing she'd set the ship on fire, or some such nonsense.

49

With no light to help, Cianda closed her eyes and concentrated. She gripped the door handle, feeling with her fingers and her mind's eye. She remembered Maisie telling her a thief alone with a lock needed no eyes, only fingers. But in ten years, this was the first time that bit of philosophy had truly been put to the test.

Sucking in her breath, Cianda used nimble fingers to twist the tool into the keyhole. The cool metal of the jemmy warmed beneath her skin, and she felt the familiar thrust of anticipation as the slim rod slipped into the opening, the mounting tension as the jemmy probed for the right place, until at last, the lock surrendered and she drowned in sweet relief.

The door creaked open. Cianda poised, waiting. Listening.

The close sound of a man's heavy, rhythmic breathing told her the closet was as cramped as she'd suspected. Just a couple of steps to the hammock where Drake slept. But where would he have hidden the emerald? Where would she hide it?

The obvious answer made her wish it hadn't been so many years since she'd picked a pocket or unfastened the clasp around a lady's neck. She had no choice but to shove aside her anxiety. Time was running out. Dawn's light hovered just at the horizon, and she had yet to retrieve the emerald and maneuver her way to a companionway or to a scuttle that opened topside. From there she must loose the lifeboat and drop into it before the watch spotted her. Could she make it to London? No matter. *I've got to try.*

All the improbabilities and pitfalls of her plan lurked at the back of her mind, nagging for attention. Cianda ignored them. She could ill-afford the distraction this moment. Drake Weston was distraction enough.

His breathing gave her hope he'd drunk his fill of ale before bed. He certainly sounded as though cannon fire couldn't wake him. Her hands stretched ahead of her, Cianda gingerly cat-footed to the hammock. The sound told her where his head lay. With a feathery touch, her fingertips found his hair. How soft it felt; and how at odds the texture was with the almost harsh, coffee brown color of it.

Concentrate!

Her fingers trailed down the thick waves at his nape and met the bare skin of his shoulder. He wasn't wearing a night shirt. *What else wasn't he wearing?* Cianda swallowed hard, forcing her thoughts to focus on nothing below his neck.

Warm flesh met cool metal. Just as she supposed, the emerald hung around his neck. In a split second, she opened the clasp.

Some things one never forgets.

Cianda cupped her hand near his chest to catch the jewel as it slid into waiting palm. She tightened her fingers around it in an almost caressing grasp, nearly giddy with her victory. With her treasure safe, Cianda turned to escape.

A large, heavy hand on her wrist stopped her before she took the first step.

"If I'd known you wanted to share my bed, milady thief, I never would have moved out of my cabin." Drake jerked her down next to him in one sweep, sending the hammock swinging. She lay snared in the curve of his arm, his hand wrapping her shoulder. At the same time, he flung his leg over hers, and the sudden slide of skin against bare skin jolted Cianda into brash speech.

"Let go of me, or I'll—I'll kill you!"

"I believe you'd like to try. But I don't intend to give you the chance." Drake shackled both her wrists with his free hand, gripping until the homemade jemmy and the emerald fell between them. "And just when I was beginning to delude myself into thinking you couldn't have killed the count."

"I didn't kill him! But I will kill you if you don't give me my emerald!" Cianda kicked and squirmed, but her frantic struggle was like the wriggling of a rare butterfly caught in a collector's fingers. Her desperate motions twisted Drake's sheet and her shirt into a tangle and she sucked in a startled breath when her belly brushed against the hot, hard evidence of his arousal.

Drake muttered a curse, then his voice came fast and angry against her ear. "If you don't lie still you're going to regret this caper of yours a damned sight more than you already do."

"I should have expected an uncivilized barbarian like you to use such a threat," Cianda spat, thankful the darkness hid her flush of fury and embarrassment.

"Outraged innocence? You're stretching the limits of my delusions, milady Marauder."

"I doubt that's possible." She wanted to fight for her escape, but the intimate press of his body stilled her. Even the shallowest of breaths caused her skin to tingle from the barest of touches against his, faster as her breathing quickened, more slowly and seductively as she fought to control her quivering.

Living in the Acre had robbed her of any innocence in knowing about the relations between men and women. But she had never lain with a man, and she abruptly realized knowing about such things and feeling a man's hard shaft pressed to her bare thigh were startlingly different!

Drake brushed a finger over the sharp edge of her jemmy. "Why didn't you kill me when you had your chance? You could have used this—" He held up the makeshift tool. "—this thing."

"Because I am not a murderess!"

"But you are a thief. And this bauble doesn't belong to you."

"Nor to you." Mustering every bit of strength, Cianda

52

gave an abrupt twist and brought her knee up as high and hard as she could.

"You bloody little—" Drake flinched back in pain and Cianda seized her chance.

Grabbing the emerald, she rolled off the hammock to her feet. Before she could make it to the doorway, it slammed closed in front of her, and she found her back pinned against the rough wood by the weight of Drake's naked body.

She gasped. His bare skin burned against her, his iron-hard body at once crushing her painfully and arousing in her strange, conflicting desires she'd never known herself capable of feeling. Part of her yearned to run and hide from his overpowering presence. But something else in her relished the moment, was anxious to savor the frighteningly delicious sensations he ignited in her.

He latched onto her wrists and yanked her arms up over her head, pinning them against the door. The emerald slipped from her hand to the floor. Cianda felt the rapid rise and fall of Drake's chest, the quick fan of his breath against her neck, the fire in his eyes branding her. Her thin shirt was poor protection. Every muscle and plane of his body seemed to plunder the softness of her own, seeking a willing match.

"Let me go!"

"Still playing the innocent? Don't you ever stop pretending? Europe's infamous Masked Marauder a virginal girl? I think not."

"You know nothing about me."

"I know a woman in your profession, with your considerable attributes, cares little for the queen's morality."

"The Queen's morality is for those who can afford to hide their sins with wealth and an aristocratic name." Enraged, frightened, stung by defeat, Cianda forgot the necessity of guarding her impetuous tongue. "Not everyone is so privileged, Captain Weston. Survival has its own morality."

"Such an impassioned speech from someone who can hardly claim to be among the less fortunate," Drake mocked. He hesitated a moment and his hand softened against her wrists. "Who are you, Cianda D'Rouchert? The Masked Marauder, a murderess, or someone I haven't met?"

"You aren't likely to find out," Cianda hissed, angling her knee upward.

The ploy failed the second time. He caught her, smashing his leg against hers before she could raise it. "I'm getting tired of that particular game of yours," Drake said, his voice dangerously low. "Let's try one of mine." Before she could protest, he bent and covered her mouth with his.

His kiss was nothing gentle. It was hungry, consuming, probing, his lips and tongue invading the sweet pleasures within. Cianda's reason screamed at her to battle his sensual invasion, but her senses betrayed her. Her resistance whimpered and died as a rush of excitement possessed every nerve, making her crave his caress, instead of prompting the revulsion she needed to keep him at bay.

It felt something like the thrill of her illicit midnight raids, yet infinitely more exalting. She felt dizzy, as if she balanced on a treacherously high ledge, a step away from a headlong fall. Her body surrendered to a seductive languor. In response Drake's hands released her wrists and slowly slid down her arms to her waist.

His mouth softened against hers and for a heartbeat, slipped away to tease the corner of her lips. He curved his fingers into her hair, letting it twine around his hand like a silken rope. "Cianda," Drake whispered against her skin, his voice savoring her name. "Did you choose the name of an enchantress on purpose, knowing you could tempt a man to madness . . . ?" Giving her no chance to answer, he kissed her again, this time slowly, deeply, as if he had eternity to learn every contour of her mouth.

She was insane, she must be. She had never let any man close enough to touch her, let alone kiss her with such bold abandon. As Drake's mouth explored her face, her chin, suckling her neck and the tender line of her throat, Cianda's will even to think fast dissipated. Why, why couldn't she react, run, hide from him . . .?

"You see," he murmured, gently nibbling her earlobe. "My game is much more interesting. Especially with someone well-acquainted with the rules."

The sly comment pierced the sensual haze befuddling Cianda. She jerked away from him. "What I am well-acquainted with, Captain, is your attempts to use me in whatever way amuses you most."

"Pretending again? A poor attempt, I'm afraid. I know passion when I taste it on a woman's lips and feel it in the willingness of her body," he said softly. He released her and stood back. "But I'll spare you the humiliation of knowing your feminine wiles, formidable as they are, won't divert me."

"The only thing more offensive than your kiss is your conceit, Captain Weston."

"You're being insulting again. It must be the strain of losing this—" He bent down and scooped up the emerald from the floor where it had fallen. "—to me. Again. And this time you *will* have to kill me to get it back."

"Gladly."

"Perhaps you'll wait long enough for me to put on my trousers."

"That I will do with pleasure," she said, turning away as he retrieved his clothes.

Dressed from the waist down, Drake opened the closet door. Red streaks of morning light from his cabin porthole met Cianda, stinging her eyes. Clutching her arms to her body, she paced to the opposite side of the room. When she whirled around to face Drake, she found him staring in wonderment at the tool she'd fashioned.

"A spoon's handle. Ingenious. But how did you make it so thin, so sharp?"

Cianda indicated the statue on his desk. "With your Indian goddess's headdress. She sacrificed it to my cause."

Drake's casual curiosity curled into a dark scowl. "Good. Now I can toss that thing overboard."

"Not a favorite trinket from your travels, Captain?"

"Neither the choice of souvenirs, nor the travels are mine. My brother sent it from the Punjab as a pathetic peace offering."

Cianda heard anger in Drake's voice, but before she could comment, he changed the subject.

"I believe you've had enough time to ponder my offer. Have you decided to agree to my plan?"

"What makes you think I intended to sell that emerald to Godfrey Thorne?"

"Don't waste my time. I have very little patience, and none at all for pretense."

"And if I refuse?"

"You hang."

Cianda silently debated her choices. If she went along with him, there was a slim chance she could escape before he sent her to prison. Which he would. She had no illusions. He didn't intend to keep his false promise to free her, any more than she intended to honor any bargain she drew with him. If she refused him: the gallows. Dear God, Jamie . . .

Damned pirate. He was her only means out of France. If she set foot on French soil again, Drake could use her mask and the emerald as evidence for theft, or worse, for murdering the count.

She paced to the other side of the cabin while Drake waited, watching. She could use the safe passage back to England, then go to Godfrey and tell him Drake unmasked her, that he knew everything about Thorne's mercenary ac-

56

tivities. Godfrey would be forced to postpone his plans for the jewels. Perhaps she could convince him to send her—and Jamie—into hiding, or out of the country until he dealt with Drake Weston. Could she trust Godfrey to help her?

One thing was certain—she couldn't trust Drake Weston. Yet a few lies to seduce him into trusting her and she might bring Godfrey's game to a hasty end and secure Jamie's release much sooner than she could have believed possible.

Cianda drew a deep breath, straightened her shoulders and, feeling none of the courage she displayed, extended her hand. "I agree."

Drake studied her face a long minute. Then, he slowly reached out and smothered her hand in his. "For your sake, milady thief, I hope you do."

Chapter Four

In the distance, through the thick morning obscuring the immense warehouses on the London docks, Cianda could just trace the hazy outlines of the Tower and the London Bridge. She leaned against the port-side railing of the *Ferret,* watching the first glow of dawn awaken the city.

It felt good to be free of the dark confines of the captain's cabin. Drake had forced her to stay below deck while the *Ferret* dropped anchor in the Thames at Wapping. Once docked, posting Zak as reluctant sentinel, he finally surrendered to her demand for fresh air.

Evidently Drake trusted his partner completely with her care for he hadn't once checked back over his shoulder toward them. He paced the quarterdeck barking out orders to his crew, focused on directing the unloading of the *Ferret's* cargo.

So close to freedom, Cianda's feet itched to take flight. A gust of ocean breeze whipped up, blowing long, silvery strands of hair across her cheek. She combed her fingers through them, twisting them back over her shoulder. At her elbow, Zak pretended to ignore her. He appeared as annoyed as she by their forced companionship. Yet he presented her principal obstacle to escape. Elude his guard, and she could easily lose herself in the growing morning crowd of fish-mongers, sailors, and peddlers milling about the docks.

But how? She'd gleaned from conversations during the voyage across the channel that the two men's loyalty to each other rivaled the best of marriages. Still, Cianda mused, their friendship might prove the key to her escape—if she turned it to her advantage.

Cianda glanced up to the man towering over her, lean and looming as the mast he propped himself against. "You don't care much for me, do you Mr. —?" she paused, waiting for Zak to take her lead. For several moments only hostile silence answered her.

Zak stuck his middle finger between his teeth, and bit off an over-long portion of nail. With the nail between his teeth he looked down and said finally, "You know the only name I answer to." He turned away to spit the nail out over the railing. "And you're wasting your dubious talents playing coy with me."

His disdainful attitude confirmed Cianda's suspicion that he had no more wish to guard her than she did to be under his watchful eye. At least we agree on one thing, she thought, carefully choosing her next words.

"Since it's obvious we hold each other in similar contempt, doesn't it seem ridiculous we should be forced to endure one another when so easily, you might be free of me and I of you?"

Zak rocked back on his heels and rubbed his scraggly red beard. "Are you asking whether I'll stop you if you try and bolt?" He held her under his scrutiny from the corner of his eye.

Cianda whirled away and grabbed the railing behind her, tossed her head back, closed her eyes, and drew in a deep, careless breath. Her hair, loosed by the movement, danced wildly in the breeze behind her. "Exactly," she said, punctu-ating the word with a short, triumphant laugh. "Just turn the other way and your nemesis will vanish."

"And leave me to suffer the consequences." Zak motioned to Drake.

"Surely you can convince him you had his best interests at heart. What was it you said at dinner yesterday evening? 'Women are trouble. We invite more than our share of that already.' " Cianda fished her boys' cap out of a pocket in her trousers. "And I agree completely. If you don't take this chance to let me slip away, you'll see just how much trouble I can be." Boldly, she held his gaze as she began stuffing her hair up under the cap.

Zak let a meatless shoulder droop against the mast. "If I had found you, I'd have left you for dead on the streets of Cayeux-sur-mer."

"And I'm delighted to have made your acquaintance too." The man was wearing on her good humor. "I'm leaving now. You can salve your wounded sense of loyalty with the knowledge you've made the right choice. Captain Weston will probably be grateful. Someday." Cianda glanced toward Drake to make certain his back was turned. "All the same, I'd consider a sudden holiday," she added, unable to resist a final jibe.

Cianda sensed Zak struggle with his decision. He glared at her, but made no move to stop her as she crammed the last strands of the heavy tresses that betrayed her femininity under her cap. Dressed in the same boys' trousers she'd donned the night Drake rescued her in the alley, she pulled her overcoat over the soft linen shirt Drake had given her.

His shirt. A rush of heat coursed under her skin at the thought of his hands exploring beneath the thin material. How freely had he touched her body? She shivered at the idea, visited by a curious uneasiness she couldn't define.

"Aren't you forgetting something?" Zak asked, interrupting her disconcerting thoughts.

Cianda hid her reddened face, furiously tucking the shirt

into the waistband sagging at her waist. He meant the emerald, of course. She'd have to leave that to Godfrey. Right now, warning Godfrey that Drake Weston knew everything about his treasonous smuggling activities took precedence.

Because as soon as Godfrey heard of Drake's pursuit he'd have no choice but to abandon his plan for her to steal the Koh-i-noor. And he would no longer have reason to hold Jamie hostage.

"You can tell Captain Weston I'll be back for my emerald." She slid a few steps away from him, testing his resolve. Would he let her just walk away?

Zak's heavy red brows furrowed over disturbed eyes. He shoved his hands deeply into his pockets and stared down at the scuffed wooden planks beneath his feet.

Cianda grappled with a slight twinge of guilt as she eased away from him. Zak might believe setting her free improved his partner's immediate situation, but the conflict on his face told her how much the choice cost him. She gauged the strength of his internal war—and took another step.

At the other end of the schooner, Drake called out to a crewman, oblivious to the betrayal underway behind him. Her confidence surged. It was now or never.

Now! Cianda bolted.

Ducking her head, she wound her way toward the gangplank, slipping behind a sailor carting off the crates Drake's men set out. Drake, his back turned to her, continued to scribble in his log. Hunched down, she slipped by him so closely the sleeve of her coat brushed the back of his thigh.

He glanced over his shoulder. Her heart froze.

But her feet kept moving, quickly forward. Weaving through the crowd of sweaty men, she used a swag-bellied sailor to block her from Drake's line of vision. Just a few more steps . . .

Her feet hit the wharf at a sprint. Dodging barrels and crates, ducking through a moving forest of fishermen and sea-weary sailors like a fox fleeing the hounds, Cianda headed straight for the first open street corner.

London! The air, foul from boats heaped with smelts and mollusks, black from the smoke of thousands of chimneys, heavy with wet fog, smelled of hope.

Eagerly, she inhaled the city's breath, as though over the stench, Jamie's freshly scrubbed scent could rise and lead her through the labyrinth of endless winding alleyways to his secret prison. She stopped, leaning against a lamppost to catch her breath and find her bearings.

"Hold on Jamie," she whispered. "Godfrey can't keep you after I tell him what's happened."

Cianda glanced up and down the narrow, cobbled street. She had to reach Godfrey before Drake discovered her absence, and to do that she needed a cab. But no driver would stop for her in her guise as a scruffy street urchin.

Think! Her eyes raced over the stream of morning strollers, settling on an elderly grand dame who stopped to rest old bones across the street.

Dashing across to stand near the expensively dressed woman, Cianda signaled a hackney cab as though in service to her. When the driver stepped down to open the door for the older woman, Cianda scampered inside. Before he could protest and toss her out onto the street, she pulled three shillings — triple the normal fare — from a secret pocket she'd sewn into the lining of her coat.

His attention perked, Cianda lifted her chin arrogantly and looked directly into the driver's bloodshot eyes. "The cab is for me. Take me to Piccadilly Terrace at once!"

The driver squinted and stared at the coins flashing in Cianda's palm.

"Are you deaf? I want to go to Piccadilly Terrace. Now!"

The driver lurched back. "Aye, sir, er — miss." He grabbed the coins. "No matter. Yer coin's real 'nough fer me."

Cianda allowed herself a small, triumphant smile as the

cab jerked into motion. The extra measure of audacity in her method of escape pleased her. Ready to challenge fate, she decided she might, with a dash of luck, be able to outwit both Drake Weston and Godfrey Thorne in the same day.

"I said Lord Thorne will not see you! Now remove yourself from his front steps before somebody spies you."

Cianda gritted her teeth and stared daggers at Pimbe, Godfrey's butler, who, under normal circumstances knew her well as Madame Cianda D'Rouchert. Pride warred against the shame of how closely she resembled the street gamin she was when Godfrey found her. Now, though, she needed the mask of the guttersnipe. She didn't dare risk revealing her identity to Pimbe, no matter how uncomfortable the charade.

Ducking her head, she shifted nervously from foot to foot. "Only a word wit' milord sir, I beg ye. I've a message from Lady D'Rouchert." Cockney came back easily, mocking all Godfrey's tutors' efforts to purge it from her. *How ironic, to be forced to rely on the past I most want to forget.*

"Message?" Pimbe was saying, "Give it to me, then be gone."

"But the lady says only ter give it ter Lord Thorne else I gets nothin'."

Pimbe scowled down, his stony face cracking slightly at the edges of his narrowed eyes. He stabbed a finger at her. "I told you Lord Thorne is not available."

"What the devil is going on out there?"

At last the thunder, Cianda thought, recognizing Godfrey's booming voice. He would see her, bypass Pimbe and usher her in immediately.

"I'm terribly sorry, sir," Pimbe apologized. "This lad simply will not leave his message with me. I shall have him tossed off the grounds at once."

Godfrey stepped past Pimbe and glared down at Cianda. The faintest hint of a satisfied smile touched the corners of his thin lips. "No. Send him around to the tradesmen's entrance."

Outrage surged in Cianda. "What!" The word escaped her lips before she could think to stop it.

"Show him to my study. But first see to it he leaves those filthy boots in the kitchen."

Cianda jerked her head up to face him, heedless of the conclusions Pimbe might draw, just in time to catch the condescending glint in Godfrey's steel eyes. He turned and disappeared into the mansion, leaving her with no choice but to follow his command.

At the back of the house the cook, a woman Cianda didn't recognize, answered the door. Godfrey's meticulously trained Dorsey must be terribly ill, she decided. He never before even considered allowing another woman to prepare his meals.

Pimbe met her in the kitchen, and she followed him through seemingly endless doorways and corridors to Godfrey's study.

"That insult was hardly necessary," she spat, after Pimbe secured the study doors behind her.

Godfrey tilted back in his chair from behind his massive desk. "On the contrary, my dear, I certainly cannot be seen entertaining street rabble on my doorstep."

Stocking-footed, Cianda slowly crossed the spacious room and took a seat opposite him. "I hardly think anyone would have taken note at this hour."

Slanting his fingertips together, Godfrey arched a brow and looked down his nose at her, studying her from head to toe. "I must admit to a sudden nostalgia seeing you dressed that way. Rather miraculous really, to consider what beauty I created from the rubbish you were when I dredged you from the Acre."

Cianda forced herself not to flinch under his sardonic gaze. She hardly needed to be reminded that he fabricated her life, her name, her pedigree. Lifting her chin, she met his eyes squarely. "You must listen to me. There's an agent for the Crown who knows everything about your taste for illicit jewels — and about how you procure them. He knows I'm the Masked Marauder."

Godfrey's sharp jaw tightened. A menacing stone facade hardened his expression. "I think you had better explain."

"There was some — difficulty in France." Cianda twisted and untwisted her fingers together in her lap. "This agent managed to abduct me. I escaped and came straight to you. He intends to expose you to the Queen. He knew everything even before he found me. I certainly didn't tell him," she added defiantly, thanking him silently for teaching her to lie so smoothly. "I didn't have to."

"Precisely what do you mean by 'everything'?"

"Just that. Everything including the Indian trio. And he intends to see you hang before you get those gems."

Lifting a letter opener from his desk, Godfrey ran the tip of his index finger over it slowly. The point nicked his skin. A drop of blood beaded up. He never flinched, but kept his eyes steadily on Cianda. "Betrayal is an ugly word, isn't it, my dear? An ugly word with ugly punishments."

Determined not to let him shake her, Cianda forced a steadiness into her voice. "I wouldn't have run from him straight here as soon as we docked if I intended to betray you."

Godfrey pulled a snow white handkerchief from his sprigged satin waistcoat to dab the crimson drop from his finger. "You came to me only because I hold your precious little brother's life in the palm of my hand. Have you forgotten so soon that you forced me into taking such extreme measures to ensure my investment in you?"

Cianda's stomach clenched. Her fault, yes, it was her

fault Jamie's life now dangled from Godfrey's fingertips. She should have simply taken him and run far and fast.

Loyalty to Godfrey prevented that. Despite his cruelties, she felt a strange indebtedness to him for plucking her and Jamie out of the Acre. And her tendency to blunt speaking led her to confess her plans to quit thieving, just at the moment he announced finding a buyer for the Indian trio.

"I see you do remember there are debts you must repay," Godfrey said, a slight smile playing with the corner of his mouth. "I trust I won't hear any more foolish prattle from you about quitting your task before you have my prize. Or retiring at all. I don't intend to give up my profits simply because you have a ridiculous whim to taste life in the country."

Clutching her hands tightly together, Cianda swallowed her fear and uneasiness. Godfrey would only prey on her weakness. "I'll get your jewels. But not now. Not with this agent at my back. When you've settled with him, I'll finish the work. And there's another problem," she went on hurriedly as Godfrey's glower intensified. "I'm wanted for the murder of Count LeDoux."

"And did you kill him?"

"Of course not! But the French and British authorities are certain to be collaborating to find the Masked Marauder now that they believe he's a murderer as well as a thief."

"And who is to blame for this latest mishap of yours? Your mysterious agent of the Crown?" He flicked an invisible speck of dust from his desktop. "I've heard nothing of your murder in the newspapers."

"It's not my murder," Cianda snapped. "Someone else tried to steal the Rajput and killed the count in the process."

"I see." Godfrey listened, his steepled fingers flexing slightly, as Cianda recounted her adventures in France, detail for detail.

"I don't know who the murderer was or how he discovered

the whereabouts of the Rajput, but I'm lucky to have made off with it."

"But did you, 'make off with it,' as you so quaintly express it?"

"Yes, of course." She decided not to mention how short a time she actually possessed it. "I went straight to the meeting place Beatrice and I arranged at the docks." She lied fast and furiously. "I didn't even take time to return to the inn. I knew the gendarmes would be looking for the thief."

"And this agent simply—found you," Godfrey waved a languid hand, "and spirited you away to his ship. Leaving Miss Dobson alone to fend for herself in France. Quite trying for her, I'm certain. It is interesting, though, that she managed to return to England a day before you."

"I told you—"

"Yes, your agent. Pray tell, who is this brilliant knight of the Crown, who not only thwarted the Masked Marauder but a host of French gendarmes as well?"

"His name is Weston. Captain Drake Weston," Cianda began, starting to describe what she knew of him. But the odd expression, a fleeting but distinct recognition of the name, crossing Godfrey's face stopped her. Anyone else would have missed it, so apt was he at masking his thoughts. Cianda knew him too well. More than once her life had depended on her ability to gauge Godfrey's intentions by the almost undetectable clues written on his face. And more than once, she'd chosen her words to elicit information she wanted. "You've heard the name."

"All of London society knows that name," he said smoothly. "But then you would have been too young to understand. Drake Weston is the one dark smear on his family's spotless pedigree. I've no doubt his mother would find it a great relief if he vanished altogether."

"You obviously share that opinion."

"I dislike anyone who interferes with my business. As you

67

well know." His even tone clashed with the coldness in his eyes.

Dislike? You hate him. But why? Cianda itched to know the truth. For once, though, she held her tongue, realizing the danger in pushing Godfrey too far. "So, you'll deal with Captain Weston while I wait for a more opportune time to finish the robbery?"

Godfrey pushed away from his desk. "On the contrary, my dear," he said approaching her with slow deliberate steps. "I'll find it vastly more intriguing to watch him sink in the mire of his own miscalculations. Besides, I have a formidable ally when it comes to dealing with Captain Weston. Someone he believes he can trust."

He loomed over her, staring down at her, a cold smile on his lips. She looked up to him, determined to resist his bold-faced intimidation. "Then the two of you can wage this war of wits without me. I can't possibly risk stealing the Koh-i-noor with Drake Weston about. That no longer gives you a reason to keep Jamie."

She remained still as Godfrey reached out and slid the cap from her head, releasing a tumble of silvery tresses over her slender shoulders. "Ah, but you will steal my diamond as planned. And you'll bring it to me by my July deadline. Don't make me repeat the obvious consequences of your failure to do so."

"I have the ruby and the emerald—"

Godfrey's face tightened. "I must have all three. Why is none of your concern. And I must have the diamond before our beloved Victoria has an opportunity to have it recut to suit her taste.

"There's something you haven't told me, obviously," Cianda said, heedless of the danger of inciting his anger.

"Didn't I mention the prince plans to present it to her in honor of the two hundred and fiftieth anniversary of the East India Company? It's to be the most glorious trophy representative of the Company's many Indian conquests."

Jerking away from him, Cianda leapt to her feet. "This is madness! Even for you. Drake Weston is determined to see you hang and I don't fancy joining you when he does. Even I don't owe you that much!"

"Don't be so certain of that, Cianda." He stared at her for a measured moment, then waved the matter away. "Enough prattle! Weston is not the first and certainly not the best man to try to ruin me. But his methods are at least entertaining."

"How nice for you. Where does that leave me? Surely you can't still expect me—"

"Exactly. I have great expectations for you. It amuses me to play this game of Weston's. So . . ." He returned to sit behind his desk. Picking up the letter opener again, he slid it between his thumb and forefinger. "You agree to go along with whatever scheme he proposes. Keeping me informed, of course. In the meantime, bring me the ruby and the emerald. I want to make certain they are safely out of Weston's reach. Without them, his word against mine is worthless."

Rage and the frustration of being caught in a trap of her own making burned through Cianda, loosing the guard on her tongue. "You'll have your jewels when I have Jamie back. Not before."

Godfrey met her furious challenge with menace. "If you betray me, Cianda, if the thought even enters your mind, your brother won't live to have regrets for your foolishness. Remember that if Weston's propositions begin to appear more tempting than my own." He gestured sharply to the door. "Now go and find my diamond."

Cianda hesitated, the urge to defy him strong and bitter. Her heart-fear for Jamie overwhelmed the flare of rebellion. She wouldn't imperil her brother's safety.

With one last searing look in Godfrey's direction, she left the study, feeling the jaws of the trap close around her as the door clicked shut.

A few blocks away at Number 144 Piccadilly, Drake Weston stormed back and forth across the polished oak floor of the drawing room of England's Foreign Secretary. He'd arrived at the stately mansion of Henry Temple, Viscount Palmerston, looking and smelling more like a pirate lost at sea for months than the son of one of London's elite families, and as a result had promptly been shown to the tradesmen's entrance.

Of course he'd given Lord Palmerston no notice of his visit, but somehow he always assumed luck would take care of the details. He glanced to the clock on the wall. For more than an hour he'd been compelled to do what he despised most on the face of the earth: wait.

Muttering a curse under his breath, Drake began to wonder if he had depleted his share of good fortune. Or, more likely, if the silver-haired witch he'd let fall into his arms had cursed him.

Feeling the urge to maim, Drake stopped in front of the huge marble mantel and, facing it, gripped it with both hands until his knuckles paled to white. Outwitted by a thief. And far worse, a woman. The thought doubled his tension. And Zak, damn him, the only man he ever even considered trusting these days, had helped her to escape. "Damn them both," he spat into the empty room.

"It doesn't sound as if you've good news for me," a voice from behind interrupted his black reverie. Lord Palmerston walked briskly into the drawing room, tossing a stack of papers on a side table as he went. "You should have told me you were coming, Drake. It's been a trying enough day as it is."

"You might say it was a spontaneous decision," Drake muttered. He stretched out his hand to grip Lord Palmerston's meaty palm.

70

"Do you ever make any other kind of decision?" Palmerston asked, returning the gesture. "Always good to see you—good God, man, what is that horrid smell—fish? Blast, Drake, mightn't you have bathed before popping in?"

"No," Drake said through gritted teeth.

Lord Palmerston stepped away. "I see. Suppose we have a drink and you tell me about it." The butler who stood at attention behind them came forward holding an ornate silver tray laden with a variety of bottles and two glasses. When both men were served, he bowed out.

Drake took a seat opposite Palmerston. The notion it would undoubtedly be given a thorough cleaning the minute he left caused him momentary discomfort. Forcing his anger at Zak and Cianda to the back of his mind, he concentrated on the considerable challenge ahead—how to reveal his plans to Lord Palmerston without appearing to have completely taken leave of his senses.

"Have you brought me Thorne's head on a platter?"

Drake tossed back the brandy in his glass. "Not exactly."

Palmerston raised a brow.

"But I do have the Masked Marauder in the palm of my hand. More or less."

"Which is it? More? Or less?" Palmerston scowled over his glass. "You expect me to believe you've captured the one thief no authority in Europe has been able to touch?"

"Naturally. You might say she fell right into my lap." He paused, pleased with the look of surprise in Palmerston's sharp eyes. "Of course I'd been trailing her for months, and my timing, that is, being in the right place at the right time, was perfect."

"Of course." Lord Palmerston shook his head in disbelief. He squinted suspiciously at Drake. "Did you say she?" The frown made his gray muttonchops look bushier.

"Yes, the infamous Masked Marauder is only a scrap of a

woman." Drake reached out to slosh more brandy in his glass. "I find it hard to believe myself."

"I do hope this isn't your idea of a joke, Drake. I'm not in the mood"

"Neither am I. It's the truth. She's responsible for all the thefts, including the Malwi. She managed to steal the emerald from Count LeDoux. By the way, LeDoux is dead."

"Good Lord! Is she responsible for that also?"

"No—at least, I don't think so. The gendarmes, of course, blame the Masked Marauder. I thought I might mention it, just in case my name ends up on the front page of your morning *Times*."

Palmerston stared blankly before stretching a hand to the carafe on the tray. "I need another," he mumbled to no one in particular. "Blast it all, do you really expect me to believe all this rot?"

"I'll prove it all to you," Drake said, beginning to unbutton his shirt.

"By removing your clothing in my drawing room? Drake, I don't—"

The dazzling gleam of green fire against Drake's chest stopped Palmerston in midsentence.

Drake gave him a lopsided smile. "She stole it from Le-Doux and I stole it from her." He took pleasure in watching Palmerston's eyes widen. Several seconds passed as he gaped, dumbfounded.

"Do I want to know how long you've been walking the streets of London with that dangling from your neck?" Palmerston said at last.

Drake smirked. "There's probably a number of things you don't want to know." He rebuttoned his shirt, hiding the brilliant glisten of green and gold.

"I'm certain you're correct. Suppose you tell me only the pertinent facts—namely, when can I expect to see Thorne implicated in these thefts?"

72

"As soon as she takes the jewels to him. As I suspected, he's her buyer."

"Why do I have the feeling that's not all there is to this?"

"Don't worry about it, Pam. There are a few minor complications." Drake attempted to sound casual. "Nothing I can't manage. With your help, of course."

Lord Palmerston leaned toward Drake. "Meaning?"

"Meaning that if my methods seem, well, somewhat unorthodox, I can still count on your backing. No matter what happens. I need your support, Pam," Drake said, urgency replacing his casual mien. "It won't work without you."

"You ask a great deal for a man who stinks of rotten fish."

"Surely you see how easily it's all falling into place. First, capturing the thief, then the jewel—next the buyer. You want Thorne exposed as badly as I do. Unfortunately in view of recent events, your relationship with the Queen and her beloved husband could certainly stand improvement. Especially if you still intend to become prime minister." Drake knew he skirted the edge of insolence with his remark. But propriety never stopped him from playing out all his aces in one hand.

"I ought to have you tossed out for that," Palmerston said, his tone only half amused.

Drake stood. "No need. I was about to leave. I do have your full endorsement then?"

"Don't presume too much. It always lands you in trouble. You haven't told me what your intentions are."

"Only the obvious, really." Drake paced across the room and back. "I'm planning on using my lady thief to catch Thorne with the stolen jewels in hand."

"You want me to approve of your collaboration with a thief?" Palmerston shook his head. "Really, Drake."

"It's more than that. She either cooperates or I'll see her hang for LeDoux's murder."

The vow earned Drake a snort of derision. "You? Send a female to the gallows? This I would like to see. Unless she's an unusually ugly one, that is."

"No." A slow smile curved Drake's mouth. "I must say, it would be a terrible waste to see her dangling from the end of a rope."

"So I imagined. But I thought, after Isabelle, you had sworn off women."

Drake's smile vanished at the mention of his former lover's name. "I have."

Palmerston set his glass down and stood, facing Drake. "Tell me, Drake, do you want Thorne for me, for the good of Crown and country? Or for yourself?"

"We both want the same thing," Drake said, meeting Palmerston's gaze squarely. "My motivations hardly matter."

"This is a personal quest then."

Drake shoved a hand through his hair. "Yes. And no. Certainly I appreciate you freeing me from that Italian cell. But even though my options were rather limited at the time, I decided to accept your offer of freedom in exchange for my services only because I wanted to see Thorne stopped too."

"I do hope you don't expect me to believe that." Palmerston waved away any answer on Drake's part. Sighing, he walked to stand before a floor-to-ceiling window. He stared out a moment then turned back to Drake. "Where is this Masked Marauder now?"

Drake shifted slightly. "In London."

Palmerston's eyes narrowed. "In London, you say?" He paused, apparently considering how much credence to give the vague claim. "I must give this matter more thought before I can give you an answer. Can I trust you to keep her and the jewels in your care until I reach a decision?"

Drake strode straight over to where Lord Palmerston

74

stood and leveled him a grave look. "Implicitly," he said, extending his hand.

Shaking his head from side to side, Lord Palmerston took the proffered hand in a grip of his own.

"You won't regret this, Pam," Drake said. With an easy smile, he turned to leave, restless to make good on the half-truths he'd told his friend.

He'd already reached the doorway leading to the tradesmen's exit when the foreign secretary, finding his hand stained with smelly dirt, pulled his handkerchief from his pocket and mumbled, "I already do."

Drake left Palmerston's home determined to find Cianda.

A bit of flattery for the pretty scullery maid who showed him out brought him the address of one Madame D'Rouchert. Servants always knew more about the coming and going of the masters and mistresses of society than society itself. And they relished nothing more than an opportunity to display their store of gossipy tidbits. Over the years, flirtatious maids and greedy footmen had unwittingly helped him more times than he recalled. Probably more times than his own partner, he thought in a rush of anger. At least with servants, he could trust a fair return for his investment, whether it be time or coin.

Frustrated and tired of the day's delays, Drake flagged down a cab to take him to the residence where the most notorious thief in Europe spent her days. As the hansom rattled and clambered over the pitted streets and narrow alleyways, his foul temper rocked and bumped back and forth from Cianda to Zak.

By the time the cab pulled up in front of a lavish town home on Dover Street in Piccadilly, he felt inclined to murder.

Tossing a few coins at the driver, he took the front steps

two at a time. "Damn you woman, you'd better be here, or I swear I'll—"

The door swept open. The woman holding the knob stepped back into the foyer, inviting his entrance.

Drake froze in mid-step, staring at her.

He scarcely recognized the mysteriously beguiling nymph he had held in his arms only days ago. Wearing a conservative, high-necked day gown, her hands folded primly in front of her, Cianda greeted him with a cool, provoking smile.

"Good afternoon, Captain Weston. I've been expecting you."

Chapter Five

Cianda perched on the edge of the long sofa, her eyes moving with Drake as he prowled her salon. After a moment's astonished pause when she confronted him on her doorstep, he'd stalked inside her house saying nothing except with the searing fury of a single glance. Now, he paced restlessly, as if he needed an outlet for his volatile emotions.

Determined to remain cool in the face of his hot anger, Cianda reached for the small bell lying on the table in front of her. She gave it a shake then held the smooth metal against her palm, giving her agitated fingers something to stroke. "Tea, Captain Weston? Or perhaps you'd prefer something more bracing to steady your nerves."

Drake stopped in midstep and whirled on her with startling quickness. "I'd prefer to stop playing these damned charades of yours. You've been to Thorne. Don't bother to deny it."

"I won't."

"You—" His eyes narrowed. "Why?"

"What purpose would it serve? You aren't likely to believe anything else."

If her bluntness surprised him, it didn't show on his face. "Did Thorne offer you a handsome bonus for delivering my head—?"

"I wouldn't need an incentive to perform that task."

"—Or are his rewards more personal?"

The taunting insolence in his voice jerked Cianda to her feet. "I care less than nothing about your opinion of how I earn my keep, and less than that for your opinion of me. But if you want my help, Captain, I suggest you exercise your gift for insults on someone else."

"The role of outraged lady of the manor doesn't suit you." His cool, provoking smile suddenly seemed more dangerous than his temper. "Especially since I know what a farce you're playing."

Cianda's gaze twitched from his. His stab at the truth disconcerted her because he probed closer to her secret shame than he imagined.

Languidly, as if he had an afternoon's leisure to explore her salon, Drake took a few steps toward her, then paused. He idly ran his forefinger over the rounded globe of a lamp. "I remember the wildcat who came to my bed and threatened to murder me with the sharp end of a spoon for this—" He slid his fingers against the gold chain lying against his neck. Through the soft linen of his shirt, Cianda could see the outline of the emerald. "There was nothing proper and civilized about you then."

He didn't look at her nor she at him, but Cianda's senses marked every breath he took, knew each movement. Her prim salon filled with his dark presence, the essence and taste and smell of danger. Next to him, she felt as insubstantial as the silver mist of a dream.

"Then we're an even match," she finally managed, her voice sounding small and light to her ears. "Because there's certainly nothing civilized about you. Not even your smell!"

His smile now was slow and wicked. "Nothing at all."

"At last we've found something we can agree on. I hope you'll be as quick to cooperate on our business."

The lazy slant of his body tightened to alert tension in an instant. Drake gave a short, derisive laugh. "Am I now supposed to believe you'll meekly go along with my plans?"

"Aren't you? Then why are you here?" Cianda seized the advantage of his hesitation and plunged ahead. "I did see Godfrey, to try to persuade him to take only the ruby and the emerald. He refused."

"A charming story."

"It's the truth." *Or at least a part of it.* She picked her words carefully. Any misstep on her part could cost her all in the treacherous game she chose to play. "You need me, Captain. And I need you. You want Godfrey. I want the Koh-i-noor. If you let me steal it, we can —"

"No we can't." Drake stood in front of her in two long strides. "I may be reckless at times, but I haven't completely lost all reason — yet. Thorne must be at a loss for clever ideas if he thinks he can hang me that easily." He swept the tips of his fingers over her neck, leaving his hand curved against her throat. His kept his touch light, but the hard tension in his hand gripped like steel. "Even with bait as enticing as you, love."

Fear and fascination clashed in Cianda's heart. She refused to surrender to either. She stood stiff under his hold, chin held high, matching his intimidating gaze with a glare. "The trap is obvious, but I thought the infamous Captain Weston would consider himself clever and resourceful enough to outwit it. I suppose I was wrong." Her mouth lifted in a mocking smile. "Perhaps after Italy, you feel you've bet on your luck once too often."

For a moment, his fingers tightened. "Are you issuing a dare?"

Cianda willed herself not to flinch. "Take it as you please."

"You could tempt a saint to sin, Cianda D'Rouchert." Abruptly, his hand fell away. "And me to attempt the unthinkable." Turning aside, he raked his fingers through his hair, pacing a few steps before dropping down onto the sofa, his long legs stretched out in front of him. "And what do

79

you gain from this adventure?" he finally asked, picking up one of the small cushions beside him and flicking at one of its tassels. "Aside from Thorne's money, of course."

My brother's life. The words trembled on her tongue. "My freedom." She glanced away from his sudden interested look. "I had an arrangement with Godfrey. But Godfrey doesn't understand partnership. He wants to own everything and everyone. I'm tired of being one of his possessions."

"Are you? The words are brave, but you deliver them with a distinct lack of conviction. Why does the idea of betraying Thorne disturb you?"

"It doesn't." *It does.* She wanted to be free. Yet it was hard to dismiss the transformation Godfrey had wrought in her life. Without him, the illusions she shielded herself with crumbled. She hated him. She owed him her entire existence. "What about you, Captain?" she asked to cover her momentary lapse. "What do you gain? Apart from the questionable pleasure of a hanging."

"Justice." He shot the word into the room with force. "A concept you're unfamiliar with, I'm certain."

Cianda turned from him, her fingers clenched into her palm. "Justice is a luxury I can't afford."

He said nothing, and in the silence, Cianda listened to the pound of her heart, the quickness of her breath, clashing like a sudden summer storm inside her body. She had dared locked doors and safes, capture, imprisonment, even Godfrey. But Cianda began to doubt the wisdom of matching wits with Drake Weston.

When his deep voice whispered in her ear, she started. "If I agree to help you *borrow* the Koh-i-noor. And if you agree to help me hang Thorne then . . ."

He slowly walked around her, his body just brushing hers, emphasizing his height and strength against her slender fragility. His eyes found hers. "Can I trust you?"

"No." The answer slipped out before Cianda had time to consider the folly of telling him the truth. She found it difficult to pretend with Drake Weston. The feelings he provoked in her were wild, angry, as heady as a walk on the edge of peril. He was right. There was nothing civilized about either of them, certainly nothing proper about her body's traitorous urge to touch him in return.

"I do consider that a dare." Drake moved until only a heartbeat separated them.

"I don't trust you either." She breathed the words, unable to find her voice.

"That makes the game more interesting, don't you agree? After all—" He circled around behind her, lifting a silver strand at her nape and letting it thread between his fingers. "I might do anything."

"Any time the fancy strikes you, I'm certain."

"Anywhere, milady thief."

It was dangerous, allowing him to touch her, infinitely more treacherous than picking a lock or purloining a cache of jewels. Yet the peril fascinated her. Illicit, forbidden, it tempted her to desires no gentle wooing could have.

Godfrey's lessons had taught her how to maintain the ruse of being a well-bred lady. But underneath the silk and polite trappings she hid the heart of the street child who lived by her wits and instincts, who had never learned to inhibit her feelings. She ached to deny it, and couldn't.

"Drake—Captain Weston . . ."

"Cianda." His low voice made her name sound like seduction.

A sharp rap at the door spared Cianda the humiliation of succumbing, even for a moment, to his potent attraction. She spun away from the sardonic amusement on his face and sucked in a breath an instant before a booted foot kicked the salon door open.

"I've brought yer tea, m'dear." A sqaubbish elderly

woman, dressed in several layers of gaily-colored cotton carried in a laden tray, precariously balancing it on her palms. "Sorry it's been a bit of a wait, but I 'ad to pull meself away from me supper."

As Cianda reached for the tray, she gave the woman an exasperated look. Maisie lied more easily than a macer with a new cheating scheme — Cianda knew she'd been listening outside the door.

With a wink for Cianda, Maisie's plump face creased into a sweet smile as she turned in Drake's direction, fixing him with a narrow-eyed stare. "I see yer pirate's still 'ere."

"Mademoiselle D'Rouchert has been talking about me, I see," Drake said as he took the tea tray from Cianda's hands and laid it on the table. His smug expression tempted her to brash action.

"That she 'as. Plenty an earful, she 'as." Maisie beamed on him with grandmotherly indulgence — the expression had disarmed many an unsuspecting gentleman and deprived him of his watch or silk handkerchief. "Things not fit fer a proper lady's ears, let alone ter come from 'er own lips. I told me girl more 'n once, I did, 'at tongue o' yers'll put ye in worse trouble than — "

"Than it's worth. Although I'm certain you wouldn't know from experience." Cianda put a firm hand on Maisie's shoulder. "Missus Cowper is my housekeeper and I know we're keeping her from her duties."

"What's that yer sayin', dearie?" She cupped a hand to her ear. "My 'earing's not as good as it were, ye know." Maisie smiled on Drake. "She's a good girl, she is. Just a bit 'ard at times, but then that's not 'er doin', poor lass. 'Specially after 'er 'usband up and died on 'er." Fishing a tattered handkerchief from her pocket, Maisie sniffed loudly and patted at her eyes. "A good man, 'e was. A good, fine fellow."

Cianda inwardly cursed Maisie's interference. Ever possessive about her security, Maisie scrapped like twenty men

82

to protect it. "Aunt Maisie, I don't think Captain Weston is interested—"

"Now, dearie, don't fuss." Maisie stumped closer to Drake, and put a confidential hand on his arm. "After all whot she's been through, pity's the man whot tries ter take whot lit'le me girl's laid back ter care fer 'erself and the poor likes o' me. Why, I wouldn't take too kindly to an evil bloke like that meself. No. Not too kindly 't all."

"I've had a taste of *Madame* D'Rouchert's temper, thank you. And I don't believe I'll risk yours at the moment."

Maisie's eyes narrowed. "Best not."

"Aunt Maisie—"

"Well, per'aps I do have a few things ter see 'bout, now that I'm thinkin' of it." Mischief sparked in her eyes as she darted a glance at Cianda. "Enjoy yer tea, dearie."

Cianda caught back a sigh of relief as the door closed behind Maisie.

"Interesting."

She frowned. "Pardon me?"

"Did you have a husband, or did you invent him, too?"

"That's none of your concern!"

Drake shrugged off her anger. "Your housekeeper also intrigues me. How large is your staff?"

His slight emphasis on the last word roused Cianda's annoyance. "I don't think you came to discuss my past or my household. We were talking about a—collaboration."

"So we were. I'd be most interested to hear your ideas. Beyond stealing the diamond, of course." Before she could answer, Drake impatiently waved her retort aside. "Never mind. You wouldn't tell me the truth anyway." He dropped down on the sofa, inviting her with a mocking sweep of his hand to join him. "Let's suppose," he said, as Cianda sat as far as possible from him, "Let's suppose I do agree, God help me. What do you intend to do while we wait? I assume this ambitious robbery will take some planning?"

"Several weeks," Cianda said vaguely. "Aside from gathering information to execute the theft, I intend to go on with my daily life. What do you envision us doing?" Instantly she regretted the question.

"I could answer that in several ways. But I was referring to our lodging arrangements." He cocked a brow at her startled look. "Did you seriously expect me to leave you free either to scheme with Thorne against me, or to disappear altogether?"

"What's the matter Captain, don't you trust me?" Cianda shot back. "I do not intend to be kept under lock and key on your floating prison, if that's what you're implying."

Drake shrugged off her barb. Picking up the teapot, he poured each of them a cup. "I'm afraid there's only one solution," he said smoothly. He handed her the hot brew.

"I'm all agog to hear it."

Well, milady thief —" He paused, the roguish glint in his eyes reflecting his obvious left-handed enjoyment of the situation. "For my peace of mind as well as appearance's sake, we will simply have to marry."

Cianda gaped at him. He was a madman on a devil's mission.

With a provoking grin, Drake raised his cup in salute.

" 'Ave you gone completely balmy?"

Cianda pressed a hand to her head, not quite sure of the answer to Maisie's blunt question. She expected Maisie to resent the threat to her hard-won security, yet it didn't make the confrontation with the older woman any less uncomfortable. "I suppose you have a better idea."

"Why, I've more than a kettle full o' shillings' worth, I do. But why should ye listen to an old woman when ye've got yer mind set on sending yerself along with the lot of us down ter Newgate ter drop one mornin' from rope collars! 'Ave ye gone off, girl?"

A gentle tap at the door interrupted Maisie's tirade. A tall woman, slender, with smooth auburn hair and a serene face, studied both Cianda and Maisie with placid gray eyes before stepping into the parlor.

" 'Ere now, it's Beatrice." Maisie sat back in her chair with a smile of relief. "Yer a smart girl, Beatrice Dobson, you c'n talk reason to 'er, now. Tell 'er whot a bleedin' fool's fancy this notion of 'ers is."

"I need your help—both of you. Not your arguments," Cianda said, trying to sound more confident than she felt. She turned to Beatrice, counting on her friend to bring her usual calm order to the chaos raked up by Maisie's outbursts and her own foolhardy decision.

Maisie was Cianda's voice of survival, willing to risk only if she were reasonably certain it meant a fat purse. Maisie, with her tricks and quick tongue, had helped keep Cianda and Jamie alive through several hard winters in the Devil's Acre. Living in fashionable Mayfair hadn't changed her. She still fought and scratched for every day of comfort as if it would be her last.

Beatrice, though, treated risk as a calculated game. Despite her good sense and clear-thinking, she secretly relished her part in Cianda's midnight exploits. It stimulated her intellect—and salved a wound Beatrice hid behind a mien of cool detachment.

"Wait until she tells ye what she's a mind ter do with that pirate she's takin' in." Maisie plunged ahead without waiting for Cianda. "She means to fob off all of London wit' some tale she married this rake—a lad no respectable lady'd think of makin' 'er 'usband—after a shameful short fortnight's wooing, then whot's more, bring 'im ter live in our 'ouse to watch and listen. 'Egots ter find out how we're planin' ter snag the diamond from under the Queen's nose. To say nothin' of tryin' ter fool Lord Thorne into thinkin' she's still workin' fer 'im! This 'ere pirate says—" Maisie snorted. " 'E says all 'e wants is ter see Lord Thorne hang And Miss Cianda 'ere 'xpects 'e'll keep his pretty promise 'bout clearin' 'er name after all's said and done. And after al that . . ." She stared hard at Cianda. "Whot's ter happen te yer lit'le brother?"

"I'm doing this for Jamie. No other reason." Cianda snapped to her feet, pacing the room, her fingers tracing quick, agitated patterns on the furniture.

"But can you betray Godfrey?"

Beatrice's soft query roused the beast of guilt in Cianda "Yes," she answered, her voice thick with a confusion of emotion. "For Jamie. I can for Jamie."

"It could work," Beatrice said, her clear voice sounding like a bell into the momentary silence. "If we're cleverer than the lot of them."

"It's a fool's brew," Maisie grumbled. She stomped to the cabinet by the fire. Pulling out the gin decanter, she slopped a generous shot into a glass and drank it back. "If ye let these pirates move in, we'll be doomed from the start." Shaking her head, she plopped back in her chair, taking the gin and her glass with her.

Beatrice raised a brow. "There are others?"

"Captain Weston has a partner. He has a cat," Cianda murmured. She stopped, poised like a sprite flirting with a moment on the earth. Beatrice's words echoed in her head *If we're cleverer than the lot of them. If we're cleverer . . .*

"Captain Weston or the partner?"

"What?"

"The cat. Is it Captain Weston's or his partner's?"

Cianda laughed. Some of the tension in the pit of her stomach uncoiled. Beatrice's passion for details was a private amusement between them, and from the sparkle in her friend's eyes she knew the comment had been calculated to relax her. "The partner," she answered. "And you'll dislike them both."

Muttering under her breath, Maisie reached for the brandy again. "I 'ate cats."

"It's only for a little while; I don't have a choice. He can prove I am the Masked Marauder. Besides, I must have the diamond to rescue Jamie." Cianda reached out and trailed her fingers over a small wooden box on the table beside her. "And I intend to get it." Lifting the lid, she drew out a slip of black silk. She caressed the satiny material for a moment, then held the dark mask up to her face. "Or perhaps I don't need it. Or our pirate captain."

A secret, satisfied smile touched her lips. "Drake Weston believes he can best Cianda D'Rouchert. But he's no match for the Masked Marauder."

Cianda tossed a few coins to the hackney driver, careful to keep her face secreted under the low brim of her cap.

"Ye lads sure this is where ye want ter be let down?" The driver looked at her then at Beatrice as though he had given them up for half-wits. "Bad lot whot lives 'ere, 'tis. I could wait fer ye . . ." He glanced around, obviously not finding the notion appealing.

"No need," Cianda answered gruffly. With a pull at her cap, she waved him on his way.

As the cab jerked into motion and was swallowed into the fog and gloom, Cianda slid her mask from the pocket over her overcoat.

She glanced to her canary, the woman she relied on to watch out for her jewels — and her life. "Ready?"

"Always," Beatrice answered softly, barely recognizable in her rough, dark trousers and coat.

The silk caressed Cianda's skin like a lover's touch as she fitted it over her face. Dressed in black, her fair skin smudged with soot, silver hair plaited under her cap, she shed the civilized skin of Cianda D'Rouchert and cloaked herself in the invisibility of the Masked Marauder.

87

Silent, swift, masquerading as shadows, they melded wit the unwelcoming midnight darkness of the Devil's Acre.

She feared the Acre at night, where life meant less tha the next meal. At least when she came back on charitable e rands, daylight offered a measure of protection.

The rough cobbled streets were so narrow they barely a lowed the passage of a single cart. Uneven outlines of th lowest lodging and tenement houses crouched over the path rank with the fetid odor of the sewers, and the sweet-sou stench of death, loud with bawdy, drunken calls and angr shouts.

Memories roiled up as the once-familiar sounds an odors circled around her. Cianda shut them out, concentrat ing on her task.

Her devil's pact with Drake Weston and with Godfre drove her back here in desperation. Thorne owned a court i the Acre. And while she knew he would never move Jami into his mansion, he might well send him here, believing sh would never return to her childhood hell. She'd been carefu to keep her charity work from him lest he censure it.

Cianda bet her stakes on finding Jack Filpucket, the ma Godfrey occasionally employed when he chose force over fi nesse. If she could catch him unaware, perhaps he would le some clue slip about Jamie.

And if she found her brother, the Malwi ruby would bu them all freedom from both Thorne and Drake Weston. Sh had entrusted Beatrice with the precious gem, after the carefully plotted their separate escapes, should Cianda fin Jamie. She would take Jamie far from England, send fo Beatrice and Maisie to join them, and forget all abou Thorne, the diamond.

And Drake Weston.

At the side door of one of the miserable, cramped dwell ings Cianda motioned to Beatrice to fish out the jemm from the small bag of tools she carried. The pointed meta rod, slender and hard in her hand, made short work of the lock.

Rickety stairs lurched upward to the third floor, creaking under their combined weight. Cianda ignored the sound. Jack would likely as not be too steeped in gin to notice the small noise.

Loud, raspy snores echoed into the hallway as Cianda eased open his door. She had only to nod to Beatrice to tell her to stay and keep watch in the doorway.

With a deep breath, Cianda drew a small knife into the palm of her hand. Catfooting to the bed, she laid the cold blade at the sleeping man's throat.

"Jack." She poked him in the ribs with her free hand.

The man grunted, stirred a little, muttering.

"Jack, wake up."

After two sharper prods to his side, Jack mumbled a string of oaths. "Wha . . .? Wha d'yer—Hell's Teeth! Whatever it is yer lookin' fer, I ain't got it."

Cianda let the blade linger in the folds of his chin. The thought of spilling his blood twisted her stomach. The thought of losing Jamie kept her hand steady and her voice low and harsh. "You've fallen low, Jack. Thorne must not be feeling as generous towards you as he once was."

"Or towards ye, neither. 'E must be a bit twigged at ye seein' as how 'e took yer brother fer payment."

Sensing pudgy fingers inching toward her hand, Cianda tightened the pressure on the knife. "Where is Jamie?"

"And ye think I'm likely t' know? Thorne's probably already sunk 'im in the Thames." His voice ended on a high note as Cianda jerked the blade. "I'm tellin' ye, I don't know! 'E ain't 'ere and that's all I do know."

"You took him."

"Maybe I did."

"Where?"

"What's it worth ter ye?"

"You might ask the same question."

"Yer a hard one, Faith, ye always were." He tried t squirm away, but Cianda held fast. "All right, all right, if did take 'im, t'were only as far as ter Thorne's doorstep Thorne said 'e'd keep the lit'le blighter 'imself. 'E probabl knew ye'd come 'ere lookin' fer 'im. Thorne's always on step in front of 'is own. 'Specially when 'e wants somefin bad as them jewels. Ye know 'at's God's truf, girl."

"Maybe. If he's not here, where would Godfrey hide him You would know Jack, if anyone."

"I'm tellin' ye, I don't! Ye c'n keep yer chiv at me throat 't dawn and I can't tell ye nuffin' more."

Cianda held the knife poised for a heartbeat longer, the eased it away. She'd known Jack long enough to be apt a winnowing the truth from his easy lies. Defeat tasted bitte welling up in her with almost painful intensity.

Stepping away from him, Cianda had her hand on th door before Jack struggled to a sitting position. "Don' bother escorting me out," she called softly before meldin with the gloom in the hallway.

Cianda met Beatrice's inquiring gaze with a shake of he head. "He's not here," she whispered, her voice trembling little. "Jack knows nothing."

Reaching out, Beatrice took Cianda's hand and gave it brief, hard squeeze. "Then we will find out who does. N matter where we have to look."

With a lift of her chin, Cianda returned her friend's warm clasp. "You're right, we will. But for now, I don't fanc spending another moment in this place."

Beatrice at her heels, they moved quickly down the corri dor. At the end of the hall they exchanged the signal to part They always separated after their night's work, each findin her own way back to the townhouse. Apart, there was les likelihood of both being discovered or, worse, both bein caught by a watchful constable. Now, Beatrice took th closest stairwell while Cianda darted on to the one they used to enter.

Anxious to escape to the open air, away from the stench of misery and her own failure, she broke into a run. Turning the corner to the stairwell, the hiss of a sharply drawn breath caught her ear.

Cianda whirled. The hallway behind her was empty.

She stood still, listening, waiting. Her skin crawled with the sensation of being watched.

There's no one, she chided herself. *Jack's not fool enough to follow.*

Putting one foot forward she took a hesitant step. Then another. A slight shuffling pinioned her against the wall. Amid the foul mix of smells, came a faint thread of a sickly sweet, almost cloying scent.

The incongruous aroma suddenly seemed more menacing than any of the Acre's familiar threats.

Driven by a spurt of fear, Cianda pushed away from the wall and ran. Without looking back, she darted down the hallway, avoiding the stairs. It would be too easy for anyone to trap her there, too likely an escape route.

She ran instead to one of the third-story windows. Yanking it open, she climbed out onto the narrow ledge, and with quick grace, lowered herself onto a rude wooden overhang that served as an awning for one of the second-floor rooms.

Holding tightly to the side, she fished in her pocket for her ladder. Fashioned of steel wire, bent at the ends, it had two iron hooks she slapped over the edge of the narrow wooden ledge. She swarmed down, dropping lightly to the cobbles below. With a slight jerk, the hooks let go and the ladder fell into her hands.

Moving back into the shadow, she hunched down, exhausted. For a moment she sunk, crouching there, her back leaning against the rough wall of the lodging house, her head hung between her hands, gasping for breath. She tugged away her mask and flung it down, letting the damp night air fan her heated skin.

She felt foolish for letting her nerves have the better of her. Yet she couldn't rid herself of a strange sense of disquiet.

She was given little time to mull it over. A cacophony of drunken voices, fumbling through the first phrases of a lewd song, drove her back into the shadow for protection until they meandered past.

Cianda tried to dismiss the incident as she neared the boundaries of the Acre where merchants' homes softened the edges of desperate poverty. It was all nonsense. Who would have been lying in wait for her? Who would have known to follow her into the Acre?

Drake Weston.

His name came immediately into her thoughts. Had he followed her? There appeared no way he could have. Besides, she reasoned with herself, if Drake had followed her, he would have confronted her in hot blood, damning the circumstances and repercussions.

She walked a few blocks before she was able to hail a passing hackney cab. Settling back against the squabs, Cianda closed her eyes and let the swaying rhythm of the cab soothe her tattered emotions.

She didn't see the man who stepped out of the darkness as the hansom started its slow journey back to Piccadilly.

Drake Weston stepped into the hazy yellow nimbus of a gas lamp, a dark figure seemingly molded from the gray brume and the night.

He stared after her long past the time she vanished into the shadows, his fist crushing a handful of black silk.

Chapter Six

The following morning Cianda woke to the sound of a bloodcurdling shriek. Instinctively she shot up in her bed. "Jamie!" she cried out into her chambers, still shrouded in blackness by the tightly closed drapes.

Was it her nightmare? The same images tormented her nightly. In the darkness, while she purloined the treasures of the wealthy, shadowed figures came and stole her only jewel.

Sitting bolt upright, she swiped the tears from her eyes and listened into the emptiness. Was that horrible scream a product of her dreams? Or was it real?

The answer came with another wail, clear enough for her to realize it came from downstairs, and not from her imaginings. A sense of relief washed over her as she discerned the cry was not one a thirteen-year-old boy would utter. It sounded like an angry infant.

"A baby?" she muttered to herself, pulling her tired body out from under the comfortable bedclothes. Everywhere she ached: head, arms, legs, toes—everywhere. The previous night's escapade, added to her adventures on the *Ferret,* had caught up to her with a fury this morning.

Her bare feet touched the ivory wool carpet at her bedside, her mind still struggling to think clearly through a sleepy fog. Another shrill yowl assailed her ears, jolting her nerves. It sounded closer, upstairs, nearer her room.

And this time it didn't sound human.

"Oh no." Cianda dropped back onto the bed. "He wouldn't . . ." Before she could convince herself that even Drake Weston surely possessed some sense of propriety, her bedroom door slammed against the wall behind it, clearing the way for a wild blur of howling fur, followed by a pack of raging humans.

The cat, which she recognized at once as Fred, catapulted to her bed, then leaped to the highest point in the room — her headboard — using Cianda's shoulder as a stepladder.

"Ouch!" she protested as Fred's claws scraped her flesh through her thin nightdress. The vault left tiny red lines of stain on her white gown.

"Don't fret, dearie, I'm on it. I'll kill that bloody cat!" Maisie scrambled after Fred, an unopened umbrella in hand. The chubby old woman climbed with astounding agility onto the bed, hoisting her awkward body over Cianda in pursuit of the cat, knocking Cianda flat against the pillows.

"Leave my cat alone you old bat!" Zak, his flaming hair sticking out at wild angles, stormed after Maisie with no apparent regard for Cianda's presence. He mounted the tall four-poster with ease, shoving his knee into the feather comforter between Cianda's ankles. "Lay one finger on Fred and you won't live to see another tomorrow, I promise."

Cianda tried to shove him away, her intended tirade interrupted by an uncharacteristically ruffled Beatrice flying in the room at Zak's heels. "Aren't you the big, brave brute! Leave her alone! You're more beast than that creature of yours. Why, I have never seen a more uncivilized man. Threatening a helpless old woman. Indeed!"

Her reprimand hit Zak's ears at the same moment Maisie's umbrella slapped the side of his head.

Cianda gasped, first from the surprise of the blow, furious enough to toss Zak backward, then from the pain shoot-

94

ing up her leg as he fell atop it. Her bruised and aching limbs shrieked in protest.

No one seemed to hear her indignant exclamation, much less care. Instead, Beatrice snatched Zak's arm in a furious attempt to yank him off the bed.

Maisie, taking advantage of the distraction, hiked up her skirts in her fists and walked on her knees toward Fred. The cat, perched at the pinnacle of the ornate headboard, sat watching the human chaos around her with feline affront.

"Aye, yer almost mine now," Maisie snarled at Fred.

"Harm one hair on my cat's head and I'll have yours!" Zak growled as he struggled to regain his balance on the rolling mattress.

"Good heavens!" Beatrice stretched out over the bed, making another swipe at his arm. "Get away from her. I'll bring you your wretched cat!" Her firm command momentarily halted Zak's offensive. He turned, and they faced off with hard stares. Even Maisie, briefly interested by the confrontation, paused in her attack.

The lull in the commotion gave Cianda the chance she needed to disentangle herself.

Exasperated beyond reason, she kicked and wriggled free of the mass of human weight pinning her to the bed and at last managed to twist and turn enough to put one foot, then the other on the floor.

Her motion jolted the combatants out of their temporary respite. Maisie lunged for Fred, causing both Zak and Beatrice to try to intervene on the cat's behalf.

Backing away from the bed, trying to decide the best way of stopping the battle, Cianda heard a rich, amused laugh from behind. She turned slowly, expecting the worst.

Drake Weston lounged insolently against the door frame, looking on with a pleased little smirk on his face. "Morning, love," he called out over the commotion.

"You!"

95

Drake held up his hands in mock innocence. "You did ask me to move in. Although I didn't expect such an—interesting welcome." His eyes roamed over her, touching her body through the diaphanous silk of her gown.

Color shot to Cianda's face. Instinctively she wrapped her arms around her body. She burned with the heat of his searing gaze, feeling naked, exposed, stirring in her a confusing combination of outrage and excitement. For an instant the mayhem behind her fell silent under the power of his gaze. A hot, curious sensation sent shivers over her skin as she remembered his hands touching the places his eyes now roved.

A slow, satisfied smile spread across Drake's face, recalling her at once to her predicament. She scowled at him and dashed to her wardrobe to jerk out the heaviest winter wrapper she could find. Safely insulated from his perusal, she lifted her chin and marched straight up to him.

"What is the meaning of this—this outrage?" she demanded, ignoring his rakehell grin.

Drake stretched his long, muscular arms and yawned. "Is that any way to greet your beloved husband on the first morning of wedded bliss?"

Cianda's temper snapped. She whirled away from Drake. "Out! All of you!"

"You can't mean me too, love."

She turned back to him and clapped her hands to her hips. "Especially you!"

Stepping close, Drake slid his hands up her arms to her shoulders. "The servants are already more than a little curious," he murmured, nodding toward the open door. "We must keep up appearances, you know. Starting now, I think." He bent and kissed her temple, his mouth lingering on the tender skin. The earthy, masculine scent of him tantalized her senses.

Cianda shoved at his hard chest, her anger strong, yet

threatened by an insidious weakness elicited by his caress. "Don't touch me," she hissed.

Drake caught her hand in his and drew it to his lips. "I'm afraid, milady thief, you're going to have to get used to my husbandly show of affection. Our little ruse will never work if we aren't convincing newlyweds. Or hadn't you considered that when you consented to this bit of play-acting?"

"What I hadn't considered is just how uncivilized you are." Cianda jerked her hand away and reached for the handle on her bedroom door. She made to fling it shut against him, but Drake had only to prop one black boot up to block the impact.

"If you'll give me a moment, I'll have them all out." Beatrice's clear, calm voice intervened before Cianda had the time to respond. "Come along, Aunt Maisie." She gave Zak's arm a final tug. "You heard Cianda. She wants you out of her room at once."

"Not without my cat." Zak finally succeeded in prying Fred from the bed—the cat's claws gripping for the headboard all the way—and back into his arms. He tucked her under his arm like a sack of flour. Unfolding his long limbs enough to ease off the bed, Zak stalked to the door, past Maisie and Beatrice, without a backward glance. "You're asking a hell of a lot this time," he muttered in Drake's direction. "Maybe too much."

"We might not be in this mess if you hadn't let her escape," Drake said. "You owe me."

"*I* owe *you?*" Zak paused long enough to throw a disgusted look at his partner. "I did you a favor! You're just too bloody bent on revenge to see it." Stomping into the hallway, Zak headed for the stairs, Fred's tail flying wildly through the crook in his arm.

"This isn't going to be easy," Drake murmured.

Cianda shot him a sarcastic glance. "How perceptive of you."

"I'm terribly sorry about everything," Beatrice said to Cianda as she helped Maisie recover her balance.

Cianda shook her head in resignation. "I should have expected it."

Maisie grabbed Beatrice's arm and inched off the bed, umbrella in tow, sputtering and cursing as she lowered herself to the floor. "I'll 'ave cat stew I will. It won't live fer long under this roof!"

Cianda and Beatrice exchanged an exasperated glance. Cianda knew she could trust Beatrice to calm Maisie. From the first day she joined Cianda's household, Beatrice began to manage Cianda's hectic life. Again and again she restored order to chaos. Cianda depended on her, trusting her with the details of her life that she hadn't the time or the inclination to manage, and Beatrice never disappointed her. They understood each other in a way only women whom men have used can.

As Beatrice led Maisie into the hallway, Cianda called after her, "I'll join you downstairs after I've dressed. We'll discuss this — this situation over breakfast."

"I'll see to it at once," Beatrice answered, ushering a still grumbling Maisie down the hallway to the stairs.

"So —" Cianda turned on Drake the moment the room emptied. "It's revenge is it?"

Drake's dark brows furrowed. "It's justice."

"I wonder." Curious, but not wishing to prolong his stay in her bedroom, Cianda stepped back and gestured toward the door. "Your partner is probably waiting for you to soothe his frayed nerves. To say nothing of his cat's."

"Are you ordering me to leave our bedroom, Missus Weston?"

"This isn't *our* bedroom and I'm not your wife. Now get out."

Drake instead closed the door behind them. "And if refuse? What will you do? Call the police?"

98

"Have you no decency at all? I need to dress so we can all at least make an attempt at discussing this in a civilized fashion downstairs."

"Please don't let me stop you. Although . . . I must say I can't imagine anything that could improve on what you're wearing under your wrapper."

"I should have killed you aboard the *Ferret*." She smiled then, a dangerous glint in her eyes. "I could have, you know."

"The way you could have killed LeDoux?" Drake eased away from the door. "I'll wait while you dress. That way we can make a proper appearance together in front of your household. Call it my contribution to the charade."

"You speak about this charade as if it were a fatal disease. It was you who insisted we *marry!*"

"We had to," he said bluntly. "And since I'm forced to endure the farce, I might as well enjoy the few pleasures it can offer."

"If you think for one minute I intend to share my room, or anything else with you, you're more insane than I took you for, Drake Weston!"

Drake walked slowly across the plush carpet, the soles of his boots crushing the soft fibers as he went. "I was generous with my modest quarters when you needed a bed." He stopped a heartbeat from her. "We've shared far more intimate moments than this, milady thief."

Why, every time the man came within breathing distance, did her mind turn to chaos? Cianda struggled to shake off the familiar langorous effect his nearness evoked. "That was quite different." She tried to imitate Beatrice's cool, prim tone. "I have an adjoining room that will suit you perfectly without raising the servants' suspicions."

"How convenient." His raffish smile did nothing to ease her disquiet. Moving a few steps backward, Drake dropped lazily onto the bed, stretching his broad back and long legs out across the rumpled satin coverlet. "I do believe I like this room. Although it's certainly nothing like the dark, secluded garret I always imagined as the hideaway of the Masked Marauder. It's rather intriguing to touch the place where the infamous thief lies each night." He bunched a feather pillow under his head, running a hand over the soft linen covering. "Your pillow smells of asters. Beguiling and provocative." He gave her his smile, the slow, easy gesture Cianda thought no doubt had broken a thousand foolish hearts. "Of you," he added, his voice low.

Mortified at the sight of a man — this pirate — sprawled across her bed, Cianda nevertheless stared helplessly at him, momentarily enthralled. His broad shoulders tapered to a flat stomach rippling with muscle beneath his thin shirt. At the center of his dark chest where his shirt split open, her emerald lay, both taunting and tempting her. The flare of stolen fire against its dangerous backdrop lured her to wicked desires. Her fingers curled at her sides. She wanted to touch it. She wanted to touch him.

The illicit and unwelcome thought shocked her. Covering her growing agitation, Cianda assumed her haughtiest demeanor. She looked down her nose to him as she said coolly, "You take far too many liberties, Captain Weston. Your rudeness repels me, and your antics grow tiresome."

Drake laughed, the rich, throaty sound filling her empty room. "I'm crushed, love. But then, so many have undoubtedly entertained you in this very bed, I must be dull by comparison."

"Quite."

"I'll do my best to improve, then." In a swift move he sat up, his tight black trousers pulling against hard thighs. "But I must wonder. How is it you prowl the night, manage a romp before dawn, *and* keep your identity a mystery? Honestly, it boggles the mind to imagine."

Cianda's temper rolled to a boil, still she refused to give

100

him the satisfaction of seeing it. For some reason, he wanted to shake her control, to prod her into abandoning her carefully-crafted facade, and perhaps blurting out her guarded truths.

She smiled grimly to herself. She had played her role too long to be bested by an arrogant rake of a pirate. "I would choose my insults more carefully, Captain. Let me remind you I can bring a hasty end to our bargain," she lied easily. "Don't push me too far. I have nothing left to lose. Your promise to set me free after I bring you to Godfrey is meaningless. It's no greater risk to me to go to him empty-handed than to cooperate with you. He needs me. I'm the best thief he's ever had."

Cianda blessed the fact Drake had no idea how desperately she actually needed the jewels. And far better not to tell him about Jamie; he would only find some way to twist the fact to his favor.

"Does this mean you prefer a cell at Newgate to this luxury?" he said, sweeping his arm out over the lavish appointments in her room. "If that's your choice, milady thief, I can certainly arrange it."

Cianda despised him at that moment. He was just like the others: her father, Legume, Godfrey, all men who wanted to use her to reach their selfish goals. Now, caught between him and Godfrey, she saw her chances for freedom dwindle again. Only her loyalties to Jamie, to Beatrice and Maisie, compelled her to endure the frustration and humiliation of her position.

"Consider it a warning," she said, affecting her finest bravado. "I'm not afraid to take chances — even with my life."

"Ah yes, love, I know." Drake moved to stand behind her, as fleet and stealthy as a predator. He lifted the swathe of tangled silver hair from her neck, whispering against her nape, "That's why we understand each other. That's why I'm so completely and foolishly fascinated by you."

Circling around, he let the captured tresses rain through his splayed fingers. "Do you believe in fate, milady thief?" he murmured, slowly drawing a few wispy strands across her cheek. "In the destiny of lovers?"

His nearness, the swanning of his fingertips over her face, tossed Cianda's senses and thoughts into a confused tumult. "No, I don't believe," she managed, her own voice sounding strange and small to her ears. "Men set out to seduce and call it chance."

"If that's so, then I suppose I'll take my own chances." Before she knew what struck, Drake wrapped his arm about her tiny waist and crushed her against him. His mouth covered hers, consuming her sweet, soft lips in a furious, possessive kiss.

Responding without thought, Cianda surrendered under the force of it, molding to his demands. It seemed madness to give in to the temptation of illicit desire, but impossible to deny it.

Drake took the kiss back from her, probing, challenging her lips, her tongue to match his fervent exploration until she had no strength, no will but to return the pleasure he incited between them.

Spreading his hand over her back, he massaged it through the heavy wool. Even through the thick covering, his touch burned her bare skin beneath. Cianda moved restlessly, craving more than just the memory of his hands on her body. Desire spread hot and fast. Nothing she had ever experienced, ever fantasized, felt so consuming, so heady; it was so dazzling and exciting as to overwhelm every other thought or emotion.

Cianda urged him closer. Slipping her hands up his strong arms, over his shoulders, into the dark curls at his nape, she invited his passion with her touch, her kiss.

Drake's mouth slid from her lips to her chin, tasting, caressing. As he moved to brush butterfly kisses over her neck, she arched her head back and moaned softly.

"How many Cianda?" he whispered hoarsely against her ear. "How many nights alone?"

The question sobered her like ice water poured down her spine. Cianda jerked back out of his arms. Shaken, she turned away, swiping the back of her hand over her trembling mouth.

"What's the matter, milady thief?" Drake's dark voice mocked her. "Are you afraid to discover you aren't as civilized as you pretend? I've no doubt none of the polished advances of your aristocratic admirers ever elicited more than the required politeness from you."

"You arrogant bastard." Cianda whipped around to face him. "You know nothing about me. You scoff at the excesses and vices of society, and yet you're no better than any of them. You were born to it, just like they were. You use what and who you want and never give a thought to anyone but yourself."

Drake leveled narrowed blue eyes on her. "Lofty words for a society-born thief."

Cianda read the question in his eyes and at once regretted her outburst. Her past was her secret shame. It was just the sort of ammunition a man like Drake Weston would use to manipulate her. "Thieving is my profession. Unlike most women, I choose to provide for myself rather than depend on any man."

"You seem to have a low opinion of men in general." Drake studied her with a disconcerting intensity. "Hasn't anyone ever loved you?"

His casual tone didn't penetrate her defenses, though his words came perilously close. Yet she resisted his probing, afraid to let him uncover too much of her heart. "I hardly think that's practical, Captain, considering my position," she said, keeping her voice level.

"Anything is possible, milady thief," Drake said softly.

Then, suddenly, a roguish smile replaced his thoughtful expression. "You know, you remind me of Fred."

"Shall I consider that a compliment?"

"By all means. I admire independence and resource in anyone, man or beast."

"Or woman?"

"Especially women," he murmured.

Somehow, even though he no longer held her, Cianda's body seemed to feel the rough urgency of his hands on her smooth skin as Drake stared down into her eyes. They looked at each other for a long moment before he at last offered her a quick, lopsided smile and stepped away.

"I'll pretend to be a gentleman and let you dress. I suppose we should make an appearance at breakfast or Maisie is liable to turn Fred into morning sausage." Taking her hand in his, he pressed a lingering kiss to her palm and then turned and strode from the room.

When he was gone, Cianda wrapped both hands around her bedpost to steady her liquid legs. Any notions she cherished of outwitting Drake Weston now struck her as improbable at best.

Her mind might be willing, but she realized with sinking heart, her body was proving to be a traitor she hadn't reckoned with.

Beatrice passed another plate of steaming buns under Cianda's nose. "Are you sure you won't take even one? Aunt Maisie will be insulted."

Reluctantly, Cianda plucked up a currant bun. "You're right, I just don't have much of an appetite yet. It's too early I suppose." The morning's events had bewildered, humiliated, excited, and enraged her all in the space of an hour. It was more than her stomach could take before noon. As she passed the breads on to Zak, she stole a glance Drake's way.

Apparently she didn't have the same effect on his appetite. He sat across from her, ravenously devouring his break-fast.

"So then," Beatrice was saying, "we are in agreement at last." She sat next to Cianda at the casual round table in the sunlit breakfast room, pen and paper in hand. She glanced around the table, counting nodded replies. "Very well, Captain, and Mister—what is your last name?"

Zak, focused on his food, reluctantly lifted his eyes to acknowledge the question. "Zak," he muttered. "Just Zak."

Several moments of silence followed, a battle of wills Cianda found almost amusing.

"Fine!" Beatrice snapped at last, breaking the odd spell between them. "Mr. *Zak* will take Aunt Maisie's room behind the kitchen and she can move in with me. Captain Weston, must, by necessity, have the master's quarters adjoining Cianda's room." Her slight frown of disapproval spoke for Beatrice's feelings on the arrangement.

Cianda scowled. "I've changed my mind about that. He can take the guest room down the hall."

"Newlyweds at opposite ends of the house?" Drake sounded appalled. Cianda, though, recognized the now-familiar taunting gleam in his eyes. "By Monday, every maid in London would know of it, and it would be news at every breakfast table."

Cianda felt the color rise to her cheeks. She bit into her bread to hide it. "What does it matter? It's not as if this were a real marriage."

"For someone whose livelihood depends on charades, you're being rather slipshod about this particular one."

"I'm afraid I must agree, Cianda." Beatrice gave her an apologetic look. "The servants find your sudden marriage curious enough, already. We mustn't take any chances. All of our futures depend on the success of this ruse."

"Wisely spoken, Miss Dobson. Don't you agree, Zak?" Drake nudged his partner in the ribs.

Zak slouched over his plate. "I just want the whole damned mess over with."

"Mister Zak, you will not use that sort of language at this table or you will not eat here." Beatrice bristled with indignation.

"You're every man's nightmare, you know that, woman?"

"And I'll thank you not to forget it."

The shock on Zak's face brought a knowing smile to Cianda's lips. "I suppose everyone knows his or her place then?"

Regaining her calm, Beatrice sipped delicately at her tea. "Yes, I suppose so. And we shall all be situated as soon as Aunt Maisie moves her belongings into my room."

"Excuse me," Drake said, reaching for another sausage on the platter. "This may sound dense, but why must you resort to sharing a room? This is a large house."

Cianda and Beatrice exchanged a glance. How could she tell him her house was not a home but a stage, for Godfrey's play, the extra rooms merely unnecessary props, left vacant, undecorated. Godfrey refused to spend the money necessary to outfit unused space, and in any case, Cianda never entertained overnight guests, due to the risks involved. Her family consisted of Jamie and the women at her side. She'd locked Jamie's room the day after he disappeared, preserving it just as he left it. No one but her little brother would sleep there.

"The rooms are in the midst of being redecorated," she lied. "And I haven't had the time to choose new furnishings. So we will simply have to make the best of it."

The doubt in Drake's arched brow told her her explanation hadn't satisfied him, but to her relief, he let the matter drop.

Beatrice sighed. Tapping her pen against her paper, she made a small check. "On to the final problem: the animal."

"Which one?" Cianda asked.

106

"Which one indeed?" Drake shot back.

Beatrice cleared her throat and looked away.

"She goes where I go, and I go where Drake goes — for now at least," Zak said, flinging a hard look at Drake.

Maisie waddled into the room just in time to overhear. "I warned ye about that beast —"

"We know what you said," Drake interrupted. "You'll just have to learn to like cats."

"You may not speak to my family in that tone." Cianda slapped her teacup onto its saucer, threatening the fragile china. "They are not common servants to be lorded over, do you understand?"

"Family? No, I'm afraid I don't."

"She means to say we strive to maintain a certain atmosphere of mutual respect here," Beatrice put in smoothly.

"Obviously that sentiment doesn't extend to uninvited guests," Zak muttered.

Cianda ignored him. "We take care of one another; we are as devoted to each other as if we were tied by blood. Even you should be able to understand family loyalty."

"No," Drake said quietly. "Only the concept."

Cianda wondered at the strange nuance in his tone. Had his family hurt him? Did he abandon them for more than purely self-serving reasons? Why did she care? The sooner she broke her link to him the better.

"Well . . . now that that's finished —" Beatrice stood, then swiped away Zak's plate and her own to take them to the kitchen.

Glowering at Beatrice's back, Zak pushed away from the table. "I guess this means breakfast is over."

Maisie reached for the meat platter, but Drake intercepted her. "I should hate to see it go to waste," he said, forking the last sausage.

"Can't you think of anything but your stomach?" Cianda asked, glaring at him.

107

"Only one other thing men ever do think about, dearie." Disgusted, Maisie shook her head at both Zak and Drake. "Reminds me, 'at bloody Thorne just sent a message by. Now where did I put it?" she mumbled, shuffling her pudgy fingers through her apron pockets.

Cianda's throat constricted. "Aunt Maisie, please—"

"Ah!" Maisie produced a slightly crumpled envelope. " 'Ere 'tis."

Taking the missive, Cianda ripped open the thick paper and read silently. Her fingers suddenly crushed it into a ball and she hurled it to the floor. "Who told him about our so-called marriage?"

Drake shrugged, leaning back in his chair. "The cabbie who brought us here this morning was a curious bloke. I might have mentioned the good news to him."

"How could you! We've scarcely had time to work out the details." She slapped her palm against the table. "You did this on purpose! Didn't you? You knew perfectly well he'd gossip to every driver he saw this morning, and they'd tell every servant. I'll bet your wretched soul Godfrey heard we were married before I did!"

"Well . . ." Drake picked up a leftover bun and tossed it carelessly into the air. "He had to find out sooner or later."

"Then I hope you're satisfied with your little maneuver, for it seems Lord Godfrey Thorne is hosting a ball to announce our marriage to London society. And we are cordially commanded to attend."

Zak laughed aloud. "You? The happy bridegroom? This I must see." He slapped Drake on the shoulder. "Back into the social whirl for you, dear chap. Old money . . . persistent isn't it?"

Cianda watched a dark cloud descend on Drake. "Well done, darling," she added, fermenting the storm brewing in his eyes.

She knew she pushed him and didn't care. He deserved

whatever torment was gripping him now, no matter the cause of it. He'd obviously believed telling Godfrey might add an interesting twist to their already convoluted game of chance. Well, it had indeed — only obviously not at all in the way he must have intended.

Drake pushed his plate aside and stood up.

"Lost your appetite, Captain?".

"Look at the bright side," Zak said. "You'll have the dubious pleasure of introducing your bride to all of your former — er — friends. At least those Thorne will deign to invite. Oh, and let's not forget your mother. Naturally, she'll be on the guest list. And appropriately appalled, I've no doubt."

A bevy of a doubts suddenly beset Cianda. She'd heard stories about Lady Octavia Weston's reputation for crushing social misfits in the most public manner. A woman with her pedigree could unmask an impostor with vicious ease. Attending Godfrey's affair in Drake's company promised to be risky enough.

"I can do without that particular introduction, thank you," she said calmly. Under the table, her fingers wrung pleats in her napkin.

Drake paced away from her, then back. "I'm afraid it's inevitable. She is your mother-in-law, at least as far as London society is concerned. But you have my sympathy, milady thief. You might want to reconsider that cell at Newgate. It might be the better choice in this instance." He faced her, his jaw tight, eyes blazing blue fire. "Welcome to the family."

Chapter Seven

"Your coach awaits, milord," Zak drawled, letting himself into Drake's room. "What's this?" He slapped a hand to his chest in an appearance of horror. "The guest of honor not even dressed yet?"

Drake shot him a black look, then circled the bed where his newly-tailored suit lay, pressed and ready for him to wear to Thorne's ball. He stared at the garment from several feet away, like a predator pacing a safe distance from its prey, weighing the risk of an attack against the hunger in its belly.

"You're worse than a woman," Zak mocked. "Your thief is already downstairs, pacing a trench in the salon carpet. In a profession where you would think patience an essential attribute, she certainly can be annoyingly short-tempered."

"Let her wait," Drake muttered.

"Not in a festive spirit, eh? Old ghosts, or new ones haunting you?" When no answer was forthcoming, Zak added, "Or both?"

"Both," Drake said shoving aside his mixed anxieties over the evening ahead. He started buttoning the dress shirt held left hanging open over his chest, flattening the Rajput against the dark mat of hair, and tucking the gleaming chain beneath his shirt.

For days he'd cursed himself for yielding to the impulse to deliberately mention his marriage to the garrulous cabbie, knowing full well Thorne would hear of it almost immediately. It wasn't the first time he'd acted before thinking—and it wasn't likely to be the last time he regretted it.

Drake fingered the snowy cravat Beatrice had laid out neatly beside the suit. Flinging it back on the bed, he turned back at Zak, scrutinizing him from head to toe. "What happened to you? You hardly look like the same man."

Zak rocked back and forth on his heels, shoving his hands into his trouser pockets. "Considering the occasion, I thought I ought to spruce up a bit. Play along, you know."

"Beatrice finally took her sheers to that mane of yours, did she? She's been glaring at your head and beard with malicious intent since the day you crossed the threshold into her territory."

"Just a trim here and there," Zak said, rubbing at his chin. "It'll grow back in no time."

Drake peeled off his black trousers, dropping them at his feet, and slid his long legs into the formal pair. At least they fit correctly, he thought, smoothing his palms over the snug-fitting material before buttoning the front. "So, you let a woman run her fingers through your hair," he said, taking up his chafing of Zak again. "Didn't feel half bad did it, old chap?" Silently, he tipped a salute to Beatrice for inveigling her way as close to his partner as she managed. Drake had yet to meet a woman hardy enough in mind and soul and tenacious enough to wear down Zak's stoic resistance to any and everything feminine.

Staring down at his boots, Zak scuffed a toe on the thick carpet. "The only reason I let that shrew come near my head was to spare myself the aggravation of her badgering."

"I'll salve your ego by letting you believe you've convinced me of that." Drake pulled the midnight-blue coat over his broad shoulders. "None too generous in the back," he mumbled, straightening the sleeves at his wrists.

"The cut looks fine to me. You're just groping for feeble excuses to avoid going to Thorne's ball tonight."

111

"A ball . . . of course Thorne would think of it. After Isabelle—" A shadow of the past visited him, bringing with it the volatile mix of anger, hatred and pain her name always roused. Drake ruthlessly shoved the emotions aside. Tonight, of all nights, he needed to keep his wits sharpened. Letting himself admit to any feelings in the matter dulled his edge. Aware of Zak's speculative perusal, he finished quickly, "After Isabelle, what better way for him to try to distract me from the hunt than to invite me back into his lair under these, of all circumstances."

Zak studied Drake, his eyes thoughtful as he stroked his beard. "Yes, I'd say after her death and your sudden disappearance from society, he imagined an event like this; he must think that slapping you in the face with your past while every London socialite looks on, might unhinge you enough to render you useless. For a time at least."

"Thank you. I feel so much better."

"You can't accuse me of being subtle."

"Neither subtle nor tactful, but unfortunately all too often right."

Drake knew Zak understood perfectly why he had tossed aside his place among London's elite, escaping into a life of recklessness. Zak rarely questioned, and even less, confided in him. Even so, Drake suspected his partner kept past phantoms of his own locked behind his sardonic facade.

Whatever the reason, the reckless way of living suited them both.

When Isabelle died Drake's no longer had any incentive to endure the pretense and hypocrisy of London society. He vowed to live life as it came to him, day to day—moment to moment at times—loyal to only himself and his own causes. As long as he lived hard and fast enough, he'd never have to think about how or why. He never had to feel.

Until now.

The past days of preparation, brushes with shopkeepers

who once knew him well, watching a beautiful woman fuss and sputter about ribbons and lace, resurrected some of the softer moments in an otherwise bitter past. A past he'd tried to drown in a sea of adventure and risk beyond reason.

He snatched up the cravat from the bed again and crushed it in his fist. Lies, betrayals, all hidden behind the mask of polite society above the law, insulated from the consequences of justice by the power of their fortunes and family names.

"You're ruining that," Zak interrupted Drake's silent tirade, grabbing the wrinkled cloth from his hand. "You know, old chap, this is exactly what Thorne intended to drive you to."

"You're a fine one to lecture me," Drake snapped.

Zak pulled the cloth taut between his hands, an effort to keep his temper in check. With a dark look, he tossed it at Drake.

Drake snatched it up, slung it around his neck, and began fumbling with the task of wrapping it. "Bloody choker," he grumbled. After so many years of dressing as he pleased, the art of tying a neck cloth had grown foreign to him.

"Here, allow me. If you pull that thing any tighter, I'll have to slit your throat to get it off."

"I am beginning to wonder if that isn't what you'd actually like to do."

Through gritted teeth, Zak continued to fold the layers of cloth. "We've been over this. Your lamenting over it is becoming rather annoying. As I told you before, all I've ever done is try to save your bloody neck. Why, I'm beginning to question."

"Forgive me if I fail to see your logic. How could you have had my goodwill in mind when you let the Masked Marauder walk off my ship and straight to Thorne's waiting arms?"

"It wasn't an easy choice."

113

"But you'd rid us of her in an instant, even now, if you had a second chance, wouldn't you?"

Zak shrugged. "This little scheme of yours has gotten completely out of hand. As usual. Only it's worse because we're depending on a woman to help us. At least before, the complications were of our own making. She's trouble. You should have learned by now, trouble is a woman's specialty. We'd have done better to go after Thorne on our own."

"It's a bit late for brilliant suggestions," Drake reminded him as Zak finished the last wrap of the cravat and stepped back to survey his work. Drake bent to pull on his boots. "Besides, we've walked the edge before. You like it that way."

"As long as I know someone's there to pull our chestnuts out of the fire. I don't think you can reassure me this time that Palmerston has sanctioned your collaboration with the infamous Masked Marauder."

Drake averted his eyes; Zak read them too easily. "He's giving it serious thought."

"Translation: don't come to me when Thorne and his *femme fatale* thief turn the tables on you and you land your ass in jail. Again."

Zak had a point, but Drake chose to ignore it. He glanced in the glass, brushing back the heavy dark wave falling over his brow. "Tell me, who worries you more, Cianda D'Rouchert or Godfrey Thorne?"

"If you must know," Zak sighed, "she does. You don't exactly have a history of successful involvements with women, do you? I don't want another woman ruining your life."

Drake turned and scowled at Zak. But he had no defense. Zak was right. Isabelle's betrayal nearly destroyed him. "Put the last time down to impetuous youth. I haven't taken a woman at her word for over six years. And I'm not about to start with a thief who lies as easily as she breathes."

114

"You haven't met a woman like her in over six years." Zak looked him square in the eyes. "If ever."

Drake busied himself, smoothing his coat sleeves to hide his discomfort. "I'm using her, nothing more," he returned gruffly.

"So you say."

"Your confidence is most touching, old friend." He realized Zak, for all his sarcasm and apparent detachment, did have his best interests at heart. He'd always gone along with Drake's wildest schemes, risking life and limb without question — as long as he believed the motives were at least partly rational.

"You can't deny your motives this time are personal," Zak said, mirroring his thoughts. "Your judgment is muddied by the past. It's my job to point it out to you, that's all."

"Well then, warning taken," Drake said, slapping a hand on Zak's shoulder in an offering of peace.

"And ignored, no doubt."

Drake swept his cloak from a nearby chair. "Didn't you say we were late?"

"And hopelessly senseless for going through with it all." Zak waved Drake toward the door with an air of martyred resignation. "But don't let that stop you."

"Imagine! Me waiting on a primping man!" Cianda stomped across the salon floor, the misty sea-green satin of her skirts swishing over the polished wood behind her. Her hair, caught up in a silver tumble of artfully contrived curls, tickled at her back. She tugged at one shoulder of the daringly cut gown, wishing she had chosen a less revealing neckline.

Beatrice was poised in the doorway, keeping watch alternately on the staircase and on Cianda. "Mister Zak went up to fetch him nearly an hour ago. I'm certain they'll be down any minute," she soothed.

Slumped in a comfortable chair by the fire, Maisie snorted. "Don't be wagerin' yer last pence on that, dearie," she muttered. "I said that man was trouble to ye the moment I laid me eyes on 'im. 'E's no more a gentleman than I am the Queen 'erself. Just the kind o' rake I always feared would catch yer eye."

"He's hardly caught my eye, Aunt Maisie." Cianda's quick fingers flitted at the low curve of her bodice.

"Do stop fussing at it, Cianda," Beatrice commanded from her post by the door. "It's meant to show your throat and shoulders to the best advantage. Although, I do think you might have taken Madame Zeile's suggestion about a necklace."

"I refuse to wear jewels. You know that."

"Yes. But for this occasion . . ." Beatrice let the words drift away as Cianda threw a scowl in her direction.

"Well, I'm through waiting for them," she snapped. "Aunt Maisie, please have the carriage brought around."

Maisie heaved herself out of her chair. "Ye're not leavin' without yer mantle. It's proper cold out tonight."

"And about to become colder." Sending a scathing look toward the upstairs staircase, Cianda lifted her heavy skirts and whipped past Beatrice. She glanced back over her shoulder. "Tell him he has five minutes. After that he can find them a cab!"

"Cianda, you are forgetting yourself. He is supposed to be your husband. You must arrive together."

"Five minutes!" Cianda called back from the entry, taking her emerald velvet cape from Maisie. She flew out the front door and down the front steps to where the driver held the coach door open for her.

As much as she would have enjoyed riding off without Drake, a few moments later he and Zak appeared at the side of the coach. As Drake climbed inside, his heavy step rocked her from side to side on the seat.

Cianda darted a glance at Drake, but the evening brume and darkness made him an imposing black silhouette. The outline of his figure alone, though, stirred wicked temptations that clashed with her annoyance. His evening dress accentuated his broad shoulders, tapering to a slender waist, and even the night couldn't eclipse the blending of danger and reckless confidence he wore so well.

His hard leg brushed against her cloak. She forced herself not to move, not to react to his disconcerting nearness. Not to feel the warmth and breath of him so close a twitch of her hand would spread her fingertips against his body.

Think of something else. Anything else.

She slanted another look at him, swiftly averting her eyes when he turned slightly and looked back, a smile hovering on his mouth.

Damn his impudence, anyway. He might look the civilized gentleman. She knew better.

A pirate in the guise of a lord. Drake detested charade, but he fit well into either role. Cianda envied him. Noble or renegade, his birthright gave him the privileges of choice she did not have.

Every time she donned the garb of a genteel lady, she carried with her the constant reminder of who she really was.

Outside the coach, the sound of Beatrice reprimanding Zak cut into her dark musings. "You should have let me trim more off of that disreputable beard of yours," Beatrice scolded.

"Let go of me woman," Zak snapped back, "you've done enough damage!" He escaped her by a hasty retreat into the carriage, folding himself onto the seat opposite Cianda and Drake. With startling quickness, he slammed the door on Beatrice's frowning face.

Despite her ill temper, Cianda smiled. The idea of Zak at Beatrice's mercy was too amusing to ignore.

At her side, Drake caught the smile and gave back one of

his own. "Glad to see me, Madame Weston? You were staring. I hope that means you approve."

The raffish twist to his smile at once captivated and infuriated her. She bristled with the confusing combination. "Actually I was thinking I might not recognize you had you not been my *husband* this evening. You or Zak. You both could actually pass for gentlemen — if I didn't know better."

Drake raked his eyes over her, his gaze lingering on the white skin exposed at the place where her cape fell open below the tie at her chin. "And you, love, might pass for a lady — if I didn't know better."

Zak punctuated the jibe with an ungracious snort of laughter.

Thankfully neither man knew how deeply the comment cut. A lady . . . the mere mention of the word from his lips cut her to the quick. So easy for him, to the manner born, to mock what he didn't understand. Arrogant bastard! "If you've finished with your insults for the evening, I would appreciate it if you would signal the driver," she said coldly, refusing to look at either of them. "We're over an hour late thanks to you. Godfrey will be livid. His god is precision. And we are the guests of honor after all, as if I need remind you."

Drake suddenly scowled. "Hardly. The less time we spend there, the better for all of us."

Even in the dimly lit interior of the coach, Cianda saw the tension etched in the hard lines of Drake's face. Had his game with Thorne gone sour so quickly? She scarcely believed it. Their mutual animosity must stem from a more personal war. And she intended to discover its source, if only to give herself more of an advantage as the one caught between their skirmishing.

The coach lurched forward, causing Drake's leg to bump against hers again. Instinctively, Cianda pulled away. Even through the layers of satin and petticoats, his touch burned her skin.

Seemingly unaware of the effect even the slightest brush against him had on her, Drake focused his attention on the passing procession of stately houses and stone garden walls. As the carriage clattered over the damp street cobbles, the diffused glow from the gas lamps intermittently cast a brief illumination on his face; then the carriage moved into the murky umbra between the lights.

A safe distance from his thigh, Cianda gathered her wits for an attack. Before she lost the chance, she resolved to gain some mastery of the situation. "Precisely how far back does your acquaintance with Godfrey go, Captain Weston?"

Drake and Zak exchanged a glance. "Too far," Drake answered flatly.

Certain she'd tapped into some aspect of Drake's past he'd just as soon forget, Cianda at once determined to dig deeper. "You've attended affairs at his home before, I gather?"

Zak choked on a cough that sounded suspiciously like a stifled laugh.

Drake looked away. "Yes."

"And you Zak?"

"This will be my first." He tugged uncomfortably at his coat sleeves. "And, with any luck, my last."

"Well, I'm certain Captain Weston will be more than pleased to introduce you to several of the guests. Beatrice assures me he's well acquainted with London society, especially its feminine members."

This time Zak laughed openly. Cianda smiled in smug triumph.

"I'm afraid many of Drake's former—er—friends won't be invited."

Drake leveled a cool gaze on Cianda. "But, I've no doubt all of your intimate acquaintances will, if only to salve their ruined hopes with the sight of you."

"Naturally," Cianda lied smoothly.

Ire flashed through Drake's eyes, rewarding her effort.

"There's one person no one has mentioned yet." Zak shifted on his seat. "But I'd wager that stone dangling from your neck Lady Octavia Weston won't pass up the chance to meet your bride."

Cianda's stomach clenched. She'd refused to dwell on Drake's mother. Most anyone else, she could fob off with vague lies and a charming smile. But only a fool would hope to be able to do the same before a woman who had undoubtedly made her social position her career. "Do you think she'll attend?"

Silent for several moments, Drake finally said, "I wouldn't gamble on it either way. If nothing else, she may see it as her one chance, after nearly seven years, to lambaste my heathen lifestyle publicly."

"A mother's righteous wrath for the sins of her son?" she asked pointedly, curious about the repressed emotion in his voice. Whether regret or anger, or something she hadn't guessed at, she couldn't tell. "I suppose you've managed to commit every unforgivable evil toward polite society."

"Perhaps." Drake glowered at her, sending an unexpected chill down her spine. "But they all 'sin,' too, as you put it. The only difference is I do it openly; they bury it beneath polite smiles, in secret rooms and between the pages of gilt-edged ledgers. Your benefactor Thorne is a prime example."

His black temper unsettled her, raising questions she dared not ask then, for the carriage pulled to a halt in front of Godfrey's mansion. The drive was a short one; Godfrey planned it when he purchased her town home. He wanted her close enough to stay under his constant watch, to be at his disposal, night or day, when the whim took him.

The driver flung open the door and Zak stepped out ahead of Cianda. She would have been offended, had he not looked back. "I'll go on in ahead of you two. You should make an entrance, after all. This is your debut as a devoted couple." With a mocking bow, he turned and loped up the long walk to the front steps.

Cianda shook her head, not certain she'd heard correctly. "I never thought Zak even considered a gracious gesture," she murmured. It somehow didn't fit with anything she'd seen of him so far.

"We're full of surprises," Drake said, slipping out. "Allow me." He waved aside the driver, offering her his hand.

Cianda shifted to the step, a draft of chill air wrapping around her as she met the night. This evening was a test she—they—must not fail. Jamie's life hinged on the success of their marriage charade. Each day the ladder she struggled to climb to him seemed to grow another rung. Beneath her cape, she shivered.

Drake reached out and took both her hands in his. The rough firmness of his touch steadied her as she stepped down. "You're cold," he said softly, searching her eyes.

Glancing away, Cianda braced herself for another typically glib remark. Something along the lines of "cold hands, cold heart." To her surprise, Drake said nothing.

Instead he led her from the carriage into the shadow of a large column, then took her small hands between his large palms, rubbing them gently. He lifted them to his lips to blow warm air over them. Slowly, the chill ebbed, replaced by a strange, soothing warmth that spread through her blood, prickling her skin.

"Better?"

"Yes," she said, her voice little more than a whisper. Who was this man touching her with actual tenderness? Not the ruffian who'd stolen kisses from her, demanding her surrender to desire. "I suppose I . . . I have a slight attack of nerves. Ironic, isn't it?"

"Devoted spouse is a new one, for both of us." He released her hands and reached into the inside pocket of his coat. "I have something to help you perpetuate the ruse."

121

Drawing out a small box, he lifted the lid, revealing a large, square cut emerald, and a heavy gold band. "Your betrothal and wedding rings. I thought your hand might appear a bit bare without them. I hope you appreciate my sense of appropriateness in choosing them."

"Your warped sense of humor, you mean," Cianda said, staring at the jewel. The sight of it unsettled her somehow. "I would rather not —"

"Yes, I know. But I insist, love." Drake removed the rings from the box and captured her hand in his. With deliberate slowness, he slid the bands on her left third finger. Then, turning her palm upward, he brought her hand to his lips and caressed her skin with a lingering kiss.

Cianda trembled at the warm, wet touch of his mouth. Her mind urged her to pull away. Her senses rebelled. She chose simply to relish the provocative feeling. His boldness made any pretense seem foolish.

"They're perfect," Drake murmured. He lowered her hand. Brushing the crushed velvet covering her shoulder, he picked up the end of one tie and wound it around his index finger. The bow at her throat gave way as he pulled the tie toward him. He slid the cloak to crumple over his arm.

Stepping back a pace, he gazed at her, with an almost bewildered expression, as if he couldn't quite believe she existed. "You look like something I've only dreamed of."

"Your dreams must be sorely lacking," Cianda said softly.

"Quite the opposite. Yet you put them all to shame."

The passion in his eyes showed plainly. Cianda refused to believe there could be more. She couldn't afford empty hopes. "I suppose we're ready to make our entrance, now, as Zak put it."

"If you insist. Although there is one more thing I can think of to make this easier." Moving close again, Drake pulled her hands against his chest, trapping her in his embrace.

The freshly bathed sandalwood scent of him, mingled with the essence of the night and the attar of her own perfume, coalesced into a heady elixir that evoked forbidden desires. "Oh?" she asked, a catch in her throat. "What might that be, Captain?"

He held her under his power with his touch, his gaze; a dangerous fascination seduced her to surrender. Yet reason warned her to do so would be her downfall.

Drake lifted her hands to his lips, kissing first the place where her skin touched his jewels, then moving to the other hand. Finally, slowly, he eased them around his neck. He bent to her, his mouth hovering near hers. "A kiss for luck," he breathed against her lips. "To seal our destiny."

Before Cianda could muster a rebuke, he covered her mouth with his in a kiss that began as an easy exploration, but quickly escalated to the consuming need any touch between them incited. She held him close, welcoming the desire that drove away thought, needing to share the fears, the past pains, the anxiety of the night ahead. If nothing else, the passion between them was real.

Drake, as if sharing her tumult of emotion, wrapped her closer, feeding her need, matching it with his, plumbing the depths of their equaling passions.

Cianda snared her fingers in the thick softness of the hair at his nape, driven by an ache to be closer, and closer still.

Drake moaned low as she beckoned his own surrender with her abandoned yielding. His touch urgent, he slid his palm up the smooth satin of her gown, over her waist and upward to mold one breast into the cradle of his hand. He massaged the soft, full flesh, stroking its tender center into a taut nub.

Cianda gasped as lightning pleasure seared through her veins. Immersed in the wildfire of feelings he excited in her, she pushed against him, avid to drink deeply of her first draught of untamed desire.

The depth of her feelings frightened her. Still she possessed no will to deny them.

Shoving down one shoulder of her gown, Drake trailed nibbling kisses down her throat, teasing and tasting each curve and valley. His hand continued to fondle her breast, arousing in her an illicit desire to strip away the barriers between them here and now, in the shadow of Godfrey Thorne's mansion, damning the risks and the consequences.

Slipping her hand down his chest, she dared to explore lower, until her fingers brushed his thigh. She whispered his name on the drift of a sigh.

At the sound of her voice, Drake suddenly started. He froze for a moment, then abruptly released her, taking a pace backward. Staring at her as if he didn't recognize her face, he raked an unsteady hand through his hair.

Cianda looked back, stunned into silence. Finally, she gathered enough of her wits together to put her cool mask back into place. Lifting her chin, she said, "I'm sorry. I didn't realize . . . I was wrong."

Drake caught a long breath before answering. "Wrong?" He sounded winded enough to have run a fair distance. "Nothing is wrong. Damn it, Cianda —" The sentence broke off. He drew in another breath and let it out slowly. "I just didn't expect . . . I didn't mean for it to —"

"Neither did I," Cianda said quietly. She felt a measure of comfort in realizing their furious embrace affected him more than he admitted. Cold comfort, though, knowing his feelings drove him out of her arms.

Without warning, Drake's mood sobered. He put another step between them, smoothing his rumpled coat. "Perhaps we'd better go inside."

Cianda busied herself with straightening her gown and taming errant strands of hair back into her elegant upsweep. She picked up her cloak and draped it over her shoulders. "I

124

imagine Godfrey will forgive us the delay," she said, matching his distant tone. "We are supposed to be newly wed after all. Shall we?" She turned and started up the stone pathway to the house before he answered.

Drake caught up to her in two strides. "Cianda," he began, then stopped. "I suppose I should apologize."

"Please. Don't."

"But it would be a lie," he finished as if she hadn't spoken. "I wanted to touch you as much as you wanted me to, no matter what either of us deny or confess." He stopped her rebuttal with an echo of his rakish grin. "At least no one now can argue we don't look like new lovers."

Unable to think of anything to say, Cianda let him tuck her hand into his arm and lead her up to the imposing double doorway.

Foreboding skulked around her, overshadowing the frustration and confusion she felt at Drake's reaction to their embrace. As the doors began to swing open slowly, her heart leaped to her throat.

Drake Weston might not be the best choice, but tonight he was her only ally.

Chapter Eight

Cianda felt a quickening in her veins as Pimbe led her and Drake down the wide, dim corridor to the ballroom. Mingling sounds of laughter, conversation, and the muted strains of a string ensemble wafted into the hallway.

The sounds should have signaled happiness, but instead provoked a nervous clench of her stomach. As they stopped in the vast doorway, Cianda unconsciously gripped Drake's arm.

"Damn Thorne, he's invited the whole bloody city," Drake grumbled low.

"What did you expect?" Cianda whispered, not looking at him. Drake muttered something under his breath that sounded like a curse and she sighed. "It's going to be a long night."

Diverting herself from Drake's foul temper, Cianda glanced over the sea of guests, many with faces she recognized, an equal number strangers to the limited circle of society she moved in. The austere gray marble and icy white of the room served as the ideal backdrop for jewel tones of silk and satin and the gold glow of the candlelight. Her every nerve tensed. She had walked the streets in London's worst teeming slums, yet stepping into Godfrey's elegant lair, knowing the stakes of the game she played, seemed infinitely more treacherous.

"Captain and Missus Drake Weston."

Pimbe's sonorous announcement momentarily disconcerted Cianda. Nearly every face in the ballroom turned in their direction, an unsettling reminder of how intertwined her and Drake's lives had become.

Through the crowd, a short distance away Godfrey's sharp features crystallized. Hearing Pimbe, he quickly excused himself from conversation and wove his way toward them. As always, his face remained impassive, except for the flicker of anger in his steel gray eyes. Cianda expected that much at least, after their shamefully late arrival. What else Godfrey intended, she didn't care to imagine.

"At last, my guests of honor," Godfrey said, lifting Cianda's hand to brush the back with his lips. His gaze briefly narrowed as it swept over the emerald on her finger. "Your new husband's powers of persuasion must be formidable indeed to convince you to wear a jewel. I fear his ability may rival my own." His fingers tightened on hers for a moment.

The gesture sent shivers up Cianda's arm. She pulled her hand back. "Your power is unmatched, as you well know."

"A charming compliment, Missus Weston." Godfrey turned to Drake, extending a hand. "And Captain. It has been quite a long while since we last met."

Drake refused Godfrey's hand. "Not long enough, Thorne."

A shadow of a scowl tightened Godfrey's features. As quickly as it came, it vanished. Smooth control eased back over his face and he became the gracious host again. "Come now, Captain, surely you can accept this little affair as a show of my desire to put the past to rest. A new bride, a new life for you. A new beginning for us."

"I prefer a new ending," Drake said. He tucked Cianda's hand back into his arm, the gesture deliberately possessive. "But I must confess, I am looking forward to showing your guests that Cianda belongs to me now."

Cianda stiffened. "I wasn't aware I had been bought and paid for, Captain Weston."

A small, satisfied smile touched Godfrey's mouth. "It appears your wife does not share your ideas of wedded bliss, Weston. Perhaps the price you paid to win her wasn't high enough."

Cianda bit back her outrage. She had no intention of entertaining Godfrey's demented sense of humor any further. But one day . . . One day, both Godfrey and her pretended husband would understand that, once she freed herself from Godfrey's hold, no man would ever lay claim to her again.

Aware Godfrey studied her every expression, Cianda composed her features. If Godfrey suspected her traitorous thoughts, or worse, if he guessed at the intimacies she allowed herself to share with Drake Weston, he wouldn't hesitate to wreak his vengeance on her innocent brother.

Assuming her prescribed role for the evening, she smoothly changed the subject. "We do thank you, Godfrey, for the opportunity to share our good fortune with our friends."

"I am quite certain you'll find a way to express your gratitude, my dear. You are quite adept at doing so." Godfrey waved a hand toward the guests. "But you must come and accept the congratulations due you. Everyone is most interested in Captain Weston's return to London, and especially in the circumstances of your whirlwind romance."

As Godfrey led them farther into the ballroom, Cianda blessed the fact she and Drake had invented and discussed every detail of their supposed courtship well in advance. At least, in that respect, she could act the part of blushing bride.

A thin, blonde woman in a startling yellow gown commanded Godfrey's attention and Cianda seized the reprieve. She pressed her fingers against Drake's arm. "Do you know all of these people?"

Drake bent close to her ear, his breath brushing her

skin. "Some. Many are family acquaintances. And you?"

"A few." Sudden mischief sparked in her eyes. "Others I know only by their jewels."

Drake laughed aloud, a relaxed, confident sound that raised eyebrows, yet eased her anxiety.

But her brief sense of relief fled when she spied a ravishing brunette sauntering straight toward Drake. Cianda took a deep breath, flashed a dazzling smile. "Why do I have the feeling she knows you very well?" she asked, keeping her smile pinned to her face.

Drake returned the brunette's obvious stare. "She does look familiar—"

"I'm quite sure she does."

"But the name . . ."

"Drake, surely you remember me?" the woman cooed, stopping close enough to lay a caressing hand on Drake's arm. Her voice was as deep and seductive as her eyes.

Godfrey, freed from his guest, moved up behind Cianda. "No one could forget you, my dear Alicia," he said, before Drake could answer. "Lady Alicia Chatsworth, allow me to present Cianda D'Rouchert Weston. Her husband I believe you know."

The voluptuous brunette, who towered over Cianda's petite frame, looked down her straight nose. "So, you're the woman who's done the impossible. You've snared the most exciting man ever to leave a trail of broken hearts across London." She frowned slightly, marring the overall perfection of her features. "You must be quite special," she said, the doubtful tone indicating she found nothing remarkable about Cianda. "I was convinced Drake would never offer any woman his name, let alone what passes for his heart."

"Cianda stole her way into my life and within hours I knew I had to make her my own," Drake said. "I've never met anyone to compare."

Cianda, exasperated by his play of words, nonetheless felt a reluctant admiration for his acting ability. He sounded so sincere, she nearly convinced herself he meant every word.

"How touching," Alicia snapped. She raked Cianda with a glance. "You must be quite pleased at snaring him. I'm simply all agog to hear about your mysterious romance. No one, not even Lady Weston, heard the slightest hint of it before now."

"It was quite unexpected. For both of us." Cianda said, casting her eyes demurely to her slippers. *Two can play this game, Drake Weston.* "I fell into Drake's arms at our first meeting and he convinced me how perfect we would be together."

Taken aback by Cianda's suggestive retort, Alicia did nothing but gape for a moment. Then, regaining her composure, she turned back to Drake. "You've been away so long," she said. "Too long."

"And I intend to leave at the first opportunity."

"You were always so tiresome about your social obligations," Alicia said, giving him a pretty pout. "I truly believe you adore that ship of yours more than any of your friends." Her voice slightly emphasized the final word. "But of course, you were rather a rake — then. I do hate to think you've lost your adventurous streak."

"I assume it has been a long while since you and Captain Weston last met, Lady Alicia," Godfrey said. His cold voice startled Cianda. During the exchange between Drake and Alicia, she had forgotten he was there, listening, watching.

Cianda caught an oddly strained look pass between Drake and Alicia. Not the sort of knowing expression she imagined between former lovers. It was more a look of discomfort, as though Godfrey trespassed on unpleasant memories.

"Yes. Quite a long time," Drake said finally, when it became obvious Alicia intended to remain silent.

"Indeed?"

Alicia's flirtatious expression turned sour. "If you must have the details, Godfrey, it was during the service for Isabelle."

"I see."

Cianda recognized the displeasure shading Godfrey's voice. He sounded as though Alicia's answer annoyed him, though, more than recalling grief from the past.

Isabelle Thorne. Cianda remembered the face of Godfrey's wife from a portrait she had once seen. Tall, elegant, raven-haired, a hint of temper and seductiveness in her fine porcelain features. It was Cianda's only memory; she had never met the living woman. When Isabelle was alive, Godfrey kept Cianda cloistered away from his public life, from all but her tutors and her mentor, Gide Legume, the master housebreaker she eventually replaced.

Though Cianda had never met Isabelle, for a time she envied her from a distance, reading about her again and again as the toast of society. Isabelle's beauty, her charm, and her spending habits were renowned. In fact, the only time Godfrey mentioned his wife was to complain that Cianda could never supply him with enough jewels to keep his most expensive possession draped in silk and gems.

And then Isabelle died. Little news ever reached the newspapers, and Godfrey never spoke her name again. It was as if, to him, she had never existed. Cianda, occupied with the life she was about to begin as the Masked Marauder, quickly forgot Godfrey's wife.

"You're unusually silent, my dear," Godfrey spoke into Cianda's remembrances.

"I do beg your pardon, Godfrey," Cianda said, lifting her chin to meet his intimidating gaze squarely. "This subject is most unpleasant."

"I agree. The death of a loved one is an unpleasant subject, especially on so joyous an occasion. Tonight is for cele-

131

brating the future, not dwelling on the past," Godfrey said, his gaze fixed on Cianda.

"Of course." Cianda quelled the tremble in her heart. Godfrey's words stabbed deeply. *The death of a loved one. Jamie. He must remind me Jamie lives at his whim.*

"You did force the issue, Godfrey," Alicia said tartly. She turned again to Cianda, assuming her coquettishness with skilled ease. "You must spare your handsome husband for one dance with an old friend. You will have him the rest of your life, after all."

Cianda returned a gracious smile. "Of course. But only one. Life is short."

Drake shot her an irritated glance as he reluctantly took Alicia's outstretched hand. "Much too short," he agreed, as he followed Alicia to the dance floor where a new set was just forming.

Cianda shrugged slightly in response. *What did you expect?*

"I applaud you, my dear," Godfrey said, his voice hushed for her ears only. "You're quite adept at mimicking the devoted wife. Just be certain it is an act." He reached out and caught up her hand, his finger sliding over Drake's emerald. "I need not remind you of the consequences if you decide to throw your lot in with Drake Weston's."

Cianda refused to flinch at his threat. "I'm positively parched. If you will excuse me—"

Before she could escape, Godfrey's fingers clamped on her wrist, masquerading the iron grip in the folds of her voluminous skirt. "Not yet, Missus Weston," he hissed under his breath. "This sport will weary me quickly if I don't have my jewels in hand soon. Very soon."

Cianda twisted her wrist painfully, but he held it fast. "You'll get them when I am able to retrieve them safely. Not before."

"I understand Jamie is in need of more medication."

Godfrey's hand tightened. "Until I have the emerald and ruby, I fear a doctor may find it difficult to locate your young brother."

A blinding rage swept over Cianda, putting tiny cracks in her cool exterior. "Jamie needs *his* doctor. You know he's the only doctor who has improved Jamie's breathing."

"Oh yes. I know."

"Cianda. At last." A familiar, laconic voice touched her ears from behind.

Instantly, Godfrey released her wrist.

"Zak." Cianda nearly hugged him in relief.

Godfrey swept Zak's tall figure with an icy glance. "I don't believe we've been introduced, Mister—"

"Zak," Cianda answered for him. "Just Zak."

A small smile visible beneath his beard, Zak dropped a small bow. "I'm Captain Weston's associate. He invited me tonight. We've known each other for some time and I wanted to be here to offer my congratulations and my praise for his excellent taste in women."

Cianda stared, imagining Zak must have brought his twin, born to proper society and reared not to forget it. "Why thank you, Zak," she managed.

"Thank me with a dance?" he asked, taking her hand and tucking it under his proffered elbow before she had time to object.

"Delighted." She accepted with alacrity, eager to distance herself from Godfrey. Before the evening ended, she knew Godfrey would repeat his demand for the emerald and the ruby. She needed time to concoct a reason why he could have neither.

How real was his newest threat against Jamie? As Zak led her to the dance floor, she reached for logic through her panic. If he hurt Jamie, Godfrey knew she would never bring him the Koh-i-noor. Even if he confiscated the other two, he needed all three. She knew him well enough to sense he had some very specific purpose in mind for the trio, though she'd seen no relation between the Rajput and the Malwi.

The ruby and the emerald alone must be expensive baubles, which, if sold separately, would bring only a fraction of the sum Godfrey could demand for the trio. It helped to know that three jewels in her possession meant bargaining power over Thorne. Whatever his reason, the lengths he was willing to go to, to gain the trio told her collectively they were her best insurance for Jamie's safety.

"You must be plotting."

Cianda sidestepped quickly to keep her balance as Zak whirled her with surprising grace through the steps of the waltz. "Plotting?"

He nodded. "I've noticed you set your jaw and scowl slightly when you're scheming. It's rather fierce."

"How flattering. I must remember to keep my mask in place or you and Captain Weston will guess all my secrets," she said lightly.

"Good luck. I don't believe even you're that accomplished an actress."

"Perhaps not." Cianda feigned a casual interest. "Tell me, what does Drake do when he's plotting?"

"He doesn't. Plot, that is. It requires too much of a commodity he is in short supply of: patience."

"That I can believe." She smiled up at him. "I've forgotten to thank you for helping me away from Godfrey. Your timing was perfect."

"You appeared to need an excuse to escape our gracious host. He looked irritated."

Cianda grimaced. "Irritated is one way of putting it."

"Thorne must want his trinkets. Difficult, when one is dangling from Drake's neck."

"Extremely difficult."

"Perhaps the gossip circulating about your alter ego's successful murder in France will put Thorne on his guard," Zak said, not sounding convinced. "Drake's return to society is the only topic to rival news of your exploits."

"I doubt it will matter much to Godfrey. The risk is to me, not him."

"And now to my partner and me."

"That was your partner's choice," Cianda reminded him. "Not mine."

"Nor mine." Zak swept her into another turn. "I still think you're more trouble than you'll ever be worth."

"Then why did you bother to rescue me from Godfrey?"

Zak's even step faltered for a moment. He stared at a spot over her shoulder. "If you're exposed, my name could be linked to you. I'm just watching out for my own ass—er—myself."

"And Drake."

Zak shrugged. "Sometimes."

The music lingered to an end and Zak stepped away. Glancing around the room, he spotted Drake standing amid a group of guests and immediately took Cianda's hand to lead her to Drake's side. "I'll return you to your husband now," he said dryly.

"If Beatrice had joined us, you could return to her and be spared the annoyance of my company for the remainder of the evening."

"Well, given the choice, I must admit . . ." Zak trailed off, then turned abruptly to Cianda. "But then that just wouldn't be the thing at all in your social circle would it? A mere servant at Godfrey Thorne's ball. Tsk. Tsk. Out of the question."

"That I didn't deserve, and you know it"

"Sarcasm withdrawn. But whether you agree or not, considering the ruse you call a life, I suppose your personal feelings about class distinction are not the deciding factor where appearances are concerned."

135

"My, my, you do sound awfully like an American just now," Cianda teased, egging Zak on with a raised brow and a sideways glance. But when he offered nothing further, she abandoned her attempt to gain information. She'd learned Zak only spoke when it suited him. "Actually, Beatrice did attend some functions of this importance at one time. She is comfortable in most levels of society."

"Is that so? I don't doubt it. But need I wonder how a woman in her station might win invitations to be included in such lofty company?"

Cianda glowered at Zak, then scanned the crowd. "That's how," she said tartly, nodding toward a tall gentleman with a bushy mustache. "Sir Arthur Gilean."

Zak frowned. "They were—an item?"

"That's the understatement of the season, I'm afraid. Sir Gilean left poor Bea devastated. She was his daughter's governess. He became infatuated with Beatrice, eventually wooing her with promises of a future together. In Lady Gilean's absence, he begged Beatrice to serve as his hostess. I believe he was trying to decide whether or not he would have the backbone to survive society's outrage and very possible ostracization if he left his wife for Beatrice. The whole episode caused quite a scandal."

"I can imagine." Zak scowled at Sir Gilean. "I gather he decided love would not conquer all?"

"To Beatrice's humiliation and sorrow, yes."

"A sad tale. Sad but oddly familiar."

Before Cianda could pursue the topic Zak alluded to, the person who undoubtedly spurred the curious comment faced them.

"I brought her back," Zak said shortly, giving Cianda a small prod in Drake's direction as if she were an unwanted parcel.

Drake raised a brow. "Thank you."

"I wouldn't if I were you," Zak muttered. Not bothering

with an explanation, he loped off toward the refreshment table.

"Such odd friends you have, Drake." A short, matronly woman in an unflattering violet gown shook her head at Zak's retreating back. Then, pulling her pince-nez up to sharp blue eyes, she turned her attention to Cianda. "So," she said tartly, "you're the one Drake chose." Having made a thorough inspection of Cianda, she lowered her spectacles. "You're nothing like the others. Is she Ashstead?"

Beside her, a stolid, refined, older gentleman nodded slightly to Cianda, but spoke to the woman at his side. "No, my dear," he remarked, examining Cianda like a trinket he didn't care to buy.

Irritated, Cianda glanced at Drake. His opinion of her must be low if he could stand by and allow these people to politely insult her without response. She bristled, opening her mouth to deliver a curt retort, but Drake intervened before she voiced a word.

"Cianda is quite different. Refreshingly so. She's the first woman who hasn't bored me." He smiled charmingly at the couple. "Allow me to present my aunt, Lady Horatia Dunn Spencer, and my uncle, Lord Stewart Spencer, Earl of Ashstead."

The mention of title kept Cianda silent. She had learned to guard each word when in the company of arrogant aristocrats, no matter how provoking they became. Her reputation in society protected her livelihood. She couldn't afford a careless comment that might exclude her from the elite circle she needed to be a part of if she was to learn who owned the most priceless jewels and where they were kept.

"You're a widow, I hear," Horatia remarked. "And French, also." She said the word French as though it left a foul taste in her mouth.

"My wife is as English as you are, Aunt Horatia," Drake said. "And it's hardly her fault her husband had the bad fortune to die."

Cianda stared at him, momentarily forgetting they weren't alone.

He was defending her. In front of his family, his peers. Yet was the show of support for her benefit or for his? Maintaining their ruse served his purpose as well as hers.

With a disdainful sniff, Horatia snapped open a large, ornate fan and waved it under her chin. "An uncommon match for you, to say the least. But then you always had the bad sense to choose unsuitable women, and the poor manners not to conceal your affairs. So unlike your dear brother. In fact, I am shocked you would bring your new bride here, of all places. After the horrid rumors about your reasons for leaving London six years ago—"

"Why are you back, boy?" the Earl ungraciously interrupted. "You'll do nothing but cause your poor mother grief. Haven't you done enough of that already?"

Drake stiffened. "She's made it clear I have. Perhaps she'll view my marriage as a sign of my intention to lead a more respectable life."

The lie cost him dearly; Cianda heard the strain in each word, recognized it in the tense set of his jaw.

Obviously, Drake's scorn for society and his scandalous lifestyle had caused a breach between him and his family.

Cianda thought of her own mother. Would she have suffered shame and disappointment if she'd lived to see her daughter grow up to be a thief? She'd promised her mother she would protect Jamie, whatever the cost. And she had. She and Jamie had survived. So far.

"Well," Horatia put in, "I, for one, am glad your mother declined Lord Thorne's invitation tonight. If your marriage weren't irregular enough there is all of this vulgar talk about murder, and robbery, and stolen jewels." She clutched palm to her fleshy bosom, grasping a diamond brooch the size of a plum. "I find it quite disgusting when the talk of the town is a wretched thief and you, Drake. Honestly—" She flung up her fan. "Traipsing about the world without a thought for your duty to the family. Then to marry without the slightest notice or thought for any of us. Most appalling."

"I think it's quite romantic," a pretty, young woman with wide doe eyes spoke up behind Horatia.

During Horatia's tirade, Cianda failed to notice several guests gathering around them, drawn by the promise of scandal and gossip.

"Fascinating," echoed a commanding voice. A stocky, graying man, distinguished by deep-set, intelligent eyes and bushy mutton chops, stepped to the forefront. He appraised Cianda with a thoughtful expression, making her feel, not for the first time, as if she were the exhibit of the evening.

Cianda recognized England's foreign secretary at once from the many sketches she'd seen of him in the newspapers.

"Pam, you've come to celebrate my good fortune," Drake said with none of the reverence Cianda would have expected in addressing a man of Lord Palmerston's political stature.

"I am as anxious as all of society to meet the woman courageous enough to take you on," Lord Palmerston returned with the same easy tone.

Cianda caught Palmerston's implication, but wasn't sure as to whether to take it as a warning or a threat. She decided the only way to deal with so powerful a man was to exude blind confidence—whether she felt it or not. Squaring her shoulders, she tossed up her chin. "I thrive on challenge, Lord Palmerston."

"Fortunate for you, my dear," Godfrey said, suddenly appearing to greet the foreign secretary. "They're a perfect match, wouldn't you say?"

"Only if opposites attract," Palmerston answered bluntly.

Judging from the reputation for outspokenness that had of late landed Lord Palmerston in ill-favor with the Queen,

Cianda expected him to speak his mind plainly. Yet instead of feeling intimidated, she found his candor a refreshing contrast.

"You were about to tell us how you and Drake met?" Palmerston said.

Several guests pressed closer, eager for every detail. Cianda knew no matter what she said, by week's end, the gossips would distort and exaggerate her story until only the barest similarity linked it back to what she'd said originally.

"We met, quite by chance actually, in France." She recounted word for word what she and Drake concocted, telling as much of the truth as she dared. For Madame D'Rouchert did in fact attend a ball, the theater, and a dinner party while waiting for the right chance to steal the Rajput.

"Oh my," the doe-eyed innocent exclaimed, a sudden realization lighting her eyes. "Then you must have been in France when the Masked Marauder stole the Indian emerald and murdered its owner."

Horrified gasps went up all around, followed by murmurs of suppositions and questions.

"I'm afraid Cianda and I were too—distracted to notice something as mundane as another jewel robbery," Drake said, the roguish gleam in his eyes eliciting tittering laughter and knowing glances from the gathered guests.

"Really, Drake," Horatia sniffed. "I, for one, have no desire to follow the sensational accounts of that criminal's antics. The police have been most lax. I blame it on the undue notoriety this horrid man has been accorded. As far as I'm concerned, a thief is a thief, no matter how infamous his feats. Justice should be met—at the end of a rope!"

"And deprive all of London of their favorite topic of conversation? Now that would be an injustice."

Cianda glanced to Lord Palmerston. He seemed to be the only one without a smile on his face.

"In your defense madame," Lord Palmerston addressed a sorely ruffled Horatia, "I quite agree. The law is the law, even when it's broken with finesse."

Thankfully, Lord Palmerston kept his attention focused on Horatia, but Cianda felt the searing power of his words as though he spoke them to her alone.

"Well, I still wonder where the jewel is," the young girl said breathlessly. "I wish it were dangling from my neck!"

With that, the crowd burst into a chorus of laughter.

When the noise died down some, Drake smiled broadly toward Godfrey. "Imagine," he said. "By now, anyone might be wearing it."

Cianda's eyes flew to Drake. What in heaven's name was he doing? She glanced to Lord Palmerston in time to see him roll his eyes, exasperated. Godfrey's gaze narrowed with suspicion.

As the crowd slowly dispersed, Cianda caught snatches of speculation about a "huge, brutish Marauder" and a "band of Marauders pretending to be only one man." People's imaginations continued to be her best protection. Not one mentioned rumors of a skinny little woman actually carrying out the Masked Marauder's exploits.

"I'm afraid I must excuse myself to another engagement, Missus Weston," Lord Palmerston said with a perfunctory bow. "You've made an excellent choice in Drake, no matter what the others may say." He lowered his voice. "I trust your future decisions will be made with equal wisdom."

"I always consider every possibility, my lord." Thoughts of Jamie made Cianda bold. Foreign secretary or no, she intended to make certain Lord Palmerston understood she wouldn't let Drake dictate her actions.

Lord Palmerston paused, considering her words. "Until we meet again, then," he said at last. "Good night Drake. Interesting guests, Godfrey. My compliments." With that, he turned and departed.

On the other side of the ballroom, a singer had begun a solo. All but a few guests clustered around to listen. "Shall we join them?" Cianda asked Drake, anxious to avoid Godfrey's company.

"Do go ahead, Captain. I shall welcome the chance to speak with your wife for a moment," Godfrey said.

"I'm sure you would. But you won't get it, Thorne."

Godfrey dropped all pretense of pleasantry. "She is still mine, Weston. Nothing has changed. I suggest you remember that."

"Quite a few things have changed," Drake said through gritted teeth.

The tension between the two men charged the air around them, as ominous and volatile as the first clash of lightning and thunder before a tempest.

"Stop it!" Cianda hissed. "This is hardly the place."

Drake smiled, but Cianda caught the dangerous glint in his eyes. "I think it is the place."

Before Cianda could react, Drake reached up and started unbuttoning his shirt. "Drake—You wouldn't . . ." Shock stole her voice.

"It's difficult to say who is at whose mercy, Thorne." Drake split his shirt open to reveal the emerald's glitter just long enough to watch Godfrey's expression turn from arrogant confidence to disbelief.

Cianda swept another glance around them. Fortunately the singer held the bulk of the guests rapt. Only one man, opposite Drake, some distance from them, seemed to be paying any attention. Cianda strained to get a better look at him. He was definitely interested in the three of them. Did his face look familiar—something in the unusually high forehead, the bulbous nose—no, it couldn't be . . .

She pressed a hand to her forehead. She was letting her nerves attack her. She looked again. The man had vanished. When she returned her attention to Drake, she drew a sigh

142

of relief as she saw him refasten his shirt.

Godfrey had recovered his aloof composure. "Theatrical, Captain. And so like you. But as for being at your mercy — I believe Cianda might disagree with you. Wouldn't you, my dear?"

Cianda paled. Jamie . . .

"Cianda?" Drake took her arm, his provoking expression replaced by a frown. "Are you all right?"

"I need a cool drink, that's all." Cianda brushed trembling fingers at her temples. "If you'll excuse me — "

"Let me." He glared at Godfrey. "I'll be right back."

"So gallant," Godfrey said after Drake moved out of earshot. "But I wouldn't count on his protection to rescue you, Cianda. You have disappointed me. Make certain it is the last time, my dear. I am not a patient man. I suggest you put your efforts toward finding a way of retrieving that emerald, even if you have to slit Weston's throat to do it."

Cianda sucked in a deep breath, gathering her resolve along with her strength. "I'll get it. And the diamond." And when I have all three, then I'll bring them to you. Not before. And if you threaten to withhold Jamie's medicine again, let me remind you that if Jamie is harmed you'll never have those jewels. Any of them!"

Godfrey cocked his head, studying her with detached curiosity. "You've become audacious, my dear. Weston's influence, I suspect. It is most unflattering. I'm beginning to have serious doubts about your loyalties to me."

"Think what you like." Not giving him time to threaten her further, Cianda gathered up her skirts and swept away, her head held high.

It was a gamble, but she had to take it. The jewels and her illicit skills were her insurance for Jamie's life, her only advantage.

Cianda headed straight for the refreshment table. Drake,

143

with a glass in either hand, met her halfway. "Your drink. Although now you don't look as if you need it. What did Thorne say to upset you?"

"Which time?" Cianda quipped lightly. "Everything Godfrey says is aimed to disturb."

"A most annoying habit." Zak walked up behind Drake. "Enjoying yourselves?"

Cianda smiled sweetly. "We're having a simply lovely time. In fact, all this excitement has left me famished. I think I'll leave you two alone while I sample a few of the sweets Godfrey's cook is famous for."

"Sarcasm ruins the charming effect," Drake murmured. "Besides, I'm not sure I should leave you open to Thorne's attentions again."

"He can't afford to poison me, yet."

Moving away from the two men, Cianda made a pretense of looking over the exquisitely appointed table. She had no appetite—for either food or any further fencing with either Drake or Godfrey.

Yet the buffet did manage to tempt her. Godfrey's cook, though British, had mastered French culinary arts. Over the years, she'd made it a habit not to eat before a party at Godfrey's, saving her appetite for the pastries and tarts Dorsey specialized in.

But tonight she saw none of her familiar favorites. The entire menu was British, distinctly British.

A maid, evidently noting Cianda's distress, came to her side at once. "Is something wrong, mum? Can I 'elp you?"

Cianda recognized the girl. She'd been a scullery in the kitchen when Cianda first came to Godfrey's home. "Has Lord Thorne hired a new cook, Hedda?"

"Why, yes mum, 'e 'as."

"When? And what happened to Dorsey? I can't imagine Lord Thorne letting her go."

The girl lowered her voice. "Well, what she told me were

144

that Lord Thorne said she were gettin' too old ter work all day in the steamin' kitchen, and that 'e 'ad somethin' else, easier on an old woman fer her ter do instead."

Something else . . . Cianda gripped the table. Of course! Godfrey could easily buy Dorsey's silence. And he had her trust already. Dorsey was his oldest, most faithful employee. Godfrey must have put Jamie in her care.

Turning to Hedda, she smothered her distress and excitement beneath her aristocratic facade. "My own cook has such a heavy hand with pastry. I would dearly love for Dorsey to teach her a few skills. I would pay her well, naturally." Cianda checked the eagerness in her voice. "I don't suppose you know how I might contact her?"

Hedda nodded anxiously. "Why she lives over in Barking now. She's rentin' a fine cottage — from gentry, she said. I been there fer tea. Twice."

"Indeed? How delightful. I know where Barking is. But might I bother you to tell me where precisely she is, so I can pay her a visit myself?"

"Oh, yes! mum. Just take the main road through town, past the market on to the corn mill. There's a lane whot goes right up behind it. Second cottage on the right."

"Thank you so much, Hedda. I'll see to it you are compensated for your help." Cianda rushed away from the beaming girl to where Drake and Zak stood conversing with several guests. She snuggled up to Drake and tucked a hand around his arm. "Dear," she said softly, "would you mind if we left? Now?"

Drake stared, his skepticism obvious.

"Marriage to Drake is most exhausting," she said with a trill of laughter.

An elderly gentleman winked at her. "A man would be a fool to refuse you, Missus Weston."

"How kind of you to understand." Making a hasty farewell, she fairly dragged Drake toward the front door, taking

145

care to avoid attracting Godfrey's notice.

"Why the haste, *dear?*" Drake demanded once they were outside the ballroom.

"I told you. I'm tired."

"I doubt it."

Cianda retrieved her mantle from Pimbe, flinging it over her shoulders. "We'll argue about this later, shall we?" she said, indicating the butler with a slight nod.

Drake matched her stride down the long path to where the carriages waited. But before Cianda could call up theirs, he stepped in front of her, blocking her progress. "Not just yet, love. I want to know the reason for our untimely exit. And I suggest you concoct a reasonable story. Zak won't be happy when he realizes we've deserted him."

"He'll have no difficulty finding a cab."

"You haven't answered me."

Cianda faced him defiantly. "And I don't intend to. I want to go back to the town house. That's reason enough. And now, Captain—" She darted around him, signaling for their carriage. As the driver pulled around and alighted from his bench to help her inside, she glanced back to Drake. "If you prefer to stay—"

"You must love to gamble, milady thief," Drake said, climbing inside and taking the seat opposite her. "Because you continually put my very limited store of patience to the test."

Cianda ignored the challenge in his voice, instead silently urging the driver to hurry. If her suspicions proved true, if she found Jamie tonight, then Drake could keep her emerald and wreak his revenge on Godfrey without her.

Her search would end. And so would the infamous career of the Masked Marauder.

Chapter Nine

A single lamp wreathed Cianda in an amber nimbus. It threaded golden light into the silver of her hair as she plaited the long strands into a neat braid. She watched the quick fingers of her reflection in the dressing table glass slowly transform her from an aristocratic lady into a midnight thief, her eyes expressionless.

"I still think ye should 'ave me along," Maisie said, grabbing Cianda's overcoat from where it lay spilling black across her ivory bedsheets. "As crows be, I sing w' the best of 'em, ye know it to be true."

Cianda smiled. "You're an excellent watch. But not tonight."

Both Cianda and Beatrice humored Maisie's refusal to acknowledge her days as a crow ended some time ago. Beatrice had taken over as watch and assistant when Maisie's speed and agility gave way to her years.

Cianda sobered, turning her attention back to the image in the glass.

"Something is likely ter go wrong if ye venture out alone. Ye've always 'ad a crow afore. And a canary. What's so special about this night?"

"I won't ask you to cross Godfrey. I'll take that risk alone."

" 'Tis a bit late for that dearie. 'E won't count the difference if 'e finds out 'bout yer schemin' behind 'is back. If I'm goin' ter get me arse kicked back ter the Acre," Maisie added gruffly, eyes averted from Cianda's mirrored reflection, "I su'pose ter's no better reason than fer helpin' ye and young Jamie."

The chance Maisie was willing to take for the love of her and Jamie warmed the chill in Cianda's heart. There were few Maisie would sacrifice her security for. "You are helping. By staying here," she said, her smile tremulous. "It will be difficult enough for one of us to slip out unnoticed. I need you here to stall our unwelcome guests with plausible lies if something should go wrong."

" 'Ave it yer own way, dearie. Speakin' of our guests—" Maisie winked broadly. "I think I'll see if they'd fancy a dish of tea before bed. Just ter be sure they won't be gettin' curious 'bout whot the rest of us 're up ter."

As Maisie closed the door behind her, Cianda glanced at Beatrice's face in the mirror. A ripple of a frown disturbed the placidity of her friend's features. "You think I should take Maisie with me. But you know as well as I, it's as much a danger to her welfare as it is to mine—or yours—to bring her now. She means well, but she simply doesn't have the strength or speed she used to."

Beatrice's expression immediately cleared and she met her gaze steadily. "Of course I agree, under normal circumstances. But this time, what if you do find Jamie at this place, and he is ill . . . ?"

She left the words unspoken, but Cianda's imagination sketched in the fears in her thoughts. Jamie was recovering, slowly, from the effects of his childhood fever. But his ability to breathe fluctuated. And the recent traumas could only have weakened him. Especially if he was out of the elixir that soothed his cough and helped him sleep.

"I refuse to believe Godfrey's lies," she announced, defying her worries. "Together, Jamie and I are invaluable—just like his precious trio of jewels." She swiveled to face Beatrice. "He thinks of us as he would valuable paintings or prized antiquities bought at auction. Things he secured at a bargain that both amuse him and add to his wealth." Bitterness edged her voice. "And we're such a safe investment. He can expose us at any time, leave us with less than nothing, not even our dignity, while he counts his profits." She tapped her fingers against her cheek. "Besides, if Jamie continues to improve, I suspect he intends to groom him to replace me. Just as I replaced Gide."

"Men are quite similar." Beatrice looked down at her neatly folded hands. "They desire everything, but will not endanger their status or wealth, or even their emotions for anyone. Certainly not for a woman."

Cianda thought of Sir Arthur Gilean and wished she could offer more than empathy. "I know. I seem to be the kind of woman men use at will, not the kind they adore and put on a pedestal to cherish and care for for a lifetime."

"Come now, you could never be content as an object of worship from a sacred distance. No matter how popular and desirable a position our beloved Victoria makes it appear, you would never be satisfied living that ideal," Beatrice murmured, eyeing her with thoughtful interest as if she were considering her attributes and weighing them carefully. "It's time you admit you are the sort of woman who demands a vital man, capable of intense passion, to equal you," She paused, a small smile teasing the corners of her mouth slightly upward. "One who can match your daring."

"It's well there's no man who meets your description. I may beard the lion in his den, but I would never risk my heart on a man. That's a true danger." Cianda snatched up her cap and began stuffing her hair underneath. "And what about you? Since we're speculating on the perfect match, I'll create one for you. Let's see . . . Someone, intelligent, of course — "

"Quiet, neat, well-mannered, and responsible."

"Now I see why you chose to work with me," Cianda said, laughing. "You'd be bored with a man like that in the space of an hour, Beatrice Dobson. You'll just never admit it. You need a challenge. Zak, for instance," she added nonchalantly, a wicked glint in her eyes.

"Really, Cianda." She looked down again. When she raised her eyes, mischief sparked their dark depths. "There's no question of that. He's completely devoted to Fred."

"Heady competition, I'll admit." Cianda shrugged, reaching for her overcoat. "It's all nonsense anyway."

Beatrice said nothing. She merely smiled a little, an enigmatic gesture that left Cianda feeling inexplicably unsettled.

With a vigorous swipe, she rubbed a little soot onto her face and picked up the small bag at the foot of her bed. "At least I won't need your imaginary marvelous man this evening. If anyone's to lay herself open to hazard tonight, it must be me."

"I wish you would reconsider. I can change my clothes and be ready in no time."

"This once, Bea, I have to go alone. Jamie is my responsibility. Besides, the household must appear absolutely normal, or Drake will realize at once something is amiss. Simply carry on the evening routine. No need for him to assume anything except that I'm asleep. I'll see you in the morning. I promise."

It was an hour past midnight when Cianda stole up to the little cottage in Barking, a town situated on the east bank of the Roding, about midway between the junction of that river and the Thames and the turnpike road to Chelmsford. Once the seat of a large nunnery, few vestiges of the convent remained. Almost the sole privilege of the place was a chartered market, a market Godfrey's cook had often mentioned for the fine quality of its fruits and vegetables.

Her cottage sat back from the river on a quiet lane behind the corn mill. Barking would suit Godfrey's stipulations for a hideaway for Jamie perfectly: quiet, secluded, but close enough to maintain his control over the situation.

Cianda paused at the low front gate. Blackened windows stared back at her, but with a quick glance, she noted a well-tended garden and a clean, swept stoop. All signs someone was in residence.

The heavy fog and moonless night were her allies as she edged onto the narrow path between the cottage and its neighbor. She looked into one of the windows and studied the ebon room, a parlor, before taking a short, stout knife and a piece of brown paper plaster from Beatrice's bag.

Leaning against the window glass, she nudged the knife into the edge, pressing with just enough force to crack it. She stuck the paper to the glass and tipped it out in her hand. Noiselessly, she set it behind her before reaching inside and lifting the latch.

Slowly she pushed up the window, her ears alert for any sound. The bag weighed awkwardly in her hand as she hoisted herself through the window, making it a challenge to drop lightly to the floor.

The last embers of a fire lent the parlor a gentle warmth. Cianda listened for any noise that might tell her where the inhabitants of the house slept. Silence answered. An oppressive stillness, as palatable as a living presence, pervaded the darkness.

Stepping cautiously, she checked the downstairs rooms, then glided up the staircase.

Her hope began to wither as she listened and glanced into each room. Some instinct, born of uncountable midnight visits, told her they all would be empty.

Standing in front of the last, Cianda closed her eyes for a moment, steeling herself against the certain disappointment. She opened the door a crack before flinging it wide.

151

I am always one step ahead of you, Cianda. No matter how clever you believe yourself to be, I play the game much better.

She heard Godfrey's voice as clearly as if he stood in the room behind her, mocking her failure with the faint, sardonic curl of his lip.

In the far corner of the room, the dim light showed her a blurred outline of an easel. Forcing her feet forward, she walked toward it and stretched trembling fingers to the smooth wood. A single tear wetted the silk of her mask when she saw the painting. A seascape alive with bright fish of exaggerated proportions and too many sea gulls flying overhead depicted her brother's favorite imaginary paradise.

For a moment the darkness faded and Cianda was back in the sunshine of her mentor's conservatory, smiling back at Jamie's triumphant face, rubbing her hand through his carroty hair, relishing his bright, vibrant eyes.

"I do think it's rather good, don't you, Faith?" In her mind, she heard him stubbornly insist on using her real name when they were alone together.

Cianda eyed the canvas he presented with mock severity. "Well . . . perhaps a little too much yellow in that fish." Her frown dissolved into laughter at his wide-eyed expression. "It's wonderful, Jamie. You have all the makings of a talented artist. I'm proud of you."

He flushed at her praise, his thirteen-year-old dignity warring with a desire to shout his pleasure. "Beatrice said I should consider studying with someone other than her. I'm thinking I might."

"You let me know if you decide," Cianda said, hiding her smile. She knew from the hunger in his eager green eyes he wanted it above all things. The years of hardship in the Devil's Acre left his lungs weakened, and though he was improving now, his activity outside the house was still limited.

Cianda was grateful for the talent that gave her young brother something to strive for, to take pride in.

Thieving seemed a small price to pay for his happiness and security. If she could do nothing else, she could keep him safe.

But I didn't keep you safe, Jamie. Cianda's vision cleared and she was again staring only at an empty easel in the blackened room of a deserted cottage. *I didn't keep you safe.*

As she slowly closed the door to the small bedroom, she left behind her heart.

Lost in the bleakness of her failure, Cianda missed any warning sound or touch of another presence in the cottage until a sudden weight flung itself against her shoulders.

She stumbled forward, barely escaping the thick fingers that groped for a hold on her neck. Her breath tearing at her throat, Cianda heaved her bag wildly behind her, in hopes of momentarily blinding or distracting her attacker.

Visions of terror in France, the Acre, revisited her. They raced over each other, tumbling together. Everything happened too fast for her to manage a single clear thought.

Dashing around the corner and back down the stairs, she choked on a scream when a hand snatched at one of her legs and tripped her headlong onto the wooden first floor. Her shoulder knocked against a table and sent a lamp crashing to the floor. The smell of oil mixed with the scent of her own fear.

Cianda tasted the metallic tang of blood on her lips as she struggled both to clear the haze clouding her eyes and to kick away from the hands clawing their way up her back.

With a painful wrench, she twisted herself around. A face shrouded in a black mask loomed over her, the menace at odds with a sickly sweet aroma.

Gloved hands reached for her throat.

153

A terrific crash of splintered wood froze both Cianda an
the dark figure above her.

"Cianda!" Drake's voice bellowed out into the darkness
"Where in the bloody hell are you?"

Hesitating for a breath of time, Cianda's attacke
abruptly jerked upward and ran toward the back of the co
tage. Cianda managed to pull herself up until she was sittin
in the middle of the parlor, hugging her chin to her knees.

Drake plunged into the room at a run, flinging her
glance as he raced to the back of the cottage on the path c
her attacker. She heard a string of muffled oaths, from fa
away it seemed, and then the sound of long streamline
strides coming back into the room.

"Cianda . . ." Drake dropped to his knees beside her. H
didn't touch her at first. She felt his hesitation, as if he wer
afraid he would hurt her. Then, very gently, very slowly, h
brushed the back of his hand against her face, coaxing asic
loose strands of her hair.

In the middle of the terror and confusion, Cianda we
comed a small, sweet thrust of relief. Whoever wanted he
dead, it wasn't Drake Weston. At least not now.

"You blazing idiot." His touch was tender, but his word
hard. "What in the devil did you think you were doing
Couldn't you do without the bloody thieving for even on
night? Was it worth this for one more bauble — ?"

"Shut up!" Cianda shoved his hand away and got shaki
to her feet. "You had no right to follow me. This is not you
business. You don't understand a damned thing about n
or what I'm doing! You don't understand anything . . ."

Her voice gave way and suddenly she was trembling a
over, shaken by a storm of grief and desperation and th
shock of realizing she had twice nearly lost her life to a fac
less nemesis.

Drake looked up at her, silent. His eyes were unreadable
the darkness, like the sea at midnight. Before she cou

move away, he reached up and took her hands, pulling her down beside him and into the protection of his arms.

For timeless moments, he only held her, soothing her with the rhythmic glide of his palm up and down her spine. When her quivering eased, he moved a little away. The unspoken current between them kept her still more than his hands on her arms.

With both hands, Drake removed her cap and mask, allowing his fingers the luxury of lingering on her face as he drew off the soft silk. Loosing her braid, he enticed her hair to fall over his hands like silver rain.

She intrigued him as no other woman had. She dared to steal into the darkest, most dangerous slums of London, and the wealthiest and most elite of homes. She upset all his plans, challenged his ideas of justice, forced him to feel things he didn't want to feel. And as soon as he was certain he had learned all the rules of her games, she outwitted him with the unexpected.

When he convinced himself she was brash, even hard, she gave him a glimpse of a beguiling vulnerability as fascinating as her boldness.

"Who are you, Cianda D'Rouchert?" he whispered. "What kind of woman hides behind your mask? A thief, a seductress, or someone I haven't seen, someone I can't see?"

"Someone you don't want to see." She barely formed the words.

Drake shook his head, whether to agree or not, Cianda didn't know. His hands tightened in her hair before he brought his mouth down against hers, enticing her to indulge in the sweet promise of pleasures to come.

He tasted like sin and temptation and the savor of him in her mouth scorned any resistance. Cianda kissed him back, wantonly, completely, forgetting every lesson she had learned about the rewards for virtuous behavior, modesty, and propriety. She longed to feel alive, as only he could make her feel, to reassure herself of her own strength.

Every feeling she ever had, every sensation, paled to a dream when he touched her. He was the one man strong enough, bold enough to match her will, the only man who didn't flinch from the passion she disguised with a virtuous facade.

It was wrong. It was right. She didn't care which.

His mouth slid away from hers to feast on the curves of her throat. Drake fought to bridle the hungry demands of his body, but they betrayed him when she clenched her fingers into the hair at his nape and brought his lips back to hers. Her low moan of satisfaction was his undoing.

He had defied reason for another draught of the lightning strike of forbidden desire between them. And now he feared he drank too deeply for his thirst for her ever to be assuaged.

She pushed closer, her surrender demanding his hands to rove over her flesh, memorizing each line and curve. But when his hand accidentally grazed the tender bruise on her shoulder Cianda winced, breaking away.

The pain flung reality in her face. "I—I shouldn't have . . . I can't be—"

"Where are you hurt?" Drake asked, overlooking her faltering attempt to explain feelings she couldn't name to herself. "Wait a moment."

She stayed kneeling on the floor, feeling dazed, as he got to his feet. She heard him fumbling about the room for a moment, then his voice sounded close again.

"This would be a hell of a lot easier if I could see," he muttered. "Ah, there." Before she could protest, a warm light sprang to life inside the parlor. "Now, I can get a better look at—"

"Are you completely witless!" Cianda jumped to her feet, snatching up the lamp and dousing the flame in one quick motion. Jerking her cap and mask back on, she groped around for her bag. "There's been enough noise to rouse the dead and you've just given a beacon to any crushers within a street's length of here!"

Drake scowled. "Crushers?"

"Constables! Policemen! Whatever you choose to call them. The neighbors have likely called a whole swarm down with all the chaos here. I've got to get out of here before—"

As if on cue, the shrill sound of a whistle screamed just outside the front of the cottage.

Without waiting for Drake's response, Cianda grabbed up her bag and ran toward the back of the cottage.

Drake, hard at her heels, caught her arm and spun her around just as she reached the back kitchen window. "It would be a damned sight easier just to confront the man."

"And tell him what? That I illicitly entered this house to look for—" Her sentence snapped and broke off.

"Yes?" Cianda wasn't fooled by the look of lazy insolence on his face. "To look for what?"

"A way to remove you from my life without murder," she shot back. Lifting up the window sash, she took a quick look around before climbing outside. "If you want to chat with the constable, please go ahead—without me! I'm sure you can find something amusing to tell him while he's putting the shackles around your wrists."

Drake hesitated for a moment, and Cianda, incredulous, decided he meant to do just that. Then, with a shrug, he moved to the window. "You know," he said as he crawled out after her, barely squeezing his tall, broad frame through the small opening, "it's interesting how you've managed to stay alive this long considering the amount of trouble you court."

"I could say the same for you," she whispered fiercely, shutting the window behind him. "At least I don't go rushing into disaster headfirst, counting on luck to rescue me."

"No, you prefer to skulk about in the shadows, until it finds you."

157

"That's what keeps me alive and my household fed and sheltered. Since I'm certain your only notion of responsibility is always to remember to thank your latest doxy, I don't expect you to understand."

"I'd forgotten what a formidable weapon your tongue is, milady thief. In more ways than one."

"Ssh!" Cianda gripped his shirt sleeve in warning. From the cottage came the sound of heavy boots tramping on the wooden floor. A beam of yellow lantern light swung back and forth against the window.

She felt Drake's muscles tense and sensed his restless urge to fling open the window and face the man inside. She wondered what kept him still, but crossed her fingers it would last long enough for her to flee to safety.

Cianda held her breath. At last, the light moved away and the footsteps faded as the constable walked back to the front of the cottage.

Slowly letting go her breath in a soft hiss, Cianda crept to the side of the house and darted a look around the corner. Moving fast, she slid out into the passage between the neighboring cottages and took the darkest route through the back gardens of several houses, emerging on the lane behind the mill.

With her concentration fixed on escape, she didn't notice Drake had followed her until she saw him step out from around a tree at the entrance to the lane.

The fog swirled in between them. Her eyes stayed on his as she took off her mask.

"The Masked Marauder safely retired for another night," he said lightly.

Aching bitterly from losing Jamie again, she said nothing as the hansom she'd hired to wait for her at a discreet distance from the mill pulled up. "Where's your lift?" she asked, making no effort to hide her anger at his interference, the near escape.

"I knew you'd have one waiting," he returned glibly, then climbed in beside her before her attempt to slam the door in his face swiped his ear.

The seven miles from the small Essex town back to London passed in near silence. When they pulled up three blocks from her home, she left him to settle with the driver and stalked down the dimly-lit street, staying in the shadow of the long stretch of garden walls. Once at the town house, instead of going inside, she strode around the back of the house into the garden.

He joined her a few moments later. Leaning an hand against a convenient rose arbor, he gave her a mocking smile. "I must thank you for a most entertaining evening, Missus Weston."

She whirled on him and with all the force she could muster, slapped him. "I should have killed you when I had the chance on your ship. I'm sorry I didn't."

He stiffened, but made no motion to restrain her. "For once, I believe you're telling the truth. I was beginning to wonder if you knew the difference between it and your pretenses."

"If you despise my pretenses so much, Captain, then get out. I don't need you."

"Don't you? What were you doing tonight?"

"Decide for yourself. You appear to prefer your versions of the truth to mine."

"I'm also interested to know what you were doing in the Devil's Acre several midnights ago," he went on as if she hadn't spoken.

He roused a fury in her as hot and uncontrolled as a fire in hell. Never had a man so utterly incensed her. Not even Godfrey. Nor had any man ever so completely disrupted her well-rehearsed act. The emotion boiling inside shot the truth

159

from her mouth before she could convince herself of the folly of it.

"I was looking for my brother, damn you!"

"Your brother?"

Regret and shame doused the angry fire in a cold wash. Drake stared at her in stunned bewilderment, obviously having expected any response but the true one.

"Your brother," he repeated the words slowly. "Why would you be looking for your brother in the Acre? Or an empty cottage, for that matter?"

Cianda slumped down on a stone bench, numb with the barrage of emotional blows dealt her this night. "Godfrey kidnapped him," she said dully. "If I don't bring him all three jewels, he'll kill Jamie. I had hoped to find him before I had to finish the deal with Godfrey — and with you." Her temper flared briefly and she glared at him. "But Godfrey outwitted me. Again." She looked down at her clenched hands, misery burning her eyes and clogging her throat.

Drake stared down at her, in the grip of unaccustomed indecision. Thorne, again, using fear and manipulation to achieve his ends. And he found himself in the role of rescuer — again. The last place he wanted to be.

The first time . . . Isabelle coming to him, begging with her body and her lilting voice for his help. For the only time in his life, he dared to allow someone to depend on him, and in turn allowed himself to depend on another, gambling with his heart.

And she rewarded his risk with betrayal.

Now this woman. Except Cianda D'Rouchert wouldn't ask for his help, not if her life demanded it. She allowed everyone to depend on her, but she relied on no one.

He looked at her, the defeated droop in her small body, the silver spill of hair masking her face, and felt an odd twist in his chest.

Cianda started when he sat down beside her. He didn't

ouch her, but she responded to the heat of him as surely as
f he had.

"Cianda . . ." Drake struggled to put a jumble of feelings
nd thoughts into words and failed.

"It doesn't matter," Cianda said, her voice sharp. She didn't
vant his sympathy. It was somehow harder to bear than his arro-
ant mockery. "We have our bargain, Captain. My reasons for
arrying it through are none of your concern."

"It's a little late for me to forget them."

"Why? I doubt you've ever cared for anyone enough even
o begin to understand."

"I did. Once."

The underlying current of anger in the terse response
idn't invite further probing. Cianda, flaunting the danger,
ersisted. "She must be a unique woman if she was able to
cratch at your heart."

"She was. She's dead."

He flung the words between them with unexpected inten-
ity, his voice thick with acrimony. From grief or fury,
Cianda didn't know. "Did you love her?" she asked, not re-
lly wanting the answer.

She immediately regretted her impulse. Drake's arm shot
ut and his fingers closed over her jaw in a painful grip.
Don't push me any further."

"You pushed first," Cianda snapped back through gritted
eeth. "Don't expect me to meekly let you try to intimidate
e. Now, if you've finished for the evening, I've had more
an enough of your company."

"Have you?"

"Quite enough."

"I did save your life." His hand gentled to shape the curve
f her face into his palm. "Surely I'm entitled to some re-
ard."

"You'll have your reward when I hand the jewels to
horne."

161

"I was thinking of something a bit more personal, milady thief."

Cianda raised her hand to slap him again. Drake caught i easily and in one quick motion, slid his free hand into he hair and pulled her against his chest. She expected him t kiss her. Instead he paused, a whisper between them, so nea she felt the rapid pace of his breath, hot and ragged agains her face.

The taste and smell of the danger and fury around then blended with the fulgurant sensations their closeness ig nited. The combination flared into wildfire, swift, angry Electrifying.

Drake's deliberate hesitation tortured every nerve unti Cianda yielded reason to desire. Reaching to pull him to he she joined his mouth to hers.

Sorely rankled by her attempt to provoke his emotions Drake meant to prove to her, and himself, she was no matcl for his strength. By sheer will, if little else, he convince himself he could purge his need for her.

But as her mouth slid hotly against his, the realizatio struck hard and fast that he held his equal in his arms. H challenged. She had the weapons to win.

His mind murmured a vague caution. His heart refused t listen.

Shoving her overcoat to a pool around her, he molded hi hand to her flesh. Stroking, grasping, he learned the shap of her as if he were blind and would never have the chance t see her in the light.

"Drake . . ."

His name on her lips, half plea, half enticement, swer away any control he might have laid claim to. Wit trembling fingers, he unbuttoned the voluminous shir and laid it open. His palms swanned the soft linen be neath, pushing it away with an urgency that felt perilousl akin to desperation. She was the last woman he should have

162

She was the only woman he wanted.

Drake's kiss smothered Cianda's startled gasp. The turmoil of sensation he aroused left her confused and uncertain, unable to protest. Even if she had wanted to.

She didn't. She couldn't.

He filled one hand with the fullness of her breast, the pad of his thumb caressing its taut center, and pleasure surged through her veins on a wave of white heat. She wanted to capture each sensation and lock the feeling away. But the combination of his scent, his taste, his touch overwhelmed her.

Unable to still her own hands any longer, she ran her palms over his shoulders and chest, sculpting the taut muscle with her fingers. Tugging open his shirt, she brushed her hands over his damp, heated flesh. The responsive quiver of his skin fed her excitement.

Cianda leaned closer, aching to feel the touch of his bared skin against hers—until her fingers slid lower and caught against the cold, hard emerald.

Drake felt her suddenly stiffen in his arms. Intoxicated with the heady force of their stolen passion, he nearly ignored her withdrawal. Using the force of the hot turmoil of desires burning between them, he could bend, if not break her will to refuse him anything now.

And in doing so, he knew with painful clarity, he would destroy his own will to resist her threat to his heart. But to what end?

Cianda pulled out of his arms, gathering her disheveled clothing around her. She answered the dazed questioning in his eyes by lifting the emerald away from his chest and letting it lie in her palm. The stone, warm from his body, seared her skin. "This, the ruby and the diamond, buy my brother's life. All they are to you are a means of justice. Or revenge. Nothing more. We're rivals, enemies even. That's all we can be. I can't let—I can't risk anything more."

She looked away, allowing the jewel to drop back.

Drake jerked to his feet, pacing a few steps away, then back again.

"Maybe. But no matter what we are together, it doesn't alter our bargain. Our goals may be different, but we both need the same thing."

"The Koh-i-noor."

"Yes," Drake's voice fell low. "The Koh-i-noor. The diamond that has brought prosperity to some and utter ruin to others since the dawn of Indian history. Do you know what the Hindu say about it?"

"I'm sure I don't," Cianda said shortly.

"They believe every precious stone doesn't suit its possessor. Streaks of light inside the stones run either parallel or in contrast to the lines of fate of the keeper. Parallel lines bring victory and joy; contrasting lines bring misery and defeat. Some jewels are not meant for some people to possess. To some the Koh-i-noor brought prosperity; to others devastation." He leveled a narrowed gaze on her." This jewel may be your downfall, milady thief."

Cianda stood and crossed her arms, swallowing the eerie sensation his words provoked. "Nonsense. I'll get it."

"When?"

"As soon as I find it." Her smile was bitter at his surprised glance. "Did you think I could somehow just conjure it up? It's not going to be that easy, Captain. Godfrey knows Lord Dalhousie annexed the Punjab at the end of March after one last awful battle. According to the treaty, all state property was confiscated by the East India Company in part payment of the debt due by the Star of Lahore to us and the expenses of the war. The Maharaja Ranjit Singh surrendered the Koh-i-noor to the Queen."

"And he was our ward to protect," Drake scoffed. "Fine caretakers we are, taking his whole territory from him. He was just an innocent boy when all of the Sikh War

164

started. . . . Ah, but no matter now. You were saying?"

Drake's concern for the wronged Indian leader both surprised and touched her. "Where the diamond is now—" She shrugged, concealing the desperation she felt with assumed nonchalance. "Even Godfrey and his magnificent contacts know only that it is presently somewhere on the road from Lahore to Bombay, and that it is in grave danger of being confiscated by robbers Indians called *Thugs*. Have you heard of them?"

Drake smiled sardonically. "Highwaymen are roughly our equivalent, except that the thieves here kill with far less finesse than the *Thugs*. To them murder is a sacred cult. They have so many disguises and dodges victims rarely know they're being followed until they feel the quick, strangling jerk of a silk handkerchief around their necks."

"How horrible! Perhaps the Koh-i-noor will never reach its destination."

Drake considered for a moment, scuffing the ground with the heel of his boot. "It will reach our shore. One way or another. You can be certain of that. Sir Lawrence has undoubtedly appointed an officer who will go to any lengths necessary to assure the jewel's safe transport." Drake glanced away, speaking as though to himself only. "And to protect his own standing in the Company." Before Cianda could ask what he meant by the offhanded comment Drake continued, "I think it's time, then, for me to make use of some magnificent contacts of my own."

"Do you have them? In India? Of course." She remembered the Indian idol in his cabin, the goddess she had destroyed to create her makeshift jemmy. "Your brother. Will he help you?"

"My brother is the most logical choice for the position I just mentioned." His jaw tightened and Cianda didn't need the moonlight to see the storm gathering in his eyes. "Contacting Charles is not an option." He paused, brows drawn, as though daring her to question his judgment.

"But if he knows where it is —"

"I'll find your damned diamond. The rest is up to you." Without waiting for her response, he turned on his heel and strode away into the darkness.

Drake pounded a fist against Zak's door for the third time, his patience long expired. "What took you so damned long?" he growled when his rumpled partner finally answered the summons. Pushing past Zak, Drake flung himself into a chair by the fire, scowling into the dying flames.

"In case it escaped your notice, it's well past two in the morning. The hour when most rational souls are sleeping." Zak sprawled into the chair opposite Drake and surveyed him with dispassionate interest. "What's the matter? Did she try to stab you with a spoon again?"

"She has a brother." Drake spit out the words as if they were the source of all his troubles.

"How inconsiderate of her. Tell me, is this the point where I am supposed to gasp in horror and immediately suggest we abandon your entire scheme in great haste?"

"Damn it, Zak!" Jerking out of his chair, Drake paced the room with long, agitated strides. He felt unsettled, without direction and control of his impulsive plot, and for the first time, uncertain if his daring and luck could pull it off. And it was all her fault.

This wasn't the way he had planned it to happen. He was going to use her without regret, capture Thorne, and forget her. Instead, she upset all his ideas about her and worse, stirred unwanted pangs of empathy and protectiveness. To say nothing of the desire he scarcely controlled.

"If you're not going to explain, I'm going back to bed," Zak drawled from across the room. "You can continue prowling about if you must."

Drake shot a glare at him. Zak gazed back, unruffled. "Thorne kidnapped her brother as assurance she would get the three jewels," he said at last. "I thought—"

"You thought she was a common thief you could manipulate with your charm and threats. Now when you find out why she's willing to risk everything to get the wretched diamond, you're mad because she's managed to get under your skin. Again." He waved a hand. "Don't bother to deny it. The question that now arises is what happens next?"

Dropping back into the chair with an explosive sigh, Drake shoved a hand through his hair. "It seems the East India Company has taken the diamond from the citadel it uses as a holding tank for jewels taken from the Punjab. As you know, Mausel is still President, ruling along with Henry and John Lawrence. John has utmost confidence in Charles. It wouldn't surprise me in the least to discover Sir John has persuaded the Board to give custody of the diamond to my brother. If so, in one sense Charles is a complication I don't care to consider at the moment." Drake heaved a discouraged breath. "On the other hand, he would know what is to become of the Koh-i-noor."

"You are desperate, old chap. Do you seriously believe your dear brother would come to your rescue? He wasn't especially accommodating over that business in Italy. And somehow I don't think Old Pam will be anxious to retrieve you if you land in prison a second time because you were outsmarted by the Masked Marauder. Again."

"You've made your point. More than once." Drake sat for a moment, scowling at the fire. "I've got it!" He jumped to his feet, drawing a raised brow from Zak. "Robert Barrett-Shaw. He's taken the *King's Bounty* on Company voyages before. If the Koh-i-noor's to be brought back as a trophy to tout our latest acquisition, as I'd suspect it naturally would be, Robert will have something to do with its transport. You can be certain of that."

"True." Zak yawned. "And I suppose Lady Barrett-Shaw will convince him to part with the information if he's at all reluctant. She dotes on you, although I can't imagine why."

"I'd hardly call it doting."

"It is. A bloody nuisance, I should imagine. Women generally are. Entirely too bad your thief turned out to be one. She's just more trouble."

"You're right." Drake leaned a hand against the mantel, and kicked a boot at the edge of the fire. "More than I ever bargained for."

Chapter Ten

Early morning sun poured gold through the tall kitchen windows, giving an illusion of summer warmth. Cianda stepped into a shaft of light and stood still for a moment, letting the heat caress her. As always, it brought both pleasure and melancholy; the sensual joy of being in the light, and the realization she spent most of her hours in darkness.

"Preparing for another spectacular snatch and dash?"

Cianda felt an irrational thrust of anger that Drake Weston somehow managed to catch her unaware and look so cool and provoking doing it. The last place she expected him to turn up was the kitchen. But then the unexpected was routine where *he* was concerned.

They had managed to avoid each other for several days, whether by unspoken mutual design or luck, she didn't care. After the night in her garden, too confused by her conflicting emotions to face him, she retreated from him, needing to reestablish her defenses and her distance from him.

He frightened her. Not with his recklessness and the threat he posed, but in the way he stripped away all of her carefully designed defenses and exposed deep, furious passions she never realized she was capable of feeling.

Drake, on the other hand, appeared to have completely

forgotten the entire incident. *How nice to be able to le.*
nothing and no one touch you, she thought, not certain
whether to envy or despise him.

He flashed his wicked grin and nodded at the large bas
ket she carried. "Rather cumbersome for your type o:
work, I'd say."

She glared at him, slapping his boots off the corner o'
the kitchen worktable where he had propped them. *If h*
wanted to ignore it all, so be it. "I don't 'snatch and dash,
Captain," she said, her eyes hard. "That's your style."

In the process of shoveling another loaf of freshly
baked bread from stove to worktable, Maisie grinned a
them both. With a snort of laughter, she turned to Drake
" 'Er tongue's a proper threat, lad. I wouldn't try my luck
with 'er in a fair fight o' words."

"I'll consider myself warned," Drake said. Plucking ar
orange from a large bowl, he swung his boots back to the
table's edge and began tossing the fruit into the air.

He reminded Cianda of a boy full of unspent, destined
for-trouble energy, and she had to smile.

"So," he threw the orange almost to the ceiling. "Where
are you going today?" The orange dropped back down
Keeping an eye on her, he caught it with one hand.

Cianda opened her mouth to tell him just what sh
thought of his constant interference in her life. But Maisi
jumped in before she rallied the words.

"She's 'eaded back ter the Acre. Or Whitechapel o
Rat's Castle. Any of 'em'll do 'er. Ye'd think a lady with ;
fine roof over 'er 'ead an' plenty ter keep 'erself busy won'
care ter be spendin' 'er days in those places, now woul
ye?"

Drake's slow appraisal brought a flush of roses to Cian
da's skin. "Yes, I would. It's fascinating."

"Fascinatin'! Not by 'alf, it ain't! Now me, I got out o

170

the Acre and ye'd 'ave to drag me by me 'eels ter get me back inside, ye would." Maisie punctuated her avowal with a smart whack to the round of bread dough in front of her.

"Yet you go there of your own volition. Aren't there safer ways to fulfill your Christian duty? Charity balls and the like? Donations to Whittington's Almshouses or the Women's Hospital?"

"Perhaps," Cianda said, averting her eyes from Drake's curiosity. "But I don't fancy the idea of my donations ending up in the hands of a wasteful administration, instead of the mouths of the needy, as so often happens these days."

Drake set the orange aside. He ran his fingers through his hair, shoving a dark, heavy wave from his brow. "You manage to keep abreast of the charitable efforts the city has undertaken since the Poor Law was revised, do you? In all of your spare time?"

"I do read the papers, Captain. And you have only to visit any of the city's slums to know the Poor Law has scarcely solved the plight of the impoverished. While I don't endorse the abolishment of the Poor Law altogether, I do feel that if fortunate individuals contributed more time and money, then the need for state services of relief could be limited—" Cianda caught herself, suddenly realizing she was saying way too much. Consciously, she softened her adamant tone. "That's why I make time to be a sort of self-appointed district visitor, for appearance's sake. You understand."

"Naturally, milady thief." Drake's penetrating gaze weighed heavily on her. "What I fail to understand is why you volunteer on your own instead of through a charitable body?"

Cianda began to feel uncomfortable with the direction

171

of his questions; he was beginning to probe much too deeply. She could hardly tell him many of the people she visited were friends from her childhood in the Acre.

"Well," she answered lightly, "as you said, I am a busy woman. I must do my good deeds at *my* convenience. I can't be restricted to visiting the poor on Sunday afternoons alone." She sighed, "I only wish I had more time to give."

"Champion of the poor. Of course, the perfect avocation to foil your true profession. Wouldn't it be to your advantage if someday one replaced the other . . ."

"Bah! Ain't nothin' ner no one worth riskin' a warm bed and a belly full o' food fer, that's whot I say. Ye c'n care ter much 'bout the wrong things an' end up wit' nothin' a' t'all. But ye won't listen ter me, will ye dearie?"

"I certainly wouldn't think of asking you to go along, Aunt Maisie, especially since it distresses you so much." Cianda smiled sweetly. "Although—of course you wouldn't be interested."

"Interested? Interested in whot? Speak up, dearie. Stop 'at whisperin'. Ye know me ears ain't whot they was."

"It's nothing. Only that I've heard there's a marvelous troupe of street dancers entertaining near Westminster. I'm going to the Acre today and you know how close by the Abbey is. The troupe is supposed to travel with a hurdy-gurdy player there who boasts to be the best in London."

"Pshaw!" Maisie spit out the exclamation. "Best in London! Best nowhere's more like it. We'll just see, shall we? Per'aps I will go along just this once. Just ter take the air." Abandoning her bread dough, she tramped out of the kitchen, muttering all the way down the hallway. "Best in London! Did ye ever 'ear such a barefaced lie?"

"Hurdy-gurdy?" Drake looked to Cianda. "Maisie is a woman of many talents."

A small smile playing about her mouth, Cianda moved behind the worktable and took up kneading the dough where Maisie left off. "Maisie used to earn several shillings a week playing the hurdy-gurdy on street corners. She pretended she was blind or deaf and it earned her more than any other street musician on the whole west side. She still takes great pride in her talent. The only way I can get her to go back with me is to challenge her sense of competition."

"Go back?"

Cianda's fingers smoothed and pressed the warm dough in faster rhythm. She carefully avoided meeting Drake's curious eyes. "To take the bread."

"You said it as if you meant the past," Drake stubbornly gnawed at Cianda's unintentional phrase. "For a woman whose tongue is more effective at times than a pistol, you've become amazingly quiet."

"I go there regularly." Cianda saw no reason to deceive him. He would only follow her and demand explanations at the most inconvenient times. "That's all I meant."

Drake sat up in his chair, eyes narrowing. "Of course. To share your good fortune."

"They need it," she answered simply. She glanced up at him and added in her most prim tone, "And as I explained, charity is expected of a woman of my means."

"Even if it's stolen?" Slowly, with languid grace, he got to his feet, moving to lean against the worktable. He bent over, resting his elbows on the surface, his fingers rubbing the rounded skin of the orange. Cianda kept her eyes fixed on the bread dough, pushing away a sudden, too-real memory of his fingers intimately caressing her skin.

Drake seemed unaware of her agitation. "Most ladies of quality wouldn't consider doing the required good works in the worst slums of London personally," he said. "You,

173

though, appear entirely comfortable with the notion."

His persistence was moving from annoying to unnerving. Somehow she must quell it at once. "If you have some observation to make, Captain, then by all means do so." Cianda massaged her palms back and forth over the long length of dough. She tried to keep her eyes from fixing on the gape in his shirt. The emerald, tied on its golden chain, hung low against his chest, swaying in a hypnotic rhythm over his heart.

Drake shrugged. "It seems an extraordinarily hazardous undertaking when you could so easily simply make donations, or engage someone else to carry out your generous works. Yet, you involve yourself personally, knowing you're venturing into certain danger. You leave me wondering what lengths you'll go to to protect our marital secrets."

"I'll leave you in suspense, shall I?"

"Mmmm . . ." The stroke of his fingers over the orange became a lazy circling. "So, tell me, what is destitution like, milady? I confess to selfish ignorance."

This time she met his eyes squarely, suppressing the nagging feeling that he knew insolence was precisely the bait to dangle in front of her to make her reveal the part of herself she wished to hide. "I must say, the image of a Weston, even a dishonored one, tramping about in the squalor of Rat's Castle is rather incongruous. To you survival means enduring the boredom between amusements. In places like the Acre, if you treat survival as a game you don't live long enough to regret it."

Drake stared at her a moment. She could see the shift of emotions in his eyes like a sea change in the moments before a storm. Curiosity, intrigue, suspicion, a reluctant admiration. "I'm beginning to think I've made a mistake in my judgment of you."

"You? The indestructible, infallible Captain Drake Weston?" Cianda said mockingly. "Why I'm appalled."

Drake dropped the orange back into the bowl, straightening. He pushed a hand through his hair, shoving back a heavy wave from his brow. "I decided you wanted the jewels. Only the jewels." The words seemed forced from him. "But that isn't it. There's your brother. And, now it seems you've adopted other causes besides the ones living in your house."

"Don't let it distract you from your plan, Captain Weston," Cianda said lightly, her eyes fixed on the warm mass beneath her hands. "Our bargain and my causes have nothing to do with each other."

"You have a way of saying my name that makes it sound like a curse."

"How fitting."

"And you're lying. Again. I'm beginning to wonder if you really intend to keep your promise. I hate to think I'm being forced into weeks of pretending to be your devoted husband just to find my neck in a noose after all."

The edge of menace in his voice brushed cold up her spine. She twisted the dough with sudden ferocity. "If it ends up that way, you can't accuse me of not warning you. I told you not to trust me."

"But I do trust you, milady thief." Drake walked close and touched his hand to a loose strand of silver hair. "If you betray me, I swear my version of hell will make anything Thorne can concoct seem like paradise."

Their eyes clashed. Danger and anger breathed in the silence between them.

Danger, anger and an echo of something that tempered Cianda's fury. For once, she risked her defenses and ignored the fire in her blood, instead listening to the whisper of her heart. She heard it in his voice, glimpsed it in

175

his face, the memory of a past hurt. A betrayal. Her thoughts resurrected the memory of the violent emotion that the mention of his past had roused in him several nights before in the garden.

"To be betrayed, you would have to involve your heart. I don't think you'll chance that—again."

His face was hard, admitting nothing. "You're right. I won't."

Cianda kept her eyes level on his. "You're using me, Captain. Like Godfrey and every other man who's wanted my skills. I don't trust you. But I won't risk my brother or the life Godfrey has given me. Just don't threaten me. I'm not the only one with something at stake."

"You're absolutely right." Drake smiled, a dangerous, provoking twist to his mouth. The glint in his eyes spoke trouble. "But my only risk is to myself. Can you say the same?"

The kitchen door pushed open and in marched Beatrice, several baskets looped on one arm and Fred draped over the other. Cianda looked at her friend then back to Drake, who rubbed a thoughtful hand over his jaw, the expression in his eyes smug.

"Fred seems to have taken to you," he said, moving away from Cianda. "She usually hates everyone but Zak."

Beatrice's gray eyes swept him in a dismissing glance. "She needed to be fed, and I don't approve of feeding animals in the withdrawing room, as your friend Mr. — Zak insists. Apart from that," she added, setting down the baskets, "Maisie was there looking for her hurdy-gurdy." She scratched Fred behind the ears, eliciting a grumbling purr from the cat. "I thought it best to avoid a confrontation if at all possible."

"Yes, I think that's best. Avoiding a confrontation. You never know who'll come out on top."

"I can well imagine you endeavor to claim that position for yourself as often as possible," Cianda muttered, slapping the bread dough into a pan and shoving it into the stove.

"I do. But I'm always open to suggestions." With a raffish grin, he tipped her a mocking salute and strode out of the kitchen, leaving the door swinging behind him.

Beatrice looked at the door, then at Cianda and arched a brow.

"If we can't locate that diamond soon," Cianda said, her eyes hot with green fire, "I swear I'll murder that man."

After weeks of cool damp and fog, the final days of April blossomed with welcome warmth. Cianda, toting her now-empty baskets, let her steps draw her from the lodging house where she had left her bread, into the patches of sunshine that dappled the narrow cobbled lane.

Costermongers driving rickety carts, balancing large baskets on their heads, or trays about their necks, crowded the warren of alleyways touting every kind of ware possible. The underlying stench of the sewers and filth intermingled with the smell of fish, rotting vegetables, and horse dung.

Cianda wove her way through the stalls and street traffic, pausing often to exchange a word or a smile with one of the sellers or the innumerable, scrawny ragamuffins darting between adults, picking pockets, playing chase, and begging for a scrap of food or a coin.

"My God—" Drake, walking close, darted around in front of her and quickly stopped, bringing her up short.

She shot a glance around them. "What is it?"

"You smiled. In fact, you're positively basking. The

worst of London seems to bring out the best in you."

Cianda let her smile linger as she looked away and slowly walked around him. "The worst of London is a maze of grimy tenements with as many starving children as starving rats. At least here in the Devil's Acre some thoroughfares allow light into the dank streets. And I spend so much time in the shadows, it seems a luxury to be in the light."

"I'll have to force you into the sunshine more often," he said, falling into easy stride beside her. "Just to see you smile."

The simple words brought a faint flush to her face for a reason she couldn't name. "I haven't had much reason for joy lately . . ." Her voice faltered away.

"You're worried about your brother." There was no mocking or prodding in the statement, and it encouraged her to confide a little of her fears.

"Yes. Godfrey's deadline is so near—"

Drake frowned. "His deadline?"

"He wants the trio of jewels by July."

"Why July?"

Cianda shrugged, not wanting to reveal the humiliating truth that Godfrey had not entrusted her with that information. She was working for him blindly. She had no choice. After so many years, Godfrey still manipulated her like a stupid puppet on a string. But Drake Weston certainly did not need to know that.

"Godfrey said it had something to do with the two hundred and fiftieth anniversary of the East India Company," she said nonchalantly.

"A gift symbolic of the Company's success in acquiring Indian holdings. The glorious Koh-i-noor, soon to be just one among thousands of jewels locked away in the Tower. Unless Godfrey does intercept it before the Company hands it over to the Queen. I wonder what powerful lord or ruler will claim the mysterious gem next? He must have a buyer eager to possess the famed idol and its missing trio of gems. Wouldn't you imagine?"

Again, Cianda felt the stab of her own nescience. "Who wins the trophy in the end matters nothing to me. My only concern is for Jamie."

Drake's voice fell tenderly on her ears, "I know." He brushed his fingers over her arm, his blue eyes sober.

It was new, this gentler side of him. A small hope trembled in her heart. Perhaps their impossible alliance could work. At least long enough for her to find Jamie and escape Thorne.

For the first time since she reluctantly allowed him to join her and Maisie, Cianda let herself relax.

She studied him surreptitiously from the corner of her eyes. Drake insisted on taking Beatrice's place and accompanying her to the Devil's Acre, out of curiosity or determination to keep her in sight, she didn't know which.

Considering the lavish Mayfair mansion he grew up in, she'd expected him to be condescending, and even appalled by the miserable little homes they visited. Instead, he tagged along with them and helped distribute the bread and other foodstuffs to families Cianda had adopted.

He hid the revulsion he most certainly felt crossing courtyards heaped with garbage, to enter filthy, sagging hovels packed with humans as unclean as their surroundings. He made no complaint when tired, rude laborers jostled and shoved against them, grumbling and cursing at the intrusion of yet more bodies into the already suffocating throngs.

When they had finished their visits, unexpectedly, she began to mellow toward him; he grated less on her nerves. Back out in the open air of the wider avenues that fringed the outskirts of the slum, her satisfaction roaming among and chatting with the people she had a certain kinship with enhanced her spirit of generosity toward him as well. She relaxed, enjoying the peaceful interlude, ignoring the sad sense of its transience.

Perpetually ill at ease sipping tea, exchanging polite niceties, and attending endless balls, she could never truly belong in that arena. Here she did belong—once—even if since, she'd stepped too far away from it ever to return.

"Don't you ever get tired of it?"

The stroke of Drake's velvet voice cut through her thoughts. "Tired?"

"Of being in the shadow." He stopped her again with a hand on her arm. "You're always there, aren't you? Even when you're pretending to be Lady D'Rouchert. You're still wearing a mask."

His perception so closely mirrored her earlier thoughts, Cianda wondered if she'd spoken them aloud. "It fits well," she said with a slight lift of her shoulders. "And I'm certain the elite of London—or you for that matter—wouldn't care to see what lies underneath."

"I wouldn't be so convinced of that."

"I am. You of all people should know society isn't forgiving."

"I do. But you and I differ. I don't care. I walked out a long time ago, and I have no intention of going back. You, on the other hand, would risk anything to stay."

Cianda caught a breath and glanced away. "I have my reasons. None that you would understand."

"I might." He avoided her eyes too, as if he were suddenly uncomfortable. "I know how it feels to live between two worlds and not belong to either of them. Is that why you come here? To try to make peace with your past?"

"I told you why I come." She tried, yet couldn't quite

disguise the catch of pain in her voice. His random words exposed too many old hurts. "Don't dig too deeply, Captain Weston. I've warned you, you won't like what you find. And neither will I."

She turned to continue her walk. Drake stopped her by plucking the baskets from her hands and dropping them at her feet. Taking her shoulders in his hands, he pulled her close and kissed her. Thoroughly, without reserve, indifferent to the laughter and good-natured calls from boys selling boiled puddings and the loud bunch of gin-sodden roustabouts who trailed a bird brainer, begging him to perform more tricks.

His mouth seduced hers open to the probe of his tongue. Fire raced wild under her skin, stealing her resistance. Remembrances of his intimate caresses rushed back with blinding intensity; she let the slide of his hands against her spine invite her to lean into his hard body. In Piccadilly she didn't dare. In the Acre, she did.

She met him equally, dizzied by the taste of honey and temptation, the match of muscle to softness, the demand and abandonment of his kiss. She willingly stepped with him into the flames, regardless of the danger, and now she wondered if she could ever retreat from him back into the safety of her shadows.

Drake's mouth gentled on hers and when he finally broke away, he held her close for a moment, his breath quick against her neck.

"Maisie will probably have left without us," he said at last, releasing her. Scooping up her baskets, he stood a pace away from her, holding her eyes with his.

The stormy blue of his gaze awakened Cianda's curiosity. She saw his turmoil in the tense set of his shoulders, his tightly drawn jaw. "What's wrong, Captain? Wasn't it what you expected? Or was it more?"

181

Without waiting for an answer, she curled her hand over his arm and led him up the lane, into the full light of the morning.

Drake stood propped against a lamppost on the back lawns of Westminster Abbey half listening to Maisie's third rendition of "Moll Brook," watching Cianda.

Happy, laughing with the noisy spectators gathered around Maisie and the rival hurdy-gurdy player, Cianda radiated childlike joy. Such a contrast to the first Cianda D'Rouchert he'd met.

The first instant he saw her was branded in his memory as clearly as if it had happened moments and not weeks ago. A creature born of ocean and moonlight, silver and ivory against the night. A thief then; a lady now. Delicate and small, yet strong and fiery when he touched her.

Drake had never known a woman as bold or as elusive. He wanted to take off her mask. He wanted her. Unconditionally. And it scared the hell out of him.

He couldn't afford to feel. He didn't want to feel.

Wasn't it what you expected? Or was it more?

More. Much more. And his only defense was she didn't fully realize it.

Yet.

"I didn't think Maisie was that off-key," Cianda's lilting voice threaded its way into his dark thoughts. "Although, I will admit seventeen verses of 'Moll Brook' is enough to try anyone's patience. And patience certainly isn't one of your virtues."

"I don't have any virtues."

"Oh, I wouldn't say that, Captain Weston." She laughed up at him, teasing him with her smile, mischief in her deep green eyes. "Perhaps virtue isn't exactly an apt description, though."

182

In his present mood, it took as much will as Drake could muster to fend off the urge to scoop her into his arms and carry her to the nearest warm bed. She knew she tempted fate—and him—and still she pushed him farther than any other woman dared.

"I'll have to follow you to the darker sides of London more often," he countered. "It brings out the lighter side of you."

"It seems to bring out the worst in you. You look like thunder and—Oh! This is my favorite." Tugging at his sleeve, she urged him closer to Maisie. When he hung back, she danced forward, caught up in the lively duet bellowed out by Maisie and her rival.

Grace in every motion, she stepped lightly to the music. For the first time since he'd known her, she looked at ease, comfortable with herself. She'd set aside the Masked Marauder and Lady D'Rouchert and become someone he'd yet to meet.

"Faith looks quite the lady now, don't she?" a rough voice said near his elbow. Drake turned, and a short, wizened man flashed him a toothless grin. He smelled strongly of fish and rank oil. A brightly painted wood tray that hung from his neck by a leather strap was papered over with newspapers and piled with shapeless brown lumps of fried fish.

The man pointed a hand at Cianda. "I knew 'er when she were just a tiny lass. She looks like 'er mama, Faith does, a little bit of a woman, but wiv a tongue ter cut yer dead."

"Faith . . . ?" Drake looked at her with puzzled eyes.

"Seein' as she's yer lady now, I s'ppose ye'd know 'bout that, though," the man went on, oblivious to Drake's confusion. He winked, his grin larger still. "I saw ye in the lane. Ye've got a way wiv 'er, ye 'ave. She's got fire in 'er,

183

but she's a good girl, still, Faith is. Always willin' ter turn a 'and ter 'elp someone, and a loyaler lass ne'er lived. Do 'er a good deed, and she'll think she owes ye fer life."

The old man's words brought an image of Thorne to Drake. Did she feel she owed him some debt? A debt misguided loyalty demanded she pay?

"It must be a long time since she's lived here," he ventured, hoping for some new scrap of information about her.

"Not since she were a scrawny little scamp. 'Er mama always brung 'er ter the Abbey back then, every Sunday, she did. I 'ope she's 'appy now, little Faith. She looks jus' like a fine lady. The real thing." He fell silent a moment, then shrugged. "Well now. I best be off 'fore I lose all me afternoon payers," he said, resettling the strap of the tray around his neck. "Ye tell Faith ol' Willie asked after 'er. She'll remember me, she will."

With a tip of his cap, Willie lumbered off into the crowd, shouting out the virtues of his fish.

Drake took a step after him, intent on taking advantage of the chance to unearth something of Cianda's past. But a shout from the crowd stopped him short and snapped him around.

At the street corner, a fracas had broken out between two hansom drivers whose cabs had collided. Spectators milled about the accident scene, calling out comments and advice.

None noticed the coster wagon until it bowled through the crowd, knocking one of the hansom drivers and two bystanders to the cobbled street. With the driver's seat vacant, loaded with potatoes, it careened wildly from side to side, dragged along by its horse at a mad gallop, aimed directly at Cianda and Maisie.

Caught up in the music and revelry, neither woman saw the danger.

Drake swept the scene in a single glance. He started to run even before his mind registered the idea of trouble. Straight toward the wagon.

A chorus of shouts erupted behind him. He heard Cianda's voice, screaming his name; he ignored them all.

Judging the distance and angle, betting on his luck, Drake sprinted out head on toward the wagon and leaped up onto the driver's seat. His shoulder slammed hard against the side, but he managed to get an arm and leg over the edge, trying to make a wild grab at the harness leathers in the same motion.

They flapped out of his reach. His boots scudded against the cobbles for several feet as he struggled to gain a hand-hold on the wildly swaying wagon. With a last-ditch effort, Drake slung his other leg up and over the wagon side and snatched at the leathers once again.

The straps cut into his palms as he gave a mighty jerk. The recoil flung him back against the jumble of potatoes. It brought the horse's head up sharp and around, forcing the frightened animal to a stumbling stop.

Drake flopped back against the lumpy load of vegetables, too winded to move.

"And you have the guts to call me a blazing idiot!" Cianda suddenly materialized beside him.

At the sound of her outraged tone, he lifted his aching head in disbelief to look at her. Her face was flushed, her body trembled. Whether with blind fury or shock, Drake didn't have the energy to decide.

She fastened her fingers on his arm and shook it hard. "Don't you ever think before you plunge yourself into danger? *Especially* the kind you might not come out of alive?"

"Never. It saves time that way." Drake attempted to sit up and pain stabbed his shoulder. "Besides, after what I've seen here today, I hardly think you're one to lecture me about exercising caution."

"It's not the same thing at all and you know it!"

Gingerly, he pressed fingers against the bruised flesh. This definitely hadn't been one of his better ideas. "By the way," he muttered, annoyed at the fury on her face, "you're welcome."

"For what? Having to watch you almost trampled to death? How kind of you."

"It was heading straight for you!" he snapped back. The woman had a way about her that made him want to put his hands around her throat and throttle to his satisfaction.

Cianda crossed her arms over her chest defensively.

"You have a penchant for near misses. Tell me — " Drake managed to sit up, stifling a groan as every muscle and bone loudly protested. "Who is your friend from the cottage? The one who wants you dead? One of Thorne's emissaries?"

"Of course not! This was an accident, and that was a coincidence, someone trying to get into the house at the same time." She looked away, and Drake knew she was lying. Or at least suppressing the truth. Right now his body hurt too much to care.

Moving slowly, he climbed down from the wagon, stopping for a moment to rest his weight against the side.

"You could have been killed." The hot anger died out of her voice, leaving it strained and bewildered. "It was insane; you didn't need to take that kind of risk. You could have called out to someone else. Why did you do it?"

Drake shrugged away the probing question. She dug deeper inside him than he wanted to look. "I was getting bored sitting in your parlor all day. I needed a little excitement."

She stared at him a long moment and then, startling him, reached up and kissed him hard on the mouth. Her face hot, her mouth determined, her eyes daring him to comment, she said sharply, "There are other kinds of excitement, Drake Weston. And by the way, thank you."

Before he could muster a retort, or even a reaction, she had motioned to a nearby fruit peddler and a pair of swarthy youths hanging over the cart gawking, to help him away from the cart. Dumbfounded, he let them lead him like a ward in his keepers' hands, while Cianda hailed their carriage.

All the way back to her house, Drake tried to decide who had won the latest battle in their ongoing war of wits and will.

In the end, he grudgingly admitted to himself the honors were hers.

Chapter Eleven

Cianda gathered her resolve around her, gripped the basin in her hands a little tighter, and rapped sharply at the door connecting her bedroom to Drake's.

She couldn't explain to herself why she had come and hoped she wouldn't have to explain it to him.

In the hours since they'd returned to her home, she relived the scene in the Devil's Acre a thousand times. His rash rescue both terrified her and earned her reluctant admiration. She might doubt his motives in partnering with him, but never his courage or daring.

Her sense of loyalty said she owed him, at least the care she would extend to anyone injured.

She told herself that. The difficulty was believing it.

After she gave several taps at the door, Drake opened it to her, a half-wary expression on his face when he saw the linens and hot water she held. "A little late for a show of wifely concern, isn't it?"

"I came to look at your shoulder. It won't take long." Pushing past him, Cianda carried her load to the low table in front of the fire. "Don't worry, Captain," she said as a frown began to creep between his eyes. "I've some experience in doctoring. I promise not to maim you any further — you do that well enough on your own."

Still standing by the door, Drake rubbed a hand over

the back of his neck. Even though evening had given way to night, he hadn't bothered to repair the ravages of his reckless ride. Brown dust streaked his white shirt, and a long rip slashed it across his chest. "I don't need your help," he said finally, his voice rough. "And I don't have the time to spare for needless fuss."

"Really? I didn't realize your calendar was so full." Glancing around the room, Cianda saw several papers strewn about the escritoire and floor. A large map, worn and shredded at the corners, covered the top of the writing desk, scraps of paper with various illegible notations lying atop it. Drake followed her curious gaze, but offered no explanation. He merely stared back at her, his face blank.

"Are you planning a journey?" she said, pointedly nodding at the map.

Hesitating, he let out an explosive sigh and shoved a hand through his hair. "More of a hunting expedition. We're leaving in one week for St. Helena Island."

"St. Helena . . . ? Is the Koh-i-noor—" A throb of excitement followed by a shot of anger vied for mastery of her emotions. "You didn't see fit to tell me you'd found the diamond. Did you intend to pursue it yourself?"

"The letter came this afternoon while we were out." Striding over to the desk, he pushed aside several papers before seizing a crumpled envelope. He held it up for her inspection. "I didn't have an opportunity to tell you. Until now."

"How did you find it?"

"Through a friend."

"I didn't think you claimed anyone, with the possible exception of Zak, as more than an acquaintance."

"Only a few." Drake slapped the letter back on the desk and turned away from her, pacing to the bed and back. The unspent energy in him stirred an uneasiness in her.

Cianda ran her finger over the rim of the basin to soothe her disquiet. The side-to-side movement turned more agitated than easy. "How can you be so sure the information you have is correct?"

"I'm sure." When she looked at him expectantly, her eyes demanding more, he burst out, "My friend is the admiral of the *King's Bounty*, the ship that will be taking your bloody diamond to St. Helena. It's set to arrive the first week in June, and the governor of St. Helena is planning a ball to celebrate the annexation of the Punjab and the acquisition of the infamous Koh-i-noor, which by the way, the royal guards did manage to see safely through the treacherous land of the *Thugs*. Does that satisfy you?"

"Quite," Cianda snapped back.

"We'll sail on the *Ferret*. The trip should take about three weeks. If we don't run into trouble with pirates near the African coast, and if the weather holds."

"With this timetable, there'll be precious little allowance for delays. Or error." After weeks of searching for the Koh-i-noor. Cianda supposed she should feel triumph, a certain relief that Drake had found it. Instead, a tightening of the desperate pressure to find Jamie and escape gripped and twisted at her nerves.

"What's the matter, milady thief? Having second thoughts about our bargain?" Drake smiled grimly. "It's far too late now. If you betray me, you'll never meet Thorne's July deadline."

And your brother will die. Cianda read the silent message in his eyes. She swallowed her fears and stared steadily back. "I suggest you concentrate on holding up your own end of our arrangement. If I don't meet Godfrey's deadline, you may be the one with your neck in a noose."

She spoke the words to stab him with the truth of his own stake. Strangely, though, the too-real vision of him standing on the scaffold at Newgate left a hollow feeling deep in her belly.

Banishing the scene from her mind, she found Drake looking at her with a curious expression. "I have no intention of letting either of us end that way," he said softly. "Only Thorne."

Cianda glanced down, saying nothing.

His hands clenched in tight fists, Drake half turned from her, his angry frustration a palpable presence in the room. "The man is a thief and a traitor. He uses you for his own gain and gives you nothing in return. And yet the idea of seeing him hang still appalls you, doesn't it? I can't explain it."

"He gave me my life, and Jamie's," she said, refusing to look at him, loath to see the disdain on his face. "I hate him for what he's done, but I owe him a debt. Without Godfrey, I would be less than nothing."

"You're wrong, Cianda." Tension rippled his shoulders. "Or is it Faith?"

"How did you—?"

He cut her short. "It doesn't matter. None of it matters except that you get your precious diamond. That's what you want isn't it?"

There were a thousand things she could have said to him. A thousand things she wanted to say. In the silence between them, all of her apprehensions magnified. "I suppose it's settled then," she said at last.

Drake turned on her, his eyes hot. "I suppose it is. You have the information you wanted. You can get out now."

His cold dismissal roused her stubbornness. She lifted her chin. "I didn't come here for that. I'm not leaving until I look at your shoulder. It will be easier here by the light," she added briskly, pointing to a spot by the fire.

"You're amazingly persistent when you set your mind to something," Drake said dryly. Slowly he walked to stand in front of her, a hand's length away. She breathed the scent, the sense of him, a provocative blending of summer heat, sudden storms, and danger. "Is this close enough?"

"Yes." She answered softly, silently cursing the insidious weakness that slipped up her spine at his nearness. After convincing herself she could repay her debt to him with an impersonal service, she now called herself a liar. There was nothing impersonal about the way Drake Weston made her feel. He stripped away her ruses and left her vulnerable to her own desires.

And there was nothing she could do about it. Giving in to his dangerous seduction meant risking everything. Including her brother's life.

The thought gave her strength to ignore the trembling in her hands and reach up to unfasten the buttons of his shirt. Drake stayed quiet, but when her fingers fumbled the first button from its slot she felt the quickening of his breath under her fingers.

For one night only, to give myself to him . . . just this once, to believe the feelings between us have the strength to erase our differences, to overcome the past. . . .

If she was holding a pistol to his heart, Drake decided he would have felt more at ease. It took every shred of will to stand motionless as she touched him, her slow deliberate movements a sweet torture.

192

He was dying of his need for her, inch by inch, determined not to want her, unable to stop any more than he could quit breathing. No matter what they denied or embraced, he could no longer avoid confronting his longing for her. He hated artifice, yet for weeks hadn't he been pretending she meant nothing more to him than a means to an end?

It was a lie.

The tremors in Cianda's heart made her fingers clumsy. She forced her hands to move slowly over each button. When she reached the last, she spread open the soft linen, her palms grazing his chest.

The gleam of gold and emerald momentarily captivated her. A flicker of firelight speared the jewel, splintering amber and green light in a lightning flash. The fire lent a copper sheen to Drake's skin. Flame shadows danced between them. Running the tip of her tongue over her lips, Cianda slowly reached up and touched a finger to the emerald.

The avid glint in her eyes brought Drake to the edge between passion and anger. As her fingers started up the golden chain around his neck, his hand shot up and covered hers, holding her palm against his restless heart.

"Which excites you more?" he said, his voice low and husky. "This . . ." With his free hand he reached up and freed the clasp of the gold chain, letting the cool metal slide between them and over Cianda's hand. "Or this—" He untied the ribbon at her nape, twisted her hair around his hand, and pulled her within a heartbeat of his mouth.

With a leisure he didn't feel, Drake gently nibbled at her lower lip, his tongue teasing the inside of her parted mouth. Her breath mingled with his on a sigh.

The emerald dropped unheeded to the carpet as she

raised her hands and pulled his mouth down to cover hers. Without hesitation, she pushed aside his shirt and rubbed her hands gingerly over his shoulders and lower, against the hard muscles of his chest, leaving no doubt of her intent to arouse. Her fingers brushed the bruise on his shoulder. Replacing her hand with her mouth, she gently laved the tender spot with her lips. Her mouth nuzzled the hollow of his throat before returning to his again.

She kissed him wantonly, with a hunger that begged him to forget the pact that divided them. The pleasure-pain of desire swept away the faint cold voice reminding him of his determination to stay aloof, to guard his heart.

The barriers seared to ashes as he guided her to her knees with the urgent pressure of his hands, shaping her body to the length of his.

Rocked by the force of their passion, Cianda clutched at his shoulders, wanting him closer. And not only in flesh. Wanting him made her ruthless, bold. In yielding, she demanded his surrender of the heart. Nothing she ever longed for, dreamed of before, seemed as important.

It was beyond reason, beyond what could or could not be.

Drake skimmed hot, hurried kisses over her throat. Moving to kneel behind her, he lifted her silver hair from her nape, igniting the sensitive skin with his kiss. His fingers ran down and back over the row of buttons, curving against the neck of her gown. Then, in one quick jerk, he split the material wide, sending the tiny buttons flying in every direction.

Far from protest, Cianda closed her eyes and leaned into his hands when his mouth moved along her spine, pushing away her clothing to fall to a crumpled heap around her waist.

When the sharp ache of longing became too much to bear, she twisted to face him. Wrapping her fingers over the corded muscles of his forearms, she pulled him with her to the soft plush of the carpet.

Dazed, possessed by a nameless driving need, she arched upward as he shoved aside the layers of dress and petticoats, until nothing came between his hands and her bare skin.

The flicker of the firelight melted gold over the ivory of her body and into her emerald eyes. Her silvery hair spread around her face like threads of mist. Beautiful, elusive, daring, she tempted him to madness. Drake longed to savor each sensation just the sight of her roused, to make love to her slowly and easily. She made it impossible. Already, her skin was damp with the sheen of desire, her lips parted for his kiss, her eyes smoky emerald, entreating his touch.

And yet he felt a whisper of hesitation. Picking up the emerald from where it had fallen, he trailed the gold chains into the hollow between her breasts. "You haven't answered my question," he murmured. The gold slid down her belly to her thigh. "Which excites you more?"

Cianda laced her fingers into his and guided his hand back up her body to her face. Her eyes holding his, she pressed a kiss into his palm. "This," she whispered. "This does. You do."

"Do I?" The jewel still lay against her. Stolen emerald fire on her ivory skin.

"Yes. Please . . . love me." She kissed him and the gem slipped aside. "Love me tonight, while we can."

The soft, breathy words twisted his heart. *Love you? Tonight? Forever? I can't. Only tonight. Just tonight.*

Then I can do what I have to do and forget this feeling.

The promise to himself should have been a charm against her attraction. Instead his heart maligned him.

Cianda vacillated between tears and laughter, as waves of pleasure, intense and sweet, rocked her emotions. By the light of day, imprisoned in her role, she quelled her passion. In the familiar shadow of night, she fanned it with her own desires, convincing herself one night—this night—with Drake Weston—with only this man—would be worth any amount of sunlit regret.

Do you believe in the destiny of lovers?

His words returned to echo in her thoughts. Did she? Did she dare?

Cianda cried out when Drake's mouth moved hot and wet in the hollow where the emerald had lain, nibbling against her skin until his tongue flicked against the nipple of one breast. He took the taut peak into his mouth, suckling it gently. Fire licked her within, coiling low in her belly.

Her low moan deafened Drake to everything except the damp silk of the flesh filling his hands, the taste of her sweetness, the scent of her arousal. Cianda's fingers kneaded his back as she pressed intimately against his hips.

Stroking from her belly to her thigh, he slipped a finger into the silver-blond nest of curls. She jerked upward as he caressed the slick flesh, her eyes beseeching.

Cianda ached to tell him how much she needed him, how much he pleasured her. Her hand brushed over his hips to flirt at the hard outline of his shaft. He groaned deep in his throat. His hand followed hers and he plundered her mouth as he fumbled with the fastening of his trousers.

The last barrier. The last surrender. The risk she dared

not take, yet dared to all the same.

Cianda's heart pounded against her chest, loud to her ears. Too loud—Her befuddled mind took several moments to realize the sound came from outside, not from within.

"If yer through with yer nursin', I've a few things to talk over with ye, dearie," Maisie's voice called loudly from outside Cianda's bedroom door. "Yer not abed yet, are ye? I see the light—" The doorknob rattled irritably.

Cianda focused on Drake's face, so close to her own. His breath came hard and fast and his hands tightened on her body. For a moment, she convinced herself he would finish what they had begun and damn the consequences of Maisie's discovery.

At the moment, she wanted nothing more.

"Are ye all right, dearie?" Maisie's rapping came louder and more insistent.

"I have to go," Cianda whispered, barely able to force her lips around the words. "If Maisie knew of this . . . I can't let her know—"

"No, I can't ask you to sacrifice your pretense, can I?" The quiet anger in his eyes frightened her more than his volatile outbursts. Drake stared at her, then bent and kissed her roughly, as if he intended to brand her with his touch.

Without another word, he got to his feet, bringing her with him. He waited, arms folded, as she hastily gathered up her clothing. "I'll be there in a moment, Aunt Maisie," Cianda called out, cursing the tremor in her voice. "I'm just finishing."

Drake caught her as she moved toward her bedroom. Shackling her wrists with his fingers, he pressed her against the wall, her hands splayed between his. The firelight played over his face, leaving his eyes in shadow.

He hadn't bothered to refasten the first buttons of his trousers. Of its own accord, Cianda's gaze followed the arrowing of dark hair from his belly to where the material gaped open.

"You're wrong, love," he said. "We aren't finished with each other. We may never be. No matter how many times you run, no matter how you hide." He kissed her again, his tongue probing deeply to spar with hers. The heat surged inside her. Drake's fingers stroked against the tender skin of her wrist, then, abruptly, he broke away, rubbing the back of his hand over his mouth.

Their eyes met like thunder and lightning. Lost in a tangle of desire and anger and confused feelings she refused to name, Cianda whirled and fled through into the haven of her own room.

She leaned against the connecting door, her ruined gown clutched to her breast, her breath erratic. Several seconds passed before she gathered enough strength to force herself to move.

Stuffing her tattered dress into the bottom of her wardrobe, she shoved her arms into a soft cotton dressing gown, belting it tightly around her body. Running a quick hand over her hair, she sucked in a deep breath and opened the door to Maisie.

Her face set with a glower, Maisie stumped past Cianda without a word. She stood in the middle of the bedchamber, arms folded, her foot tapping a jerky rhythm on the carpet.

"I'm sorry to keep you waiting, Aunt Maisie," Cianda said, holding her voice level as she closed the door. "I've been—"

"Bedding that pirate! Don't bother to deny it, dearie. From what I 'eard outside 'is door, ye weren't doin' much doctorin'. Not that I expected ye would be. Every time the two a ye looks at each other, it's plain what's in yer minds."

Cianda raised her chin. "I should have guessed you would be listening at the keyhole. And you deliberately took it upon yourself to intervene."

"Someone 'ad to. Do ye realize the trouble you're courtin' by lettin' that rake into yer bed?"

"I did not let him into my bed!" *So close. Though I was so close. And I would have. I would have, and gladly. For a moment, I did believe . . .*

"Pshaw!" Maisie snorted. She waved a hand up and down indicating Cianda's undress. "Ye only 'ave to look at ye ter know what ye've been at."

Cianda glimpsed herself in her long dressing mirror, hair tumbled, lips slightly swollen from Drake's passionate assault, skin flushed. She blushed more deeply as she realized how wanton she did indeed appear.

Her silence encouraged Maisie's tirade. "Did ye ever stop to think whot'd 'appen if 'e got ye with child? Thorne'd turn ye out on yer ear without blinkin' an eye. And then where'd we be? Where'd ye and yer little Jamie be? Ye look and act like a fine lady, dearie. Thorne's almost turned ye into the real thing. But bein' almost a lady ain't good enough ter keep us in Piccadilly if ye lose Thorne's protection." Cianda winced at the cut, but Maisie forged ahead, ruthless in her defense of her home and hearth.

"Did ye ever consider the rest of us 'fore ye let yer feelings fer that pirate 'ave the better o' ye?"

"My feelings? For Drake Weston?"

"Ye care about 'im. Don't deny it, now."

"No!" *Yes.*

"Yes," Maisie said heavily, shaking her head. "Ye do, no matter how many times ye try ter say otherwise. I've

199

seen from the beginning that lad were goin' ter be trouble fer ye, and I were right. 'E's no weak-kneed, fancy talkin' gent tryin' ter woo ye wit' pretty words and promises. 'E's the wild kind that I've always known would catch yer fancy. Nothin' civilized 'bout 'im. The question is now, how do we rid ourselves o' 'im and that friend o' 'is?"

"We don't." Cianda dropped down in a chair beside the cold fireplace, drawing her knees to her chin.

"Look 'ere now—"

"We don't," she repeated firmly. She met Maisie's frustrated gaze squarely. "I need Captain Weston if I'm to steal the diamond. I can't do it alone. And I must have the diamond to rescue Jamie. There's no other choice. They both stay."

Maisie glared hard at her for a full minute. Cianda stared back, undaunted. She knew Maisie was only protecting her hard-won security in the only way she knew how. But it didn't make it any easier to accept the circumstances. And it didn't make it easier for her to forgive the older woman's untimely interruption, whatever the motive.

"Well," Maisie said at last. "It seems there's no changin' yer mind."

"There isn't. Captain Weston stays."

Maisie shuffled to the door. "We'll see about that, dearie," she said before closing it behind her. "We'll just see about that."

By the following afternoon, preparations for Cianda and Drake's extended "holiday" abroad were in full swing. The house bustled with activity under Beatrice's firm command. Cianda instructed her staff to work with

200

Zak, stocking enough food and clothing for over a month's cruise aboard Drake's schooner.

The pretty young parlor maid Cianda employed during the day only, for appearance's sake, thought the notion of an intimate journey at sea terribly romantic. As she went about her tasks, tidying the salon, she chatted incessantly. Cianda allowed herself a smile at the girl's silly notions. *If you only knew the half of it.*

The journey's true purpose aside, romantic was hardly the term she would have used to describe the intimacies she and Drake exchanged. Desperate, furious, dangerous, perhaps, their attraction had never been a matter of tender wooing and gentle caresses; it ruthlessly consumed her senses. Irrational. Raw desire. Aching need.

In the fury of their mutual hunger, burned a common inner void, the loneliness of the lives they'd chosen. Cianda felt they shared an unspoken understanding, both existing between the lines of right and wrong, misfits, alone. Except with one another.

Lost in her thoughts she almost forgot why she came in search of the parlor maid in the first place. "Do you know where Missus Cowper is? I haven't seen her today, and neither has Miss Dobson."

The girl paused and looked up from the lamp shade she'd been dusting. She shook out the feather duster to her side. "I saw 'er on 'er way out, when I come in first thing, early today. But not since then."

"Did you say anything to you about where she was going?"

"No. I says mornin' to 'er, but she passed right on by without so much as a nod. 'Er ears don't work so good no more, though, so I ain't 'oldin' no grudge."

Her ears worked perfectly last night. Pushing aside the disconcerting memory, she said swiftly, "Well, if you

201

do see her, tell her I need to see her at once. There are a number of details we need to discuss before I leave."

" 'Yes, mum," the girl nodded and curtsied, and Cianda turned to go back upstairs and resume her packing. As she moved out into the hallway, Beatrice met her, looking oddly out of sorts. From directly behind her another woman, taller and considerably older, stepped forward, a stately woman of straight-backed regal bearing whom Cianda had never seen before.

"I am sorry to interrupt, Cianda," Beatrice said, her eyes troubled. "But Lady Weston insisted on a word with you."

Cianda's knees nearly buckled beneath her. She glanced down at her worn day gown, feeling every bit the guttersnipe before royalty. Drawing in a steadying breath, she lifted her chin, assuming her best look of gracious bearing. "Shall we sit in the salon? The sun is quite warm there. Please have tea sent in, Beatrice."

"I shall not require any refreshment." Octávia Weston raked Cianda with a look of loathing. Then, with a disdainful sniff, she strode past her into the salon.

The parlor maid was still cleaning the room. Cushions lay askew upon the settee, and several small decorations—painted vases, Jamie's framed watercolor portraits, tiny enameled boxes—lay on the floor beneath the side table she was dusting.

"Oh! Didn't know you were expecting a visitor, mum. I'll 'ave this straightened up in no time," she twittered.

Cianda had no choice but to stand awkwardly and watch. Her cheeks heated. Drake's mother chose the worst time to pay a visit to her new daughter-in-law. If that was indeed the purpose of her visit. If so, surely she would have sent word of a formal call ahead of time.

Unless her unexpected call was deliberately designed to catch her and Drake off their guards.

Just then, the maid, in her haste, dropped a vase. It hit the wood floor with a resounding crash. Cianda resisted an exasperated sigh.

Where is Drake? He and Zak must have finished their jaunt to the *Ferret* to oversee preparations by now.

"Dear me!" the parlor maid cried. "I'll go and get me broom and—"

"Leave it!" Lady Weston's imperious command sent the maid scuttling backward.

Wide-eyed, she looked to Cianda. Cianda gave her a brief, reassuring smile. "Go tend to the bedrooms." Relief washed over the young girl's face before she ducked quickly out of the room.

Cianda walked ahead to arrange the cushions. "Please, do sit down. I apologize for the inconvenience, but we are preparing to leave on a long journey."

Lady Weston's long, slender neck seemed to grow another inch as she lifted her sharp chin and clasped her gloved hands in front of her solemn gray skirts. "I have no intention of staying here," she said icily as she perched on the edge of a chair.

Cianda narrowed her gaze. *So that's the way it's to be.* She'd dealt with arrogant aristocrats many times before. Only never under *these* circumstances. She was supposed to be this woman's daughter-in-law, her son's devoted wife. After last night, devotion sounded tame. She seemed better suited for the role of ardent lover.

Cianda almost smiled as she pictured Octavia Weston's shocked reaction if she did adopt that particular role. Yes, she could play the charade, especially if it meant defending Drake before this blue-blooded matriarch of the *beau monde*.

"As you wish," she said with a perfect smile, "I must assume the matter you wish to discuss is of the utmost urgency."

"Don't be tart with me young woman! I know what you are, and I know what you have done to snare my son into marriage."

"Snare?" Cianda laughed aloud. "I assure you, no one traps Drake into doing anything he doesn't choose to do. Considering his way of life, you must be well aware of that."

Lady Weston's mouth drew into a hard line. "I suggest you guard your tongue or I will make certain you regret it. It would be quite easy for me to ruin you with a few well-spoken words."

"I care less for the opinion of society than your son," she lied for his sake.

"I should have known Drake would marry a low-minded chit. I refuse to sit and banter insults with you any further. I have come for one reason—to tell you I intend to do all I can to have your marriage declared invalid on the basis of your deception. Drake, I am certain, had no idea you are carrying another man's child or he would never have married you. For all his faults, he is not witless!"

"Another man's—that's absurd!" Cianda didn't know whether to laugh or rail at the ridiculous and cruel accusation.

"I will not have my family name ruined by your French bastard! Drake has done enough to tarnish the Weston name." Lady Weston's hands clenched in her lap. "I have endured his scandalous affairs and his sordid adventures abroad, but this I will not endure!"

Cianda rose to her feet, all attempts to be polite gone. "You've no choice in the matter. And I don't intend to endure your company any longer."

Lady Weston glared at Cianda. Her voice became a low hiss. "You are cheap and common. I knew it before I laid eyes on you. You, *Madame D'Rouchert,* or whatever your name is, are a fraud. You are certainly no lady."

"Considering your treatment of my wife, I don't know how you would recognize a lady, Mother," Drake's low voice rumbled into the salon. He didn't bother to disguise his fury as he strode to Cianda's side.

Cianda nearly collapsed against him. Instead, she accepted the warm pressure of his hand against the small of her back as welcome support.

"I see your manners have not improved," Lady Weston said, rising to her feet.

"Not in the least. Why are you here?"

"Your mother is under the impression I am with child," Cianda quickly answered. "Another man's child. Perhaps you would care to set her mind at ease."

Drake looked squarely into eyes that matched his own piercing blue. "The child is mine."

"Well!" Lady Weston stared at him for a stunned moment, her expression vacillating between shock and anger. Finally, regaining her haughty mien, she drew herself up and snapped, "After meeting your little strumpet, I'm not sure whether I am relieved or revolted. How could you do this to us? To me? Why can't you simply be more like Charles? *He* took a respectable position and sought my approval before he married."

"That's always been the problem hasn't it? I'm not Charles. And I never will be. Why did you have another child, Mother? You had your heir; you should have stopped at one. Or was I conceived as insurance? Unfortunate for you. If Charles meets an untimely demise, I'll make a poor excuse for an heir."

Cianda turned and put a hand on his arm, feeling his fury in the tension of his muscles. "Drake . . ."

"It is most unfortunate for me and for our family name," Lady Weston said tightly. "You will both regret this. I can assure you of that." With a last look of hatred for Cianda, she swept by them both and out of the salon, nearly cannoning into Maisie.

"Beg yer pardon, yer ladyship," Maisie muttered, glancing at Cianda, her eyes guilty.

"Don't believe you will get anything more from me, you wretched creature," Lady Weston spat. "This unfortunate incident is due entirely to your meddling."

Cianda stared, her fingers tightening on Drake's arm. "Aunt Maisie, you didn't —"

Lady Weston halted her march toward the front door long enough to look back at Cianda with malicious triumph. "Of course she did. Being one of them, you should know the loyalty of the lower classes can always be bought."

As Lady Weston left the salon, Maisie disappearing in the opposite direction, Cianda looked up at Drake. She wondered, as she tried to read the expression in his eyes, if he shared his mother's opinion. Did he think Godfrey had bought her loyalty with his promise of security?

Cianda's gaze slid to the touch of gold chain at Drake's throat and then back to his face. She wanted to deny it. But, in her heart, she feared that without knowing it, Octavia Weston had spoken an unwelcome truth.

Chapter Twelve

"Her ladyship is gone," Beatrice stepped into the salon, glancing from Drake to Cianda. "I am going to the kitchen rooms now to see if I can soothe Lily. She is in a state over a broken vase, although I suspect it's more to do with your visitor."

Cianda moved away from Drake, nodding her thanks to Beatrice. "I'm going to find Maisie. Obviously, she's the reason for Lady Weston's unexpected appearance."

Drake watched her glide out of the room, a delicate, ethereal sprite of a woman. Yet with an inner strength that endowed her with a undauntable spirit. A lady by heart, not title, he thought, realizing how much he despised women like his mother who were the opposite. Born to the title, but lacking the courage and compassion of true stature.

He paced restlessly in front of the mantel. When Cianda returned she'd undoubtedly ask him why he claimed her nonexistent child. He ought to have a logical reason. He didn't. He'd made the claim on impulse, not from any rational motive.

The lie came easily, springing from a sudden, overwhelming urge to protect Cianda from his mother's wrath. But why? His mother read Cianda expertly. Cianda D'Rouchert was a fraud, a thief. His mother embodied society's quintessential "lady": proper, self-righteous, strictly ruled by protocol, never the lower side of human nature — emotion. Everything he scorned.

None of it made sense.

Swiping a small porcelain figurine from the mantel, Drake began tossing it from hand to hand as he strode back and forth. Why should he care what his mother thought about Cianda? Their marriage wasn't real. Neither were his feelings for his pretended bride.

He was using Cianda, nothing more. Wasn't he?

She lived a charade and stole to preserve it. He couldn't afford to understand the choices she made. Could he?

But was it any less a crime than theft every time his mother turned her back to the bribes and dark favors that aided his father's political career? When she destroyed innocent people's reputations with untrue rumors, just to further her own ambition in society by eliminating competition, was it any less deceptive than Cianda's pretense?

No. And it was why he defended her. Living so close to her, watching her loyally sacrifice and care for her makeshift family (and even in an odd, disturbing way he might never fully understand, for Thorne), he realized her only purpose in thieving, living a lie, rose from selfless devotion. In his mother, his father, his brother, Isabelle, pretense served selfish ambition.

"Aunt Maisie has locked herself in her room. She says her heart is troubling her and she can't talk to anyone." Cianda shook her head in mixed disbelief and irritation as she walked back into the salon. She walked near enough for Drake to catch a drift of the disturbing spicy-sweet fragrance of her perfume. "I know she did it out of worry for her security, but she doesn't realize the trouble she's caused. Please be careful. That's Jamie's favorite figurine."

"What — ?" Drake stopped pacing and stared at the china dog in his hand, seeing it for the first time. "This?

208

It's your brother's?"

"Yes. I gave it to him on his eighth birthday. He wanted a real puppy. But the doctor said the fur might aggravate his condition."

Drake's brows drew together. "What condition?"

"Jamie has trouble breathing. Ever since . . ." Cianda looked away. "Oh, for a long time. I'm very worried. Godfrey threatened — "

Her sentence broke off and Drake sensed her concern for her brother had led her to a confidence she regretted. Reaching out, he tipped up her chin with his forefinger. "Tell me."

"He threatened to withhold Jamie's medication." The emerald of her eyes blurred with unshed tears. "He suffers so without it," she ended in a broken whisper.

Drake looked at her a long while, his heart twisting at the pain on her face. If she ever did bear a child, the little bastard couldn't be luckier, he thought. Jamie might as well have been her own, as much as she obviously loved him. He wondered how long she'd been Jamie's only parent.

And if anyone — any man — had ever loved her with the fierce devotion she had for her brother.

"I almost forgot." Cianda pulled away from him, briefly turning aside while she fumbled in the pocket of her gown. Her fingers swiftly dashed at the corners of her eyes before she turned back, holding out a small envelope. "This came for you."

The urge to fold her into his arms nearly overcame his good sense. Yet no matter how he wanted to comfort and protect, it would only annoy her to be coddled when she struggled to shove back her tears and appear strong. Instead, Drake took the note, ripped open the thick envelope and scanned the few hastily scripted lines.

"Is it important?"

"It might be." He crumpled the missive into a tight ball. "I've asked a friend of mine for help in finding your brother. He's agreed to make inquiries."

"You . . ." A frown crept between Cianda's eyes. "Why?"

"Because if we find him, it takes away some of Thorne's advantage."

"And yours. What reason then would I have to help you?"

Sliding a finger against the gold rope around his throat, Drake said, "I have the emerald. I can still expose you as the Masked Marauder."

"Yes. You could." She continued to study him, her expression thoughtful. "But would you?"

Would you? He glanced at the clock on the mantel, evading her question. "It's not too late. If we hurry, we can still meet him."

"Him? Who? Where are we going?"

Drake grinned at Cianda's sudden suspicion. "To Epsom Downs, love. I'm taking you to the races."

Cianda spent the better part of the drive to Epsom Downs fretting at the time they wasted in attending such a frivolity when so much work remained before they set sail. But Drake insisted, promising her the afternoon would not only be a perfect diversion after the disastrous encounter with his mother, but that it might yield information about where Dorsey had taken Jamie.

As they neared the race track, Drake instructed the driver to stop and fold down the top of the cabriolet for a better view. Obediently, the old man, his shoulders rounded from years of sitting in the same position, hunched forward to hold the reins, climbed off his high perch. He pulled his bollinger off to wipe drops of sweat from his brow before he went to work.

The top flapped back behind them, exposing them to the hot, dusty haze billowing up from the thousands of shoes and wheels and hooves clogging the race track grounds. Perched on the leather seat next to Drake, Cianda opened her tasseled parasol to shield herself from the intense sunlight.

As they neared the heart of the crowded track, Drake laid an arm across the back of the seat. Not bothering with a coat, he had rolled the sleeves of his loose, white shirt to the elbows. "I'm going to place a wager at the betting post. You're welcome to join me, if you don't mind being trampled. All manner of pickpockets and criminals haunt these events, you know," he said, a devilish twist to his mouth.

"I'll wait here, thank you," Cianda said, endeavoring to ignore the brush of his forearm at her nape. "These race meetings are overall vulgar and detestable spectacles."

"Now you're sounding like my mother. Come on now, show me the *real* Cianda D'Rouchert," he taunted. "Place a bet."

"I don't gamble."

"Your life is a gamble."

"Well then, what else is there to wager?"

Drake lifted a brow. "I could make a suggestion," he murmured.

Cianda put her chin in the air. "You'd better hurry, the line is long already."

A satisfied smirk on his face, Drake climbed out of the cabriolet. "I'll bring you the lists for today. Perhaps a name will strike you as lucky."

Cianda watched Drake's long smooth strides as he melded into the crowd. He towered above the bulk of people, his dark hair glistening in the sunlight. He turned, showing her his chiseled profile, as sharply aristocratic as his mother's. Yet he lacked Lady Weston's civilized finish. He exuded a sense of danger, of power, an incongruent mixture of untamed sensuality and arrogant superiority. Cianda suspected the former was a gift of nature, the latter a gift from his parents.

She felt relieved Drake seemed as willing as she to avoid discussing his mother. The confrontation disturbed Cianda more than she cared to admit: Lady Weston's brutally accurate assessment of her, the ever-present threat of exposure to society as an impostor, and the devastating reminder she could never hope to be a true lady, one born to the role.

Cianda supposed Drake's desire to ignore the visit meant the incident roused demons of his own to contend with where his mother was concerned.

Sighing, she adjusted her parasol to better shield her fair skin from the sun. It hardly mattered what Drake's mother, or any of his family or friends, thought of her. She ruthlessly reminded herself she and Drake were only playing a game, one that placed them on opposite sides.

To distract herself from her moody reverie, Cianda focused her attention on the teeming activity of Epsom Downs. In front and behind her cabriolet, over-crowded brakes and wagonettes shoved and pushed their way along in procession all around her. She was only half surprised when a heavy thrust from behind knocked her carriage, jolting her hard against the side.

From somewhere close by, she caught a whiff of the same sickly sweet scent she'd smelled the night she was attacked at the cottage. But when she turned to find the source, she came face to face with a grizzled, drunken coster leading a donkey cart, who reeked of cheap gin and sweat—hardly a sweet combination. The rickety cart scraped against her carriage, its wheels kicking dirt over her pale apricot gown.

The drunkard whooped a crude, lusty call, then promptly relieved himself on the back wheel of her cabriolet.

Disgusted, Cianda blocked her view of him with her parasol. But the loud, pained grunt, that followed made her look again. The rude driver now lay in a crumpled heap on his bench, hunched over his huge belly, moaning.

Nearby him, Drake slapped the donkey's rear and sent the cart clattering into the crowd. Dusting his palm against his thigh, he strode back to Cianda's side.

"Thank you," she said tentatively. "But was that absolutely necessary?"

"I've no doubt the Masked Marauder could have fended for herself, but I thought it might look suspicious if I didn't defend my wife's dignity."

He climbed back in beside her and signaled the driver. The old man cracked his whip over the backs of the team of dappled mares, sending them forward.

"Here—" Drake handed Cianda the broadsheet. "Maybe you'll change your mind about placing a wager after you look this over."

"You're amazingly persistent, Captain," Cianda muttered, as the cabriolet lurched ahead, trampling the outskirts of a Gypsy caravan. Its wheels tore over a bright carpet, inciting the olive-skinned men and women with mystic eyes to shout what Cianda knew must be vile curses.

Drake scouted the suffocating masses, the line of carriages and drags outside the overflowing stands struggling for a view of the horses.

"We'll never be able to find a seat," Cianda said. She hoped to discourage Drake into abandoning the whole silly notion. He'd probably used the story about meeting somebody at the track who could help find Jamie as a trick to lure her out of the house.

"To the grandstand," Drake called to the driver over the pandemonium.

"You have a box?"

"The family does. But we won't be using it today. We'll be using Lord Palmerston's."

"We will? I don't think—" Cianda's question was lost in the thunderous noise of the mob swarming around them.

Near the base of the grandstand, Drake swung out of the carriage. He reached up as Cianda stood, wrapping his hands about her tiny waist. As he slowly lowered her to the ground, he held her close for a moment, bringing his face near to hers. "The scent of you alone could tempt me to create a scandal here and now," he whispered in her ear.

Cianda stood in his embrace, unable to either deny or invite his touch. "I'll smell like a stable before this day ends."

"I'd still be tempted, love." Laughing, Drake released her, tucking her hand into the bend of his arm. As he led her past the stands, the crowd pressed in on them. Drake pulled her to his side, sliding his hand around to cradle her back.

Cianda considered moving away, knowing she should. But the shelter of his arm, the pressure of iron muscle rubbing against her spine in rhythm with Drake's confident strides, felt too warm, too right. Just this once, she indulged the secret pleasure of basking in his attention, in seeing the jealous stares from women ogling him as she walked by with Drake's hand possessively holding her beside him.

His touch recalled vivid memories of his hands urgently caressing her skin. With those remembrances came the recollection of Maisie's warning, and Lady Weston's hurtful accusation. "By the way," she blurted out without pre-

214

amble, "I'm not with child."

Drake stopped and looked down at her. An indulgent smile lifted the corner of his mouth. "Did you really think I believed you were?"

"You were very convincing with your mother. Why did you tell her I was expecting your child? It would have been simpler to tell her I wasn't expecting any child."

"She wouldn't have believed it."

"She'll only believe what she chooses anyway," Cianda said, scowling. "Now, everyone will be waiting for us to produce a baby."

Drake's smile widened to a rakish grin. "I'll be happy to oblige you, love. Although, the image of the Masked Marauder with a belly the size of a pumpkin, crawling through a second-story window is rather amusing. I can picture the headlines in the *Times*." He framed an invisible banner with his hands. *"Marauder Snared By Windowframe. Or, even better, Marauder, Master Thief— Mother Of Twins?"*

Cianda rolled her eyes, both embarrassed at his audacious comment, and exasperated at his teasing. "If someone hears you, Captain Weston, I'm going to swear you're the Masked Marauder. I don't think I'd have any difficulty making them believe it."

"Yes, you would," Drake said as he led her toward the boxes. "The mask you keep leaving behind is too small. Incidentally, why do you keep leaving it in various safes and lock boxes?"

"The first time I left it by accident," Cianda said, avoiding his amused gaze. "One of the newspapers somehow discovered my carelessness and dubbed me the Masked Marauder." She lifted her chin and bravely met Drake's laughter. "Since then, I've felt obligated to add that artistic touch to each of my burglaries."

"I always knew you were a woman with imagination."

From the sudden smolder in his eyes, Cianda knew he intended to make some outrageous comment about her creativity, and that it would have nothing to do with thievery. Only their arrival at Palmerston's box spared her.

The box presented an excellent view of the track. As Drake and Cianda stepped inside, the single occupant, Viscount Henry Palmerston, stood and greeted Cianda with a dip of his head. "I was beginning to think you wouldn't make it today," he said, lifting her fingers to his lips.

"I apologize for the late arrival, Pam," Drake said. "My mother decided to pay Cianda and me an unexpected visit."

Lord Palmerston chuckled ruefully. "Then I'm surprised to see you here at all. Octavia can be quite formidable."

"Yes," Cianda said vaguely. She looked from Palmerston to Drake and back again. "You're Drake's mysterious friend? The one helping to search for Jamie?"

"Drake can be very persuasive, when he chooses," Palmerston said. "You have my deepest sympathies for your brother's predicament, Madame D'Rouchert. And, in fact, I have a bit of good news for you. An acquaintance of mine, Inspector Davidson, is making inquiries into your brother's whereabouts. I can't make promises, but Davidson's a clever chap. I've no doubt he'll turn up something."

"An inspector?" Cianda swallowed hard. "I could never have risked —" She stopped, savoring the small hope that kindled in her heart. "How can I thank you?"

Impulsively, before she thought to mask her emotions, Cianda stretched up and kissed the foreign secretary on the cheek.

Palmerston beamed at her, a twinkle in his eyes. "And I thought when I lost on my favorite today that luck was against me."

216

Cianda flushed, faltering back a step. "I beg your pardon. It's just that I—"

"Don't apologize. It's not every day a man my age is kissed by a beautiful woman. But I'm afraid you're giving me credit for Drake's scheme. He's the one who convinced me to intervene on your behalf."

Feeling an unfamiliar shyness, Cianda turned to Drake. She touched his sleeve lightly. "Thank you."

"I want to be sure your mind is on business. Worry is distracting," he said a little too gruffly.

"I see." Cianda smiled, her eyes shining. "Well, I thank you all the same."

"When we've the time, you can show me your appreciation," he returned, flashing his familiar roguish grin.

"Speaking of time," Palmerston intervened. "Mine is quite limited. I'm interested to hear what progress you've made in your plan to entrap Thorne."

Cianda glanced to Drake, her throat tightening.

"We're making excellent progress," Drake said easily.

And if he believes that . . . Cianda restrained a sardonic laugh.

The suspicion in Lord Palmerston's narrowed gaze confirmed he did not. "I am in a particularly awkward and delicate position at the moment, Drake, as I'm sure you are aware. My decision to take action against the Greek government is as unpopular in the House of Lords as it is with the Queen and Prince. As I'm certain you've read in the *Times* numerous accounts of my management of the whole affair, every action I take at present is under scrupulous criticism by my colleagues as well as by the Crown."

"I must say, through all of the doubts the Cabinet has expressed over your policies in general, this situation seems to have escalated to a frightening pitch," Drake mused.

217

"Precisely my point. I know I've made the correct choices in dealing with Greece. But convincing my peers, hah! therein lies the difficulty. Most are enraged that I refuse to back down and submit to Russell's dictates."

"But surely the Prime Minister and the Cabinet cannot ignore your many successes," Cianda interjected, unable to stop herself from defending a man she had long admired for his bold defenses of human rights. "If it wasn't for your careful, patient negotiations, Belgium wouldn't have gained independence. And what about the alliance of Spain, Portugal, and France? Your diplomatic initiative gave the constitutional parties their only hope against absolutist monarchies."

Lord Palmerston smiled broadly. "I thought you said she was a thief, Drake, not a politician."

"Cianda never fails to surprise me."

"I can well imagine," Palmerston said, appraising Drake thoughtfully before returning his attention to Cianda. "You could scarcely have been born when I was immersed in those particular disputes. How is it you know my career so well?"

"I had excellent tutors, my lord," Cianda said, a touch of pride in her voice. "And I made it a point to learn as much as I could about the wealthy and powerful. For my own purposes. You understand," She added with a touch of teasing, "But I must admit, I've always found your political style fascinating. You follow your instincts, even when you suffered grave opposition. And your frank manner is most entertaining, my lord."

"You're rather outspoken yourself, Madame," Palmerston noted. "Perhaps I should send you to intervene with Albert and Victoria on my behalf."

"You don't sound optimistic," Drake said with a frown.

Palmerston turned suddenly grave. "I'm not. I'm afraid even now they're looking for a way to dismiss me. And it is for that reason that I cannot afford to promise you any further support in this venture of yours."

"But stopping Thorne will only work to your credit."

"*If* your search ends successfully. And frankly Drake, I cannot help but have my doubts about where it will end. Timing has become an issue it was not when we first began." Palmerston rubbed a weary hand over a bushy gray mutton chop at his jawline. "I know it was I who first initiated this pursuit, but now, I believe it would be prudent to delay it until I can stabilize my situation."

"No, blast it, I can't," Drake burst out. He restlessly paced the confines of the box. Shoving a hand through his hair, he confronted Lord Palmerston with an expression compounded of frustration and impatience. "I'm going to help Cianda steal the Koh-i-noor."

"You're going to — ? Good Lord, Drake. Have you gone completely mad?"

Cianda tried tactfully to intervene. "The plan isn't as insane as it sounds," she said, knowing it was.

"Don't ask for an explanation, Pam," Drake broke in. "It's too complex —"

"You mean you, as usual, only have the vague outline of a plan, and — as usual — you expect me to trust blindly in your infernal luck."

"This is the only way to snare Thorne." Drake flung out a hand. "Damn it, if I don't have your sanction, I'll end up hanging even if I do catch Thorne with the jewels."

The intensity in Drake's voice gave Cianda a start of surprise. *What hasn't he told me?*

"There's obviously something you haven't told me," Palmerston echoed Cianda's thoughts.

With a heavy sigh, Drake dropped into a seat. His fingers rapped against the arm in an agitated rhythm. "Admiral Barret-Shaw wrote to tell me Charles is overseeing the Koh-i-noor's journey to England."

"Good Lord," Palmerston repeated. Fishing a handkerchief from his waistcoat pocket, he mopped at his forehead. "I needn't remind you Charles is the reason you spent six months in an Italian jail."

"Charles?" Cianda looked at Drake. "So that's why you feel such anger toward him. But—"

"Charles Weston is one of Thorne's associates," Palmerston said. "He informed Thorne when Drake was in Italy to recover the Malwi Ruby. For once in your life, heed a warning, Drake. I cannot bail you out this time. If your brother or Thorne outmaneuvers you, I'll be forced to turn my back and claim ignorance of the whole affair." Hesitating for a moment, he stepped up and laid a hand on Drake's shoulder. "Let it go—for now. Put the past— put Isabelle to rest. Don't risk your career and your life for something you cannot change. Thorne will pay. It will just take more time than we hoped."

Isabelle? Cianda tried to make sense of the rapid hail of developments. How did Godfrey's wife fit into Drake's past? If they had been lovers—the notion stabbed at her heart. Was Isabelle Thorne the root of Drake's burning desire for justice?

Abruptly, Drake pulled away from Palmerston and stood to face him. "No, it won't take more time. Thorne is going to pay for everything and very soon."

Cianda saw the battle of wills, the concern and conflict in the depths of Lord Palmerston's eyes as he glared at Drake. Drake met his objections with stubborn eyes hard and cold as cut sapphires.

"Then I wish you Godspeed." Lord Palmerston said, regret heavy in his voice. "And to you." He bowed slightly to Cianda and picked up his hat and cane. "Please keep my box for the day. The next race is about to begin."

The words were abrupt, perfunctory, spoken from a man who had already washed his hands of anything and anyone connected to Drake Weston.

Drake, his tanned brow glistening with sweat, reached around Cianda and pointed to an exquisite colt. He bent close, his lips near the sensitive skin at her nape. "There's my choice. His jockey's wearing the Duke of Turcotte's colors—gold and green. He's running the next race."

The heat enhanced his earthy, masculine smell. Cianda inhaled a scent not fresh, but all man. It aroused something frighteningly primitive deep within her. His body heat seemed to add to her own rising temperature. She folded her parasol and plucked a kerchief from her reticule.

Leaning her head back slightly, she dabbed tiny beads of moisture from her neck slowly, pressing down and over the two ivory mounds above the scoop in her gown. As she tucked her kerchief away, she noticed Drake staring at her, a strange, mesmerized look on his face.

"For a man who is almost certainly doomed to hang, you've recovered quite nicely," Cianda said tartly.

He blinked, then said abruptly, "Read the lists. Maybe you'll choose the same name I wagered on. If you do, the winnings are yours."

"I suppose this means we're not going to discuss the latest complications in our plan? Complications you didn't bother to warn me of, I might add."

"Would it have mattered if I had?"

Cianda thought of Jamie and shook her head. "No. But I do like to know the risks beforehand. Tell me, Captain," she asked, mischief glinting in the depths of her emerald eyes, "Was your wager deep?"

Surprise flickered briefly across his face. He recovered quickly. "Very," he answered smoothly.

"I must say, the odds are too favorable for me to decline, then." Cianda glanced over the lists. Most names struck her as downright silly. "Billingsgate Bounder, Padwick, Turk's Head, Teddington." As she read, she felt Drake's heated gaze roam freely over her sweat-damp body. Despite the heat, she shivered.

"Oh, here it is! Emerald Fire. What other choice could there be?"

"My sentiments exactly."

"Are you suggesting we're of like minds?"

"Only in matters of importance, love."

"We'll see, won't we?" Cianda squinted against the blinding sun, examining the sleek, chestnut colt. "He seems smaller than the others. You know he'll lose, that's why you're offering me your winnings."

"Don't abandon hope so quickly," Drake said, appraising the colt. "He looks to be about thirteen hands. He *is* the long shot in this race, though, twenty-to-one odds last I heard." He grinned disarmingly. "Just the kind of odds I like."

"The longer, the better, I'm sure."

A row of constables herded the crowd off the track. Excitement swelled in Cianda, despite her anxiety over all Palmerston told them. Drake's life was as much at risk as her own. They only had each other now.

The sun beat down on the restless horses lined up at the starting gates. An electric current of expectation shot through the stands. Horses snorted and pawed anxiously, their anticipation infecting her. She wiped the perspiration from her throat and forehead with her bare palm.

Beyond, on the track, the starter stepped to the foreground and flashed the jockeys one last look. Every nerve in Cianda's body tensed, her heart beating a wild rhythm. At last the starter dropped the flag. A bell pealed out the final signal.

"They're off!" the crowd cried in unison.

Cianda heard her own frantic voice joining in. All around spectators screamed their horses' names, waving hats and gloves. The horses lurched forward, and instead of release, she felt a clutching low in her belly.

The horses sprinted forth furiously, every breath a pant, their wake a whirlwind of dust. Cianda felt as though she ran with them, unfettered, flying. Her own breath came in short gasps, her heart thumped against her breast. It was a familiar thrill, like the surge of danger, of the coming prize, after weeks, sometimes months of planning, watching, waiting, the moment she reached inside a safe to cup a coveted jewel in her hand for the first time.

Bouncing up on her toes, she tugged at Drake's sleeve. "He's behind!" she cried. "Why doesn't he hurry up?"

Drake laughed, a rich, throaty sound that only enhanced her pleasurable agony. "C'mon boy, take 'em. One more round. Run you bloody beast!" His robust baritone boomed out over her head.

The horses' hooves pounded the track, their rhythm an echo of Cianda's heartbeat. All around the crowd's screams reached a hysterical pitch. One more furlong.

"Emerald Fire is going to lose to that black colt," Cianda wailed. Her proper pretense drowned in the fury of the moment's passion. She cried out with all the gusto of a lusty gin-shop wench, "Take 'em Emerald Fire, take 'em right on out!"

She didn't notice the ladies in the next booth clap their hands to their mouths.

"I thought you considered race meetings 'vulgar and detestable spectacles.' "

Her eyes riveted on the track, Cianda waved a dismissing hand in Drake's direction. "Run Emerald Fire!" she yelled. "Run!"

As the horses drew near the finish line, a wave of sudden, superstitious fear overtook Cianda. Emerald Fire em-

223

bodied Drake's and her desperate race for the diamond and the prize—Jamie's life.

Emerald Fire must win! The colt, oblivious to her mind's images, persisted in remaining behind the lead black and the second horse, the day's favorite.

"Push, c'mon push yourself harder." It was a strange and urgent plea. The favorite inched closer to the lead running nose-to-nose for a few seconds. But with the step that overtook the lead, something spooked him.

He reared, whinnying a loud, anguished cry, then landed in a confused tangle of dust and blurred reds and blues of the fallen jockey's coat. Gasps flew up all around as the crowd looked on in horror.

The horse ran on, helter-skelter across the track disrupting the other runners. But Emerald Fire, undaunted by the turmoil, boldly seized the others' moment of vulnerability to edge past them into a fierce competition with the lead black.

Drake grabbed Cianda's hand, unaware he squeezed so tight it stung. "You have to do it for us," he urged, his words a manifestation of Cianda's thoughts.

She gripped his hand in return, feeling infused with his tension, tension that matched her own. As the horse made a last surge toward the finish line, Cianda's breath caught in her throat.

The two front runners crossed the finish so closely she couldn't tell who won. She waited the endless seconds in tortured silence until word rang out that Emerald Fire finished first.

Elation surged through Cianda; she turned to Drake beaming, clapping furiously. "I knew he would win! I knew it!"

Drake's hands swooped down around her waist lifting her to swirl her around. Shouts and curses flew through the stands; winners were clapping and hugging, losers swearing, stomping their feet.

But as Drake held her in his arms, the world around them disappeared. Cianda's breasts brushed Drake's sweat-damp chest as he let her slip gently to the ground. He looked down at her, slowly lifting her chin in his palm.

"We're going to win, love," he murmured. "Together." Bending to her, he sealed his promise with a fervent kiss, oblivious to the stares and whispered comments of the surrounding spectators.

Cianda returned his kiss with equal fire, feeling the emerald pressed hard between their bodies. Despite the mounting obstacles in their path, in that moment, she believed him.

"I don't believe you're actually serious! If you go now, we may as well walk straight to the Newgate scaffold." Drake threw up his hands. *Damn, the woman was stubborn.* "We'll never get the diamond if you traipse off to some godforsaken hole! We're shaving the time too close as it is. Have you forgotten Thorne's deadline?"

"If I find Jamie, I don't need the wretched diamond and Godfrey can go to blazes!" Cianda confronted him, chin defiantly high, eyes hot.

Drake stood amid the last of the crates and trunks he had been loading. It was now midmorning, and he had been looking forward to setting sail this afternoon for St. Helena, more than ready to have the journey started.

What he hadn't been ready for was Cianda's arrival, hours earlier than their agreed upon time, and her announcement that she planned to follow a lead on her brother's whereabouts given to her by Palmerston's blasted inspector.

Slamming his palms against the railing of the *Ferret,* he worked to tame his fury. "You may not need the wretched diamond, but I do."

Cianda turned away from him, one hand twisting the thin lawn of her skirt. "That's why I came here to tell you before I left. So you can make other arrangements. There are other thieves—"

"Oh, yes. I'll just go and pluck one off the streets. Any pickpocket will do, I'm sure." Drake raked his fingers through his hair. "To think that I was actually beginning to believe, fool that I am, that you were the first truly loyal person I'd ever met."

"I am loyal. To my brother. When Inspector Davidson came this morning, he said Dorsey had gone to her sister's home up in Stowmarket. But Godfrey never lets them stay anywhere longer than a few days." She swung back to face him, her gaze beseeching. "I have to go. I have to try to find Jamie."

Drake stared at her, conflicting impulses warring within him. To go, and to hell with her. To stay, and risk everything.

"Stowmarket, about four hours by rail," he said finally. "If we leave today, we could check on Davidson's information and be back in time to set sail early tomorrow morning."

"We? I didn't ask you to come along."

"I'm inviting myself," Drake snapped.

He wanted to hate the woman. After all his work, all the hours calculating the time they needed to find and retrieve the Koh-i-noor before the deadline, she wanted to gamble it all on the very uncertain chance of finding her brother.

Obviously, though she knew what he had at stake, she didn't care.

The thought instantly struck him as both selfish and frightening. What bothered him most was that he *wanted* her to care.

"You would help me find Jamie?" Cianda asked softly.

"If I go along, I can make sure you return in time to set sail."

"I see. You're a fine example of loyalty, Captain. Loyalty to yourself. I suppose it's easier than acknowledging any irksome feelings you might have." Cianda crossed her arms over her breast. "You should reconsider. I can think of any number of reasons we might be delayed."

"I'll be there to see that we're not." *And to extricate you, if it turns out to be another of Thorne's traps,* he thought grimly.

"Have it your way. I'll see to the tickets at once." Without waiting for his reply, she whirled and strode off the *Ferret,* back to her waiting carriage.

Drake watched her leave, troubled by a vague, persistent longing. She loved her brother so deeply, so completely. What would it be like, to hold her heart that way? To know she needed him without reservation, without reason?

He didn't need to know, he reminded himself. He didn't need the trouble caring and depending on a woman would bring. Not again.

Heaving up a nearby barrel, Drake started toward the hold. As he turned, he nearly stumbled over Fred. The cat, forgiving him the affront, curled around his ankle, purring loudly.

"Welcome aboard again, you hideous beast." He bent to scratch her ears, but as soon as his hand brushed her fur, Fred wriggled between his legs and dashed away.

"You're smarter than I am, animal," Drake muttered after her. "I should have run, too. We're both better off alone."

Chapter Thirteen

Witnesses Describe Horrifying Encounter With Infamous Masked Marauder.

Cianda curled a lip at the sensational headline bannering the afternoon *Times*. The story brimmed with colorful adjectives supplied by two tweeny maids who swore to seeing a "fearsome, black-masked giant" rip open a safe late the previous night and leave with their mistress's jewels clutched in his great fist.

"Some petty pilferer with a sack over his face who fancies he can blame it all on the 'infamous Masked Marauder,'" she muttered low.

"Someone who lacks the talent you have with your hands, I'm certain." Drake tossed out the comment without taking his eyes from the slowly passing scenery outside the railway car. He stood with his arms stretched out on either side of the small window, glaring as if everything in the world displeased him.

"A talent you've seemed to appreciate on more than one occasion, Captain Weston." She smiled sweetly when his glower shifted to her. Setting her newspaper aside, Cianda arranged herself more comfortably in her corner of the padded seat in their first-class compartment, eyeing Drake with a mixture of exasperation and amusement. "It's nearly four hours to Stowmarket. Do you plan to pace the entire journey?"

"I don't like being shut up in this damned closet, waiting," he grumbled, turning from the window. Pushing a hand through his hair, he dropped down on the seat opposite her. With a quick jerk, he tugged off his cravat, threw it in the direction of his carelessly discarded coat, and unfastened the first three buttons of his shirt.

"That's obvious. Between prowling and sulking, you haven't sat still for more than five minutes since we left London."

"I'm not sulking."

Cianda arched a brow.

"I don't sulk."

"You must have another name for it."

"I'm used to traveling on the *Ferret* — "

"Or on the run."

Drake grinned, his wit reasserting itself. "That too. Idling away hours on a train isn't my idea of getting this problem of yours resolved. We're losing time, and we have to leave London tomorrow as planned, or we'll never reach St. Helena in time to meet the *King's Bounty* and be back in London by July."

"I'm willing to take that risk."

"Don't remind me I agreed to share it with you. You have a singular talent when it comes to convincing me to join you on your rescue missions."

"I'll consider that a compliment." She looked down at her hands, stilling the nervous play of her fingers. "The waiting isn't easy," she said, for his benefit or hers, she wasn't certain. "I know you prefer solving a problem by spitting in its face, daggers drawn, but there's little we can do until we get there and . . ." *And find Jamie.* Cianda desperately wanted to believe they would. But after so many failures, she dared not hope.

"If he's there, we'll find him," Drake said, somehow divining her thoughts. "Of course, if we do, I'm going to be sorely disappointed."

"You—!"

"I was just beginning to look forward to watching you perform this fantastic robbery of yours. Zak and I laid bets as to whether or not you'd actually be able to steal the diamond." He winked. "I put my money on you."

Drake's raffish smile teased her and Cianda relaxed a little, knowing he intended to distract her from thoughts of Jamie and the task ahead. "It was money well spent. You can trust me," she said, answering his smile.

"Zak didn't think so. But then Zak swears women aren't to be trusted. He even winces when I refer to the *Ferret* as a she."

"Speaking of your partner . . ." Cianda leaned forward with a conspiratorial gleam in her eyes. "I have been wondering. What is his name? Surely he wasn't christened Zak. I'm hoping you'll satisfy my curiosity on at least that point."

"Not a chance." Drake lifted his hands in mock defense as Cianda's coaxing smile turned to a frown. "He'd slit my throat. Besides, if Beatrice wants to know so badly, she can ask him herself." He paused and arched a brow. "Not that he'd tell her."

"You knew all along, didn't you?" she said, laughing. "And I'll bet you my emerald you're wrong about Beatrice. She'll find out his name before he leaves London."

"I'll take your wager, but *my* emerald is safe. Zak would sooner be drawn and quartered than reveal that to any woman."

"Hmmm . . . well, we'll see, won't we? Perhaps I won't have to steal it again after all."

"I won't remind you what happened when you tried to

accost me, while I was sleeping, the first time."

"Please don't."

"Although I don't understand why you weren't able to get the better of me considering that you're a . . ." He picked up her discarded newspaper. " ' towering hulk of a man, with eyes glowing as red as flame.' Quite an apt description, I'd say."

"As long as that claptrap convinces the police, I've little chance of being unmasked. They wouldn't believe me even if I confessed. You've not heard half of the trumpery that's been written about the Masked Marauder. Jamie and I used to laugh for hours over—over . . ." Her words crumbled away under a torrent of memories and emotions she had deliberately kept sequestered in her heart. To acknowledge them would erode her resolve, blur her focus; shunning them made them all the more painful.

"Have you always taken care of him?" Drake asked gently.

Cianda stared blindly at the window glass. "Since I was seven. Our mother wasn't strong. She died when I was nine. I promised her then I would always keep Jamie safe. I haven't done an especially good job of it though, have I?"

"You aren't responsible for what Thorne's done."

"If it hadn't been for Godfrey taking me in, Jamie would have died. And if I hadn't told Godfrey I intended to quit thieving, Jamie would still be safely at home."

"You wanted to quit?"

She turned to him, a bitter smile twisting her mouth. "Does it surprise you, Captain? I told you I wanted my freedom."

Drake's expression was unreadable. "From Thorne? I had the impression you enjoyed the thieving."

"The challenge of it, even flirting with the danger perhaps. Like you," she added. "The smuggling, your work

231

for the service, Palmerston's missions, you do those for the excitement, the thrill of a dare. It's easier for you to risk your neck than to risk your heart on a cause." Her voice dropped to a whisper. "Or someone."

She struck a vulnerable point, she saw it in the sudden tense ripple of muscle, the flare of emotion in his eyes. It should have warned her away but didn't. She suddenly wanted him to admit it, to say he didn't care and never would. Maybe then she could exorcise him from her thoughts and dreams.

"You don't know a damned thing about gambling with your heart, milady thief," Drake shot back. "You only care when you feel indebted to people for service or loyalty, like Maisie and Beatrice. Or for investing in you, like Thorne. That's why you can't bear the thought of seeing Thorne hang."

"That's not true!"

"It is. You've never cared about someone without reason, wanted them beyond everything else that mattered regardless of the risk."

"Am I supposed to believe you have?"

Drake jerked to his feet and moved to stand by the door. His jaw was clenched tight. "Believe what you wish. But the truth is, yes, I did take that chance. Once."

"She must be one special woman," Cianda said gently. "Who is she?"

Drake stared hard at her, his inner struggle brewing dark and stormy through troubled eyes. "Isabelle Thorne *was* a very special woman, indeed."

Godfrey's wife's name on Drake's lips, even years after her death, revived poignant anguish in his voice. It jolted Cianda into facing what she'd suspected but talked herself into denying. Drake and Isabelle. A secret love affair. The mysterious scandal surrounding her death. Rumors in society, first whispered, then hastily hushed.

The years Cianda was envying her from a distance, Drake was holding her in his arms. Isabelle Thorne was in reality all Cianda only pretended to be: high-born, refined, elegant, a true lady. A woman loved by Drake Weston. Cianda gritted her teeth against the shock waves shooting through her and forced herself to focus on what Drake was saying.

"I was young and impetuous and I believed heart and soul that she loved me with the same passion I had for her. She didn't. She played the part of abused wife and devoted lover expertly, but from the beginning she never intended to give up her prestigious role as Thorne's wife for the lesser glory of being tied to a second son with dubious prospects."

"That's why you took to smuggling. And why you agreed to work for Palmerston." It wasn't a question. Somehow she knew the answer.

Drake's smile was a twisted, sardonic shadow of his rakehell grin. "Why not? I don't disguise what I do. I was fed up to the teeth with the hypocrisies of society. I hated it. I still do."

Cianda groped to put words to the tumult of feelings churning up inside her. "Drake . . ."

"Spare me trite, meaningless phrases of understanding," he snapped, cutting her short.

"I do understand."

"I'm certain you do. You're a professional actress, playing whatever role circumstances demand."

"I understand how you feel!" she snapped, the sneer in his voice feeding her anger. "How you felt about — her." She couldn't bring herself to say the name.

"Do you? Is that the way you feel about Godfrey Thorne?"

"No!"

"Isn't it?"

"No. It's the way I feel about you!"

The words, propelled by an unstoppable current of emotion, hung between them, echoing in the silence. Cianda wished them back with every ounce of will she possessed. Except it was too late. Too late to regret them, too late to deny they were true.

"I'm sorry," she whispered, turning from the arrested expression on his face. Her courage in her hands, she looked back. She tipped her chin up, her eyes steady on his. "No. It's a lie. I'm not sorry. Not any more. I have a very difficult time pretending when I'm with you. You make me feel . . . reckless. I should despise you for what you are, for what you could do to me. But the way you make me feel defies reason. As if . . . as if—"

"—Nothing else mattered but being together," Drake finished for her, as if they shared the same forbidden desires.

Before she could answer, he sat down beside her and pulled her into his arms. Combing his fingers through her neatly arranged hair, he scattered pins until it tumbled free. He slid his hands into the silver fall, and dismissed any possible answer with the hunger of his kiss.

Cianda's mouth opened under his as she willingly surrendered to passion, to wanting more than just the taste and touch of his mouth plundering hers.

When Drake finally broke from her, he buried his face in her hair, holding her tightly against him. His breath came fast and warm on her skin, his heart pounded against hers. "How many hours did you tell me it was to Stowmarket," he murmured.

"Too many, you said."

"No. I was wrong." He leaned back far enough to hold her eyes with his. Touching a finger to her mouth, he traced the moist line between her parted lips. "There aren't enough, milady thief. Not nearly enough."

234

* * *

Drake stood on the crowded platform at Stowmarket Station, arriving and departing passengers dodging and jostling him while he culled the odds over in his mind. Did he stand a better chance of completing his mission by appeasing Cianda and carrying out her scheme to track down Thorne's errant cook, or by slinging her over his shoulder and dragging her back to London and the *Ferret?*

At the moment, it seemed he had a choice between a bad plan and a bad plan.

"I get the impression every time you scowl like that, you're thinking of me."

Her voice, cool and steady, provoked a ridiculous feeling of annoyance. After her impulsive confession in the rain, even as he held her, he felt her withdraw behind her protective facade. The moment he thought he glimpsed the vulnerable, elusive Faith behind her mask, she turned on him and became poised, polished Cianda, his elusive midnight seductress.

Fueling his ire were the simultaneous feelings of wanting her to abandon her ruses completely and admit again he cared, and a fear of ever hearing those same words again. What the hell would he do if she managed to force him to concede both to her and to himself that he felt the same way?

Suddenly aware of her curious appraisal of him, he shoved aside the onerous dilemma. "I was thinking how bloody hard it's going to be to find a carriage and driver in this mob," he said, scooping up her light carpetbag. "Unless you fancy walking the streets of Stowmarket looking for this cook of yours."

"If we have to walk, we'll walk." Cianda straightened her shoulders, putting more bravado into her pose than

235

she felt, as well as Drake knew. "Dorsey's sister lives near a rest house owned by the monks of St. Osyth's. She's married to the grounds keeper, Inspector Davidson said. Jamie and Dorsey must be there; it's the perfect hideaway." She looked around them, the poignant tremble of her soft mouth just perceptible.

"Of course," he said, rubbing the back of his hand over her cheek. She gave a swift nod and Drake returned what he hoped was a reassuring smile. Taking her arm, he propelled her forward through the crowd. "I've been practicing the art of stopping vehicles, working my way up from carts to carriages." The brief quiver of her smile rewarded his slight attempt at humor, making him feel ridiculously pleased. "Trust me," he said, not realizing the reckless look in his eyes contradicted the words on his lips.

He managed to hail a carriage just outside the railway station whose driver knew the way to the monks' retreat. "Course I c'n take ye there. But don't count on gettin' inside. Private lot, they are. Don't hardly never open their doors.

"We're in a hurry," Cianda urged, augmenting the asked for fare with an extra shilling. "We don't want to go to the rest house itself. We've come to speak to the grounds keeper. Surely you know where he lives—?"

" 'Ole 'Enry knows fine folks does 'e? Well, well now I'll 'ave you on his doorstep in no time, mum," the driver beamed, suddenly remembering to help her to her seat.

Her urgency gave Drake pause. He held onto her hand a minute longer after he had handed her into the carriage studying her face. Her green eyes stared back into his wide and haunted. "We were on the train for hours and the Abbot's retreat doesn't sound far from here. Why the sudden hurry?"

Cianda shook her head. "I don't know. I just feel a if—as if I'm wasting precious time." She rubbed two fin gers against her temple, letting go a long breath. "I think I've lived too long with Godfrey one step in front of me. I'm beginning to believe he'll always be there." Tugging at his hand, she pulled him in beside her, then let go as the carriage jerked into motion.

"You're as jumpy as Fred before a storm," he muttered as the agitated drum of her fingers against the seat drew his attention. "You're beginning to make me nervous."

"Sorry." Cianda flicked the short draperies aside from the small window glass and stared for a moment at a lone shepherd in a grassy field, ambling up a hill after his flock. The pastoral scene struck an uncomfortable chord in her. *Was life so simple for some? Was it supposed to be?* She shrugged the notion away, thinking it absurd. She'd never have the chance to find out.

"Are you always this tense before one of your expeditions?"

"This is different," she answered without looking at him. "You can hardly compare it to filching a necklace or brooch from a library safe."

Her terse replies convinced Drake to abandon any attempt to distract her. Watching her only increased his own growing uneasiness. When they left London, the task before them had seemed more tedious than potentially dangerous. But Cianda's mention of Thorne evoked his presence and Drake fleetingly wondered if she were right, if Thorne was already one step ahead of them.

More disturbing, though, was his own reaction. He expected to experience the familiar, underlying surge of excitement, the thrill of the hunt. Instead, he felt restless and vaguely unsettled. He didn't care for the stakes in this game, especially because they meant so much to her.

"It can't be far," Cianda's voice broke into his thoughts. "It should be—oh!"

Her words broke off as a sudden sharp lurch flung

them both against the wall of the carriage. Drake glimpsed a quick flash of galloping horses and the black sides of a buggy perilously near their own before another wild swale tossed him and Cianda toward the opposite side.

Their own carriage swung from side to side and then surged forward in a burst of uncontrolled speed.

"What the bloody hell—?" Drake managed to jerk up a window and lean out. The driver sat askew on the box, holding for dear life to one of the reins while the other flapped in a mad dance over the horses' backs.

"They nearly hit us!" Cianda shouted as she leaned close to him for a better look.

The indignation in her voice might have been amusing if not for their precarious predicament, Drake decided. "Move back," he ordered, swiping an arm behind him to push her aside. Shoving open the carriage door, he assessed the distance to the box in a quick glance and then eased out onto the narrow step.

Cianda gaped at him as comprehension dawned. "Are you totally insane?"

"I came along with you, didn't I?"

His focus on her caused him to slip backward an inch on the slender foothold. Cianda grabbed at his shirtfront righting him against the carriage side. "You're making a bad habit of this," she said, shouting to be heard over pounding horses' hooves and the rumble and crack of wooden wheels on the pitted, gravel road.

"One of my many." Flashing her his best daredevil grin, Drake found a handhold on the rack on the roof and kicked one leg up and over, hauling himself onto the top of the carriage.

By moving slowly and deliberately, and clutching every hold for dear life, he eventually eased himself onto the box beside the whey-faced driver.

238

The man stared at him with dumb incomprehension as he snatched up the reins. Throwing his body backward, Drake used the momentum to aid his jerk on the straps. Gradually, after several minutes of tugging and pulling, the frightened team slowed to a trot, then stomped to a halt.

The driver pushed back his cap with a hand that trembled. "Bless me. In ten years o' drivin' I ain't never 'ad anyone come that near to runnin' me down." He swiped at his face with a large hand. "The bloke drivin' damned near run 'is rig right into me own."

Drake nodded, looking back at the billows of dust behind them. Accidents were common enough. What was uncommon was the driver's deliberate refusal to stop and return to lend a hand.

"It were a fine thing, what ye did, gov'n'r, stoppin' them 'orses like ye did. I'll 'ave somethin' ter tell the lads this night, I will." He gave a shaky laugh, wiping at his face again.

"Glad I could help," Drake said, climbing down from the box. "If you'll return the favor, we'd like to get on to our destination."

"Right, gov'n'r. But 'tis only up the way." He pointed to a small house, just visible ahead.

Drake nodded, walked around to the carriage door, and pulled it open. He looked in expecting to find a ruffled and anxious Cianda ready to barrage him with admonishments.

"You were rather a long time," she said coolly, arching a delicate silver brow.

"My sincere apologies, milady. I'll try me 'umble best to save your pretty neck without delay next time." With a flamboyant bow Drake crawled inside, taking the seat beside her. He signaled the driver on with a rap on the roof of the carriage. "I think the horses gained a little time in

239

their frenzy. We're nearly there."

She heaved an exasperated sigh. "How comforting." Cianda hesitated a moment before laying her hand on his arm, lightly swanning her fingers down his shirt sleeve. "Drake . . . are you all right?"

His name spoken in her low voice sounded like an intimate invitation. He laid his hand across hers, loving the feel of her warm flesh tightening against his through the thin barrier of his shirt. "Perfect." He lifted her hand and kissed the palm, letting his mouth linger in the soft hollow. "What happened to Captain Weston?"

Her fingers curled in response to his touch. "Mmmm?"

"Captain Weston." His lips teased against the rapid pulse at her wrist. "You say it in that prim and provoking way you have. You only say my name when you're pretending to be my wife. Or my lover."

"I'm not pretending then," she whispered. Leaning forward, she guided his face near hers with the touch of her hand and brushed her mouth over his.

The light caress roused a slow-burning heat. The meaning of her words incited fire.

He reached for her just as the carriage jolted to a sudden halt.

Tension swiftly replaced Cianda's languor. She gripped his hand for a quick second before turning to the door, fumbling anxiously with the latch. Drake reached over and unfastened it. She scrambled out, nearly bowling into the driver in her haste to reach the door to the diminutive thatch-roofed house.

Drake strode after her and made it to her side a heartbeat before the door opened. A wiry old man with a long face eyed them with suspicion. "What d'ye want?"

"I'm looking for Dorsey, and the boy with her. Please spare me needless explanations," she pleaded, pressing sovereign into his withered hand. "Are they here?"

He clutched the coin, and squinted hard at Cianda. "They've gone. Gone, and took me wife with 'em."

"Gone?" Cianda looked at Drake and back. "Gone where? Please, I have to know. . . ."

The man sagged. "Wish I knew. A nasty-lookin' gent came callin' fer me wife's sister. Me wife done took me buggy. Then the free of 'em went tearin' out o' 'ere a bit ago like the devil 'imself were chasin' 'em." He shook his head. "If ye ask me, that boy's trouble. Me wife done fixed a room special fer 'em so Dorsey could keep the brat real close. I gave 'em both me food and me home and put up wiv his coughin' all night. How do they fank me? Why, they up an'—'ey, now!"

Cianda bolted toward the carriage. Drake paused long enough to toss the man a few more shillings. By the time he caught up to her, Cianda had hoisted herself onto the box and snatched up the reins.

"Now ye jus' can't take me rig and leave me 'ere, miss," the driver called up to her, waving his hands in ineffectual protest.

Turning the pair and carriage back toward town, Cianda ignored his pleas. "I'll send someone back for you."

She snapped the leathers across the horses' backs and set the rig in motion, giving Drake scarcely enough time to haul himself up beside her. "Leaving without me, milady thief?"

"I have to get to the station. I'm sure that's where she's taken Jamie."

Her mouth settled into a line of grim determination. Drake let her concentrate on her task in silence, admiring her command of the horses as she drove them at breakneck pace into Stowmarket

She'd barely jerked the team into a halt in front of the railway station before jumping down from the box to run toward the trains. Drake at her heels, she frantically searched the face of each passing person and each window, pushing her way through the crowd, blind to everything but her desperate need to find the one person she sought.

At the last platform, between two trains, she stopped cold. "Which one?" she cried, expecting no answer.

"You take the one on the left." Drake's familiar, commanding voice rose above the noise of the crowd and the hisses and groans of the trains.

"But it's beginning to pull away! I can't get on."

"Just stay here near the engine and watch every window." He turned to dash to the end of the train parallel to the one Cianda faced. "I'm going to search that one from the rear forward. The stairs are still down," he called back over his shoulder.

The train nearest Cianda snorted and ground its great iron wheels to a roll, slowly picking up speed as it pulled away from the station. Cianda strained to peer into each passing window. Car after car chugged by, window by window revealing only nameless faces to her aching eyes.

As the engine moved farther away, the entire train gathered speed, pulling faces quickly past her, transforming crisp images faster and faster into expressionless blurs.

Her heart in her throat, only the two rear cars hadn't yet passed her when Drake, breathless from running the length of the other train, yelled to her from the doorway of that train's first car.

"Any luck?"

"No. No sight of him," Cianda called back, not letting her gaze slip for an instant from the now swiftly departing train.

Suddenly, she gave a strangled cry. Her fingers groped blindly for Drake's arm, but grasped only empty air. "Jamie!"

From the bottom step of the opposite train, Drake turned just in time to glimpse the window of the last railway car. Before it lumbered away, he caught the flash of a boy's face, tousled red hair and wide eyes, his hands pressed against the glass as if in mute appeal. As quickly as it came, the image vanished and he was staring at the end of the last rail car.

Cianda started to run in the direction of the train but Drake caught her arms, spinning her around and holding her fast between his hands. "It's too late."

"Jamie is on that train!" She struggled to look after the train, her face and voice anguished.

"Cianda." Drake shook her a little. Her despair knifed through him. "Cianda, there's nothing we can do now. He's gone."

"No . . ." She looked to him, to the wake of the train, and back again. "No. Not again." Rallying a little, she looked wildly around them. Her fingers dug into his shirt-front. "We can find out where they've gone. We can go after them. Drake—please."

The tortured plea nearly broke him. Drake wanted nothing more than to say yes. It took all his resolve to tell her no. "By the time we discover anything, they could be anywhere. Our only chance now is to find the Koh-i-noor. We'll save your brother. I promise. But we need that diamond first. Before Thorne's deadline."

White, trembling, Cianda froze in his grip, fighting the tears welling in her eyes. "I don't have a choice. Jamie . . . . Oh, Drake, my Jamie is gone." Her voice faltered and she crumpled against his chest, shaking with the force of her silent misery.

Her grief was as palpable as if it were his own. Drake pressed her against his aching heart, eyes closed against the pain, silently racking his mind for a solution that would allow them to abandon what they had started.

But the same answer, the only answer, played over and over in his thoughts. The Koh-i-noor. He'd once teased her about the diamond's power to bring prosperity or ruin to the fate of the one who held it. Now, secretly, so close to claiming it, he wished the diamond's history didn't make that superstition seem so very real.

Cianda crouched in a corner of the seat, knees drawn to her chin. She leaned her head on the cool pane of window glass and watched the grays and blacks of the night slide by like melting watercolor. The rhythm of the train rocked her, its low rumble the only sound in the midnight stillness.

She had promised Drake she would try to sleep some of the hours on the return to London. At her request, he had reluctantly left her in solitude.

She hadn't even tried to keep her promise. Instead, she sat alone attempting to revive her determination and regain the inner strength she depended on to once again overcome her failure and keep her pushing toward her goal. To take the Koh-i-noor. To rescue Jamie.

Hot tears scalded her eyes, mocking her efforts. She put her hands to her face and felt the dampness on her skin.

At the sound of a familiar tread in the corridor, Cianda hastily swiped at her eyes, struggling to compose her face into a mask of control. The expression in Drake's eyes as he stepped into the small berth told her what a farce her efforts were.

He said nothing as he sat down beside her. Slowly, he reached out and touched a finger to her face, following the wet trail of a single teardrop.

She endured the pleasure-pain of his touch until he made to gather her into his arms. Pulling back, she turned her face back to the window. "No. Don't."

244

"Let me help you."

Cianda saw his reflection in the glass, dark and positive, mingling with her own pale, shadowy image. "I can't." She spun back around before he could protest. "I don't want to take anything from you I'll be indebted for. We have our bargain, that's all I have to offer you. I'm a thief. You want justice. All I want is my brother. I can never be anything more to you than a pawn in your game to trap Godfrey."

From the fleeting flinch of pain crossing his face, she knew she struck near the truth. "In the beginning, maybe," he said, his voice husky.

"And now." She smiled bitterly. "You despise my pretenses. And I don't think you'll risk another betrayal no matter how your heart tempts you. You've made that clear."

Drake shook his head. "It doesn't matter. It's too late now."

He silenced her denial by kissing her, hard and fast, almost roughly. The hunger and the desperation she felt in him matched her own.

When they parted, he pulled her close and sat with her cradled in his arms, his hand stroking along her spine. In the glass, she saw him staring out into the night and knew neither of them found comfort in the embrace. Yet neither could pull away.

They stayed together until the train pulled up at Euston station in the early hours of the morning. As she prepared to leave the berth, Drake stopped her at the door.

"There's not much time. We'll have to leave London almost immediately."

"I know."

"The journey begins, milady thief." The smile he gave her was a ghost of his raffish grin.

"To St. Helena."

245

"To St. Helena," he agreed.

But his expression now was faintly sardonic and as they stepped out into the predawn fog, Cianda wondered exactly where he intended the journey to end.

Chapter Fourteen

Cianda dipped her cup into the scuttlebutt and gulped the tepid water down greedily. For days the *Ferret* had slowly limped along the west coast of Africa toward St. Helena. Sea-salted air hung hot and heavy over ship and crew, weighing down hope and good humor. The *Ferret* cracked and swayed, her dry masts creaking with the effort to sail onward in the deadly-still afternoon swelter.

No one spoke, a common gnawing tension breeding voluntary isolation. Unless the wind kicked up and cooperated, they'd never reach St. Helena in time. They'd weighed anchor off London Dock nearly a week ago today, and Cianda knew from nightly discussions over dinner, Drake had expected to be much closer to their destination by now.

The fact they were tarrying in waters infested with French pirates multiplied his frustration. Except when barking out orders to his small crew, he closeted himself in his quarters to pour over his ship's log and the stack of maps and papers on his desk.

But today, though still uncommunicative, at least he'd stayed up top. Cianda stole a sideways glance to where he stood on the prow, gazing out over the shimmering waters of the South Atlantic. His broad back to her, arms stretched forward to grip the railing, he stood, black boots spread wide for balance on the undulating planks beneath him.

At his nape, wisps of curls glistened raven-dark in the scorching afternoon sun against the white of his collar. Knowing he couldn't see her, Cianda allowed herself a lazy perusal of his beautifully sculpted form. Black trousers stretched like a second skin over the sleek, rock-hard lobes of his buttocks down over long, lean thighs and muscular calves molded by his high boots. Here on the *Ferret,* surrounded by sea and sky, elements as wild and primitive as he, Drake exuded a raw, hypnotizing sensuality.

Cianda drew her hand from shoulder to arm, her fingers sliding from the soft linen of her borrowed shirt to the sweat-damp skin of her forearm. She had taken to wearing Drake's shirt over her boy's trousers, finding the makeshift apparel much cooler than piled petticoats and clinging skirts. Although draped loosely over her body, the material seemed to retain Drake's masculine scent, enough to suggest his presence even when she was alone.

As her eyes roved back up his legs and backside, Drake reached back to push his shirt off his shoulders. He shoved it slowly back off one shoulder then the other, revealing a wide berth of sun-bronzed back. Pulling his arms out of the sleeves, he let the shirt slip to hang loosely from its tuck in the waistband of his trousers.

Leaning back against the water barrel, Cianda watched each languorous movement of his corded arms. The deep copper skin on his sinewy back gleamed with sweat as he reached around behind himself to massage the gentle curve at the base of his spine.

Cianda's fingertips stretched wide with longing to touch that hot, wet skin, to press the balls of her thumbs slowly up his spine and hear him groan with the sheer pleasure of her caressing touch. She yearned to be the woman to ease his tensions, to give him sweet relief in the soft comfort of her body.

Lost in the images her heat-inebriated mind conjured, when Drake turned toward her, Cianda for a moment believed he'd somehow divined her fevered desires.

The glint of green fire from the emerald nested in the mat of crisp dark hair on his chest drew her eyes to the heart of the gem, then lower. Her gaze gravitated to where the line of ebon curls narrowed and trailed downward like a dark shadow slipping over his glistening skin and disappearing tantalizingly into the taut material covering his loins.

Cianda shivered as desire flared hot in her belly. With a trembling hand, she lifted her cup up to her lips again. The slight gesture caught Drake's attention. His eyes met hers, and she saw her passion mirrored in his face.

He held her entranced, a willing prisoner to his probing gaze, his eyes fathomless, deeper than the ocean, bluer than the heavens.

Part of her cried out to flee in embarrassment at her open lust. The rest of her begged to stay ensnared by the power of their mutual need. She ached for him, body and soul. She knew she should have felt shame, or at least fear of the dangerous desires one glance from him provoked. Yet the risk only made it more exciting, and she felt no shame, only surprise in the strength of her emotions.

"Cap'n look aloft!" The call heralded from the lookout in the crow's nest nearly one hundred feet above the masthead.

Cianda tore her eyes away, breaking the strange, silent spell between her and Drake.

"Weather's turnin' to be sure," the lookout called down.

At once Drake shifted his gaze skyward, shielding his eyes from the sun—and from her—with the side of his hand to his brow. He scanned the horizon to the south, the direction the lookout was waving to.

Feeling drained, Cianda slumped against a mast. Was it the midday heat or the fire beneath her skin sapping her energy? She didn't care to dwell on the answer.

Fortunately, distraction, in the form of a slight shuffling sound, rescued her from probing too deeply into the question. She turned to see Beatrice surface from below deck, tottering on shaky legs.

Cianda rushed to her side to offer support just as Zak's wild red mane appeared in Beatrice's wake.

"Damned woman insisted on coming out for some air. As you can see for yourself she *still* hasn't got her sea legs," Zak grumbled to Cianda.

"The air should help." Cianda smiled reassuringly at her friend. "I'm glad you felt able to come up even for a few minutes. I was afraid you were beginning to molder down there."

"Smother is a better word," Beatrice muttered, nodding her head toward Zak. "Mr. Zak is quite the persistent nursemaid."

Zak scowled, stroking a hand over Fred, who lay draped around his neck like a cheap fur piece. "The woman is overflowing with gratitude. Every time I tried to leave the cabin, she started retching up her guts again."

"That is an exaggeration," Beatrice snapped. "I have always been able to care for myself. I am —" Suddenly pale, she put a hand to her forehead.

As she swayed precariously, and Zak reached up to steady her by the shoulders. "Now who do you believe?" he asked with open disgust.

Zak's sudden move woke Fred. The cat lazily opened her eyes, lifted her head in affront, then dropped back to sleep on Zak's shoulders.

With a visible effort, Beatrice regained her straight carriage. "Mr. Zak, if you would simply help me to a comfortable spot, I'm certain I shall fare better up here than below."

Cianda smiled. Beatrice was proud and proper; dignity fit her like a garment tailor-made. *She deserves to be a gentleman's wife,* Cianda mused. Ruefully acknowledging her own domestic ineptness, she thought how easily her friend would fit the role, managing household staff and social calendar with confidence and grace.

"Certainly, your ladyship. Whatever you wish." Sarcasm edged his tone, but he wrapped his arm around Beatrice's waist with a gentle firmness that belied the sarcasm and revealed the tenderness she stirred somewhere hidden beneath his gruff indifference.

"A bit testy today, Zak?" Cianda couldn't resist.

"Aren't we all?" Zak shot back, with a cool look first to Cianda, then up to where Drake, scowling, stood talking with one of the crewmen.

Cianda, her eyes drawn to Drake, murmured, "It's this heat. There seems to be no relief." Realizing she stared, she snapped her attention back to Zak and Beatrice. "The lookout did say a storm may be brewing, though."

"Storm?" Zak lowered Beatrice carefully onto a bench, sitting her in a spot where a sail created a spot of shade. "Bad?"

"I'm not sure. You'll have to ask the captain." She gestured to Drake. "Go ahead. I'll watch your patient."

Zak glared at her a moment, then, muttering under his breath, he stuffed his hands in his pockets and ambled off toward Drake.

"Are you certain you can tolerate this heat?" Cianda asked Beatrice. She moved to the bench and reached over to brush lank auburn strands from her friend's pale face.

"It's worse below. At least there is some air moving up here."

251

"I suppose." Cianda snatched up a nearby rag she'd washed out early in the morning and hung on the railing to dry. Dipping it in the scuttlebutt, she wrung it dry then pressed it to Beatrice's brow.

Beatrice leaned back, closing her eyes. "Thank you. It does help."

Sitting down next to Beatrice, Cianda stared off into the endless melding of blue against blue, shading from the deep blue-green waters to the turquoise horizon to the palest powder-blue sky. The only break in the monochromatic seascape were the white-tipped crests on choppy waves that looked like dollops of meringue topping on an endless berry tart.

Not a breath of breeze stirred the oppressive stillness. Cianda could almost taste the heat as it embraced her skin with a heavy dampness.

"Cianda," Beatrice broke the silence at last, "I must ask you a question I know you would rather avoid."

Cianda drew a deep breath. "Yes?"

"I understand why you must go through with this scheme to steal the diamond. But if we are successful, what then?"

"Then Drake will use our jewels to entrap Thorne."

"That is not what I meant."

Cianda opened her mouth as if to say something, hesitated, groped for words, then gave up.

"I have nothing to go back to, except for the life we have made," Beatrice said softly. "Nor do you."

"I know. Neither does Maisie." A flicker of pain crossed her face. "Or Jamie."

"You have taken care of all of us. You took me in when no one else in London would employ me. Arthur blackened my name so thoroughly, I feared my only recourse would be the workhouses—or worse."

Cianda managed a laugh. "In some people's estimation

ending up a housebreaker's assistant is worse."

"I've loved every minute of it. It's thrilling, you know." A slash of color tinged Beatrice's ghostly white cheeks. "Even though all I've ever done is carry your tools and act as watch, it has been the most exciting thing I have ever done. The danger, the secrets, the headlines . . . and most of all the wonderful sense of revenge on *them*."

Cianda knew she referred to the aristocrats who scorned her after she admitted her affair with Sir Arthur Gilean. Such alliances, though common, were considered scandalous, not to be acknowledged. Especially by a mere governess.

"We have had some marvelous, and some terrifying moments."

"Had." Beatrice took Cianda's hand. "We cannot go on like this forever. Especially if Captain Weston is successful in exposing Lord Thorne."

Not looking at her friend, Cianda said hesitatingly, "We could leave London, move to some quiet spot. . . ."

"Oh, Cianda." Beatrice shook her head, a small, knowing smile lifting her mouth. "This time you must be realistic. I know when you told Godfrey you wanted to retire, you said your plan was to move us all to the country where we could live quietly and inexpensively, and you could spend your days tending Jamie. Surely you must realize that is an impossibility. You would never be happy in some isolated, obscure village. You are singularly illsuited to a life of quiet domestic bliss. Even if you could afford it."

Cianda winced. "Next you will remind me that age will also thwart me."

"Just as it did your mentor, Gide Legume."

"Yes, I think he hated me, because Godfrey forced him to teach me his skill when arthritis crippled his hands. By the time Godfrey banished him to France, he had become

253

so embittered . . ." Dark remembrances clouded her vision. "I don't want to end that way."

"You won't. If the risks we take are carefully planned. Between the two of us, we surely can find a way to outwit all these men."

Cianda averted her eyes from Beatrice's piercing gaze. "How come you are so wise and I'm so hopelessly foolish?"

"You are nothing of the sort," Beatrice insisted. "You are a dreamer, an actress, an artist. I would give anything to have one particle of your talent and vision. I am, I fear, doomed to be eternally practical. One of us has to be," she added with a twinkle in her eyes.

"Then we need each other?"

Beatrice pulled Cianda close. "Always."

Cianda returned her hug. Drawing away, she smiled. "From the look of your face, you need me to help you back to bed. You should rest for an hour or so before luncheon. I will need your clear mind when we finish planning the robbery of the Koh-i-noor."

"Considering our choice of partners," Beatrice said, grimacing as she rose to her feet, "we will need more than clear thinking if we're to succeed. I fear we are going to need a considerable measure of luck."

Hints of Domenique's decadent delights spilled out of the galley with the enticing aroma of butter and herbs. Cianda preceded Beatrice into the room, where Drake and Zak were seated already, deep in conversation.

Zak looked up as Beatrice entered the room. "You look almost human again."

Beatrice gave him an icy stare, smoothing the tight roll at her nape. "I wish I could return the compliment, Mister Zak. You have reverted to mongrel. You look as scruffy as your cat with that unruly beard and mane of yours."

"I consider that a compliment."

Cianda and Drake exchanged an amused glance.

Drake leaned back in his chair, waving a hand at the empty seats opposite them. "Dom has been waiting for you."

As Cianda took her seat, she noticed he had shaved and donned a fresh shirt. She cocked her head and thought of the earthy, reckless pirate on deck only a short hour earlier. Compared to that image, this man looked tame and refined, a true Weston. One she found thrilling; the other intimidating. But which one was he? And which did she prefer?

"You both look refreshed," Drake said, openly admiring the soft drape of Cianda's borrowed shirt.

Cianda tried to remain cool and collected despite the smolder in his eyes. She knew her breasts pressed freely against the thin fabric of a single chemise beneath the over-large shirt. Without a corset to control her shape, his shirt and her trousers clung to her slender waist and rounded hips, leaving little to the imagination.

A picture of Drake's finely honed body outlined in broad strokes of sunlight and shadows crossed her mind. If he could dress—or undress—for comfort, then so could she, she thought with a burst of defiance.

Lifting her chin, she challenged his bold gaze with one of her own. "I'm quite refreshed, Captain, thank you."

"I must admit," Beatrice put in, with a quick look at Cianda. "Even though I've been too ill to sample much of your chef's cooking, what I have tasted is superb." She lifted a spoonful of soup. "This vessel is surprisingly well outfitted."

Drake swirled the wine in his glass. "The British navy seized the *Ferret* in a raid. When I acquired it, I had a few amenities added here and there for comfort."

"Soft through and through," Zak put in, talking around a mouthful of soup.

"If you want to feel more like a sailor, you and Fred are welcome to sleep with the crew below and eat with them on deck. I'll even stock in hardtack and let you drink salt water. You can bet your cat they won't share their grog the way I do my wine."

"So thoughtful," Zak muttered.

"If you two are through insulting each other," Cianda said, at the same time the soup bowls were removed, replaced by a succulent plate of tarragon lamb and new potatoes. "I believe we have the small matter of burglary to discuss?"

"Ah yes," Drake said, raising his glass in a mocking salute. "Do tell, milady thief. How do the infamous Masked Marauder and her trusted assistant plan to purloin the coveted Koh-i-noor?"

A sly smile curved Cianda's lips. "Why, I plan to let you do it, Captain."

Drake choked in mid-swallow, a coughing fit temporarily preventing his retort.

Zak threw back his head and laughed. "One for the thief!"

A frown puckered Drake's dark brow. He tipped his chair backward, balancing it on two legs. "I've no doubt I could crack a safe. Come now, how hard can it be? I'll wager I've executed far more technically challenging tasks in the course of my assorted jobs for Palmerston."

"If that's so, then why weren't you able to extricate yourself from that Italian jail?" Zak taunted with open disregard for his partner's bruised pride.

Dropping his chair forward, Drake threw a glare at Zak. "That was entirely different," he muttered. "I still say anyone could be a thief."

"What manner of thief are you referring to, Captain?

256

Weston?" Beatrice asked in typically matter-of-fact fashion.

"The kind that steals."

"That includes housebreakers, pickpockets, snoozers, cracksmen, and gonophs," Cianda detailed. "Which do you think you might aspire to?"

"None of them, love. I only meant it can't be that difficult a profession whatever specialty one chooses."

"Well then, suppose I handed you a petter-cutter, an outsider, a set of bettys and an American auger. How would you use each one?"

Drake grimaced and stuffed a forkful of lamb into his mouth so he couldn't answer.

"I thought as much," Cianda said, satisfied she had shut him up. "Now, can we please move on to the matter at hand?"

Pushing aside her plate, Beatrice turned to Cianda. "It seems we have very few facts with which to create a plan."

"That's true." Cianda sighed, idly rearranging the meat and vegetables on her plate. "All we know for certain is that the East India Company took the diamond from the jewel house of the Ranjit Singh, the Sikh ruler, when they annexed the Punjab."

"And that Thorne has the idol," Drake said, stabbing at a chunk of lamb.

"Yes . . ."

"Thorne didn't tell you about it. Did he?"

Cianda considered lying again. But it suddenly didn't matter if Drake realized how little Godfrey had told her about the jewels. Facing him, she let go of pretense. "No, he didn't."

Satisfaction flashed in his eyes. "I don't know many details. When the Pandavas acquired the diamond about 500 B.C., they had it set, along with the ruby and the emerald, into a spectacular gold idol. Well, through centuries of

257

wars, the idol was stolen and re-stolen by other conquering peoples. Somewhere along the way, the jewels were removed and scattered. The Koh-i-noor at last ended up the property of the Sikh ruler in the Punjab. Until our own expansionists decided it was our turn to claim that coveted trophy of conquest."

"That's why Godfrey wants all three so badly," Cianda murmured. "The jewels restored to the original idol would be priceless."

"Exactly. Though they have undoubtedly been re-cut too many times to fit where they were meant to."

"And now the diamond is on the *King's Bounty* on its way to England to be presented to Queen Victoria on the two hundred and fiftieth anniversary of the East India Company only weeks from now."

"July. Thorne's deadline," Beatrice said softly.

Cianda nodded. She thought of Jamie and her resolve hardened. "The problem isn't where the diamond will be, but when we'll have the opportunity to steal it."

"There's going to be a ball."

"What?" Cianda stared at Drake, who grinned at her, the rakehell glint back in his eyes.

"A ball." He leaned back in his chair again, waving a hand. "Music, dancing—"

"Drake—" Cianda began, slapping down her fork.

Drake held up his hands. "I surrender, love. My friend, Robert Barrett-Shaw, the admiral of the *King's Bounty,* informed me there's going to be a ball when the diamond reaches St. Helena in honor of the diamond's escort, Sir John Lawrence."

"That is our chance," Beatrice said.

"It seems so," Cianda agreed, her mind racing over all the probabilities and possibilities.

"I hate to take the shine from this glowing plan," Zak drawled. "But how do you intend to get invited to this grand—and very private—affair?" He looked hard at Drake. "Especially with Charles on the *Bounty*. He's likely to be suspicious of your turning up unexpectedly, especially after that fiasco in Italy. He'll probably guess you've come to purloin the diamond. Or had you forgotten your dear brother?"

Watching Drake, Cianda saw his expression darken dangerously. "Not quite," he said tightly. "Trust me. Charles won't stop me from getting an invitation to that ball. Robert will make sure my bride and I—" He tipped his head to Cianda. "And my dear friend and his wife are on the guest list."

Cianda exchanged a doubtful glance with Beatrice.

Zak looked appalled. "Now wait a minute—"

"Does the idea of being my husband offend you, Mister Zak?" Beatrice asked coolly.

"The idea of being anyone's husband revolts me, Miss Dobson."

"Perhaps you would prefer the notion of traveling with your mistress?"

Zak's voice went flat. "I prefer to travel with Fred."

"You are an uncivilized boor," Beatrice shot back.

"So they tell me." Zak plugged a whole potato into his mouth.

"It's as good a story as any," Cianda interjected before Beatrice bit into Zak again. "At the ball it will be up to you two to provide a distraction while Beatrice and I steal the diamond. Will the ball be on the ship?"

"I imagine," Drake said.

"That simplifies things. We won't have to worry about learning our way around the governor's home." Mentally, Cianda checked off one major worry. "Of course, we'll set sail as soon as the robbery is over. There will be less risk of our being discovered that way."

"I agree," Beatrice said. "It won't take long for the

259

ship's crew to miss such important cargo."

"Or for your friend, the Admiral, to suffer the consequences. Not to mention your brother. Anyone with any sort of responsibility for the diamond's safety will be implicated after its theft," Cianda said. "I assume you understand that aspect fully, Drake."

A raffish smile spread across Drake's mouth. "Just as I supposed. Experts are you? Well, it seems you've overlooked one key item that I, luckily for you both, didn't. It will protect the admiral, and my brother, long enough for us to reach the authorities in London and make the necessary explanations."

"Oh? Pray tell, Captain, what miracle might that be?"

Reaching into the pocket of his trousers, Drake produced a small pouch. Delving inside, he held up a glittering, blue-white stone.

Cianda stared, struck speechless. "It's not—"

"Real? Of course not. I had it made. I know a lapidary who excels at producing paste replicas. Clever, isn't he?"

"I don't believe it!"

"I knew you'd be surprised," Drake said, triumphant.

"I don't believe how stupid and careless you are!"

Drake's good humor vanished. "This duplicate will buy valuable time. An element you obviously overlooked."

"And what happens when your friend the lapidary lets slip he made a replica of the famed Koh-i-noor for you?"

"Antoine wouldn't dream of crossing me," Drake snapped. "He knows I'd wring his scrawny neck. Do you think I'd take that kind of chance?"

"I think you take too many chances altogether," Cianda returned angrily. But then again, she reasoned, since Drake and Zak would be immediately suspect to Charles, the fake gem might buy them all some much-needed time. Cianda took a deep breath. "Well, it's done now. And I'll admit it—I suppose it might prove useful. We can only hope that you and your partner can manage to act your parts the night of the robbery."

"Zak is a master at playing the decoy. Aren't you, old chap?" Drake nudged Zak in the ribs.

"The tune sounds familiar to me."

Their arrogant flippancy grated on Cianda's frayed nerves. "You two are so damned confident, it would serve you right to have to carry this off without us!"

"It might be amusing to try," Drake said.

Lifting her chin, Cianda confronted him with cold fury. "I don't find anything humorous about it, Captain Weston. My brother's life depends on the outcome of this theft. Or had you forgotten that small detail."

"No." Drake held her hot gaze with his own. "I didn't forget."

"I hope you also remember our necks could be fitted for a noose if this little scheme fails," Zak said, his tone characteristically bland.

"Of course," Drake mused, "if we do stop Thorne, you and your brother will be free of him. That *is* what you want isn't it, Cianda?"

"And you'll make sure Palmerston will appear the noble countryman for exposing a traitor. That *is* your motive, isn't it, Captain? Or is it revenge?"

Drake's eyes darkened. "Palmerston is a noble countryman already. Aside from his accomplishments as foreign secretary, you have only to look at his efforts to bring about reform for the poor, to see that."

"And your revenge?"

"I'll have that, too. With your help, or without it. Which is it going to be, Madame D'Rouchert? Or should I call you Faith?"

Scraping his chair back, Zak got to his feet. "I need some air," he mumbled, obviously anxious to avoid becoming entangled in the confrontation.

Cianda suddenly realized she and Drake were leaning over the table, noses practically touching, locked in a private battle. Flushing, she jerked back.

"Might I prevail upon you one last time to see me to my cabin, Mister Zak?" Beatrice asked, slowly rising. "I believe I ate a bit too ambitiously. I don't relish the idea of collapsing alone on my way to my cabin."

"I *was* about to offer." Zak stuck out his elbow, not looking at Beatrice as she hesitated, then took the proffered support.

As Zak led Beatrice from the salon, Drake looked at Cianda, his expression unreadable. "How about taking a walk around the deck with me? I need to check on a few things."

Cianda pushed away from the table. "I'd enjoy that," she said matching his casual tone. "Perhaps it's not as hot out there as it is in here."

Drake's fingers brushed her waist as they moved to the companionway that led topside. "Don't count on it, love."

Light, billowing clouds mottled the afternoon sky above white sails snapping in the fitful breeze. To the northwest, the sun streaked smoldering waves of heat through the sultry summer air. But to the south, bloated, gray thunderheads crowded the horizon, carried closer on the wings of the rising wind.

The watch was changing, and Drake snagged the sailor grabbing the rat lines to begin his ascent to the crow's nest. "Look sharp. I don't care for the way this storm is moving on us." Drake slapped him on the shoulder.

"Aye, Cap'n. Be keepin' me eyes peeled fer St. Elmo's light, I will." Confident and agile as a young monkey, the boy scaled the mast to his post.

Drake turned to where Cianda waited nearby. He

paused for a moment, allowing himself the luxury of studying her, unnoticed.

Resting her elbows on the railing, she cupped her face in her palms and leaned to look out over the swelling ocean. Her hair gleamed with a silvery light to rival the sun. Heavy waves tumbled down over her delicate shoulders, falling in platinum streaks down her back almost to her waist. Smooth supple hips curved provocatively beneath her snug trousers, and the zephyr off the water molded her loose shirt to her breasts.

Except for the watch, the rest of the small crew had gone below to eat and take a brief reprieve from the heat, leaving them alone with the sky and sea. The coming storm charged the elements around them with a feeling of restless anticipation. Above them, the wind keened through the sails. It snapped the stiff cloth back and forth against the masts, uncertain what direction to take.

Compelled to action, Drake moved up noiselessly behind Cianda and wrapped his arms around her waist. When she didn't shove away, he rested his head in the soft hollow between her neck and shoulder, breathing her elusive scent, the attar of crushed asters, warmed by a midnight heat. As the *Ferret* swayed with the wind, Drake rocked her in his arms, in time with the rhythm of his ship.

"Sometimes I don't believe you're real," he whispered against her skin. Gently guiding her around to face him, Drake tried to put his uncertain feelings into words. "You're like an apparition, something I dreamed after too many days alone at sea. Maybe that's all you are. I don't know." He brushed several errant silver strands from her face. Her skin slid like rose petals beneath his fingertips. "Who are you? Cianda? Faith?" Hesitating, he leaned nearer and kissed her temple, letting his mouth linger on her face. "Don't hide from me any longer."

Pulling backward, Cianda went rigid in his arms.

He held fast, determined to overcome her resolve with his own. Suddenly, right now, nothing seemed more important than hearing her speak the truth. "Don't. I want to know who you are. Who you really are."

Cianda wrestled against herself. Part of her longed to tell him the truth about her past. To have it over with. The rest of her begged to cling to any hope he might yet learn to care for her, if he didn't know what lay behind her mask.

In the end, reason overtook her heart. He would find out, one way or another, sooner or later. Let him reject her now, before she fell hopelessly in love with him, before the pain of his contempt was too much to bear.

"I don't exist." There was an ache in her voice. "I came from nowhere. That is the truth."

Drake stilled. Then, slowly, his hands tightened on her shoulders. "You came from the Acre."

Her eyes darkened to an infinite frosty shadow. "So gracious of you not to mention you knew sooner."

"It wasn't exactly a topic open for discussion."

"I'm nothing like your mother. Or Isabelle Thorne."

"No. You're nothing like them."

Cianda stopped herself from flinching at his blunt assessment. She kept her eyes steady on his. "Yes, your mother was right. I am a fraud. Godfrey's creation."

"I've known that all along." Frustration laced his voice.

Cianda jerked away and clutched her arms about herself. "Damn you Drake, are you determined to humiliate me?" she lashed out. "Do you want me to say it? Will it satisfy you to hear I'm nothing but a low-bred, common guttersnipe? That I'm not a lady, born and bred to the role? Not like your mother. Or Isabelle."

Drake caught the bitterness and shame behind her words like a blow to the heart. He had wanted to hear her admit her past, to strip aside her pretenses. But he hadn't expected it to be so hurtful. He didn't expect to care so much.

"I see you're impressed," Cianda said, a sardonic twist to her mouth.

"I'm interested in your opinion that birth and breeding creates a lady."

"Doesn't it? Women like Isabelle—"

"Isabelle Thorne wasn't a lady," Drake spat. "She was greedy and selfish and I was a fool to ever imagine I cared for her."

"But you did care for her." Cianda forced herself to say the words. "And you're angry because you still care, even though she betrayed you."

"No. I stopped caring a long time ago."

"You're a liar." She took the force of the fury in his eyes without backing down. "You accuse me of living a charade, yet you pretend nothing or no one matters to you but the thrill and excitement of the risks you take. Can you tell me Isabelle has nothing to do with your determination to hang Godfrey?"

"No. It has everything to do with it."

"I see."

"No, damn it, you don't see." Whirling about, he paced away from her, raking a hand through his hair. Turning back, he slapped her with a hard stare. "Thorne killed her."

"He—" Cianda floundered for words, feeling a cold chill settle over her.

"Yes. He did. Godfrey discovered Isabelle and I were lovers. He couldn't stand the thought of losing one of his prized possessions so he had her murdered. Then he used my brother's influence to have me thrown in that Italian jail."

Not wanting, and yet needing to know the whole truth

Cianda prompted him, "How did Godfrey—?"

"Discover our illicit alliance? Isabelle told him." He smiled grimly at her evident disbelief. "She convinced me she hated Thorne, and that her feelings for me gave her the courage to leave him. And I believed every word of it. When I heard she'd been killed—" He leaned both hands on the railing, clenching it tightly. "I went to Thorne. It was all very polite. He received me in his study and calmly handed me a letter. From her. She'd written it the night before. In the end Thorne had his revenge on both of us. Isabelle had decided marriage to one of the Queen's most powerful diplomats was preferable to her grand passion for me."

"I'm sorry," Cianda said softly. I can imagine . . ." She stopped, realizing how much hurt lay behind his words. "How did she die?"

"Thrown from her horse. Or so Thorne said. I knew from the look in his eyes that he'd killed her. And took great pleasure in doing it." Drake fixed his gaze on the distant horizon. "I couldn't do a damned thing about it. My entire family believed Thorne. He'd insulated himself with enough wealth and status to guarantee their loyalty. Charles still courts his favor. He just pretends he knows nothing about how Thorne accumulated his fortune. You'll be amused to know it was my father who helped give him that autonomy. My father always admired Thorne's avarice and ruthless ambition, traits I sorely lacked. He arranged for Thorne to get a high-ranking position in the diplomatic service."

"I-I . . ." Touching shaking fingers to her forehead, Cianda tried to sort out her wildly churning emotions. She had long suspected Godfrey of using force where manipulation failed. But murder . . . A vision of Jamie, alone at Godfrey's mercy, haunted her.

Drake straightened, facing her with a tight smile. "Sorry

266

to have destroyed your illusions of a generous benefactor. Although I'm certain it won't affect your loyalty to Thorne, either."

"It's so easy for you to scoff," Cianda shot back at him, her resolve returning, on a surge of anger. "Let me tell you a story of my own, Captain. My mother earned nine pence a day weaving cages and baskets out of cane to feed us. My father was a drunken bastard who beat her until she was too weak and broken to keep up her only trade. Rather than go to the workhouse and leave us alone with him, she took to selling watercress in the streets. She died in my arms, of pneumonia when Jamie was just a baby. I promised her I'd keep Jamie safe, so I took him and ran as far as I could. We lived with the rats and the prostitutes and the thieves, moving from lodging house to lodging house. We were always eventually tossed out because I couldn't pay the rent."

Cianda paused, the harsh, painful memories eliciting a torrent of searing emotions that threatened to overcome her strength.

Drake watched her, offering neither sympathy nor pity. Lightning cracked overhead, followed by a low grumble of thunder. A rush of wind wailed between them.

Returning his gaze, she waited for him to say something, to make some response.

"Don't stop," he said, his voice low and taut as if voicing the words had been an effort.

Overhead smoky clouds with heavy black bellies rumbled and rolled. Cianda stared down at the planks beneath her feet, debating, agonizing over each word that would inevitably drag his opinion of her further and further from his ideal of what a woman ought to be.

Yet, she had begun and now the words could not be stopped.

She drew a tremulous breath. "I had two choices. Sell

my body, or steal to keep it alive so I could care for Jamie. I chose to be a thief. That's when Maisie took me under her wing. She taught me a great deal about manipulating people into positions to pick their pockets. She lived on the street, pretending to be deaf and blind. She played the hurdy-gurdy, attracting a crowd, while I emptied their pockets of watches and coins."

"And Thorne?"

"He'd sent Gide Legume, his master housebreaker to the Acre to search for a pair of talented young fingers to replace his ailing ones." Her tone grew wistful. "Godfrey took Jamie and me in, setting us up in a small cottage with Gide, a governess, and a variety of excellent tutors. For a time, it seemed like a fairy story to me. We were warm, dry, fed. And safe. For the first time, Jamie was safe."

"And then?" Sharp streaks of light split the sky behind him. The storm loomed closer and with it a chill mist swirled in over the deck of the *Ferret*.

"Then . . ." Cianda's mouth twisted. "I grew up. And I hated what I'd become: Godfrey Thorne's private creation. He gave me a name and a pedigree and forced me into society so that I could learn the habits of the wealthy, and know when and where to steal from them. I hated him for it and yet—"

"Yes," Drake urged harshly. "And yet?"

"I owed him everything. I still do. He took me from the gutter and gave me my life. He gave me Jamie's life." She dashed a single tear from her cheek. "But I wanted to quit. I threatened to quit. That's when he took Jamie from me."

A loud clap of thunder reverberated around them. Drake's gaze flicked up to where the mainsail swelled and snapped furiously above them. On all sides, angry waves slapped the *Ferret* to and fro. When he looked back to

268

her, Cianda saw the burgeoning tempest reflected in his eyes.

She grasped at the railing as the ship lurched in a gust of wind. Drake's silence lanced her heart. There was nothing more to say. She had gambled and lost.

Forcing her emotions deep inside, she held herself straight in a show of coolness. "I won't delay you any longer, Captain," she said, twisting around to walk away before the tears of vulnerability showed through her crumbling mask of strength.

Chapter Fifteen

Drake's hand caught her arm before she took a pace from him. "You're not running and hiding this time, milady thief," he said, raising his voice above the growl and wail of the advancing tempest.

"You've said nothing to make me stay." *Say something! Say anything!*

The wind whipped between them, sweeping away her unspoken plea. Cianda's mind screamed protest at Drake's silence. She had pushed him, she knew, almost dared him to use her revelations as an excuse to reject her. If he did, if he said the words that embodied her worst fears aloud, maybe he could convince her mutinous heart that loving him wasn't worth the risk.

"I see I've again left you speechless," she finally forced out, reaching deep for a scrap of bitter humor. "Quite an accomplishment on my part."

A confusion of emotions struggled for mastery of Drake's expression. He half raised a hand, then dropped it.

Cianda wrapped her arms about herself, her fingers digging painfully into the soft flesh of her upper arms. A dazzling streak of lightning shot an instant's light from the hovering overhang of clouds. She started, feeling exposed by the brief glow.

The white light chased the shadow from Drake's face and

in the instant of brilliance, she saw resolve had replaced hesitation. Thunder beat above them. The first spatter of raindrops slashed the deck.

Drake, as if he took the storm as an omen, and it had forced a decision, took a stride toward her.

Cianda dropped her arms. Waiting.

Before either of them could breach the barrier of silence, a tall shadow thrust between them. Zak, his flame-red hair and beard wildly tossed by the wind, glanced once at Cianda then turned to Drake. "I'm certain you've been far too occupied to notice," he glared at Cianda—"But it is getting a bit rough underfoot. Any suggestions, Captain?"

"I was just about to go below," Cianda said, returning Zak's scowl. "He's all yours."

Drake wiped his brow with his shirt sleeve. "Check the glass Zak, and—"

"I already have. It's still falling."

"Hell. Then we're in for a heavy sea. I'll take the wheel."

"Glad to hear it. Grindel's probably taking us to South America instead of St. Helena by now."

Her emotions honed to a fine edge, Cianda had to press a hand to her mouth to choke back an hysterical laugh. Zak's way of making the most dramatic sound as mild as an invitation to tea struck her as an anticlimactic finish to the intensity of her confrontation with Drake.

Drake looked at her then turned back to Zak. "Prepare to drop the mainsail."

Zak scratched at his beard. "But then we'll lose our headway and she'll start to drift."

"I know. But this close into shore, the chop can be so hard we might founder. If the roll gets too bad we'll rig a sea anchor. I just don't want to end up on those reefs."

"That's reason enough for me then," Zak said, shrugging. "I'll see to it."

The sea rose and broke heavily against the *Ferret,* forcing Cianda to spread her feet wide to keep her balance. She knew she should leave him to his work, yet something stubborn and demanding inside her wanted to finish what they had begun. Her lifelong defenses stripped away, she felt disturbingly vulnerable. Her past, her shame, hung out before her, before Drake's scrutiny as defenseless as the thin sail whipping and snapping above her at the mercy of the squall.

She didn't notice Drake followed her gaze to the mainsail. Already, his men worked furiously along the mainmast, greasing it with tallow and lowering the ropes. "Be sure the rigging is lashed down," he called out to them. A young sailor stood idly by gawking skyward. "You there! Turn to! And slap the tacker on those booms."

The boy jumped to attention. "Aye, Cap'n."

The *Ferret* lolled to one side and back with the force of the wind, and he steadied himself with a hand to the railing. "Get everyone topside. We'll need all the hands we have."

Zak answered, touching two fingers to his forehead in a mock salute and ambled toward the quarterdeck.

Drake put his hands on Cianda's shoulders to brace her as the *Ferret* lurched again. "You'd better get below."

"Aye, Captain," she flipped back, struggling to ignore the warmth of his touch.

"Don't worry." He tried a smile. "If we go belly up, I'll consider sharing my cork."

"Thank you, but I'll find my own."

Drake dropped his hands. He paused, searching her face, then turned and started to the quarterdeck. Stopping in mid-stride, he looked back.

Her body pressed to the railing, Cianda kept her own gaze steady. Wind and sea clashed; the wooden skeleton of the *Ferret* creaked in protest.

Drake took two steps and pulled her into his arms. She went willingly, seeking sanctuary. He held her tightly, his face buried in her silver hair. "We'll finish this," he murmured, so low the storm nearly stole the sound. "I vow we will."

As quickly as he caught her to him, he released her, striding into the face of the tempest.

Cianda waited until his tall figure vanished into the gloom before letting go her breath in a trembling sigh. She stood for a long moment amid the furious blending of elements until the sudden pelting rain forced her reluctantly to descend to safety.

She dared to enter Domenique's domain, certain the cook would be aft where his strength was invaluable. She laid her palms flat on the worktable to brace herself against the *Ferret*'s pitch and sway. Outside, the storm buffeted the schooner with wind and water. Inside, just as fiercely, the turmoil of her emotions battered her heart.

She desperately wanted to believe she had found the one man with whom she might finally relinquish her facade. If she was given one chance for a man to accept her past, her one chance was Drake Weston.

His silence haunted her. What did he think? Had he already guessed? Did her confession shock or repulse? Did she have his pity or his loathing? Could she ever steal his heart or would that treasure always elude her? And even if the impossible happened, what future could there be in it?

Questions, and only her fears to answer.

"You're still here." Beatrice suddenly appeared in the doorway, a hand on either side, lurching slightly with the motion of the ship. "They're all topside. I do hope this doesn't delay our making port at St. Helena tomorrow." She managed her way on unsteady legs across the room and sat down beside Cianda. "I confess, I don't think I will ever be a good sailor. I'm looking forward to having my feet on solid ground."

Cianda nodded in response. Beatrice's gentle voice soothed, giving her time to regroup her emotions. It was a technique Beatrice used well.

Thunder echoed off the walls of the galley and Beatrice

lifted her face to the sound. "It seems bad, but then I have little to compare it to."

"It's a summer storm," Cianda said, surprised she could sound so calm. "They come swiftly, without warning, but they rarely last."

She felt Beatrice studying her. "Sometimes they do," Beatrice said softly. "And then comes the difficulty of reconciling yourself to the truth that they're going to linger." She waited, then asked gently, "Is that what you want?"

"I don't know. Perhaps I want something I can't have."

"So did I once. At the time, I decided I had made a foolish gamble."

"And now?"

Beatrice smiled a little. "Now I realize loving someone is a perilous undertaking. But it's the one chance in life you must take if you intend to live fully." Her smile widened at Cianda's surprised glance. Smoothing a hand over her hair, Beatrice stood and moved to the great stove that sat atop a brick pad, warming the small galley. "Well —" She lifted the kettle to check for water. "We can at least make ourselves useful."

"Are you certain you're up to it?" Cianda asked, studying her friend's still-pale face.

"It's no better trapped in that tiny cabin space. At least here, I can keep myself distracted. I don't know how bad it will get, but I have the feeling it will be a long night."

A long night. "Yes," Cianda agreed as she rose to help. "It will be at that."

Hours later, well into the heart of the night, the storm's furious bluster abated into a steady rainfall, the crack and rumble less spectacular. Cianda aided Beatrice in dishing out hot mugs of tea to the half-drowned crew in the shadow of the fo'c'sle. But her hands worked independently of her thoughts, which refused to leave Drake.

274

Now, back in the salon, she busied herself wiping clean the empty mugs on her tray as Zak and Beatrice sat finishing the last of the tea. "It's time I pried the captain away from the helm for a spell," Zak said, unfolding his long legs from under the table. "He's been at it seven hours steady. Long enough to be seeing double, if he hasn't drowned yet in this wretched squall."

As he scowled at the ceiling in a silent curse of the weather, Beatrice laughed. "I believe you hate being wet more than Fred. She hasn't come out from under my berth since yesterday afternoon." As she rose to follow Zak out, she glanced over her shoulder. "Are you coming back to the cabin, Cianda?"

A pewter cup clanked to the planks as Cianda's hands suddenly fumbled with the cloth she held. "No. I—I'll just finish here. You go ahead."

"There's nothing to be done." Beatrice sent a pointed look around the room.

Cianda avoided looking at either her friend or Zak. "I want a breath of air before I subject myself to a moving bed for the rest of the night. I'm feeling trapped in here." She managed a self-conscious laugh. "There's not even a port-hole to remind me that there is an outside."

"Damned odd night for a stroll on the deck," Zak muttered. "But then there's no accounting for a woman's taste." With a shake of his head, he shoved his hands in his pockets and made for the door. He glanced back at Beatrice. "I suppose you want me to see you back to your cabin."

Beatrice paused briefly, looking at Cianda. "If you can spare the effort, Mr. Zak," she said at last. "Be careful on deck, Cianda. Storms can be dangerous."

Cianda nodded sharply and waited until they'd left before flinging aside the cloth. "Damned odd night indeed, Mister Zak."

Dousing the salon lanterns, she kept her promise to herself to brave the weather. As she climbed up onto the deck, a

275

spray of warm rain, tangy with brine, showered her face. She moved carefully over the wet, slippery planks, making her way to the railing and curling her fingers tightly around the hard, wooden support.

Cianda leaned back and let the wind and water embrace her. Thunder and lightning chorused in sound and fury above her. The swell of the sea licked at her legs. She closed her eyes and abandoned herself to the crashing rhythm of the ship as it plunged again and again into the rolling waves.

The taste and feel of the untamed fury of sea and sky exhilarated her. *This is why Drake loves the sea. This feeling. This freedom.*

She opened her eyes to watch the raw splendor of it — and found him watching her.

He stood, legs spread on the deck, braced against the gale. Cianda stared, uncertain if he were real or if her longings had conjured him from the wild elements of the storm.

Drake seized the advantage of her hesitation to simply look at her, as if seeing her was a wish granted only this night. Wind and rain combed through her hair and molded his shirt to her slender body. The image recalled his first vision of her, a creature born of moonlight and sea. More strongly now, her power to enchant tossed his senses into a whirl and flung his reason into the tempest.

Clearly she expected a rebuke for challenging the storm. Drake could think of nothing but the desire to hold her. Before he convinced himself of the folly of acting on his emotions, he strode to her side and caught her hand, guiding her to the scant shelter of the sail locker.

Cianda twisted to face him. A strike of brilliant light across the ebony sky illuminated a hungry excitement in her eyes that mirrored his own. The primitive coupling of wind and water around them drove away uncertainty. She lifted her hands to his shoulders.

Drake's fingers closed around her wrists, keeping her body from touching his. "This is how you've haunted my dreams," he said hoarsely. "Without your masks. The siren who fell into my arms. I wanted to tell you, before—"

He stopped, his expression uncertain. A glimpse of vulnerability, so unlike his usual fearless bravado, stirred hope again in her heart. "Before . . . ?" she echoed.

"Nothing you've told me matters. None of it."

"None of it?" Cianda searched his face for the truth. She longed to believe him without doubt. Yet she was compelled to ask the painful questions. "Not what I am, what I've been?" Slipping her hands free, she lifted the emerald from beneath his shirt. "Not this?"

Each motion deliberate, his eyes fixed on hers, Drake unfastened the golden chain and let the jewel drop into his palm. Threading the chain between his fingers, he slowly unfastened the first several buttons of her borrowed shirt. Slipping his hands beneath the wet cotton, he pushed the clinging fabric from her shoulders, taking the thin straps of her chemise with it, exposing her heated skin to the soft play of the rain.

Drake laid the emerald in the hollow between her breasts, his hand covering it, then moved the chain up her throat and around her neck, linking it at her nape. "None of it matters. Especially this. I don't want Cianda D'Rouchert or the Masked Marauder. I want Faith."

Cianda almost didn't trust her ears. "I—I've pretended so long to be someone else, I've nearly forgotten I ever was Faith Newman." She touched the emerald around her neck. "I never thought I could go back to her, never dared to hope I could give up the pretense."

"And now? Are you still pretending? With me?"

The bite of his fingers into her shoulders told her how much the answer meant to him. "No," she answered, holding his eyes. "Not now."

"You never have to. Not again. I've known for a long time you're the only woman who could understand me, the choices I've made. No other woman has ever moved me the

277

way you do with that blasted, blind sense of loyalty. And your drive to tempt fate, as though you're daring it to intervene and disrupt your schemes. The way I do. In some ways we're so frighteningly similar. Do you realize that?"

"Yes. And, you're right. To our discredit, no doubt. We seem compelled to take chances."

"All of them. We live moment to moment."

"There's no other way."

He stepped close enough to let the length of him press against her body. "You've utterly destroyed my resolutions, made me forget all my good intentions."

"You have good intentions?" Cianda's mouth swanned at the hollow of his throat with each word.

"I did. Not to care. Not to need anyone like this. Not to need you."

Cianda lifted her mouth to meet his. His kiss demanded and offered surrender. Her tongue thrust against his, tasting temptation. Rainwater slid in rivulets over her skin, laced with lightning when Drake's hands moved warm and wet on her flesh. The thunder now beat a driving tempo in her blood.

His hands ran along her shoulders to the back of her shirt. Pulling it to her waist, he let his fingers chase the raindrops up and down her spine.

The emerald pressed between them, flooding Cianda with the wonder of Drake's sacrifice. He willingly put his fate in her hands. But why? He was giving her his trust. But were trust and love one and the same?

Drake's lips nibbling hot, hurried kisses over her throat made it impossible to think. All the sensations, all the feelings, forbidden and seducing, combined to create the fiery elixir of passion unique to them alone. With each touch, she drank deeply of it, yet each touch left her as wanting as if she'd never tasted it at all.

There was no reason in it, only need. Tugging open his shirt, she explored his body in return. Water slicked his skin.

278

The marriage of wet and firm under her fingertips created frissons of excitement with each stroke. She leaned forward to taste what her hands touched and he stumbled a pace.

"You're inviting danger, milady thief," Drake muttered against her ear.

"Am I?" She flicked her tongue to the salty rain on his chest. His muscles tightened in response, making her bold as she realized the power she had to arouse him in return. "Are you accepting?"

"You don't need to ask twice." Her shirt and chemise fell to the deck as Drake's impatient fingers pushed them aside. His palm teased the taut peak of her breast and she arched to his touch. Returning to claim her kiss, he used the callused flat of his hand and the rainwater to invent a banquet of pleasures.

Drake tried to move slowly, to linger over each step of the journey. But she pushed him, as she always pushed him, to give her everything, without reserve, damning the danger. And she held nothing back. No pretense sheltered her now, nor any longer protected his heart.

He loved her. The simple truth struck a hard blow. It was crazy, and impossible, and begged trouble.

And he didn't care.

Her hands stripped away his shirt from his shoulders and his razor edge of control with it. He tossed them both away. Bending her into the curve of his arm, he traced a trail with his mouth from the hollow of her throat to the soft swell of her breasts. She tasted of rain and sea. The scent of her skin matched that of the summer tempest, echoed with the faint incense of asters.

Cianda's fingers dug into the muscles of his shoulders. She gasped in startled pleasure when Drake unfastened the buttons of her trousers and curled his hand over the curve of her hip. When she pushed closer, flattening her breasts against his chest, he groaned deep in his throat and shoved the clinging material from her body.

The slide of his hand over her belly sent a wild excitement racing under her skin. Cianda kicked away the confinement of material and boots at her feet and wrapped one leg around his, intimately pressing his hard arousal against her thigh.

She felt no fear, no confusion. Only a swell of urgency breaking over her with increasing strength, steady as the ebb and flow of the tide, strong as the storm-tossed sea. It was fire, sweet and hot. And she wanted to burn.

The rain fell faster, dancing in a swirl of wind around them. Thunder rolled long and slow above, and Cianda felt it tremble through her body as Drake lowered to his knees in front of her. His fingers splayed over her hips, caressed her sensitive skin. The touch of his mouth where his hands lay elicited a gasp of startled pleasure.

"I asked you once if you believed in the destiny of lovers." He inflamed her soft skin with a light, tormenting kiss. "Do you, love?" His tongue traced a line from the point of her hip just to the juncture of her thighs. "Do you believe in the power of this feeling between us?"

Cianda's eyes fluttered closed as a thousand new sensations struck her nerves. She forgot to answer, forgot even his questions. Words, even thought fled with the rush of the wind as Drake's mouth lingered in the hollows and swells of her flesh. Fire raced under her skin. She had never craved a man's touch like this, so desperately. As if her body had been made for his touch alone. As if they belonged together, a coupling of fate.

She rhythmically kneaded her fingers into his shoulders, gripping tight the moment he slid his hand into the silver curls covering the center of her passion.

All her senses rioted as he stroked lightning into her belly. When his tongue replaced the touch of his fingers, she cried out.

Hearing her call his name in passion and joy, Drake lost any last resolve to seduce her slowly. It was never that way between them. He pulled her down with him to the rain-wet bed of folded sails.

He would have guided her beneath him, but she stopped him by sliding her hands between their bodies. She lightly brushed over his chest, the flatness of his stomach, then lower. He watched her, his breath ragged, as she slowly unbuttoned his trousers and shoved them low on his hips.

Trembling inside, Cianda looked up before she touched his hard shaft. Her first intimate caress rocked him against her. His shuddering response made her hands bold and his heart pound against hers. Drake's kiss was wild as he shoved away the last barrier of clothing between them and lowered her back against the sails.

The storm swept them beyond control. His leg parted hers and she reached to pull him against her, unafraid of the consequence. Avid to feel his hot skin on hers, she willingly stepped into the flames.

The tip of his shaft slid into the slick fold of flesh between her thighs, caressing the core of her desire. "Is this what you want?" Drake's voice whispered warm and intoxicating against her ear. He moved the emerald to the soft swell of her breast. The coolness of the gem clashed with the heat of his thumb circling her taut nipple. "Once we've begun, I'll never finish with you, my thief. Not now, not ever."

Cianda writhed under him in sweet agony from his sensual torment. "It's what I want. Please — Drake . . ."

Still, Drake held back, keeping them both balancing on the brink of fulfillment, wanting more than just her surrender to passion. "Tell me," he urged softly. "Tell me you believe."

Moving her hands down his back to his buttocks, Cianda wrapped her legs around his hips and took him inside her. She gasped as the sure thrust of his body breached the barrier of her innocence. But, almost at once, the brief pain burned to ashes with the fire of pleasure. "Make me believe," she boldly entreated him. "Make me a believer."

Drake's mouth took the plea from her lips as he succumbed to the demands her hands and body made of his. She gave him no chance to tenderly and slowly seduce her into a gentle rhythm of lovemaking. She wanted no half-measure from their joining. Not a rain shower, but a fierce tempest in all its wild glory. Everything he wanted and more.

He quickened his deep strokes, abandoning any reticence. This woman matched him in daring and in strength. Her yielding, total and without hesitation, defeated the defenses of his heart, leaving him at the mercy of his desire for her.

Cianda drowned in a flash flood of sensation. She wanted to capture each feeling and hold it to savor. But it was like trying to catch a shower of falling stars, each brighter and hotter than the last. Each plunge of Drake's body against hers, each slide of flesh against flesh sent her rushing, racing, flying toward some culmination she could not imagine.

He felt it too. She sensed it in the tight grip of his hands on her back, his fevered plundering of her mouth. She encouraged, begged his hungry touch. Knowing he wanted her as fiercely as she did him made it all the sweeter, all the more exciting.

Drake rocked harder and faster against her. The primitive tempo incited the tempest inside her to a fury of pleasure and aching need so powerful it screamed for release.

At the moment Cianda thought she would die of it, suddenly lightning struck her with spine-shattering intensity.

Cianda cried out as heaven and earth moved in her soul. She jerked upward, dashed on wave after wave of an ecstasy that felt like the culmination of every moment of laughter and tears she ever had experienced, or would experience in a, lifetime of joy.

Almost simultaneously, she felt Drake stiffen and tremble inside her. Holding her tightly in his arms, he buried his face in her silver tumble of hair as they both shuddered to the final echoes of their shared passion.

It lasted forever. Yet it wasn't long enough.

When it finally ebbed, Cianda lay spent in his arms, her longed-for haven from the storm.

Drake rolled to his back, too exhausted to do more than cradle her languid body against his. Gradually, the shaking inside eased, and he realized the gale around them had abated to a soft patter of raindrops.

The wonder of what had happened between them washed over him as warm and gentle as the summer rain. In all the times he'd bedded a woman, even in the fire of his passion for Isabelle, lovemaking had never been so consuming, so wild. So beyond his control. So completely fulfilling.

He tenderly brushed his hand over Cianda's silky face. She turned at his touch, lazily kissing his palm. "Is it always like this?" she murmured. "Always so . . . so—"

"Breathtaking?" He pulled her closer to his heart. "Only between us, my love."

"I was afraid that would be your answer."

"Afraid?"

He tensed beside her and she laughed, lifting her head to look into his eyes. "If it's always like this between us, Captain Weston, I fear neither of us may survive even this night."

"Then at least I'll have seen paradise before I die." Taking her chin in his hand, he kissed her, a deep, gentle caress that renewed the warm quiver in her heart.

The sweet intensity of it shocked her. She let the fire of their passion disguise the truth of her feelings. Now it was too late to deny she had lost her heart to Drake Weston. And it was the one jewel she could never steal back.

As he continued to kiss her, his hands moving over her in confident possession, Cianda drowned her troubling thoughts in a new wash of desire. Drake's touch rekindled it like a flame to a dry field. It spread quickly, wildfire to the wind.

Drake suddenly sat up, taking her with him. Getting to his feet in one fluid motion, he pulled on his trousers. He bent and scooped up first their sodden clothing, then Cianda from the pile of drenched sails, swinging her into his arms. "I believe we're in danger of drowning," he murmured, smiling into her eyes.

"Speak for yourself, Captain," Cianda teased. "Tonight I've developed rather a fondness for wind and water."

He nuzzled the curve of her neck as he carried her below. "Indulge me this once, love."

The moist heat of his cabin wrapped around them as Drake kicked closed the door and moved with her still in his embrace to the narrow berth. He laid her among the crumple of bedsheets and she listened to his wet trousers drop onto the floor. Fumbling near the head of the bed, she smelled the scent of burning oil.

Cianda's fingers closed over his hand just as the small amber flame of the lamp on the nightstand sprang to life. "I'm hardly afraid of the dark," she said lightly. In the warm black of the night, she could pretend their lovemaking erased all the barriers dividing them. For a few more stolen hours, at least, she wanted to hold tight to that illusion.

"Hiding again?" Drake pulled her hand away from the lamp. The flickering fire cast planes and valleys of shadow on his body. She tried to look away. His fingers caught her chin and forced her to meet his stormy eyes. "In less than three hours it will be dawn. You'll have to face this in the light and then what will you do, milady thief?"

"I don't know. When you touch me, it all seems so simple. Yet in truth we've only complicated everything," she finished miserably.

"Is that how you see me? As a complication?"

"No! I — yes! You are a complication. This was never part of the plan." She punched a fist into the tangled linen in frustration. "Just when I believe I know what your stakes are, you do this . . ." As she touched the jewel hanging between her breasts, the green and gold of the emerald caught the lamplight. "It's just the sort of unpredictable, reckless thing you *would* do."

"At least I don't bore you." Drake's wicked, seductive smile turned her spine to water. He traced a forefinger over the surface of the emerald, just grazing her skin with each stroke.

"You confuse me. I could easily betray you with this. But you surrendered it without a thought, trusting me to help you carry out your justice. It's as if . . . as if—"

Drake leaned forward until his lips brushed her ear. "As if I loved you?" he whispered.

Shock froze Cianda. Before she recovered her wits, Drake's mouth slid over hers, his tongue slipping between her lips to taste and probe.

Desire licked her skin, whirling her thoughts into a maelstrom of chaotic emotion and sensation. Had he said he loved her? Or was he asking her to say it for them both?

She couldn't decide, couldn't think, couldn't remember. Every touch of his hands distracted her more. Drake shifted to stretch out on the berth, pulling her atop him, and she forgot to care about any of her questions or doubts.

Her cool damp flesh upon his melded to a sultry dew. Sliding her legs to either side, Cianda raised herself up to watch his face as she moved intimately against him. "Perhaps there are advantages to being in the light after all," she murmured, loving the way passion tightened his jaw and darkened his eyes to midnight blue. Looking at his dark hands tensed on her ivory skin aroused her, making her curiously breathless.

"Allow me to demonstrate a few," Drake said, in one moment ending any need for more words.

Hours later, Cianda curled into his arms, sleepy and sated. Her cheek rested on his heart and one hand cradled the emerald between them. As she listened to the steady rhythm under her ear, her fingers absently stroked the jewel.

How could she choose? Jamie, her loyalty to Godfrey, the

lure of the promised fortune for the trio of gems, the security of her false identity. All at risk because she dared to fall in love with Drake Weston. The choice seemed clear.

Yet as she drifted into an uneasy sleep, she knew nothing was further from the truth.

Chapter Sixteen

James Bay scooped into the rocky coast of St. Helena, the nearness of their destination stirring a flurry of conflicting emotions in Cianda. She'd lingered portside for the first glimpse of the island since the first shell-pink glow of dawn kissed the now-quiet sky. Resting her elbows on the railing, she let the faint drift of cool breeze waft over her face, soothing her warm skin.

Last night's tempest almost seemed a dream. In its aftermath, the scent of rain lingered in the sea-kissed air. Gentle waves lapped the *Ferret's* hull in a soft, rhythmic wash.

Cianda wished her thoughts were as peaceful. In the quiet of the predawn, she'd slipped out of Drake's arms, leaving him asleep, alone in the narrow berth, hoping the cool silence of the early morning would clear her mind. Instead, it roiled and churned with memories of the night before. Her body ached pleasantly in the most intimate places. And in others it just plain ached.

How she longed to spend the day basking in love's afterglow, letting herself freely relive each touch, every sweet-hot caress. She'd relinquished the darkest secrets of her past to Drake. And he surprised her heart by accepting them without question, without censure.

His acceptance, his passion for her was real, stripped of

all pretense, all lies. He wanted her, Faith Newman. The knowledge both frightened and exalted her. The more so because she knew she wanted him with an equaling fire. A fire neither of them could quench.

And yet . . . A poignant sorrow touched her heart. Today, did last night matter anymore? Had anything changed between them? Drake was still a British agent. She was still a thief.

But the emerald—Cianda fingered the gem where i rested warm and safe in the deep cleft between her breasts. He gave it back to her willingly. How dearly that act cos him, after Isabelle's cruel betrayal, she could only imag ine. The jewel symbolized his readiness to risk his hear again, to believe in the love of a woman. To feel again.

To feel again. A cold frisson of guilt stole up Cianda' spine. Could she trust herself not to betray him?

The question hammered her aching heart. She longed t beg him to take back the sacrifice, because she couldn promise him her loyalty. She had to do whatever was nec essary to protect Jamie and her little family. Even if meant lying to Drake.

Once she had the Koh-i-noor, she could easily slip a three jewels into Godfrey's hands, take Jamie, and fle England at once. And why shouldn't she? The risk woul be so much less to Jamie if she avoided Drake's scheme t entrap Godfrey altogether.

But how could she? She loved Drake deeply and irrevo cably. How could she do something that would destro him?

But could she trust her heart?

What if he was playing her for a fool? Preying on he sense of loyalty, using her passion for him to his advar tage—

Cianda shook her head in frustration. Questions, ques tions and more questions. Her head throbbed, her hea wept. She felt tossed in the middle of a hopeless storm, without chance of rescue.

I have to stop pretending I have any choice. I know what I have to do.

Drawing her self upright, Cianda forced her thoughts to order. The Koh-i-noor was practically in her grasp. Once she had the diamond, she would have Jamie too. That was all that could matter. Ever.

Her foolish dreams and private desires threatened her brother's life.

"Couldn't you sleep either?" Beatrice's clear voice came from behind. When Cianda turned, she smiled, her eyes still bleary from her restless night.

"What? Oh, good morning. No. No, I didn't sleep at all." That, at least, was the truth, Cianda thought ruefully.

"It was difficult, I must say, with the storm rocking the ship most of the night."

"Yes, very difficult," Cianda murmured, averting her eyes. "How are you feeling this morning? Did the extra motion make your stomach worse?"

Beatrice smiled, smoothing a hand over her hair. "Surprisingly, no. I seem finally to have gotten my sea legs — now that we're about to drop anchor."

"I'm glad you've recovered. I'm afraid you're going to need all the strength you can muster in the next few days."

"The burglary isn't actually what worries me most," Beatrice said, with a slight frown. "It's afterward." She paused, then asked softly, "Where will it end, Cianda?"

Cianda tried a smile. "I'll take care of us. Haven't I always?"

"Yes . . . but you haven't always been in love with Drake Weston."

"I—"

"It would be rather useless for you to deny it." Beatrice

touched her arm. "You didn't come back to your cabin last night."

Hot color flooded her face, but Cianda bravely held her friend's calm gaze. "No. I didn't. And even if I did—care for Drake, what difference would it make? It doesn't change our plans."

"Doesn't it?"

"No. In fact," Cianda said, forcing a false lightness into her voice. "Our situation has improved." Reaching under her shirt, she drew out the emerald, letting it swing between them.

"Good heaven—" Beatrice stretched out a hand to touch the jewel, then pulled it back. "Drake gave it back to you?"

Cianda nodded, not trusting herself to speak.

"Oh, Cianda." Beatrice bit at her lower lip. Her expression wavered between sympathy and distress. "If he trusted you enough to give you the emerald, then he obviously cares for you. Even if you're given the chance, you won't be able to betray him now. I know you too well."

Beatrice's words so closely echoed her own thoughts that Cianda winced. "You also know I would do anything to rescue Jamie."

"Yes, I do. But what if you're forced to choose?"

Gazing out over the cluster of vessels anchored on the leeward side at James Bay, Cianda blinked away stinging tears. "I made my choice years ago, in the Devil's Acre. Nothing can change that now. Not even Drake Weston."

"Fool! Fool! Fool!" Drake cursed himself under his breath.

Zak dropped down on an upside-down half-barrel. "Dare I ask what you've done now?"

Drake whirled on him, his eyes blue flames. "No. You can't."

"Must be quite a blunder this time. Let me hazard a guess. You bedded the bloody little thief. Didn't you?"

Drake slammed his palms against the railing, his back to Zak. "Worse."

"What could be—" Zak broke off. After a considerable silence he sighed, "Turn around."

Reluctantly, Drake slowly faced him.

Zak stood and walked up to Drake. He slapped a palm against the center of Drake's chest, his fingers probing the fabric of his shirt for the emerald.

"Well, hell and damnation. That's all we need, isn't it? Once she has the diamond, what's to stop her from running straight to Thorne with all three jewels? Without us!"

Drake shrugged. "Me?"

"You're damned right! You'd better find a way to get that wretched emerald back. All she wants is that brat brother of hers. If you think for one minute she cares about you, you haven't learned a goddamned thing about women since Isabe—" His sentence broke. "Sorry, old chap. I only—"

"I know. And you're right." Leaning heavily on the railing, Drake stared out blankly over the rippling water of the bay.

"Maybe she's different," Zak said uneasily.

Drake snorted out a derisive laugh. "Nice try."

"Unless you plan to wrest it back by force—which I gather is not an option—you haven't left us much choice but to gamble that her supposed passion for you rivals her loyalty to Thorne. And her determination to rescue the boy."

"I wouldn't even bet Fred on that."

"Then you'd better think ahead for once and start planning a way to get that diamond out of her hands the minute she lays them on it. Without the Koh-i-noor, we're out of aces, old chap."

Drake wished he could counter Zak, promise him the jewels — and their futures — were safe in Cianda's hands. He couldn't. "I know," he muttered at last. "I know."

A gust of wind whipped a fine spindrift over his face. Drake shoved a hand through his hair, letting go a long breath. He looked out beyond the prow of the *Ferret* to where the bay cradled numerous ships anchored in the roadstead for refitting and revictualing, scanning for the *King's Bounty*. There was no trace of the East India Company ship among the confusion of masts and rigging and sails.

Maybe fate would gift him with the time to undo his rash act before the *Bounty* arrives. Maybe he could beg, steal or charm the damned emerald back into his hands. The way he felt about her now, the use of force to get it back was simply out of the question.

But did he want it back? Or did he want to believe Cianda's feelings for him were strong enough to overcome her reluctance to betray Thorne?

His eyes moved unwillingly to the sail locker.

The answer came easily; the solution did not. With the emerald, he had entrusted his heart to her. That much he could never take back. If she betrayed him, so be it. Only so much more hung on her every decision. Zak's future, Thorne's fate, Palmerston's reputation.

His own life.

If she disappeared, the blame for the theft would fall on him.

The *Ferret* cut a path into the sea on its way to Jamestown, but Drake's eyes stayed fixed on the sail locker. He would never look at it again without seeing Cianda. Her hair molten silver in the flashes of lightning, her skin wet and warm with summer rain, her emerald eyes inviting the passion of his embrace.

"So — what's the decision?"

Drake glanced over his shoulder at his partner. "You know me," he said, turning back to the view of the bay. "I'll make it up as I go along."

That evening, an ebony-skinned servant unlocked the door and ushered Cianda and Beatrice into their room at the Porteous House Inn.

"We'll be in the adjoining rooms," Drake said, setting down Cianda's trunk in front of the bed.

Beatrice looked around the simple, but pleasantly attired room. "This is charming. How did you find it?"

"Napoleon's family once stayed here for a time during his detention on the island at Longwood. When I heard of it, I had hoped that if the Bonapartes were willing to rest their heads here it would at least be livable." Drake moved to the door. "It doesn't appear to be much more than that though," he scoffed, suddenly sounding like the aristocrat he was born to be. "I'll leave you to settle in," he said, shutting the door behind him.

"I daresay I'll have no trouble sleeping tonight," Beatrice murmured, easing onto an overstuffed chair. "By the time we finally dropped anchor this afternoon and took a tour of the town, I was more than ready for a decent night's sleep."

"You're not back up to your usual strength yet," Cianda murmured. She tossed her wide-brimmed straw hat onto one of the beds and began plucking the pins from her hair.

Her feet ached from walking the streets of the island's capital. To everyone's relief, the *Ferret* had arrived at Jamestown before the *King's Bounty,* giving them precious time to explore St. Helena. Cianda felt it essential that they orient themselves with the layout of the town. Too many unexpected narrow escapes in the past had taught

293

her to familiarize herself with her surroundings in daylight before attempting to negotiate them in the nighttime shadows.

St. Helena welcomed passengers from homeward-bound vessels anchored for supplies and repairs inland to spend time and money locally during their wait. To the east, north and west of the narrow valley where Jamestown lay, perpendicular cliffs of volcanic rock towered skyward like the walls of a Gothic cathedral. The natives, largely freed slaves of African descent, introduced the small company of visitors to their beautiful lace and drawn-thread work.

Cianda retained the servant long enough to help them unpack and fold back the beds. She and Beatrice helped each other undo the fastenings of their gowns. Cianda hesitated, then left the Rajput emerald around her neck, the jewel nested between her breasts.

Beatrice slid under the cool linen sheets with a sigh of pure pleasure. "Ahhh, a bed that doesn't move. Yes, I shall sleep well tonight."

As often as they traveled together, Cianda always envied Beatrice's ability to fall asleep in any environment. Cianda could never sleep soundly unless she was safely in her own bed in familiar London.

"I only have one question," Beatrice said, snuggling against the down pillow with a slight yawn. "You aren't intending to leave me to fend for myself again, as you did in Cayeux-sur-mer, are you? I don't fancy having to depend on Zak and Fred for passage home."

"No, certainly not," Cianda laughed. "That was a highly irregular situation."

"And this is normal?"

"Nothing we do is normal." Cianda lay down on her own bed. "Good night, Bea."

Cianda tried to let the soft song of the ocean and the light breeze from the open windows soothe her to sleep.

For nearly an hour, she wrestled to and fro, but her thoughts and her aching body refused to give her any peace. She longed for a soak in a cool bath. But it was far too late to have one drawn.

Still . . . Cianda suddenly remembered Drake mentioning the island was rich in natural springs; he had pointed out a natural pool nestled into a hill a short walk from the back of the inn. The night was uncommonly hot, even for summer in the temperate island climate, and on a whim, Cianda decided to venture outside to search for the pool and perhaps soak her tender feet.

Moving quietly so as not to disturb Beatrice, she pulled on a thin wrapper and tiptoed out the French doors. The doors led her onto a small patio and out into a circular compound. A drift of wind lifted the edge of her wrap, fluttering the soft silk against her legs. Feet bare, she padded up a walkway, with each step relishing the feel of bare earth between her toes. At the end of the path, illuminated by the silvery starlit glow, her eyes traced the lava rock perimeter of the pool.

Cianda sat on the edge, letting her fingers play in the cool, gurgling water. The water ran through her splayed fingers, tempting her to abandon decorum and drench her whole body.

Why not? Who will know?

Tossing her wrapper on a rock, she quickly twisted her chemise to the top of her thighs and dipped first one toe, then her whole foot into the smooth, swirling water. The heated ache left her leg in a ripple of cool pleasure. With a sigh of relief, Cianda stepped over the low edge of the pool and waded into the center.

The water rose to just under her breasts, painting her thin shift to her body. Feeling almost wicked in her delight, she walked farther into the pool, finally sinking to her chin in its welcoming embrace.

Lost in the delicious feeling, Cianda didn't see the tall figure move into the shadows near the pool.

Stopping still under a nearby banana tree, Drake's eyes feasted on her body as she arched back into the water, her hair spilling silver onto the surface of the pool.

Golden moonlight danced over her ivory skin. Tiny droplets of water clung to her bare limbs, enveloping her in a glistening halo. In the coolness, her nipples hardened and the wet, clinging shift left little to his memory of her. Every graceful, languorous motion enticed. She had transformed into his sea-born sprite again, luring him with each sensual arch and sway.

Drake wanted to touch her, to lose himself in the delights of her sweet flesh.

He ought to walk away. She was trouble. More than he'd ever bargained for.

Cianda scooped her hands into the water, held them up to the stars and let it drizzle down her arms and between her full, pointed breasts. The water trickled against the glimmer of emerald and gold exposed by the low neckline of her chemise. The moonlight struck sparks of stolen fire on the surface of the gem.

He shouldn't want her.

He had to have her.

Against reason, against every warning instinct, Drake strode out from the umbra into the canopy of starlight that stretched over the pool.

Cianda froze, crossing her arms over her breasts. "Who's there?"

She saw him standing at the pool's edge, legs apart, hands at his side, the familiar outline of his powerful figure. His loose white shirt hung open as if he had carelessly pulled it on as an afterthought. The breeze ruffled his hair, over-long after the weeks at sea, and the suggestion of a beard darkened his jaw. He looked as she'd first seen

296

him, the pirate captain who had boldly taken her captive.

A small tremor, part joy, part anticipation, part fear, shot through her veins. "Drake," she said, her voice a breath of sound.

They stared at each other for a timeless moment, each hopelessly ensnared by an enchantment born of desire and moonlight.

"I went to your room. You were gone," Drake finally murmured, feeling strangely uncertain, off-balance. The sound of his name on her lips left him shaken by a surge of disquieting emotion. Emotion he didn't need or want.

It angered him that a woman, this woman, should have the power to so thoroughly disturb him. Restless with a need he didn't want to name, Drake sat down at the edge of the pool, cupping a palm full of water and letting it slip through his fingers.

Cianda watched him with hungry eyes. The night sketched him in hard lines of black and gray. Slowly, forgetting her fear and doubt, she walked through the water to his side. She reached up trembling fingers to brush a heavy wave back from his brow. As she did, Drake caught her palm and brought it against his mouth, kissing the hollow of her hand.

His piercing gaze held her with a look so burning, so intense, Cianda nearly glanced away. The emotion struck her as both angry and wanting. And perhaps, between them, the difference between the two was hard to define.

"Damn it, Cianda." Drake turned away, then back, his hands dropping to grip her shoulders. The heat of his touch through the thin cotton of her damp chemise seared like a fiery brand, marking his possession on her soul. "I must be insane to want you like this." He slid one hand down between her breasts, spreading his fingers over both the emerald and her soft flesh. "I can't think of anything else but wanting you."

"Then we're both mad," Cianda whispered, reaching up to curl her fingers around his neck. Laying her head on his heart, she breathed the earthy scent of him, rubbing her face against the soft mat of hair on his chest.

Drake wound his fingers into her hair and drew her head slowly back to look at her face. As their gazes locked, he saw her eyes blazed with mindless desire that matched his. "It won't change what I am. What I have to do."

"I know," Cianda said, her voice soft and steady. "I know. But tonight I can pretend it doesn't matter."

"And tomorrow . . . ?" Drake's mouth brushed hers with each word.

"Tomorrow may not come. If we make tonight last forever." Without giving him time to think, Cianda kissed him with the wild abandonment he had taught her in the midst of the summer storm. Shoving aside his shirt, she matched her softness to his strength, seducing him into joining her in loving away, for a few stolen hours, despite the obstacles between them.

She felt hesitation leave him and passion take its place. Briefly disengaging from her embrace, Drake kicked aside his boots, and stripped his trousers from his legs, dropping them in a forgotten heap beside the pool.

As he stepped in the cool water, Cianda sucked in a breath. He was magnificent. She ran her fingertips over the hard muscles rippling beneath his bronzed chest and shoulders. Her fingertips drifted down the center of his flat stomach, glancing over his hard shaft. She stroked him gently, loving the feel of him in her hands. He was beautiful—strong and dangerous. Her pulse throbbed. The water melted on her skin like liquid fire.

Drake moaned softly. Avid to touch her bared skin in return, he slipped urgent hands up under her wet shift, skimming the sides of her breasts as he pulled it over her head, leaving her clad only in the emerald. When Cianda raised her arms to allow him to strip her of the clinging material, Drake gently shackled her wrists with one hand.

Her sensual stretch lifted her breasts for his touch. With his free hand, Drake cupped her full flesh in his palm, massaging the sensitive crest with his thumb. The jewel drew cool patterns on his skin; the feel and scent of her burned. He watched as her head fell backward, her lips parted, her breath quickening with his.

If only his longing for her could be sated in one night, in a hundred nights of pleasure. But he knew better. She'd blazed a path deeper than flesh and desire, straight to the heart he thought he'd locked away forever.

What was he doing? Why torture himself tasting the forbidden, when instead of satisfying his hunger, she only left him starving, ravenous for more?

Abruptly he released her, letting his hands fall away.

Cianda slowly raised her head, her emerald eyes clouded with passion. "What is it? What's wrong?"

"We're wrong. All wrong."

"Don't you believe in the destiny of lovers?" she murmured, echoing his own words back at him. She smiled faintly, the gesture teasing, yet touched with sadness.

All too clearly Drake remembered the moment he last spoke them. "I—" He raked a shaking hand through his hair. "I don't know what I believe anymore."

"I'm not asking for promises you can't keep. Only for tonight. Just believe for tonight." Cianda reached up and guided his mouth to hers. Tomorrow be damned. She needed him now, needed to feel the spine-shattering power of their joining. Wanted him for whatever stolen moments she could believe he was hers.

Drake's desire pressed hard and hot against the soft curls between her thighs. He crushed her to him, plunging his tongue deeper and deeper into her honeyed mouth, his body succumbing to the demanding pace of their shared passion.

Cianda clung to him, rocked in his embrace. This was more than passion. It was something desperate and driven, insisting on culmination. She wrapped her leg around his thigh to bring him closer. Drake's tongue flicked down her chin and neck, his mouth searing a trail to her breasts to suckle one taut peak.

Leaning back to encourage his tender assault, Cianda dug her fingers into the hard muscles of his back. She forgot how even to breathe, gasping as the pleasure built, layer upon layer of blinding, racing sensation, until she nearly begged for release.

Drake, as if answering her silent plea, slid his hands behind her thighs, lifting her legs to wrap them around his waist. Holding her with one arm, he slipped his hand between their bodies and into the core of her desire, stroking and probing until Cianda cried out in sweet agony.

Gripping him tightly, she opened her eyes to his. "I need you. So much . . ."

"More than I have words to tell you," Drake whispered.

"Then love me," she urged. "Love me."

Always. No matter how many times I tell myself it isn't true. The thought struck him as he thrust inside her, joining them now, forever.

Her small, incoherent cry spurred him to push faster, hotter, riding the tremors of pleasure that strengthened with each rock of her body. His need to possess her drove him into a frenzied rhythm, commanded by desire.

Around them, the waters of the pool surged in time with their lovemaking. Diamond-bright droplets mingled with the sultry dew of passion, slicking their skin.

Craving the ecstasy Drake promised, Cianda matched his motion, shuddering moans of delight slipping from her lips. Each time he loved her, the fire raged hotter, the feeling intensified, more exciting, dangerous, more exalting than she believed possible.

"Cianda, my love." Drake's voice came hurried and hot in her ear just as Cianda reached the final peak of desire and the world exploded in a consuming, swift fulfillment.

Still joined together, they slid low into the cooling water. She panted against his chest, listening to the agitated beat of his heart, the only voice between them.

Cianda longed to tell him she loved him. Looking straight into his eyes, she longed to convince him that her feelings for him were the only reality she knew.

Yet it would only make their inevitable parting more painful. Perhaps he did care for her—but love? How many women had he loved like this? Even if, impossibly, he could give her his heart, she knew their conflicting stakes in Godfrey's game would eventually poison any feeling he had for her.

They had no tomorrow.

Drake absently rubbed his palm over her back, wishing he could promise her more than one night's passion. But how, when he had no guarantee she wouldn't bolt, jewels in hand, the moment the *Ferret* docked back in London. Jamie was all that mattered to her; she would sacrifice Drake without second thought if it came to a choice. He had no delusions.

In his arms, Cianda shivered. "I should take you back to your bed." He eased her away from him, lifting her out of the pool.

When she wrinkled her nose at her soaked clothing, Drake picked up his discarded shirt, wrapping it around her. "I've become rather fond of seeing you dressed in my clothes," he said with a teasing smile.

Pulling on his trousers and boots, he took her hand in his and they walked in silence back to the French doors leading into Cianda's room.

They stopped in the shadows near the doors, hands touching.

"What will you do—afterward?" Drake finally asked.

"Does it matter?"

"I want to know."

Cianda stiffened, drawing her hand from his. "I'm a survivor. Remember? If I survived the Devil's Acre, I will survive whatever end this escapade brings us to. And you, Drake Weston." Whirling about, Cianda strode into her room, firmly shutting the doors behind her.

"That's what scares me the most about you, love," Drake said, staring at the closed doors. "You may survive me, but will I be able to say the same?"

The next afternoon, Robert Barrett-Shaw sent word inviting Drake, his bride, and their guests to tea aboard the *King's Bounty*. As the sailor manning the skiff rowed out over James Bay harbor toward the impressive three-decker, Cianda clapped a hand to her hat to keep from losing it to the wind.

"I'm looking forward to meeting your brother finally," Cianda said to Drake, raising her voice to be heard over the rush of water slapping the sides of the small boat.

"You shouldn't be. He won't be eager to meet you," Drake returned with undisguised bitterness.

He treated her with distant politeness today, more often than not finding ways to avoid even looking her direction. Cianda tried to mirror his cool demeanor, yet couldn't quite banish a lingering and hurtful disappointment. *What did you expect? You made it clear one night was all you wanted.*

Except, in truth, she wanted so much more.

"Well, at least Admiral Barrett-Shaw sounds like a pleasant gentleman," Beatrice put in.

"Don't let his easy manner fool you," Zak said. "He's sharp as a dagger's blade."

"You may rest assured, Mister Zak, I am quite capable of measuring people's worth for myself."

"I don't doubt it. I just hope you're as good an actress as your partner."

Cianda didn't miss Zak's narrowed glance in her direction as the skiff pulled alongside the *King's Bounty*. She ignored him, reaching to take the hand of one of several sailors who waited to escort the small party aboard. A distinguished older man Cianda recognized at once by his uniform as Admiral Barrett-Shaw, stood a few feet behind the sailors. A pillar of a man, he towered a full head above every other man except Drake. The two men met at eye level. His hair was a light almond color with streaks of gray at the temples. Everything in his straight-shouldered stance spoke of refinement, and pride in himself and his position.

As Drake led her toward him, the admiral doffed his hat and she felt his appraising eye, as though she were his daughter-in-law and not merely a good friend's bride. Old insecurities urged her to run and hide like a frightened child. But, as always, she managed to bury her fear. Lifting her chin, she walked toward the waiting captain, practiced grace and confidence in every motion.

"Robert, good to see you," Drake said, taking his friend's hand in a strong grip. Turning to Cianda, he wrapped his fingers around her elbow and led her a step forward. "Allow me to present my wife, Cianda. And these are our guests, Zachariah and Beatrice—"

Before Drake gave a last name, Zak stuck out his hand. "The pleasure is ours, Admiral," he said quickly.

From the corner of her eye, Cianda saw Beatrice glance at Zak with a raised brow and silently mouth "Zachariah?"

303

Zak glared back at her, thrusting his hands in the pockets of his coat.

"Welcome aboard, all." Tucking his hat under his arm, Admiral Barrett-Shaw lifted both of Cianda's hands in his, his eyes grazing over her with open appreciation. A slow smile spread across his face. "Well, by George, you finally found yourself a *real* lady, my boy. You must be a saint to tie yourself to this man for the rest of your life," he said to Cianda with a wink.

Cianda laughed. "I daresay I'll be one by the time I've lived out my life with him."

Admiral Barrett-Shaw laughed with her, a full, robust sound that warmed and cheered Cianda. "Come, let me introduce you to our honored guest, Sir John Lawrence. He is the royal escort for the Koh-i-noor. An interesting fellow."

Drake's hand touched Cianda's waist as they followed the admiral. "I'd hoped you brought Amanda along. Since you spent so many months in India, I assumed she'd be with you."

"This time you're without an ally, Drake. Amanda's sister fell ill just before we were ready to leave England. She will be disappointed to have missed meeting your bride. Perhaps you'll have time to pay her a visit when you return to London."

"Of course." Drake paused. "And Charles?" He attempted to keep his tone casual, but Cianda felt the sudden tension in his hand.

"He is aboard, yes," the admiral said, frowning slightly. "I believe he is in the coach just now. I didn't tell him about your arrival. I thought, after Italy . . ." He let the sentence trail off.

"My wife, for whatever reason, is anxious to meet her new relation," Drake said tightly.

"Not all that anxious, darling." Cianda regretted eve

304

mentioning Charles Weston's name. She turned to the admiral, smiling. "If it wouldn't be too much of an intrusion, I should like to see your glorious ship before tea."

"Why, there's absolutely nothing I'd rather do, if you ladies are certain such a tour wouldn't bore you."

"Certainly not," Beatrice put in. "I simply adore sailing."

Cianda glanced over her shoulder in time to see Zak elbow Beatrice in the ribs. "Oh yes," Zak said. "Beatrice is quite the sailor. In fact, I may have to sell my home so we can spend our lives on board ship, traversing the Atlantic."

To avert an argument between the pair of them, Cianda took the admiral's arm, plying him with questions about the *King's Bounty*. To anyone listening, her queries sounded like innocent curiosity. But Cianda carefully noted the admiral's response, learning critical details about the ship and its layout.

Admiral Barrett-Shaw led the group up to the poop deck to gaze out across the rest of the ship, pointing out structural improvements in the deck beams and hulls of his ship with pride, all the while introducing them to officers and crew members who approached him with questions or comments.

After a leisurely perusal of the topside, the admiral ushered them into the coach. Inside, his back to them, a man sat at a large round table pouring over a pile of papers.

"Ah, Charles, I thought we might find you here." Cianda heard the note of forced heartiness on the admiral's voice. He looked to Drake, concern in his eyes.

Charles Weston pushed out of his chair and turned to face them. His eyes, a pale gray-blue, locked with Drake's fathomless cobalt depths. The resemblance was keen—the same straight, narrow nose, high cheeks and strong jaw. But overall, Charles appeared to Cianda to be a thin, diluted version of his arrestingly handsome younger brother. Perhaps Charles realized early on he could never compete with Drake in physical appearance, and hence the bad blood between them.

"This is certainly unexpected," Charles said at last. He turned to the admiral, his expression icy. "You didn't tell me my brother was planning to visit."

"You'll forgive me Charles, but it was hardly your business. Drake and his wife are on a wedding trip, and as St. Helena was one of their stops, I asked them to my ship." The admiral put slight emphasis on his last two words.

Charles glared at him a moment before turning his attention back to Drake. "I hadn't heard of your marriage."

"No?" Drake smiled, a dangerous twist of his mouth reflecting the glint in his eyes. "I can't imagine why."

"This must be my new sister-in-law." Charles' eyes flicked over Cianda. He made no move forward to greet her.

"Cianda, my brother Charles," Drake said. "You see, he's as charming as I told you."

An angry flush stained Charles's face. "And you are as arrogant and uncivilized as always. If you did indeed marry him," he said to Cianda, "then you're either a fool or madder than he is."

Fists clenched, Drake started forward, the swift fury etched on his face leaving no doubt of his intention.

Zak caught his shoulder, pulling him back. "Not here, old chap."

"I think it's best if we move on," Admiral Barrett-Shaw said quietly, moving his imposing figure between Drake and his brother.

For a moment, Cianda feared Drake might damn the consequences despite the intervention of his friends. He looked murderous. Charles had backed up a few steps, his face pale.

306

"This time," Drake said at last. "This time." Whipping around, he stalked out of the room.

Cianda followed him outside to where he stood gripping the railing. Tentatively, she touched his shoulder. 'Drake—?"

"I want this over with. Now."

"I do, too. I wish—"

Her sentence was left unfinished as they were joined by Beatrice, Zak, and the admiral. They finished the tour of the *Bounty* in subdued fashion, each affected by the unsettling tension still rife in the air.

As they were leaving the admiral's quarters and filing into the gangway, a flustered man bumbled into them. "Oh, there you are Robert. My, my, I've been combing the whole bloody ship looking for you." He scratched his head, looking confused. "Only what was it I wanted . . . ? Yes, yes, I recall. Do tell, will the ball in my honor be held aboard ship or off to the governor's mansion? Not that it matters of course, but—oh, I say, you have guests."

Admiral Barrett-Shaw introduced his party to Sir John Lawrence with an indulgent smile. "We decided to have the affair on the *Bounty*. You remember, don't you, Sir John? It was your idea."

"My idea? Of course, of course."

"A ball?" Drake asked, all innocence.

"Yes, and naturally you're all invited," the admiral said.

Cianda saw a glance pass between Drake and Admiral Barrett-Shaw, and she could easily read the admiral's silent message to Drake. *As if this wasn't what you had planned all along, my friend.*

"It's to be tomorrow night," the admiral went on. "You will join us in celebrating the Company's good fortune in acquiring the Koh-i-noor, won't you?"

He knows Drake has some scheme, Cianda thought.

307

And that makes the game all the more dangerous. Drake and Robert Barrett-Shaw might be fast friends, but she doubted the admiral would approve Drake's idea to steal the Indian treasure from the admiral's own ship.

Drawing in a breath, Cianda flashed the admiral a brilliant smile. "We'd be delighted." She looked up at Drake, slipping her hand over his arm. "Simply delighted."

Chapter Seventeen

Cianda twisted to critically appraise her reflection in the long glass one last time. Part of her scoffed at her careful primping. The elegant trappings were only a tool necessary to maintain her ruse as Madame D'Rouchert, and now as Drake's wife. Tonight, though, she secretly admitted for the first time to a purely feminine desire to make Drake oblivious to every other woman at the ball.

Studying her reflection, she decided she'd chosen well. Her gown was watered silk the color of dawn, a pale silver gray with the barest hint of rose. Cut simply, it was skillfully trimmed and overlaid with gossamer white silk illusion dusted with glittering silver. Beatrice had coaxed her hair into a crown of curls, interwoven with tiny pearls attached to invisible wiring so they seemed to float.

She was twitching her skirts into a more flattering sweep when Drake rapped at the connecting door between their rooms. "Beatrice said you were finished," he began, striding into the room without waiting for her invitation.

"I am finished." Cianda turned to face him, smiling at his arrested expression. "I had thought of borrowing your shirt again, but this seemed more suitable."

Drake took both her hands in his and brushed a lingering kiss over each. "You're fetching in my shirt, but this . . ." He shook his head slightly, as if at a loss for words. "You're

309

asking the impossible of me again, expecting me to concentrate on our impending caper."

"You've managed this far. I'll simply trust in your devil's luck."

"It's talent, love, all talent. And before we go —" Taking the cloak Cianda had picked up from her hands and tossing it aside, he dipped into his coat pocket and retrieved a small gilt box. He put it in her hands, his eyes full of mischief and anticipation, saying, "It occurred to me this afternoon I never gave you a wedding gift."

"But . . ." Cianda stared down at the box, then at him. You gave me my beautiful ring."

"That was a necessity. This . . . is just because I want you to have it."

Covered with confusion, Cianda hesitantly lifted the lid. Inside, a string of creamy pearls lay nested in black silk. She slowly touched a tentative fingertip to the gems, feeling at any moment they would vanish like a dream at dawn.

"I thought you might miss having a treasure around your neck," Drake said. "I know you've stowed it safely in your reticule, but you could hardly wear your emerald."

"No," she whispered. Without warning, tears welled in her eyes, blurring the image of the jewels in her hand.

Drake gently raised her chin with his hand. "What is it?"

"Nothing. It's just that —"

"Just that . . . ?"

Unable to escape his hold, she forced herself to meet his eyes. "I've never had any jewels of my own. I didn't want to desire something I had to steal to survive. And — and it's silly but — but no one ever gave me a gift without reason." She shifted her shoulders, trying to minimize her foolish reaction to his gesture. "Either they felt an obligation, or they gave because they wanted or had something from me in return. I'm sorry. You must think —"

"— That you're the most beautiful, intriguing woman I've ever met. And I don't want anything in return except the promise you'll wear these tonight. For your own pleasure, not mine."

Unable to speak around the knot in her throat, Cianda nodded and let Drake turn her toward the mirror. Reaching around, he picked up the pearls and fastened them around her throat. As he closed the clasp, he bent and kissed the nape of her neck, making her shiver.

Her own image in the glass seemed a stranger. The reflection of an ethereal sprite, a perfect foil for the dark, handsome pirate captain at her side. *If only it were true. If only this was who I was.*

"Scowling spoils the effect," Drake said lightly. He stepped in front of the glass, blocking her view. Sliding his hands around her face, he kissed her, long and deep, stealing her breath with his fire. "Better," he murmured when he finally released her. "That hot flush is very becoming."

"Thank you so much," she muttered, torn between irritation and longing for more than just the feel of his mouth. She scooped up her dark gray cloak, tossing it over her shoulders. "Everyone will now assume I've just come from your bed."

"I have to keep my sordid reputation somehow. It isn't easy, you know, now that everyone believes I'm a respectable husband."

As they left the room, Cianda tossed a tart smile over her shoulder. "Trust me, Drake, only a fool or a madman would ever believe that of you."

The ride in the skiff out to where the *King's Bounty* was anchored was brief, but by the time Cianda and Drake arrived, the grand formal room of the ship was already filled with elegantly-clad guests, mixed among the crew in their crisp naval blue and white. Flickering light from a hundred lamps lent a flattering glow to the polished oak floors and walls, and warmed the mingled scents of a garden of perfumes. The soft strains of music from a string ensemble wove in between the surrus murmur of conversation.

311

Admiral Barrett-Shaw, heading the receiving line at the entryway, clapped Drake on the shoulder as he stepped into the room. "Well, I should have known you would be late." He winked at Cianda. "Drake always did take pleasure in flaunting convention."

"I don't enjoy boredom. It's why I married Cianda."

Cianda shot him a scowl and the captain laughed, taking her hand. "From the fire in her eyes, I would say you've met your match, Drake. Now, if you'll allow me the pleasure, I'll introduce your lovely bride to our guests."

He led her from Drake's side to introduce them both to the governor and his family, several officers, and then to a short, stout man with an air of being permanently preoccupied. "And this is our most exalted guest, Sir John Lawrence. Sir John recovered the Koh-i-noor in India. You must let him tell you the story, Cianda. Ah, Drake I see your partner has arrived."

Cianda turned to see Zak, Beatrice on his arm, stepping into the ballroom. Beatrice looked striking in the midnight blue satin Cianda chose for her, but she noted the unnatural stiffness in her friend's motions. Knowing Beatrice must feel uncomfortable among the elite who banished her, Cianda took a step toward them, intending to ease the way.

"I'd like a word with you and your partner," the captain said to Drake. "But please stay, Cianda. I'm certain Sir John will amuse you with his tales while I monopolize your husband's attention for a few moments."

Cianda and Sir John spoke simultaneously.

"Delighted, I am sure—"

"Oh, that's not necessary—"

"I'll leave you in good hands then, my dear," Drake said, tossing her a raffish smile over his shoulder as he let the captain guide him to a corner of the ballroom.

Cianda found herself alone with Sir John. He stared at her as if he'd never seen, let alone spoken with a woman before. *Damn you, Drake,* she silently cursed. *You'll regret this, I promise you.* Drawing in a breath, she mustered a polite smile, expecting Sir John to make some attempt at conversation. He didn't.

"Are you enjoying your stay on St. Helena, Sir John?" she finally said, more to break the awkward silence than because she wanted an answer.

"Enjoying . . . ?" Sir John seemed to ponder the question. "I haven't paid it all that much attention. Rather bleak spot, I'd say. And an annoyance to have all this fuss when there are so many things to be done once we are back in England. The music is rather pleasant."

"Music? Yes. Quite nice."

"Should you care to dance?"

She could hardly refuse, considering his status as honored guest, without appearing rude.

After two waltzes, Cianda began to seriously weigh the consequences of telling the exalted guest to choose some other unfortunate for a dance partner. Clumsy and unmindful of her feet, he held her too tightly, said little, and his eyes feasted on her face with the expression of a starving man offered dinner.

She firmly fended off a third turn in his arms by insisting on some refreshment. Sir John, equally insistent, volunteered to fetch a drink from one of the trays of refreshments that waiters roamed about the outskirts of the dance floor with.

Cianda was standing alone, dreading his return, when Drake's dark voice brushed her ear. "It seems I have a rival for your affections."

"Where have you been?" she hissed, whirling on him. "I've been trapped with that wretched man for nearly an hour. I can hardly steal a teaspoon, let alone the diamond, with him tied to my heels."

"Shall I run him through for you, love? I'm sure Robert has a saber lying about somewhere."

"Will you at least make an attempt to be serious? Damn.

313

He's coming back." She prodded Drake's ribs with the end of her fan. "Act your part for once and tell him you're claiming your husbandly rights."

Drake raised a brow. "Here?"

Sir John's arrival quashed Cianda's impulse to tell her *husband* just what she thought of his mockery. "Your drink, Missus Weston," he said, proffering her the glass with a little bow.

Cianda reached out to accept the glass and as she did, she glanced over Sir John's shoulder and met the eyes of a face in the throng. The cup slipped from her fingers and fell to the floor, shattering in a hundred crystal shards and splattering Sir John with champagne.

"Forgive me, Sir John. I—I . . ."

"Are you all right?" All the mischief vanished from Drake's face, replaced by sudden concern. His hand closed tight on her arm. "You're very pale."

Searching each stranger's face, Cianda felt a wash of sick fear. The one she recognized had vanished. *Gide. It couldn't be; he couldn't be here. You're letting your nerves have the best of you.*

And yet . . .

"Cianda—"

Drake shook her a little. She looked up at him, dazed for a moment, as if suddenly awakened from a dream. "What . . . ? Nothing. It's nothing. I'm fine. I'm sorry," she added quickly, smiling for Sir John. "I felt faint for a moment. Perhaps it's the heat. If you'll excuse me, I think I'll go take a little air."

Pulling away from Drake's hold, she hurriedly moved away from him, weaving into the crowd to elude him. She heard him call after her, but she ignored the urgent summons. At the far end of the ballroom, a set of long doors led to the balcony at the stern of the *King's Bounty*. Cianda slipped outside, certain this was where she had seen her phantom figure disappear. A slight wind caught the fragile silk of her skirts as she closed the door behind her, bringing with it a faint, sickly sweet scent.

Cianda wrinkled her nose. The odor stirred a memory. Where had she—?

"Bon soir chérie," a familiar voice spoke out of the shadow. "It has been a long time, *ma petite.*"

"Gide!"

The short, pudgy figure of Gide Legume stepped into the narrow glow of one of the ship's lanterns. The light swayed slightly in a drift of breeze, glinting off his sleek, dark hair. "You don't seem pleased to see your dear Uncle Gide. And when I have come all this way simply to congratulate you on your marriage. Quite an accomplishment, *chérie,* an alliance with one of the Queen's agents. Godfrey surely must be pleased."

Cianda ignored the mocking insinuation in his voice. "What are you doing here?"

"I told you—"

"You lied. Did Godfrey send you?"

Legume's face twisted into a sneer. "Hardly, *chérie.* I am, let us say, here at my own pleasure."

"The diamond."

"A worthy prize, you would agree. And the reason for your coming to this godforsaken rock. I knew Godfrey would send you here once he had the ruby and the emerald. The value of his precious idol demands he have all three. A pity you will never be able to bring him the trio, but there it is *chérie.* The best thief will win."

"Yes, I will." Cianda's cool composure slowly returned to cover her trembling shock at seeing Gide. "Even if you managed to steal the Koh-i-noor, you'll never get the Rajput or the Malwi. And Godfrey would hunt you to the ends of the earth merely for the end satisfaction of killing you slowly if he discovered you betrayed him."

"You are confident, *ma petite,* too confident. As you were in France when I nearly—"

His sentence snapped off and broke but the words were enough for Cianda. She remembered in a rush where she last smelled the same cloying cologne assaulting her nose now. "You killed the count. And then you tried to kill me. In France, in the Acre, and again at the cottage. It was you."

The little man's shoulders lifted in a shrug. "My only regret is that I did not succeed." Legume's eyes narrowed. "The fool Thorne should have trusted me from the beginning to steal the trio. Instead, he betrays me with you, a low-bred pickpocket. I taught you the skill of housebreaking. If not for me you would have ended up another whore in the Acre."

His smile was cruel when he knew his blows had struck hard.

"Perhaps you shall still end up there. What would your agent of the Crown say if I told him what you really were?"

"He would take great pleasure in slitting your throat."

Cianda whirled as Drake's voice, hard and dark with anger, answered Gide. He stood behind her, half in the shadow, half illuminated by the swaying light of the lantern. She didn't need any light to know he was roused to a volatile fury. She felt the tension in him, could smell and taste the danger.

"Ah, Captain Weston. It has been many years, has it not?" Gide's retort was flippant. The nervous twitch of his mouth was not.

"Not nearly long enough." Drake made a quick bending motion. In the next instant, Cianda saw the lantern light glint off the blade of the dagger in his hand. "And I'm going to make damn certain it's never again."

"You—you would not . . . here." Gide took a few stumbling steps backward. His back pressed against the railing.

"Drake!" Cianda caught his arm, clutching tightly. "Don't. Please—"

The fury on his face nearly crushed her courage. "Is he another bastard to whom you owe your undying loyalty?"

"It's not that!"

"Then what?"

Cianda wrenched her hand from his arm as if his flesh suddenly burned. "Go ahead then! If you're so determined to have your neck broken in a noose, don't let me stand in your way."

In the hot moment of silence, neither of them noticed the doors open and shut again behind them until Zak laid a hand on Drake's shoulder. "She has a point, old chap. The Bean is hardly worth sullying your dagger for."

For a terrifying second, Cianda believed he would defy them all and kill Gide. Then, letting go an explosive sigh, he shoved the dagger back in his boot. Stabbing Gide with a cold glare he said, "Get the hell out of here before I decide not to let someone talk me out of murder."

After the Frenchman scuttled into the darkness, out of sight, Drake pulled away from Zak's hold and stalked to the railing.

"I wish you would give me fair warning when you make a determined attempt to have yourself thrown in prison again," Zak drawled, shoving his hands deep in the pockets of his coat. Rocking back on his heels, he raised a brow at Drake's fierce glower. "You should be thanking me for rescuing you from your brief flirtation with gallantry. If I hadn't taken the notion to follow you—"

"Then we would be rid of at least one problem. Thank you so much."

"You wanted to murder the little weasel over a woman. Bad choice, old chap."

Cianda stared at Drake, a warm, sweet feeling curled in the pit of her belly despite her disquiet at Drake's brash display of temper. Was Zak right? Had he wanted to kill Gide merely to defend her honor?

The thought seemed so alien she brushed it aside as nonsense. Yet when he looked at her, the fire still kindled in his eyes, a small hope ignited in her heart. The hope he might care for more than just a few fleeting days.

Silence lay heavy between them until Drake shoved a hand through his hair and asked roughly, "What is Legume doing here?"

"I didn't invite him, if that's what you're insinuating, Captain," she snapped, fighting for her composure. "He's bitter over losing his prestigious position as Godfrey's head thief to me. Ever since France, he's been trying to thwart my plans to steal the trio. The diamond is his last chance."

"Wonderful. That's going to make this robbery of yours so much easier."

"I hate to add agony to misery," Zak put in. "But things aren't exactly going smoothly inside. Sir John Lawrence seems to have taken a fancy to you, Miss Cianda," he said, looking her up and down. Shrugging, he went on, "He's done nothing but ask about you since you vanished for some night air. Beatrice is keeping him occupied for the moment, but if you disappear again, it could be beyond our creative capacity to invent reasons why. Especially if the Koh-i-noor conveniently vanishes in your absence."

Cianda heaved an exasperated sigh, her fingers curling and uncurling the handles of her reticule. "Damn. I don't have time nor the inclination to appease him. It's getting late and this grand ball can't last forever."

"Then we don't have a choice," Drake said shortly.

"We can't abandon the robbery," Cianda cried. "Not now. We may not have a better chance and—"

"I have no intention of abandoning the plan."

Zak rolled his eyes, shaking his head. "Must you say it aloud?"

"Say what?" Cianda looked from one man to the other, then fixed Drake with a hard stare. "Exactly what do you have in mind?"

"Well, since you can't go through with it without endangering the plan and all of us in the bargain, that leaves—"

"No. Absolutely not."

"That leaves me." His reckless, daredevil smile matched the dangerous glint in his eyes. "Come now, milady thief, how difficult could it be? Beatrice can still tag along, hand me the proper tools and provide instructions, if that will ease your mind."

"It doesn't," Cianda said flatly, crossing her arms in front of her.

"Then I suppose you'll just have to trust my infamous luck. We don't have any other choice."

"There's always another choice. You just prefer to choose the most insane, risky, and improbable one."

Zak gave a derisive snort. "Are you just now figuring that out?"

"Do you have a better idea, Missus Weston?"

"I —" Cianda faltered, desperate scrabbling amongst her thoughts for some sensible alternative.

"I didn't think so." Drake's expression was smug. "It seems it's settled then. Tonight, I'm going to play the part of the Masked Marauder."

"Was it necessary for both of you come along? This will be difficult enough."

Drake glanced at Beatrice, her mouth set in a disapproving line. "Robert is hardly going to leave his cabin unattended considering the treasure he has tucked in his safe. Besides — " He nudged Zak in the ribs with an elbow. "Zak is occasionally useful when it comes to creating a distraction. With any luck, we should be in and out in minutes."

Zak, loping slightly ahead of them down the darkened gangway, ignored the jibe. Beatrice raised a brow. "You'll need more than luck to use a petter-cutter quietly and effectively. It takes considerable experience. Experience none of us have."

"I'm a fast learner."

"If you open a safe as smoothly as you make promises, I

won't doubt it." Before Drake could think of a return, Beatrice reached for Zak's sleeve and pulled him up short. "The cabin is just ahead. And there is a watch — one man only. We will have to be on guard for the regular watch, also."

"Lovely," Zak muttered. With a shrug, he dug his hands in his pockets and started toward the cabin door. "Best get this done with."

"I wish this weren't necessary," Beatrice whispered as Zak approached the guard.

"Zak can take care of himself," Drake began, then realized from Beatrice's pained expression she thought his partner intended to use force to get past the watch. He choked on a laugh, keeping his voice low. "Don't worry. Zak might lacerate him with sarcasm, but that's all. He never gets close enough to a confrontation to have to avoid it."

As if on cue, Zak and the guard strolled away from the door, moving up the gangway, deep in conversation.

Drake, silently congratulating his partner's verbal prowess, slipped silently up the narrow corridor to the cabin entrance.

With a quick look around, Beatrice reached under the folds of her voluminous cloak and removed a picklock from Cianda's black bag.

Drake turned it over in his hand once before sliding it inside the lock. He cursed as the slim metal rod caught fast against the delicate mechanism of the lock. Metal scraped metal as he slid the rod out and then slipped it back into the narrow opening.

"Quietly," Beatrice cautioned. "You have to coax it inside, then move it slowly until you find the correct location."

Drake focused on her instruction and was rewarded with a soft click as the lock gave way to the persuasion of the rod. "I think I've got the hang of it," he told her triumphantly.

"You've only started, Captain. We've a lot of work ahead of us yet." She reached out and eased open the door, her hand arresting on the handle when the sound of voices and

heavy footsteps sounded in the gangway. "Hurry. Inside."
Both slipped inside the cabin.

"Where's Jeffers?" a growling voice demanded just the other side of the door.

"Probably off catchin' a wink when 'e thinks the cap'n ain't lookin'. Let's try the sail locker. 'E's sure t' be there. Sir John's bloody rock is safe enough in the cap'n's safe."

Drake let go a long breath as the two sailors moved away. More than ever, he admired the patience and cool nerves Cianda must rely upon each time she willingly stepped into danger's embrace.

Beatrice gently nudged him out of his reverie. "They're gone, thank heaven." Moving away from him, she fumbled in the dark for a moment. Suddenly, the room lit up with a tiny spot of light, no bigger than a shilling. "It's a dark lantern," she explained. "It becomes terribly hot, but it's safer than working with the large lanterns. We can focus it on the safe."

"I didn't know I'd be working blind. How does Cianda manage?"

"Her fingers see more than her eyes. It took her years to develop that talent. You have—" she glanced at the watch she carried, "—approximately two minutes." Reaching into the bag again, she pulled out a complicated contraption and slapped it into his hands.

Drake eyed the tool with a dawning sense of being far out of his element. Picking locks was one thing. But this—"It looks like some sort of drill."

"Clamp it over the keyhole. You must hurry," Beatrice chided as he fumbled with the unfamiliar tool. "It won't take them long to realize Mr. Jeffers isn't in the sail locker."

"Damn. This blasted thing—" Drake cursed the petter-cutter. "Can't I just stick a jemmy into it and have it done with?"

"Captain, please. This is difficult enough as it is. If you would just set your impatience aside for a few minutes and

take a little care, this will be much better for both of us."
Drawing a deep breath, Beatrice pointed to the key points of
the lock. "Put it there, and then tighten it. Like that.
There—you have it. Finally."

"Thanks for the compliment," Drake grumbled. "I suppose Cianda would have had the bloody thing attached by
now."

"Cianda would have had the safe open, the diamond in
hand and been back dancing at the ball by now."

"Jolly good for her. What now?"

"You should be able to apply leverage to the cutter. It will
bite a small opening over the lock, and then you can attempt
to get past the wards and open the lock."

Drake pushed against the petter-cutter. The cutter ground
against the metal of the safe, emitting a loud *scritching*
noise.

Beatrice closed her eyes in frustration. "Captain—"

"Don't say it." *If a wisp of a woman can do this, so can
you,* he berated himself. *She'll never let you forget it if you
don't.* As he struggled to use the cutter quietly, Drake vowed
never again to underestimate Cianda's skills, however illicit
they might be. "She must be a witch to be able to get this
damned thing to do more than just groan and screech."

"It's coming," Beatrice urged. "Just a little more and
you'll be finished. If the watch doesn't decide to return before then."

"Did anyone ever tell you what an optimist you are, Miss
Dobson?" With a final push and shove, the cutter finally cooperated. "There!"

"Now the lock. Do hurry."

Drake twisted a picklock into the small opening and at
last managed to overcome the lock. He jerked open the door
of the small safe just as Zak's raised voice sounded outside
the cabin.

"Seems a bloody shame to be tied to watching a locked
door all through the night. Sure you won't come for just one

322

pint, Jeffers?"

Jeffers response was muffled, but Drake had no trouble understanding Zak's warning. Reaching inside the safe, he yanked out a smallish, silver box, embossed with the Queen's seal.

"Open it, anyway" Beatrice ordered, as she hurriedly doused the dark lantern and began shoving tools back into the bag.

"It's got the seal. Why—?"

"Open it. You don't know for certain. Cianda always checks to be sure we retrieve what we came for."

Drake gave the box a shake. He reached into his pocket for the fake diamond to leave in place of the Koh-i-noor. His pocket was empty. "Damn! I left the other one with Cianda."

"Amature," Beatrice muttered. "Well, there's nothing to be done about it now, is there? Just open the box, anyway to be certain, then we can leave."

"Trust me. It's in here," Drake said, thrusting it into his jacket pocket. The voices outside the door became more distinct and Drake realized Jeffers had moved back to his assigned post.

"I wouldn't worry about what Cianda does with boxes about now," he whispered close to Beatrice's ear. "You better start telling me how she gets around doors with guards in front of them." He looked at her, half expectant, half resigned to her probable reply.

Beatrice stared back with her usual placid expression. "I am afraid for that answer, Captain Weston, you're on your own."

"Where are they?"

"Excuse me, my dear? Did you ask me something?"

Cianda hastily crafted a smile for Sir John, realizing she'd spoken her worries aloud. "No, nothing. I was merely wondering why the musicians were taking so long to return. I was looking forward to the next dance."

Sir John beamed on her. "I'll go and see about it, shall I?"

"Do take your time," Cianda muttered under her breath as he walked away. With a sigh, she turned to find a secluded corner to retreat to and nearly collided with Gide Legume.

"You appear worried, *chérie*," he taunted softly, a sneer pulling at his mouth. "Perhaps you would care to confide in your Oncle Gide."

Cianda met his mockery with cool disdain. "I'm surprised you found the courage to show your face in the light, Gide. If my husband were to find you here —"

"Ah, but he will not. We both know he is busy elsewhere." Gide shook his head. "I am disappointed. I had prided myself on having taught you the best of my skills. Yet you send your lover to do your work. A fatal error. He will not succeed. Even now, he has put himself and his companions into a fine stew." He rubbed his hands together, smiling. "He will be caught and then you will be exposed to all these fine friends of yours as the fraud you are. A pity. You play the role so well. But all games must end, no?"

Determined to maintain her impenetrable facade, Cianda said haughtily, "The only thing more detestable than your company is your conceit. I should have let Drake slit your throat when he had the chance." Raking him with a contemptuous glance, she twitched her skirts up and swept past him.

She wore her arrogant demeanor like a shield until she was certain he was out of his vision. Only then did she let worry and apprehension surge to the surface.

It had been far too long. Even without Gide's taunting revelation, she knew Drake and Beatrice must have met with trouble. Her stomach clenched, but she forced calm into her thoughts. Panic would only confuse matters. She had to think of something. Absently, she lifted her fingertips to rub at her temples, only to be knocked in the ear by the weight of

324

the reticule dangling from her wrist. She froze. The fake diamond. It was in her reticule instead of in Drake's pocket!

"There you are my dear." Sir John strolled up to her, taking her hand and tucking it in his arm before she could protest. "The musicians are back and I have asked them to play a favorite of mine. You will honor me with this dance, won't you?"

Cianda murmured a vague assent, her mind whirling as she allowed him to lead her to the dance floor. She couldn't wile the hours dancing with this fop not knowing where Drake and Beatrice were. Even Zak had disappeared.

Her mind consumed with considering and discarding possible plans of action, Cianda failed to take notice of where Sir John's feet were. In their previous dances, she had managed to keep him from trampling her by being quick on her own feet. Now, distracted by her dilemma, she made an awkward move.

Sir John stumbled over the toe of her slipper and fell forward against her. Cianda put out her hands to ward his body away from hers and in the process, her fingers caught against a large, hard shape.

For a moment, her hand froze in embarrassment. Until she realized the object she touched was egg-shaped and very hard. Diamond hard.

Maintaining the pretense of being shaken by his fall, Cianda encouraged Sir John's effusive apologies, keeping one hand fluttering against his ruffled shirt front, while the other swiftly found the edge of his jacket pocket.

"Oh, Sir John, I do hope you are not injured." She could hear the sweet plea in her voice as if it came from the lips of a stranger.

A quick motion. In, out, cupped in the palm, into the reticule. Maisie's lessons repeated themselves over in her mind.

Her fingers dipped into his pocket. She touched the cool faceted surface of the jewel. The thrill of stolen fire raced over her skin.

"Do let me help you, Sir John."

One more moment of distraction. Just one more moment.

The diamond slid into the cradle of her palm. Her hand slipped out of his pocket.

"My handkerchief. I feel quite warm."

Cianda nimbly dropped the diamond into her reticule, fumbling for a moment on the pretense of retrieving her handkerchief. As she did, she switched the real gem in her hand for Drake's paste replica.

Patting Sir John's coat sleeve again in a gesture of concern, she managed to drop the fraudulent diamond unobtrusively into his pocket.

The entire process had taken less than a minute.

With a brilliant smile, she stepped back, pressing her handkerchief to her face to hide her triumphant smile. "I do believe I need a little air. If you will excuse me, Sir John."

She was gone before he could refuse.

Cianda took her prize to the solitude of the open quarterdeck. Glancing about her, she drew it out of her bag and nested it in her palm, letting the lantern light fleck it with gold. She caught her breath.

The Koh-i-noor. Jamie's freedom.

Victory felt exhilarating, a rush of fiery, intense pleasure.

That lasted all of ten seconds.

Cianda stuffed the diamond back in her reticule with a fierce thrust. Her success was an unexpected gem. Except for one ugly, glaring flaw.

Drake was at this moment trying to steal something she already had.

Chapter Eighteen

Drake stood with an ear to the door of the Admiral's quarters listening to Zak's last attempts to woo Jeffers away from his post. He heard the edge in his partner's voice—not growing desperation, but annoyance. Zak never panicked. He got exasperated at futility and walked away.

He was sure to come up with another plan, but Drake didn't have the time to spare.

Thinking fast, he turned to Beatrice. "Give me your cloak."

It was the first time he had seen a look of incredulity mar the serenity of her features. "My cloak?"

"Quickly," he whispered, gesturing impatiently. "The bag, too." Beatrice thrust the items at him as if he were a madman she didn't want to get too near. Drake flung the voluminous cloak on his shoulders, drawing the loose hood over his head. He took a swift glance around the room. "The closet. Get in and stay there until either Zak or I give the word."

"The closet—? Captain Weston!"

"I don't have time to argue the matter, Miss Dobson." Taking her firmly by the arm, he pushed her inside the narrow space in between several hanging uniform jackets.

"Cianda isn't going to be pleased."

"She'll be less pleased if I let you get arrested as an accomplice to the Masked Marauder."

"If this idea is anything as well thought out as the rest of

327

your schemes, you'll be the one in irons, Captain."

"It won't be the first time." With a flash of his rakehell grin, Drake tipped her a mocking salute and closed the door on Beatrice's disapproving grimace.

Beatrice safely stowed, Drake stuffed Cianda's bag under the cover of his borrowed cloak and took one long, last look at the barrier of the door. "Get ready partner," he told an unsuspecting Zak. "The Masked Marauder is about to make a fast exit."

He took two strides backward, squared his shoulders, and hit the door at a run. The combination of his weight and momentum flung it outward. It smacked into Jeffers, sending him flying into Zak. The two ended in a tangle of flailing arms and legs.

Drake grabbed the advantage of confusion. Swerving sharply to avoid the two men, he dashed toward the closest companionway out to the quarterdeck, his cloak flying out behind him.

"It's 'im!" he heard Jeffers shout from behind. "It's the Masked Marauder! 'E's stolen the diamond!' "

"Not quite yet," Drake muttered through gritted teeth. He made a quick dodge around a corner and pulled up sharp. He couldn't go galloping around the ship carrying a king's ransom in stolen diamond under his arm. And if he didn't return to the ball soon, someone was certain to notice his absence. The only solution was to hide the bag and box until he could safely retrieve them.

He scoured the deck for a safe spot to secrete his stolen treasure away, weighing pros and cons of each idea in rapid-fire form. His head throbbed. And then, suddenly the solution seemed so simple. He threw his brief attempt at logic overboard and gave a quick scan skyward. A million bright diamonds shone against a black satin backdrop. Fair weather was a promise luck was guiding his choice. "Where else for this gem of stolen fire?" he whispered, then darted straight to the sail locker.

A chaotic chorus of voices and footsteps erupted in the companionway below. Drake jerked open the door and stuffed the box with the diamond in Cianda's bag, then shoved it under several layers of cloth. He wrenched off Beatrice's cloak and pushed it over the top of his cache and closed the door on the lot.

Drake drew a long breath, combed his fingers through his ruffled hair, and straightened his jacket. He sauntered to the railing, leaning against it in apparent unconcern just as two sailors and Jeffers burst onto the quarterdeck, followed closely by a rumpled Zak.

"Did ye see 'im, sir?" Jeffers cried.

"Him?" Drake turned slowly, as if drawn from a deep reverie. "Who? Is something wrong?"

"The Masked Marauder! 'E's stolen the diamond from the Admiral's safe! Couldna' been more than five minutes past. Are ye sure ye didn't see anyone, sir?"

Drake appeared to consider the matter, avoiding the sardonic expression in Zak's eyes. "A man in a cloak hurried past a few moments ago. I'm afraid I didn't pay him much mind. I thought perhaps he was anxious to breathe freely. It's terribly cramped below. Why, I came up for a bit of air myself."

"That 'ad ter be 'im," Jeffers said grimly. " 'E can't be far." Turning to the sailors, he motioned them ahead. "Ye go on. Call up every hand. I'll go and tell the Admiral. 'E's goin' ter be bloody red-faced, 'e is, ter say nothin' of Sir John and Lord Weston."

Shaking his head dolefully, Jeffers moved off toward the ballroom.

"Next time you decide to turn yourself into a battering ram," Zak drawled as he stepped up the railing, "you might have the courtesy to inform me."

"If you had kept your guard friend occupied a little longer, I could have spared myself the pain. As it is, I had to leave Beatrice ensconced in a closet. She ought to be about as delightful as Maisie's stewed rhubarb by now.

"Ready to run you through. She did manage to slip out when I joined our friend Jeffers on the hunt for you, old chap. I'll do my duty and escort her back to the ball in due time."

"Which is where I should be," Drake said, clapping a hand to Zak's shoulder.

"One question. You did get the bloody diamond, didn't you?"

Drake nodded to the sail locker. "It'll keep until we can extricate ourselves from watchful eyes."

"You hope."

"I know."

Zak raised a brow. "You have a plan?"

"Of course not," Drake said, grinning. "But trust me. I'll think of something."

Cianda knew from the dark expression on Admiral Barrett-Shaw's face the worst had happened.

I should never have let Drake attempt the robbery. Yet, the silent recrimination posed a devil's dilemma. If she had done the work herself, she never would have discovered the Koh-i-noor in Sir John's pocket. She would have left St. Helena empty-handed.

But her friends, her lover, would be safe.

Fidgeting with the handle of her reticule, Cianda chased around several alternate plans in her mind, seizing and discarding them as too risky or impossible. She was verging on tossing caution to the wind and trying anything even vaguely reasonable when Drake strolled through the door of the ballroom.

She blinked. He looked impossibly dashing, wearing his cocky smile and a smug air of assurance. Cianda's emotions warred between an ecstasy of relief and a surge of hot-blooded anger.

Drake walked up to her, still smiling, and took her hand. He brushed a light kiss over her palm before tucking her fingers over his arm. "Miss me, love?"

"Miss you? I thought you —" Cianda stopped, gathering up her wits. "Where have you been? What went wrong?"

"What makes you think anything went wrong?"

She gave an exasperated sigh. "Admiral Barrett-Shaw just left the room looking like thunder, followed by several of his officers and your brother. I can only think of one reason."

"Well . . ." Drake shrugged. "We had a little trouble. Let's just say I had to make a rather hurried exit."

"Someone saw you?"

"He saw a man wrapped in Beatrice's cloak."

"You didn't leave her behind!"

Drake looked pained. "Of course not. I left her locked in a closet."

"I should never have let you go," Cianda moaned.

"I didn't do too badly," Drake said. "I did get the diamond. And I managed to add a little more color to the legend of the Masked Marauder."

"The diamond?" Cianda stared at him, then realized he didn't know his night's risks had been in vain. "Drake —" she began.

The entrance of Admiral Barrett-Shaw and several sailors cut short her attempt to explain. Cianda gripped Drake's arm. Her reticule swung between them, a heavy reminder of the illicit prize dangling from her wrist.

"I'm sorry to inconvenience you," the captain began. "But there has been an unfortunate incident. Someone has stolen the Koh-i-noor diamond. Until we discover the thief, no one will be allowed to leave the ship."

A collective gasp rippled through the crowd of guests. Then several voices raised in a chorus of questions, demanding Admiral Barrett-Shaw make explanations.

Cianda turned to Drake. "I've got to find a way to leave the ship. If there's a search —"

Drake slid an arm around her waist, drawing her to his side. He pressed his lips to her temple. "Don't worry, sweetheart," he murmured. "They'll be looking for a tall, dark man in an ill-fitting cloak, not a sprite of a woman in a ball gown."

Her reticule rested against his thigh. To Cianda, its weight felt like a boulder chained to her arm. "You don't understand. I've got the diamond in my bag."

"They won't find it. And if they do, anyone who knows gems will soon realize it's a fraud.".

"No. They won't. If you would just listen to me —"

The sudden stiffening of Drake's body momentarily distracted Cianda from her predicament. She looked up and found him staring toward the entryway.

Charles stood at the door. His eyes searched the room until they settled on Drake and Cianda. A tiny, triumphant smile touched his mouth.

"Damn him," Drake muttered. His hand tightened at Cianda's waist. "He wouldn't dare. Not again."

Cianda glanced from Charles to Drake. His face was hard, his eyes stormy. "What is it?"

"We're about to find out."

Admiral Barrett-Shaw followed Charles into the ballroom. Charles ignored the hand of warning and the hurried word the captain spoke to him. Catching the attention of the guests, he waited until conversation had died.

"I know you are all quite anxious for this wretched affair to be resolved," he said. "No more than I. And so I am pleased to tell you I know the identity of the infamous Masked Marauder."

Drake gave a start forward. Cianda clenched her hand on his arm in mute appeal. Surely Charles wouldn't —

"The thief is here among you even now." Charles flung out an accusing hand, pointed straight at Drake and Cianda.

"The Masked Marauder is my brother, Drake Weston."

* * *

Drake felt the jagged edge of betrayal slice into an old, festering wound. Beyond pain, beyond anger, his brother's accusation left him unable to feel anything but a dull sense of knowing his instincts about Charles had been right.

You bastard. You'd do anything to save your precious reputation. Just like in Italy.

"It grieves me unspeakably to have to dredge up my own brother's sordid past," Charles said, sounding more satisfied than regretful. "But in the interest of recovering the jewel, which rightfully belongs to our Queen, I must. Mere months ago, Italian officials, having found Drake at the site of the theft of the famed Malwi ruby, only moments after it disappeared, concluded he was responsible for that theft also."

You blamed that on me too, dear brother. To curry Godfrey Thorne's favor. All the time you knew it was Thorne, and you still know it. Drake nearly spoke the words aloud. He wanted to rip away Charles' mask of good breeding and righteousness, to ruthlessly expose him for the supercilious coward he was.

At the very least, he wanted to throttle him.

The touch of Cianda's hand as it curled around his quelled the urge to impulsive action. Drake looked down at her. Her fingers tightened on his. Her eyes burned with the fire inside he loved to rouse. Without words, she encouraged him to jump headfirst into the fight.

He couldn't. Not this time. Not without risking having Charles drag her down too. If they found Antoine's replica in her bag, Charles would have no qualms over incriminating his brother's wife in the bargain.

"So convinced were they," Charles was saying, "my brother was held in an Italian jail until, I suspect, a powerful ally of his had his name cleared. But the evidence remains as it was. Twice now he has been present when valuable jewels were stolen. I am told by reliable sources he was also in France at the time the Rajput emerald was taken and its owner murdered. And now tonight, he was conspicuously absent during the time the diamond was being stolen. You may draw your own conclusions."

Murmurs rustled through the crowd of guests. Drake felt the rake of accusing eyes. He tried to release Cianda's hand, to put her away from him, sparing her the scrutiny of a hundred gazes. She stubbornly held tight, the determined set of her mouth allowing no argument.

"I believe you've said enough, Charles." Admiral Barrett-Shaw stepped forward, his imposing presence causing Charles to falter back a step. "You're set on condemning a man based on the weakest of evidence simply because of your embarrassment at losing a gem that was placed in your care. I will not stand by and allow these dramatics of yours on my ship."

"I'm appalled anyone would stand and listen to such claptrap," Cianda spoke out clearly.

Drake stared at her, too amazed to stop her fierce defense.

"My husband was unjustly accused in Italy, as his release proved. And we were together in France, where I can assure you he did not commit either a theft or murder. As for tonight . . ."

Cianda paused, her words apparently faltering. She brought her handkerchief to her face. Drake felt a rush of admiration for her acting ability. Everyone in the room was convinced she was the devoted wife, overcome with emotion. Only he could see the anger burning in her eyes.

"Tonight," she went on, a catch in her voice. "Tonight we had a small disagreement. We are newly wed and my husband became upset over Sir John's innocent attentions to me. I foolishly encouraged his jealousy. But instead of causing a humiliating scene, Drake left the room for a little time. If anyone is to blame for this wretched accusation against

him, it is me. I don't know how he can ever forgive me."
With a little sob, Cianda pressed her handkerchief to her
face again and rushed from the room before Drake could
move to stop her.

Drake was left standing alone, a hand half-raised, gaping
as Cianda ran out the door. From the sympathetic glances
and the impotent fury on Charles' face, he knew her histri-
onics had turned the tide in his favor again.

What he didn't know was Cianda's reason for wanting to
flee the ballroom. But he intended to find out.

Ignoring his brother's halfhearted protests, he pushed his
way through the crowd, determined to find his loyal wife.

Near the stern of the *King's Bounty,* Gide Legume scurried toward a hatch that led down to the gun deck, a large
bundle tucked under his arm.

Cianda smiled to herself as she stepped into the glow of
lantern light. She'd seen him maneuvering his way to the
back of the room while Charles held the audience captive
with his accusations. And she guessed his intentions.

"You seem in a hurry to leave, *cher* uncle," she called out.

"You!" he spat, freezing in place, poised to open the
hatch.

"You taught me well, Gide. Always know every way of escape. Your first lesson." Moving quickly, Cianda hiked up
her skirts, and stepped on top of the hatch, blocking his escape route. "I see you also found Drake's treasure," she said,
pointing to her bag and the cloak she recognized as Beatrice's.

"He has no imagination. And he was hurried. It was quite
simple to retrieve it once he had distracted the guard," Gide
sneered. "You cannot stop me, *chérie.* Now get out of my
way."

"You'll have to remove me yourself," Cianda said, crossing her arms in resolve.

"*Merde!* Move, you little bitch, or this time I will make

335

certain I kill you!"

He shoved at her with his free hand and Cianda stumbled off the hatch. It was the provocation she needed.

As Gide tugged at the hatch, Cianda dropped to the deck and deliberately ripped the sleeve of her gown at the shoulder, exposing a wide swathe of white skin.

Before Gide could react, she screamed, loud and long. Within moments, several sailors rushed to the sound, finding her huddled in a corner, seemingly terrified.

Among the sudden throng of bodies, Cianda recognized one familiar figure. Letting a sailor help her to her feet, she flung herself into Drake's arms, clinging to him. "Oh, it was awful! I saw him trying to go below and he . . . he attacked me!"

She felt his swift anger in the tensing of his hands on her back. Raising her head a little, she glanced up and gave him a small smile. He rolled his eyes in return, shaking his head, and pulling her back against his heart.

Admiral Barrett-Shaw stepped forward to where several sailors held a struggling Gide. He picked up the cloak and bag. Fishing inside the bag, he plucked out the jewel box and held it to the light. "Well. It appears we have our thief."

Cianda, her face turned to Drake's shirt, held her breath, mentally crossing her fingers. Employing Drake's favorite technique, she gambled.

To betray her alter ego, Gide would be forced to expose Thorne also. The British authorities, long thwarted in their efforts to snare the Masked Marauder, wouldn't be too quick to take the word of a French thief. And Gide knew better than to expose Thorne, even if it meant being accused of the Masked Marauder's crimes. Prison, even hanging, would be welcome compared with Thorne's merciless vengeance.

Still, she couldn't hope her ruse would last. Once Sir John discovered his diamond was a fraud—She banished the thought. With any luck, the discovery wouldn't be made until they had left St. Helena and were well on their way to England. She had to get the Koh-i-noor back to London and use it to rescue Jamie. Then, only then, would she worry about the consequences.

Behind her, Gide kicked at the men holding him, hurling accusations in French and broken English at Cianda. His rantings were ignored as the crowd surged forward to catch a glimpse of the lost treasure.

A sailor slapped a hand over Gide's mouth, quelling his foul curses as Admiral Barrett-Shaw drew a key from his pocket and fit it in the lock of the box. "Let's make certain, shall we?"

"By all means." Sir John suddenly appeared at his side. "Let's have this wretched business done with. It's all been quite annoying."

As the captain opened the lid of the box, Cianda smiled up into Drake's face. His expression was a mix of warring relief and bitter disappointment and she wanted to laugh aloud when Sir John gave a exclamation of dismay.

"By George, it's bloody empty!" Sir John blurted out.

Drake's mouth dropped. He scowled down at her, clearly not amused by her lighthearted reaction.

Before anyone else could react, a tidy little man interrupted. Bustling through the crowd, murmuring apologies, he made his way toward Sir John with small, mincing steps.

"And who, by God, are you?" Admiral Barrett-Shaw demanded, glaring at the man who hit him mid-chest.

"Don't fret, Robert. This is only my valet." Sir John turned to his servant. "Really, Hughbert, what are you doing here?"

"I heard the diamond had been stolen. Such a commotion. Men rushing about, being quite rude."

"Yes, yes, Hughbert. But what are you doing here?"

"Sir, don't you remember sir? You told me you wanted the diamond close to you, so you had me put it in your pocket." The valet pushed close to Sir John, plunged his hand into

337

his employer's jacket pocket and drew out the diamond with the effect of a conjurer.

Sir John flushed ten shades of red. "Oh my. Why, so I did. In all the fuss, I had quite forgotten."

Drake stared at Cianda, his confusion evident. She smiled sweetly and shrugged.

"I'm afraid there's been a misunderstanding," Charles muttered.

"Largely due to you, I'd say," Admiral Barrett-Shaw said icily. He turned to Drake and Cianda. "I must apologize. For everything."

Drake grasped the captain's hand in a strong clasp. "You have nothing to apologize for Robert. I should be thanking you for coming to my rescue."

"Well," Admiral Barrett-Shaw said with a smile, "at least some good has come out of this fiasco. We did manage to unmask the Masked Marauder!"

Drake slammed the door to their room at the inn behind him. "We're alone now, so suppose you tell me just what the bloody hell is going on, milady thief."

Cianda set her heavy reticule on the dressing table and slowly pulled off her gloves. "That was very rude of you to force Zak and Beatrice to take a midnight stroll so you could harass me without allies."

"Answer my question." The edge to his tone told Cianda his temper was in danger of snapping free.

But he had this coming, and furious or not, she intended to take down his arrogance a peg or two. "You're the expert cracksman. You tell me what happened."

Drake paced to one end of the room and back. "Legume must have followed me after I left the admiral's quarters and saw me stow the box in the sail locker. I'm guessing he didn't have time to jump ship before the watch herded him back into the ballroom with everyone else."

"The guard discovered the robbery rather quickly,"

Cianda mused. Sitting down at the dressing table, she ran her fingers over the pearls at her throat.

"I ran into him with a door," Drake snapped. "There wasn't much doubt in his mind after that."

"You also left the safe door wide open."

"I didn't have time to be tidy."

"And you left Beatrice in a closet."

Striding to her, Drake put his hands on her shoulders and spun her to face him. "If I hadn't, she might have ended up in the brig with your dear Uncle Legume."

"Perhaps. But I think you merely saved Gide the trouble of opening the safe. All he wanted was the diamond. That would have been his revenge on me."

"And now neither of us have it." Drake abruptly released her. Jerking off his jacket, he flung it onto the bed along with his ascot, then began his furious pacing.

Cianda tried to ignore him. With deliberate languor, she removed the pearls from her ears, then unclasped her necklace and laid them on the dresser table. "This was my last robbery," she said softly, caressing the creamy gems. "A pity in a way. It wasn't exactly a jewel in my career."

Drake stopped in midstride. "What are you talking about?"

Cianda forced a nonchalance she did not feel into her voice. "Just that you can go back to London and continue your life, your work for Lord Palmerston, even if you don't implicate Godfrey. Your name has been cleared as far as the theft of the diamond is concerned."

"And so is yours."

"For now. The Masked Marauder is in the brig. And even when they discover Gide is not the thief, I am out of work. If I attempt even one more jewel robbery, everyone will certainly doubt Gide is the Masked Marauder and there will be new suspicions. Only this time, thanks to your devoted brother, they will be directed at you. And you would, naturally, have to clear your name by exposing me."

She looked down at the jewels in front of her and they blurred and wavered. She wanted to tell him she would be willing to sacrifice all her pretenses for him. Because she cared. Because she loved him.

But there was too much at stake for her to trust her heart.

Drake walked up behind her and brushed his hand over her bared nape. Gently, he wove his fingers through her hair, freeing it from its confining combs. He let the silvery mass tumble around her face. It spilled to the torn shoulder of her gown, and Drake traced the gleaming strands where they lay against her white skin. "I would never do that. Not to you."

Cianda turned to face him, his touch at that moment more pain than pleasure. "Why not? You told me you were only loyal to yourself. You said you didn't need anyone else."

"I was wrong."

There was nothing she could say, no words for the sweet depth of feeling threatening to crumble her defenses.

Drake slid a finger under her chin and forced her to meet his eyes. "I was wrong. I'm no thief, as Beatrice no doubt told you. I thought I could do it on my own, but I discovered just how much I needed you. And not just to steal a bloody rock. Is that what you want to hear?"

"Drake . . ."

"Is it?"

"Yes," she whispered. Standing, she reached to curl her fingers around his neck and bring his mouth close to hers. With each word, her lips swanned against his. "It's what I wanted to hear."

She kissed him, not tenderly, but with fire, tasting the flame of his response. Drake bent and lifted her into his arms, his kisses deepening as he took a step toward the canopied bed.

A sharp knock at the door stopped him short of his goal.

"Cianda? May we come in?" Beatrice softly queried. "We've had quite enough walking for one night."

Cianda thought Drake might refuse and part of her wished he would. Instead, he set her on her feet and moved from her to the window, shoving a hand through his hair.

Sucking in a steadying breath, Cianda called out, "Of course. Come in." As Beatrice and Zak stepped into the room, she picked up her discarded reticule. She avoided looking at either of them as she dipped into the silk bag. "I was just about to show Drake the prize I managed to remove from Sir John's pocket."

With great care, Cianda drew out the Koh-i-noor. She held it in her palm, letting it reflect shards of golden lamplight from every blue-white facet, transforming it into a star alone in the universe she held in her hand. "Sir John has the replica," Drake said slowly, staring at the diamond as if he couldn't quite believe it was real. "You picked his pocket and replaced this with the fake stone."

"Damned clever," Zak said in grudging respect.

"For a woman, I presume you mean," Beatrice said, raising a brow.

Zak shrugged. "For anyone."

"So, Captain Weston—" Cianda forced a smile. She offered him the diamond. "A fair trade for my emerald. With the two of them, we can both still get what we want."

Drake looked down at the gem, then at her, his face hard. Without making an attempt to take the proffered jewel, he strode to the door, jerking it open. "At least one of us can, milady thief," he said, then walked out, leaving Cianda holding the cold stone.

Chapter Nineteen

Alone at the wheel of the *Ferret,* Drake scowled at the relentless blue-on-blue of the horizon. If cursing and sheer will could have made the coast of England materialize in place of ocean and sky, his ship would have arrived in London days ago.

For nearly three weeks, a brisk, even wind had pushed the *Ferret* back over the white-capped waters of the Atlantic toward England. Though the schooner fairly flew over the calm sea, to Drake, his ship couldn't sail fast enough.

Despite the danger of pirates, he pushed closer and closer to the coast of French-occupied Africa to shave time off their trip, to end the whole bloody mess. What started as another adventurous lark, the mere stroke of luck he'd come almost to expect as a matter of course, the night the object of his search — the Masked Marauder — landed in his grasp, had turned into a nightmare of pain, betrayal, and regret.

Bitter wind slapped Drake's sunburned face and chest. Long, scorching days of pacing the quarterdeck beneath the merciless assault of sun and wind left his skin as raw and tender as his insides. The elements beat against his body; tortured thoughts of Cianda against his soul.

All three jewels at her fingertips, halfway to reaching her goal, Cianda was almost finished using him. The only thread tying her to him now led to Jamie. Once she rescued her brother, she would abandon her temptress' hold on his heart and leave him.

Alone again.

Drake slammed the palms of his hands against the wheel. After Isabelle, when time finally dulled the pain, only the burning desire for justice remained in place of the love he learned to live without.

He would have willingly chosen to live without it — except for Cianda D'Rouchert. Faith Newman. She challenged and coaxed, provoked and enticed until he relinquished all his heart's defenses.

Fool! He had to face the truth: vengeance was an empty substitute for love. But accepting that resolved nothing.

Thorne. The name had haunted him constantly, growing into an obsession. Very soon, he'd finish the mission he'd begun over six years ago, the day Thorne told him Isabelle was dead.

Soon it would be over. . . . Drake rubbed a hand over his eyes, squinting into the late-morning sun. The shape of a ship wavered just at the edge of his vision.

He stared at it for a long moment before picking up the spyglass to bring the vague outline into sharp focus. Another ship, this near, traveling in the same direction, in pirate-infested waters.

Drake had no doubts. It was trouble.

Domenique clomped from the galley into the salon carrying a tray laden with four steaming bowls of turtle soup. He swept the table in a glance and frowned. "Bah! Again, he does not eat? I cook hiz favorite, and still he does not bother to come inside and sit at my table. Bah!" he growled, splashing soup on the saucers in front of Zak, Cianda, and Beatrice.

"My sentiments exactly," Zak grumbled. He took his seat.

"If he keeps this up, he'll starve to death before he reaches England. Or one of us will get fed up with his vile temper and run him through."

Cianda sighed. "I'll take a tray up again." Fred, attracted by the smell of food, wound around her ankles. "Maybe I should take you along," she told the cat. "I may need protection." Reaching down, she fed the cat a scrap of meat.

"It appears the captain is as anxious to reach England as he was to leave St. Helena," Beatrice said.

Zak glowered at his soup. "He's got good reasons in both cases, I'd say."

"At least Admiral Barrett-Shaw will defend him against accusations once the false diamond is discovered," Cianda said. "Hopefully, his word will be enough to discourage a pursuit."

"Don't count on it," Zak said with a derisive snort. "Charles won't be happy, to say the least. Blame for the theft is going to fall on him. You can bet he'll be looking for a scapegoat. Drake is more than convenient." He looked at the bowl in front of him, then pushed it away.

The subdued loathing in Zak's voice sounded foreign to Cianda compared to his usually flippant tone. "As he was in Italy?" she ventured.

"Just like in Italy."

Her back to the passageway, Cianda didn't see Drake step into the doorway. "I'm glad my absence at meals is providing you an entertaining topic of conversation." His dark voice commanded their attention.

Cianda opened her mouth to protest, but Zak spoke ahead of her. "Trouble?" he asked, getting to his feet.

Drake nodded. "We've got a shadow."

"Pirates? Or our friends from St. Helena?"

"I don't know. But I want the guns at ready. If it is trouble, I want the first shot." Drake turned to Domenique, lumbering out of the galley at the sound of his voice. "I think you're going to have to trade that apron for a pistol, Dom."

"Merde! All my work! And for what! Zat ugly cat!" Domenique's tantrum disturbed Fred, who had nimbly leaped onto the table and was now leisurely lapping at Zak's abandoned bowl of soup. The cat glared up at him before returning to her purloined meal.

"I'm coming too," Cianda said, pushing away from the table.

Drake slammed his hands flat on the table in front of her, leaning over from his imposing height. "Wrong."

"But I can—"

"I know, I know. You can match any man. I've heard it often enough. But bravado won't stop a cannon shell. On my ship you do as I say. If they are mercenaries, the sight of a woman is sure to incite an attack."

Cianda stood up. "I'm not a member of your crew."

"Exactly. Which is why you're staying below."

"Of course, Captain, we will do as you ask," Beatrice intervened. She moved to Cianda's side.

"Wise choice." Pushing away from the table, Drake motioned to Zak to follow him up the ladderway.

As Zak trailed his partner out of the salon, he glanced back at Fred, her nose pushed in a corner of his bowl. "I want a dog," he muttered before disappearing up the scuttle.

"Of all the arrogant, high-handed—" Cianda slapped her arms across her chest and marched to the opposite side of the narrow room. "Drake knew better! Why did he have to sail so close to the mainland? Why does he do anything! I was right from the beginning. He is a madman!"

"Mad, yes," Beatrice said, sitting back down. She folded her hands on the table. "About you. Only you're determined not to see it."

Cianda whipped around. "I think we've had this conversation once before."

"Yes. And I was right then, too. He loves you."

"Love? Him? Oh, come now, you of all people should know better. For now, he needs me. Nothing more. Once he has Godfrey, that will be the end of it."

"Unfortunately, it will not. I do know love when I see it in someone's eyes. I once saw the reflection of it in my own." Beatrice lowered her gaze and began meticulously to refold the napkin in front of her. "You love him, too."

"I love Jamie, and you, and Maisie. You're my family, the only people I'll ever trust. Drake Weston is using me, just like Godfrey uses me. Just like—"

"Arthur used me?" Crumbling the napkin between her fingers, Beatrice stared at it in silence before finally raising her eyes back to Cianda's. "I thought the same of Drake once. But no longer. Not after St. Helena."

"The robbery changed your opinion?" Cianda asked with an edge of sarcasm.

"No. I changed my mind when he put the diamond back into your hand. It might as well have been his heart."

This time, it was Cianda who averted her eyes. She wanted to believe, yet didn't dare trust her feelings.

"Oh Cianda . . ." Beatrice sighed. "If you lose each other in the end, none of this will have mattered. Even if Drake does manage to entrap Lord Thorne. Can't you see that?" Her voice softened. "Or are you afraid to?"

Beatrice's pointed question, echoing her own thoughts, struck a vulnerable spot in Cianda's heart. To be forced in the end to choose between betraying Drake and ensuring Jamie's safety—She touched the golden chain around her throat. Would it come to that?

"Jamie's life is all that matters," she said at last. "It's all that ever mattered."

"I know that and so does Drake. What he doesn't know is how you feel about him. I cannot help but believe he could accept any action you must take on Jamie's behalf, if only he did know."

"Love is a risk I can't afford to take."

"Then surviving is all you will ever do. Is that living, Cianda?"

Cianda slowly sat opposite Beatrice, gripped with uncertainty. "What choice do I have?"

"Only you can answer that." Beatrice stretched out her hand to cover Cianda's. "I only want you to stop pretending. You can't hide behind Godfrey's illusions anymore."

"No . . ." The realization came like a sea change, gentle and insistent. She couldn't hide. Cianda met her friend's knowing gaze. "Beatrice, I —"

A sudden thunderous roar splintered the air. The *Ferret* lurched sharply to starboard. Furniture and bowls and silverware slipped sideways, crashing to the floor. With a piercing yowl, Fred dived under the scant cover of the table.

Cianda and Beatrice clutched at the table, struggling to stay upright. "My God!" Cianda cried. "It's cannon fire. Drake's fired on them!"

Another volley of booming shots thundered above deck, jerking the schooner sideways. Wild shouts and the stampede of running footsteps sounded overhead. The acrid smell of gunpowder impregnated the air.

Without warning, a series of explosive cracks rocked the *Ferret* in the opposite direction. Cianda and Beatrice simultaneously looked up as the last burst of cannon fire resulted in a long, agonized creak, followed by an enormous crash.

"They've hit a mast." Cianda grappled against the force of the tossing ship to get to her feet. "I'm going topside."

"No." Beatrice grabbed at her arm. "We must be careful. Remember Drake said —"

"Not this time." Cianda had to shout to make herself heard over a new onslaught of cannon fire. A faint haze of smoke began filtering into the salon. "I won't stay here waiting for Drake to get himself killed. I'm going up."

Beatrice managed to move close enough to latch onto

Cianda's wrist. "There's nothing we can do."

"There has to be." Pulling free, Cianda made a lunge for the ladderway.

"Then I am going with you."

"No! Bea—"

"Yes," Beatrice said, pushing her toward the opening. "Someone has to watch out for you."

The hail of noise and confusion made argument impossible. As Cianda pushed open the hatch, black smoke and a blast of heated air hit her face, briefly forcing her backward. Sucking in her breath, she hauled herself up on the deck, reaching back to drag Beatrice after her.

Cianda scarcely recognized the topside deck as that of the *Ferret*. Crouching behind a jumble of rope and barrels, she and Beatrice exchanged a horrified glance. The clear calm of the early afternoon now resembled a version of hell.

A thick smutty haze hung over the schooner, lit here and there by small fires. The bellow of the cannons and carriage guns reverberated around them. Drake had all the *Ferret*'s guns mounted portside and crewman swarmed around the battery in the endless ritual of loading, tamping, firing, and reloading.

One of the smaller spars lay split in half across the stern, cut down by a cannon shot. Gaping tears rent two of the sails.

Through the confusion, Cianda could see the outline of the larger ship bearing down on Drake's schooner.

"What the bloody hell are you doing up here?"

Cianda jerked to find herself staring into Zak's incredulous eyes. Disheveled, smudged with soot, he looked as if he'd like to toss her overboard to spare himself any added grief. "Where's Drake?" she demanded.

"At the wheel. He's trying to rake the ship about to bring the guns to bear on their bow. He's gambling on getting a lucky shot at another of their mainsails. It's the only chance

348

we've got. We're outgunned and outmanned." Zak glanced at the approaching ship, now less than one hundred feet from the *Ferret*. "I'm going to break out the small arms. I suggest you get below. We're about to be boarded."

He started to push past them. Cianda stepped into his path. "There must be some other way to even the odds."

"Sink them. But we'd need one amazing distraction to keep them from slitting our throats while we tried to blow them to kindling."

"A distraction . . ." Cianda scanned the deck. Then she looked up at the sails of the pirate ship.

"What are you thinking?" Beatrice asked.

"Fire. The wind is in our favor. Then if Drake were able to knock out the mainmasts—"

"Woman, you're crazier than Drake," Zak muttered.

Despite his scowl, Cianda caught the glimmer of interest in his eyes and seized on it. "I can do it. From up there." She pointed at the *Ferret's* rigging.

"I was wrong. You aren't crazy. You're flat out insane." Zak jabbed a finger overhead. "They're aiming for our masts as well, in case you hadn't noticed. And apart from that minor detail, what makes you think you can scale up a mast and rigging, to say nothing of finding some way of carrying a torch along with you. Without getting your head shot off."

"I've managed to climb down from fourth story windows with a wire ladder. I can climb a mast. And I don't need a torch. I need a pot of pitch. I'll leave it below and take a rope with me. When I get to the top, Beatrice—" She glanced at her friend, who nodded. "Beatrice can light it right before I haul it up. It will work," she said firmly in answer to Zak's raised brows. "Besides, you yourself said I was an accomplished actress. I can play the part of scared witless cabin boy taking to the rigging in a desperate attempt to escape the mayhem."

Zak glared at her a moment, then threw up his hands. "Why not? Come on," he motioned to Beatrice. "We'll find some pitch. And work out a signal. If by some miracle this scheme works, someone is going to have to get to the wheel and make sure the *Ferret* swings hard to starboard. Otherwise, we'll burn with them." Glancing over his shoulder at Cianda he added, "Just keep in mind, if you get yourself killed, I won't have to worry about any pirate running me through. Drake will do it himself."

Drake manned the helm of the schooner, half his mind on the assault on his crew and ship, half of it busy calculating the odds of winning a distinctly unfair fight.

Wrenching at the wheel of his ship, he willed the schooner to starboard. To have any chance of hitting the remaining mainmast, he had to maneuver the *Ferret* into position for a clean shot. Hit the mainmast, then aim as many guns as he could spare at the hull below water level. The mercenaries were firing from beneath the top deck, and with any luck at all, toppling the mainmast would trap at least a dozen of them under the deck.

It was a gamble, but if it worked, he had a good chance of sinking them before they returned the favor. If it didn't . . . he'd at least guarantee them a good fight for their trouble.

"It'll only be a few minutes, Cap'n, and they'll be near enough to board," a burly crewman shouted to him from the stern deck.

"I can always use good news," Drake muttered.

It didn't make sense, he thought as he grabbed his pistol and cutlass from the side ledge, jamming the gun in the waist of his trousers. The attack had come from nowhere and the marauders were flying the Portuguese flag, not French. Besides, they wouldn't have much to gain raiding a small schooner, one not likely to be carrying any valuable cargo.

Valuable cargo. A clear vision of Cianda, the Rajput emerald hanging from her neck, flashed before him. If they found her, or Beatrice on board—

Drake shoved the unsettling thought away. He had a bad feeling about the whole damned situation, but he didn't have time to dwell on it. Giving the wheel one last hard turn, he dashed off the quarterdeck and down into the heart of the battle.

He found Domenique shoving a length of chain into the barrel of one of the cannons. "Better for clearing the deck, no?" the cook grinned at him. "And this—" He held up his immense cleaver. "For discouraging ze pirates."

"I pity the one that gets in your way, Dom," Drake agreed, briefly clapping the cook on the shoulder before running farther down the line of artillery.

A shell from a carriage gun hit in his path, knocking him backward. Steadying himself, Drake peered into the inky haze, gauging the angle of the salvo and the position of his target, the last mainmast.

Thoughts racing, he moved up to one of the largest cannons positioned near midship. He took the place of a young crewman struggling to load a large ball into the barrel. "Go and help Dom with the chain," he ordered. "We've got to keep them from boarding as long as possible."

Long enough for me to make this shot.

Shoving the ball into the barrel and tamping it into place with the long staff, Drake swung the cannon around to aim in the direction of the mast. The smoke made accurate targeting near impossible. Cannon fire thundered around him, rocking the *Ferret* as the iron balls smashed into her sides.

One shot.

Putting all his chips on his mercurial luck, Drake lit the fuse.

351

Cianda had waited for the hatch door to close on Zak and Beatrice before plucking up the thin coil of rope at her feet and dashing for the closest of the *Ferret's* mainsail masts.

Now, brazen courage her only ally, she snatched at one of the wildly swinging ratlines and began the long climb to the top.

Halfway there, the schooner rocked with another salvo of cannon fire. A ball flew at the aft mainmast, barely missing a direct hit. The second ship had maneuvered close enough for several of the crew to toss grappling hooks at the *Ferret's* side in an attempt to bind the two ships together. Several missed, falling to slap the side of the mercenary vessel. From the corner of her vision, Cianda saw one arc between the ships and catch against the railing.

She kept climbing. Looking up. Ignoring the shouting and the new snapping pistol retorts. Hanging onto the rope with resolve more than strength as it swaled with the motion of the ship.

The *Ferret* staggered with the concussion of its own guns. A deafening crack arrested Cianda. Her eyes riveted to the pirate ship as the second of its mainmasts teetered then fell lengthwise along the ship, crashing through the topside deck.

A triumphant cheer went up among the *Ferret* crew. From her vantage point, Cianda picked out Drake's tall figure in the midst of the men, standing near one of the carriage guns, a tamping rod in his hand.

"Bloody good show, Captain," she whispered.

Judging by the flurry of activity on deck and the lessening of opposing cannon fire, Cianda guessed the mast had trapped several of the pirate crew below deck. If she could manage to catch the vessel's rigging afire, it might give Drake and his crew an extra edge.

Below, several more grappling hooks flew and caught. In minutes, the *Ferret* would be boarded.

The realization doubled her determination. Nearing the top of the mast, she lunged for a handful of rigging and pulled herself close to the wooden support.

Bracing herself with her foot in a cradle of rope, she sucked in a deep breath and looked down.

For a moment, the chaos on the deck underneath her swayed and whirled in a dizzying kaleidoscope of smoke and fire and bodies. Cianda closed her eyes to it. She opened them and amid the pandemonium, at the foot of the mast, she saw Beatrice.

Saying a prayer, mentally crossing her fingers for luck, Cianda lashed one end of the rope to the mast and threw the other end down to Beatrice.

She watched as Beatrice managed to grasp the rope. And then she waited. Waited for long, restless moments while her friend tied on the makeshift pot of pitch and lit it with the flare from a lantern.

On the portside, about a dozen mercenaries now swarmed over the side of the *Ferret*. Pistols abandoned in the close confines of fighting, Cianda caught the glint of cutlass and dagger blades.

A tug at the rope signaled her. As quickly as she dared, Cianda jerked up the flaming pot.

A cannon ball slammed the side of the schooner. The rope slipped in her hands, scalding her skin.

Teeth clenched, Cianda hurriedly unfastened the rope from the mast. Hefting the end tied to the pot, she turned toward the pirate ship. *One try. One try. I can't miss.*

She focused on her target. The rigging of the last mainsail. Back to the *Ferret*'s mast, Cianda gathered her strength, held her breath, and heaved the pot and rope toward the pirate ship.

It sailed in a perfect arch and landed in the mainsail rigging. Pitch rained over the sails and deck, scattering a shower of fiery sparks. Almost immediately, several small fires ignited. The splattering of pitch spread the flames to a hundred different places on the mercenary ship, making it impossible for the crew to douse them all. Left burning, the fires chased and fed each other, beginning an unquenchable inferno.

Hugging the mast, Cianda nearly collapsed with relief.

The moment was short-lived. She looked below. Beatrice had disappeared.

Grabbing at the ratline, Cianda scaled down to the deck. Her legs wobbled a little as she fought to regain her balance once her feet touched the planks.

On the broadside, the crew of the *Ferret* battled the mercenaries on board and those still trying to leap to the schooner's deck. Cianda caught sight of Domenique, wielding a large hatchet, chopping at the grappling lines, while Zak worked furiously to wrest the other hooks free.

There was no sign of either Beatrice or Drake.

Heedless of the danger, Cianda turned and ran toward the quarterdeck.

As she neared the back of the schooner, she pulled up short.

Drake stood at the point of the stern, a bloody cutlass in his hand. A discarded pistol lay at his feet. His shirt had been slashed across the middle, revealing a long angry gash and his face was bruised and sooty. Behind him and to his side were the crumpled bodies of two of the pirate crew.

Cianda glanced from Drake to the four men he faced. Three of the mercenary crew; a fat man armed with a pistol and two wiry, unshaven sailors with cutlasses. The fourth man stood a little aside from the group, an arrogant sneer curling his lips.

Stunned shock froze her in place. The fourth man was Charles Weston.

Backed into a corner, down to his final roll of the dice, Drake had one thought. Before he took his last breath he was going to kill his brother.

His bad feeling had materialized into grim reality.

The attack on his ship had been no chance clash with pirates. Charles had discovered the false diamond and had hired a ship full of mercenaries to track them down and recover the Koh-i-noor. And his brother would stand by and watch his hired pirates murder everyone on the *Ferret* to get back his treasure.

Everyone including Cianda.

"You do have the devil's own luck, Drake," Charles said, flicking a glance at the fallen pirates. "But I'm afraid, dear brother, your good fortune has run dry. This time, we end it once and for all. I want my diamond."

"I tossed it overboard."

"I suppose you consider yourself clever. I'm not impressed. Where is the diamond?"

Drake tasted his own blood and swiped the trickle from the side of his mouth against his shoulder. "Go to hell," he snarled.

"Considering the circumstances, I believe it will be the other way around. And soon, I hope."

"At least I'll have the pleasure of your company."

"As if you could touch me," Charles taunted. "You're a thief and a traitor, a disgrace to the family. Do you think your word means anything against mine?"

"Your word!" Drake spat blood at Charles' feet. "You don't even have the guts to fight your own battles."

Charles's face flamed to bright crimson, his fist knotting and unknotting in front of him. An incongruent combination of fear and loathing flashed hot and cold in his eyes.

"Go ahead," Drake prodded, uncaring of the risk. "I

could best you blindfolded and shackled."

Charles took one step in Drake's direction, then stopped. He looked to one of the mercenaries. With a malicious grin, the pirate raised his pistol.

"No!"

Drake gaped in disbelief as Cianda darted out of the shadow of smoke to stand between him and his brother. Surely she wouldn't risk — "Get the hell out of here," he ground out.

Cianda ignored him.

"You bloody coward," she hissed at Charles. "Drake doesn't have the diamond."

"Cianda!" Drake grabbed at her arm and yanked her backward. "That doesn't matter now." *Don't take off your mask now, love,* he silently urged her. *Not now.*

She faced him defiantly, fire in her eyes. " 'It matters more than ever." Twisting out of his grip, she whirled on Charles. "The truth is I have the diamond. And the emerald and the ruby. I stole them. I'm Godfrey's thief. I'm the Masked Marauder."

Drake's heart caught in his throat. *His* thief was trying to protect him, but she had no idea of the damage she'd just done with her impulsive words.

Charles glowered, confusion making his expression uncertain. "The Masked Marauder is in the brig of the *King's Bounty.* You expect me to believe you — you . . ." He waved a hand up and down at Cianda. "I'm not the fool my brother is."

"No, you're definitely not your brother." From behind Charles, Cianda snatched a glimpse of brown and auburn. Beatrice. Her friend must have came to the quarterdeck at Zak's signal, intending either to warn Drake or take on the helm herself.

If I can create one more distraction —

"I can prove what I'm telling you is true," Cianda said,

dipping her hand into her shirt.

"Damn it, Cianda." Drake lunged out for her hand. "Don't do it!"

Evading him with a quick sideways step, Cianda yanked the emerald out from under her shirt, holding it high in front of Charles's face. "Do you recognize it? It's the Rajput. I stole it from Count LeDoux in France. Just like I stole the Malwi in Italy. And the diamond from Sir John's coat pocket on the *Bounty*."

For a moment, they all stared at the gem as a moment of sunlight cut it into brilliant emerald shards. Around them, the sounds of fighting and intermittent pistol shots chorused into the silence. The heat of the smoke and fire burned the air.

Then, as if in answer to Cianda's prayers, the *Ferret* lurched hard to starboard.

The tallest of the sailors lost his footing, careening into his companion. Drake, without hesitation, charged at the group.

Catching the fat man by surprise, Drake shoved him up and over the railing before the other two had time to react.

Charles backed up a few steps, twisting his head from side to side as if seeking escape. Rushing past him, Cianda kicked at the shorter of the sailors, drawing his attention away from Drake, who was fending off a slash of the tall man's cutlass. Metal blade struck metal blade as Drake pressed his attack, driving his opponent closer to the rail with each thrust.

Cianda, after rousing the ire of the pirate, instantly regretted her impulse when he swiped at her with his dagger. She was rapidly considering and discarding escape plans when Drake, dispatching the tall man with a final, furious offensive, dashed up and grabbed the short pirate by one bony shoulder.

Whirling Cianda's attacker around, he delivered a crushing blow with the handle of his cutlass, then shoved the short sailor into a mast, leaving him in a senseless heap.

When he wheeled back to face her, Cianda could only stare in dumbfounded relief.

Drake stared back, a chaos of powerful emotions surging through him. He couldn't find any words strong enough to express even a fraction of what he felt. Instead, swearing under his breath, he strode over to her and pulled her into his arms, heedless of his gashes and bruises, and the mayhem around them.

"Beatrice said you needed help," Zak's voice drawled from behind. Drake turned to look over his shoulder. Zak propped against the mast, glanced down at the unconscious pirate. "I see she was wrong."

Keeping an arm around Cianda, Drake gave his partner a weary grin. "You're a little late. Do I want to know how you managed to start that fire just at the opportune moment?"

"No. You don't." Zak looked at Cianda. "Does he?"

"I don't think so," she murmured.

"Anyway," Zak continued quickly, "we're pulling away now. Beatrice is quite handy with the wheel, I must say. And Domenique is tossing off those that haven't been scared off by the sight of him wielding his cleaver and roaring like a starved bear."

Cianda sighed. "So it's over."

"Not quite," Drake muttered. He swept the deck around them in a glance. Then, dropping his arm from her shoulder, he trotted to the railing and scanned the choppy sea below. "Damnation. I should have known the bastard would try that way out."

Zak loped to his side. "Well, hell."

At his shoulder, Cianda leaned over the railing in time to see Charles lower himself into a small skiff. "He can't possibly hope to escape that way."

"You're damned right." With a hand on the rail, Drake

leaped over the railing and jumped overboard.

"Drake! No!" Cianda screamed after him. "Are you crazy?"

"Yes," Zak grumbled. "He is."

Drake hit the skiff with a painful sounding thud. The small boat rocked furiously, tottering to its side so far Drake lost his footing. As he slipped over the edge he grabbed Charles' shirtfront, yanking him into the icy water.

For nearly a minute, Cianda saw no trace of either man. "Do something!" she shouted at Zak, frantically searching the water through the still-thick haze.

Zak stared down into the fathomless ocean, hands shoved deep into his pockets, shaking his head, disgusted. Finally, he bent down to pull off one boot.

A loud gasp from below brought Cianda back to face the water. Drake, Charles limp in his grip, broke the surface, shaking water from his face. Hauling his brother behind, he dragged himself back into the skiff. He laid back on the wooden bench, eyes closed for brief seconds, panting, then glared up at Zak. "Thanks," he called up.

Shrugging, Zak put his boot back on.

Drake pulled himself up and picked up the oars, rowing back toward the *Ferret*. Behind him, the late afternoon sky, smoked with black, glowed with the orange and yellow reflections of the flames that were rapidly consuming the pirate vessel.

Several of the crew came forward to help as Drake climbed back aboard his ship.

Cianda pushed between them, her eyes feasting on his bedraggled figure. "Let me help."

Exhausted from the struggle in the frigid water, Drake draped his arm around her, lightly leaning on her slender strength. Nodding to Charles, held upright by two burly crewman, he said to Zak, "You better take him or I might decide to throw him back in."

359

"A tempting idea," Zak answered, as he motioned to the sailors to take Charles below deck. "But you've probably had enough excitement for one afternoon."

Carrying a box full of medical supplies, Cianda rapped firmly at the door to Drake's cabin.

In the past hours, the *Ferret* had managed to pull away from fiery remains of the mercenary ship. The schooner had been severely battered in the attack. One of the mainsail masts had been lost, and Drake and his crew had rigged a jury mast as a temporary measure to give the ship the sails needed to finish the journey back to England. Rends and holes, ripped by the cannon salvos, had to be patched, and sea water pumped from the hold.

Despite his exhaustion and injuries, Drake worked tirelessly alongside the crew, feverishly trying to repair enough of his ship to keep it afloat for the few days they needed to reach London.

Now, well past midnight, he had finally returned to his cabin. And Cianda had determined to make sure *he* survived the final days at sea along with his beloved *Ferret*.

When no answer to her knock came, she pounded at the door with her fist.

"What is it?" Drake's voice through the door sounded harsh and tense.

"Let me in," Cianda called back.

There was a deadly silence that seemed to Cianda to last an eternity before the door opened. Drake stood in the narrow opening, one hand propped against the frame. His shirt hung open and in the dim lantern light, Cianda's eyes traced the ragged gash across his abdomen and numerous cuts and bruises.

Without waiting for an invitation, she pushed past him, setting her box on his desk. The smell of brandy and sweat hung in the close confines of the cabin.

"Come to play nursemaid again?" Drake said, closing the door. He moved to the desk and picked up a half-empty glass, downing the contents in a single swallow.

"You should know by now I won't take no for an answer."

"I should." Refilling his glass, he raised it to his lips, then set it back on the desk, untouched. "What you did out there today—"

"I did what I had to do," Cianda interrupted. She didn't want to hear his recriminations. Or his gratitude. She wanted to pretend she never confessed the truth to Charles Weston. That her love for Drake hadn't exposed her to the very real threat of being stripped of her identity as Madame D'Rouchert, of being imprisoned as the Masked Marauder.

"I'm going to thank you, whether you like it or not," Drake said. "You could have been killed. Several times over."

"It's not the first time."

"And, unfortunately, it's not likely to be the last."

"You mean Godfrey, of course."

Drake retrieved his brandy and drank it back as he paced the room. "Who else is left?"

"You."

"I'll admit, I considered wringing your neck several times this evening. But, I decided you did more damage with your outburst than I ever could."

"I'm so sorry, Captain," Cianda snapped, lifting her chin to meet his hot eyes. "Next time I'll let them shoot you."

"Don't you realize what you've done?" Drake slammed his glass down. "No, you don't. Let me tell you. Unless I can find a way to keep Charles's mouth closed, he'll tell all of London about your confession. The best you could hope for is being ostracized from society. More likely he'll do his best to make sure you hang, if for no other reason than to hurt me. And if that happens, milady thief, I'll be up there beside you. Even Palmerston won't be able to save my neck."

Cianda fought back angry tears. She hadn't considered any consequences, she had only acted for him. And in her heart, she couldn't find room to regret it. "I know what I've done. And you should be pleased," she taunted. "You wanted me to strip away my mask. Well, I have, and in your best dramatic fashion."

Stopping his restless pacing, Drake frowned at her, then moved close and put his hands on her shoulders. "I wanted you to stop pretending. But not at this cost."

"Don't worry, Captain," Cianda said, struggling to keep her voice even. "You can keep Charles locked away long enough to make sure you get your justice. That's all you want, isn't it?"

"And all you want is to rescue your brother."

"Yes." Her vision blurred. "That's all I want."

"We're both liars, love." Wrapping his arms around her back, Drake pulled her against his heart. "God, what a bloody mess."

"And there's no answer to it." Cianda raised her head to look at him. "Is there?"

Drake said nothing. He looked back at her, his face half in shadow, taut with a cross of uncertainty and pain.

Cianda let one tear slide down her cheek unheeded. "Let me stay tonight," she whispered, brushing her fingers over his jaw.

One last time. One more memory that I can hold in my heart when I can't hold you in my arms.

After a heartbeat's hesitation, Drake took her hand and led her to the narrow berth, slowly lowering her to the cool linen, his eyes never leaving hers. Bending one knee on the bunk, he spread her silver hair over his pillow. "Let me love you, Faith," he said, the low throb in his voice making her tremble. "That's all I want."

In the silence of the night, they came together with the

362

force of need and desire. When, after long hours, their passion was spent, Cianda lay cradled against her lover, waiting for the dawn, knowing when the day came she would leave behind her heart.

Chapter Twenty

Like a wraith through the predawn fog, the *Ferret* limped slowly into the London harbor. Cianda stood on the bow deck watching the vague, fuliginous shapes of the wharf as they materialized through the gray mist. Overhead, a whisper of wind sang through the tattered sails of the schooner. She shivered, pulling her cloak a little tighter.

She didn't turn as the sound of a familiar tread cut into the silence, knowing it was Drake. She felt the heat and restless energy of him even before he stepped up close behind her. "We're nearly to the dock," he said.

"Yes."

"Yes." Impatience, frustration edged his voice. "And we have to talk about our plan." Without touching her, Drake moved so they stood face to face. The bruises on his temple and cheekbone were still a vivid reminder of the attack on his ship. "You've managed to avoid the subject for days. You can't avoid it any longer. I want the damned thing done and over with. We both do."

Cianda shrugged. She had wrapped herself in her facade of the Masked Marauder. Cool, professional, nothing of her true self involved in the business that lay ahead

That was the way it had to be. She could no longer trust her heart when it came to Drake Weston. No matter how much she longed to.

"There's little to discuss," she said. "When we reach the town house, I'll send word to Godfrey. Since we're nearly a week into July, he'll be anxious enough to hear from me. Then, I'll retrieve the jewels and—"

"—You'll take the bloody stones, shove them into his hands, and collect your reward. How simple you make it all sound." Drake strode to the railing and gripped the wooden support with clenched hands. Abruptly, he whirled back to her, his anger no longer leashed. "Damn you, Cianda. We can't just leave it like this. You can't pretend you can betray Thorne, then simply walk away."

She thought of Jamie. Of Isabelle Thorne. "I can now. And I will."

"And what about me? Can you also walk away from everything we've shared and convince yourself you don't care?"

"What are my choices, pray tell?" Suddenly her fury matched his. "Your brother will do his best to ruin us both. You have Palmerston and your pedigree to protect you. I have my charades. They end when you arrest Godfrey."

"I'll still be there."

"Will you? How long after Charles tells all of London society what I really am?"

Drake caught her shoulders in a tense grip. "Long enough to convince you I don't give a damn where you came from or what you did to survive. And I have a feeling that will take me more than a lifetime." Before she could answer, he pulled her against him and, capturing her face in one hand, covered her mouth with his.

For a moment, Cianda struggled against the tide of desire he unleashed with the rough demand of his kiss. The fight was futile. A half sob caught at her throat as she succumbed to the torrent of feeling and sensation that, with frightening ease, swept aside her resolve to remain unmoved by their shared passions.

She clung to him, desperate for this last taste and touch of him. It was a luxury she never should have allowed. Yet she couldn't deny her love for him. Part of her ached to say the words, to give up the one last ruse she clung to in defense of her heart.

But saying the words wouldn't change the truth. In the end, his need for justice would force him to betray her.

Drake broke their embrace, his last kiss lingering as if he were reluctant to release her mouth. Threading his fingers into the silver mass of her hair, he held her face between his hands, searching her eyes.

With a trembling touch, Cianda reached up to brush her fingertips against the shadowed line of his jaw "Promise me."

"Anything."

The husky caress of his voice nearly crumbled her facade. "Promise me that — afterward . . ." Her voice faltered. She willed her strength back into it. "Afterward Jamie, and Beatrice and Maisie will be safe."

Drake's hands tightened on her skin as a familiar fire ignited in his eyes. He let her go and stepped away in one quick motion. "Is that all you want?"

"I won't go through with it unless I have your promise."

"Are you certain you can trust my word?" he said, his sarcasm not quite swift enough to mask his flinch of pain

"I trust you," she answered softly.

"You're a liar, milady thief."

She wanted to deny it. But it would only be another lie "Promise me. Or it ends here."

"It could, couldn't it? End here."

"You wouldn't." Cianda didn't trust her own confi

dence. She thought of the diamond in his cabin safe, felt the weight of the emerald around her neck, and knew he made no idle threat. "You want too badly to see Thorne hang."

"Perhaps I want you more."

They stared at each other in silence for a long moment until a call from one of the *Ferret*'s crew bellowed through the fog, drawing their attention to the fast approaching pier. Cianda became aware of the sounds of activity around them as the crew readied the schooner to make port.

"Drake—" She stretched out a hand to him.

He stepped back before her fingers touched. "You've got your damned promise. As soon as we dock, you contact Thorne. This will end today. One way or the other."

Without giving her time to reply, he turned and strode away, disappearing into the gray shroud of fog.

Cianda stood in the shadow of the stone wall that guarded Godfrey's manicured gardens, clenching and unclenching her hands to spend some of her restless energy.

It was well into evening, hours since the *Ferret* docked. It had taken from morning till twilight to lay the necessary plans. Although Beatrice protested, Cianda had insisted she stay with Maisie at the town house. If anything went wrong, she wanted to give her friends time to make hasty plans to flee.

She'd seen little of Drake after they left his ship, leaving Charles behind under the watchful guard of Domenique. He'd kept his feelings about the impending exchange with Godfrey well hidden. Only once, when she received Godfrey's note confirming their nighttime meeting, had a flicker of emotion flared in his eyes. Whether satisfaction or anger she didn't know.

Now, dressed in her thief's clothing, the stolen bounty in hand, Cianda counted the moments in nervous anticipation. When a piercing cat's mewl suddenly sounded nearby, she jumped a pace backward. Zak's signal.

Cianda sucked in a breath, straightened her shoulders, and touched the gems in her pocket for luck. She slipped inside the garden wall and up to the side door Godfrey had indicated would be left unlocked. The cavernous house was quiet and dim, her soft footsteps the only faint sound as she moved quickly toward Godfrey's study.

The heavy door closed with a click behind her, a brief echo in the empty room. A fire snapped fitfully against the grate. The wavering glow from the flames was the only light in the room save for a single lamp on the desk.

"Godfrey?" Cianda's softly spoken query went unanswered. She pushed away the uneasiness that crawled over her skin. "Damn you, if you've lied to me—"

"Your language is quite unbecoming, my dear," Godfrey's voice seemed to come from the air around her. She whirled as the narrow door at the far end of the study opened and he stepped into the room. "I am pleased to see you again, Cianda. I confess, I had begun to doubt your talents. I do hope you brought my jewels."

"Where is Jamie?"

"Well, my dear . . ." Godfrey examined the nails of one hand in casual perusal. "You are several days past my deadline."

The blood left her face in a rush, leaving her lightheaded. She balled her hands into fists and dug her nails into her palms, the pain helping her focus her strength. "We had a bargain. My brother's life for your jewels. Your precious treasure is mine unless I leave with Jamie."

"You've become quite bold. Another unattractive trait."

"Where is Jamie?"

"Don't become tedious, my dear. There is still the little difficulty of Drake Weston."

"His brother discovered the theft of the diamond in St. Helena and accused him of being the Masked Marauder," she lied without hesitation. "Considering their respective reputations and your influence, I have no doubt everyone will accept Charles Weston's word. Just as they did in Italy."

"Ah, you know of that." Godfrey rubbed a finger over his jaw. "Interesting. Did Weston tell you?"

"What does it matter?"

"Perhaps it doesn't. Well, it seems you've accomplished your task satisfactorily. Let's see the results of your labors, shall we?"

Cianda glared at him, her mouth pulled in a stubborn line. "I want to see Jamie."

Godfrey returned her straight gaze for a moment. Then, with a sigh, he made an imperious gesture toward the open door behind him.

Jack Filpucket's fat bulk appeared in the door. And with him, the slim figure of a boy. A boy with bright auburn hair and wide green eyes full of the joy Cianda felt in a dizzying surge. "Faith!"

Cianda started forward. Godfrey's raised hand stopped her. He motioned again and Jack pulled Jamie back behind the door. "My jewels," he said. "After all, we do have a bargain."

Cianda flirted with the idea of murder. It took every ounce of resolve she possessed to walk slowly to Godfrey's desk and remove the bundle of jewels from her pocket. Spreading open the linen cloth, she set the diamond, the emerald, and the ruby in a row on the desktop.

The lamplight caught the points and planes of the gems and splintered into a thousand shards of green, and gold, and crimson rays. The gem fire was the only warmth in

Godfrey's eyes as he feasted on the sight avidly before brushing a finger over the hard shape of the jewels. "Perfect," he murmured. "Just as I imagined."

With a reverent touch he picked up the ruby and held it to the light.

As if the jewel in his hand was a signal, the study suddenly erupted in a chaos of noise and bodies.

The door flung open with a crash and Drake strode in. Zak followed behind, flanked by a short, authoritative looking man in neat tweeds, and three constables. Cianda stood between them and Godfrey, the evidence of her guilt and his plain to see in the display of gems.

A warm gladness washed over her as Drake came up to where she and Godfrey stood and touched her shoulder. The pressure of his hand was a reassurance. She wondered if he knew how strongly at this moment she felt the chasm caused by their pasts, their loyalties, and how much his display of support meant to her.

Godfrey looked from Drake's grim face to Cianda, his expression one of stunned disbelief. "It appears I misjudged you, Cianda, and your loyalty to me. I created you and I foolishly trusted you would repay your debt. You have nothing now. Not even a name." His hand clenched around the ruby and he smiled, a cold, cruel curve of his lips that struck Cianda harder than a blow. "You miscalculated, my dear, putting your trust in Captain Weston. You are a fool, just as Isabelle was. He couldn't protect her and neither will he be able to rescue you. Before you hang, you'll spend your last hours in a Newgate cell knowing your brother died first."

"There's only going to be one hanging, Thorne. Yours." Drake strode forward and pushed between Godfrey and Cianda. Grasping Godfrey's wrist in a crushing grip, he forced his hand open. The ruby fell to the floor at Godfrey's feet.

Godfrey attempted to wrench his hand free. Several men moved forward to subdue him as he made a lunge for the jewels on the desktop.

A scuffling sounded in the back of the room. Cianda cast a wild glance at the narrow door. Jack. And Jamie with him.

You have nothing now.

Before you hang . . .

Godfrey's words pounded in her head, driving out everything but the instinct to survive, to escape. She shot a look at Drake. His eyes were fixed on Godfrey.

. . . your brother will die first.

She made her decision in a split second of panic.

Darting under Drake's arm, Cianda snatched up the Koh-i-noor, slipped between them and dashed for the door.

Ignoring the shouts and scrambling boots behind her, she jerked open the door and slammed it in the face of one of her pursuers just as he reached for it. Cianda turned the lock, knowing the action bought her only a minute or two at best.

The small parlor she found herself in was empty. "Jamie!" she shouted, praying he still could hear her.

There was an agony of silence before she heard sounds of a scuffle, a muttered spate of curses and then, "Faith! Here! In the corridor!"

Cianda raced out of the parlor into the long hallway and nearly cannoned into Jack. He held a struggling Jamie with one hand, his other fumbling with a short-handled knife.

"Not so close," Jack said, brandishing the blade near Jamie's throat as Cianda made a move toward him. " 'E's goin' out with me. I ain't lettin' the crushers put the blame on me fer Thorne's dirty business."

"They'll catch up with you a far sight faster if you take

Jamie with you." The slam of a shoulder against the parlor door punctuated Cianda's words. "Let him go and we'll all get out of here. Godfrey is the one they want."

Jack hesitated. The thump against the door grew more determined until finally the wood gave way. The resulting crash decided him.

Shoving Jamie into Cianda he turned and ran.

Cianda threw her arms around her brother and hugged him to her in an ecstasy of relief just as Drake came dashing into the corridor.

The two men with him raced off in Jack's wake, leaving the three of them alone in the hallway.

Drake stared at her, not moving, his face expressionless, as Cianda raised tear-filled eyes to his. "You found him," he said at last.

"Yes." Cianda pulled away from Jamie to lovingly brush her fingertips over his long-missed face. "I found him." She looked him up and down. "Are you all right? You seem thinner. Have you—"

"You're still fussing, Faith," Jamie said, grinning. "I rather missed it after a while." Turning to Drake, he smiled tentatively in recognition. "I remember you from the train. You and Faith made a jolly good try at a rescue." He held out a hand. "I wanted to thank you."

Drake accepted the gesture with due solemnity. "You seemed to have managed well enough on your own. You must have a fair share of courage and fight. Just like your sister. Faith took on hell and high water to find you."

"Faith loves adventures." Jamie turned to her excitedly. "You have to tell me everything."

Cianda smiled as she smoothed an errant lock of hair from his brow. "I will. I promise."

"I'll leave you to your reunion then," Drake said.

Cianda glanced up as he turned away. The diamond.

She slid her fingers around its cold, hardness. It could buy her safety, her future.

But suddenly she knew—and it seemed she had always known in her heart—she couldn't build a future on the betrayal of the man she loved.

"Wait for me," she said, putting Jamie from her with a quick smile.

Cianda caught up to Drake halfway across the parlor. She stopped him with a hand on his arm. "You've forgotten something."

When he looked at her, she nearly flinched back from the pain and fury in his eyes. For the first time she realized how deeply he trusted she would choose her feelings for him over her misguided loyalty to Godfrey, even over her need to protect herself from exposure.

And she realized how much he risked to put that trust in her. Much more than just his reputation or his plan to snare Godfrey.

"Drake, I—"

He cut her short. "You want it so badly, then keep the damned thing. Inspector Davidson is in league with Palmerston. He's not pleased, but he's agreed to let you go on my word you won't leave London. I'll see to it Palmerston clears your name. And I'll make up some clever explanation about the Koh-i-noor."

"No." Ignoring his stiff withdrawal, she took his hand in her own. She reached into her pocket and fished out the jewel. Without hesitation, she put it into his hand and closed his fingers around it. "I don't want it. Godfrey has to answer for what's he done. Especially for Isabelle. And I have to finally stop pretending."

The ache in her heart was almost beyond bearing as she let go his hand and stepped back.

Drake looked down at the jewel in his hand and then up, their eyes locking. Cianda sensed his internal struggle.

She held her breath, the blood pounding through her veins as she waited. Waited for him to say something. To send her away.

To ask her to stay.

"Faith?" Jamie stood in the doorway, his eyes full of curiosity as he looked from Drake to Cianda. "They're all getting ready to leave. Shouldn't we leave, too? I'd like to go home."

Cianda wanted to laugh and cry. How could her heart be so full of joy and gratitude at finding her brother alive and safe, and yet at the same time feel as if it were shattering into a thousand pieces she could never repair?

She looked at Drake, at the unyielding expression in his eyes. There was only one answer to Jamie's question.

"Yes, of course." Her heart cried out at the effort it took to smile. "It's all over now."

Not trusting herself to glance back, she took Jamie's hand and walked with him into the dark embrace of the night.

Drake slammed another barrel onto the deck of the *Ferret,* shoving it forcefully against the six others stacked in a haphazard row.

"Going on the run again?"

Glancing up, he glared at Zak in response. His partner stuffed his hands in the pockets of his overcoat, and rocked back on his heels. Draped around his neck, Fred opened her eyes to give Drake a disinterested glance, before settling back to sleep. "If you aren't careful, old chap," Zak drawled, "you're going to sink what's left of the *Ferret* in pickled herring. Or whatever that is you've chosen to vent your ill temper on."

"Is there something specific you wanted," Drake growled as he bent to pick up another barrel. "Or did you

374

just come to annoy me?" He was hardly in the mood to cross wits with Zak this morning.

"I had the foolish notion you would be celebrating. After all, Thorne is being fitted for a noose. His associate is decorating a Newgate cell. The jewels are safely in the Queen's hands. Palmerston must be pleased for once."

"He's thrilled. He thanked me and said he'd contact me when the Crown needed my unsavory talents again."

"That's not what I heard. I heard Palmerston mentioned a commendation."

"All claptrap. And I'm not interested."

"Really? I heard your reward for our little adventure was your lady thief's freedom. Palmerston has apparently agreed to forgive her illicit past."

"I hope you don't think I had anything to do with that," Drake snapped, not looking at his friend. "It was Pam's idea."

"I see. What about Charles?"

"I've decided to throw him overboard once I get to the middle of the channel."

Zak shook his head. "You're lucky, old chap, you have my genius to rescue you from your impulsive afflictions." With a sigh, he started off toward the lee side cabins.

Drake threw up a hand, knowing how useless it was to pry Zak's intentions from him. He resumed his loading, only to be interrupted by an earsplitting wail of off-key singing. Fred dashed around the corner, crouching behind a barrel, her ears flattened.

"What in – ?" Drake began, breaking off as Domenique lumbered onto the stern deck.

Flung over Domenique's shoulder in a graceless sprawl was Charles.

"What happened?" Drake demanded as Zak strolled up beside him. He winced as Charles broke into another unharmonious version of a popular tavern tune. "He sounds like he's been—" His eyes narrowed. "He sounds like you've been feeding him my private stock for meals."

"Oui, capitainne." Domenique fought back a smile. "Monsieur Zak suggested eet might give you an idea for solving your problem."

Drake glanced at Zak, who merely shrugged. "Well, you can tell Monsieur Zak . . ." He stopped, a slow, wicked smile spreading over his face. "You can tell Monsieur Zak he's a bloody genius."

"Where have I heard that before?" Zak muttered.

"Charles is in enough trouble over the supposed robbery," Drake said, ignoring him. "No one's likely to believe anything he says about St. Helena when he shows up in this condition—"

"On your mother's doorstep, perhaps?" Zak looked pleased at his artistic touch. "Anyway, when he hears of the arrest, he'll be anxious enough to deny any link to Thorne. It's Charles's way."

Drake clapped his friend on the back. "I'm in your debt."

"You always are," Zak said. With a few quick words, he sent Domenique to put Charles in a hansom, rewarding the driver generously to deliver him to the Weston estate. "Well, one of your problems solved."

The deliberate blandness of Zak's expression raised Drake's irritation. He sat down on the barrel nearest him, crossing his arms over his chest in resignation. "I knew it would come to this. Go ahead. Say it."

Pointing a finger at his own chest, Zak looked back in wide-eyed innocence.

"I'm waiting for your usual lecture about women, and the trouble they've caused me. Let's have it. I want to get underway before month's end."

"I won't delay you further then," Zak said, scooping up Fred and starting toward the dock. "Have a good trip."

"Wait a minute." Drake nearly fell off the barrel in his haste to catch up to his partner. "You're staying behind?"

Zak stared at a point over Drake's shoulder, absently stroking a hand over his beard. "I thought I'd visit the old estate for a few weeks."

"You haven't been back in months, years more likely. It would take weeks just to scrape off the dust."

Still averting his eyes, Zak said nothing.

"You—" Drake burst out laughing. "Beatrice is quite efficient at getting what she wants."

"She has a new post at a girl's school in Southampton. Palmerston's meddling again, I suspect. It's just as well," Zak said, scuffing the toe of his boot against the deck. "That boy she used to be governess to is beyond the age of needing her. You know, the boy your thief risked all our necks to rescue."

"If you say so. Convenient for you Southampton is so close to your fair village of Gosport."

Zak turned on him with a look of offended dignity. "I said I was visiting the estate."

"So you did. You know," Drake mused. "I don't know what Beatrice sees in you. She doesn't even know your real name."

Zak shrugged. "Minor detail." He glanced up as a carriage rolled up to the edge of the dock. "Finally. I was running out of ways to entertain you."

Drake glared at him in sudden suspicion. "You didn't."

"Probably not." With a languid wave of his hand, he loped off the ship and started down the dock.

Drake opened his mouth to call after Zak, but the words froze in his throat when the carriage door opened and the driver handed out the sole passenger.

As the driver set his horse into motion, he found himself staring, a foolish gaping expression on his face, at the woman walking toward him. Dressed in a simple blue day dress, her silver hair in a thick plait down her back, she was neither the Masked Marauder nor the elegant Madame D'Rouchert.

She still carried herself with the familiar sureness. But there was a touch of uncertainty in her eyes that made him look at her anew, as if seeing her for the first time.

The emotions flickering across his face — surprise, suspicion, heartache — nearly caused Cianda to change her mind about confronting him. After their exchange at Godfrey's house, she resolved to stay away. Until she realized she only chose a different way to hide.

The knowledge emboldened her. She walked straight up to his ship, hesitating at the railing. "May I come aboard?"

Drake wanted to say no. It would be easier to say no. It would spare him any amount of grief and trouble to say no.

Instead, he gave her a sharp nod in reply and held out his hand.

Slowly, she raised her own and put it in his, simply holding on for a moment. Her fingers felt small and cold and he felt a slight tremor when her hand closed on his.

The feel of her skin, the elusive attar of asters she brought with her, the steady emerald gaze, roused all the emotions and longings he had sworn he could live without. Letting go her hand, he stepped back, raking his fingers through his hair, trying to gain some control.

Cianda made no comment. His reaction to her touch kindled a small hope. She glanced at the haphazard arrangement of barrels. "Are you leaving again?"

"As soon as possible. There are still repairs to finish."

"I see."

"I suppose you know Palmerston has cleared your name. You can go on being Madame D'Rouchert, if it pleases you. And if you're worried about Charles—" he said quickly, fighting to keep the disappointment from his voice. She appeared unconcerned, but she had likely come to make sure he kept Charles silent.

"I'm not worried," Cianda interrupted. "That isn't why I came."

Her uncanny ability to surprise him made Drake's reply sharper than he intended. "Why did you come then?"

"There's something I needed to tell you." Cianda looked away from him. When she raised her gaze to his again, unshed tears glimmered in her eyes. "I should have told you before. I didn't have the courage." She swallowed and lifted her chin. "I love you."

Drake stared at her, stunned, uncertain whether or not he really heard her say the words. A sweet, powerful feeling trembled in his heart, making it hard to recall the pain and the doubt.

Cianda smiled slightly at his astonishment. The truth sounded strange and wonderful to her own ears. She only prayed, after all the pretense between them, she could make him believe it. "You were right. It was my last charade, pretending I didn't care for you. At Godfrey's house, I took the diamond because I was afraid. I was afraid to risk everything on my feelings for you. I realized too late it was the only risk worth taking."

Drake finally found his voice. "Too late?"

A single tear slid down her face. "I know you think I betrayed you. But all I could see at that moment was a future without hope. I took the diamond, yet even then, I knew I couldn't leave with it. I left the Masked Marauder on St. Helena, and Madame D'Rouchert in Godfrey's study. I've decided to be who I am — Faith Newman. And to put as much effort into helping the people I grew up with as I have stealing from society," she added with a rueful smile. "I have no idea yet how I'm going to support myself and Jamie and Maisie honestly. But —" A spark of mischief flashed in her eyes. "I've decided I'm resourceful and stubborn enough to make it work. Your determination to remove my mask finally made me accept the reality of who I am and what I can be." She paused, drawing a steadying breath. "But the only truth I am certain of is the love I feel for you. Finally, I'm ready to believe it."

Cianda drew a tremulous breath. She gambled everything on her feelings for him and the hope he might care for her in return. If he turned away now, it would crush her heart. But she at least took pride in finally being able to discard her facades.

Their future, with or without each other, was his choice.

Two instinctive urges called Drake to action. The first, was to turn and walk away. How could he chance his heart again? Love betrayed him once. Was it worth the risk again?

And the second . . . The second was the stronger, the more dangerous. A perilous adventure, fraught with the unknown, demanding everything, promising nothing.

His hesitation erased the flicker of hope in Cianda's eyes. She turned away, the rigid set of her shoulders and back belied by the waver in her voice. "I apologize for taking your time, Captain Weston. I'll take my leave now."

She took two steps toward the dock. Drake reacted without giving himself time to reason why.

Wrapping an arm around her waist, he scooped her into his arms. "That's the third time you've tried escaping my ship, milady thief."

Cianda stared up at him, disbelief fighting joy for command of her face. "Are you objecting this time?"

"This time I intend to make certain you stay."

Laughter mixing with the tears in her eyes, Cianda curled her arms around his neck. "And, pray tell, how do

380

you intend to do that? If I remember correctly, I did manage to escape you once."

"Once and the last time, my love. Before you invent another husband, I intend to make true our story of a wedding trip at sea."

Cianda glanced down, her fingers idling with the hair at his nape. "You'll be wedding Faith Newman. I never really was Madame D'Rouchert."

"I know the woman I love."

"And your family?"

"I finally have a real family," Drake said, brushing a kiss over her lips. "My wife and her brother, and Maisie, if she'll forgive me for bringing a cat into her domain. By the time Charles arrives home—drunk as a lord, I might add, hardly lending credibility to any story he might care to tell—and my mother hears of Thorne's arrest, we're going to seem very respectable by comparison."

"I hope not," Cianda said, laughing. "I prefer you at your most uncivilized."

"That's the way it will always be between us, love. We don't belong in proper society, we never will. It doesn't matter anymore. We've found what matters." Drake let her feet slip to touch the deck. Taking both her hands in his, he kept his eyes steady on hers. "I swear to God, I never loved anyone as I love you, Faith. Never. You taught me to trust. And to love."

"You're the only man I've ever dared to love," she said, smiling through her tears. "Then, I should have known at the beginning only a rogue pirate captain could be a match for the Masked Marauder."

"And only a thief could steal my heart." Sweeping her off her feet again, he kissed her thoroughly, tasting the passion he loved, the only fire to equal his own. "I suppose it was destiny after all."

"The destiny of lovers?" Cianda slid a caressing hand to

his face. "I don't know if I'm quite convinced of that," she mused.

"Persuasion is one of my many talents, my love."

"I'll give you a chance to prove that, Captain." Reaching up to draw his lips to hers, she whispered against his mouth, "Make me a believer."

About the Author

Danette Chartier is the pseudonym of the writing team of Annette Chartier-Li and Danette Fertig Thompson. Annette, a former free-lance journalist and columnist, and Danette, currently an editor for a St. Louis area newspaper, met nine years ago while working for the same publication. They have been writing together for four years. Annette and Danette share a love of history, gourmet cuisine, travel, and odd animal companions. When Annette writes, she is kept company by her ferret, her African pygmy hedgehog, and her daughter's cat, and Danette by her two Chow-Chows and a female cat named Fred. They are also the authors of *Alabama Twilight,* an historical novel published by Pinnacle.